THE COUNCIL OF THE CURSED

Also by Peter Tremayne and featuring Sister Fidelma:

Absolution by Murder
Shroud for the Archbishop
Suffer Little Children
The Subtle Serpent
The Spider's Web
Valley of the Shadow
The Monk who Vanished
Act of Mercy
Hemlock at Vespers
Our Lady of Darkness
Smoke in the Wind
The Haunted Abbot
Badgers Moon
Whispers of the Dead
The Leper's Bell
Master of Souls
A Prayer for the Damned
Dancing with Demons

THE COUNCIL OF THE CURSED

PETER TREMAYNE

headline

First published in 2008 by
HEADLINE PUBLISHING GROUP

1

Cataloguing in Publication Data is available from the British Library

ISBN 978 0 7553 2840 6

Typeset in TimesNewRomanPS by Palimpsest Book Production Limited, Grangemouth, Stirlingshire

Printed and bound in Great Britain by
Clays Ltd, St Ives plc

Headline's policy is to use papers that are natural, renewable and recyclable products and made from wood grown in sustainable forests. The logging and manufacturing processes are expected to conform to the environmental regulations of the country of origin.

HEADLINE PUBLISHING GROUP
An Hachette Livre UK Company
338 Euston Road
London NW1 3BH

www.headline.co.uk
www.hachettelivre.co.uk

To the memory of a great friend,
Peter Haining (2 April 1940–19 November 2007),
Sister Fidelma's 'godfather'.
His humour and support will be sorely missed.
His like will never be there again.

AD670: . . . et ad sacrosanctum concilium Autunium, Luna in sanguinem uersa est.

Chronicon Regum Francorum et Gothorum

AD670: . . . and at the sacred Council of Autun, the Moon became the colour of blood.

Chronicle of the Kings of the Franks and Goths

PRINCIPAL CHARACTERS

Sister Fidelma of Cashel, a *dálaigh* or advocate of the law courts of seventh-century Ireland
Brother Eadulf of Seaxmund's Ham in the land of the South Folk, her companion

At Autun (the religious)

Leodegar bishop and abbot of Autun
Nuntius Peregrinus the Papal Nuncio or envoy
Ségdae abbot and bishop of Imleach
Dabhóc abbot of Tulach Óc
Cadfan abbot of Gwynedd
Ordgar bishop of Kent
Brother Chilperic steward to Leodegar
Brother Gebicca a physician
Brother Sigeric a scribe
Brother Benevolentia steward to Ordgar
Brother Gillucán steward to Dabhóc
Brother Andica a stonemason
Abbess Audofleda the *abbatissa* of the *Domus Femini*
Sister Radegund the stewardess of the *Domus Femini*
Sister Inginde
Sister Valretrade

At Autun (the city)

Lady Beretrude
Lord Guntram her son
Verbas of Peqini
Magnatrude sister to Valretrade
Ageric a smith and husband to Magnatrude
Clodomar a smith
Clotaire III King of Austrasia
Ebroin his mentor

At Nebirnum

Arigius abbot of Nebirnum
Brother Budnouen a Gaul

HISTORICAL NOTE

The events in this story occur at the Council of Autun. The city is situated in what is now Burgundy, in France. It had been a vital stronghold in Roman Gaul when it was called Augustodunum. The Council of Autun was an important Christian Council for it decided that the Rule of St Benedict would be the normal monastic code, overturning the practices of the Celtic monastic religious establishments in Gaul. The decisions of Autun put the Celtic Church once again on the defensive as Rome sought to challenge its rites and customs and bring it under Roman control. Autun attempted to reinforce the decisions made in Whitby in AD664 when Oswy of Northumbria adopted Roman Church practices in his kingdom and rejected those that had been introduced with Christianity by the Irish missionary monks. Oswy's decision to go with Roman rules gradually influenced all the other Anglo-Saxon kingdoms.

The Council of Autun also ordered all ecclesiastics to learn by heart the Athanasian Creed. Cardinal Jean Baptiste Francois Pitra (1812–89), in his *Histoire de Saint Léger* (Paris, 1846) believed that this canon or decision was directed against the ideas of monothelitism which were then spreading among the Celtic Churches of Gaul. This was an idea developed to explain how the human and divine related in the person of Jesus Christ. It taught that Jesus had two natures (human and divine) but only one divine will. Monothelitism enjoyed considerable support in Fidelma's day but was officially condemned as heresy at the Sixth Ecumenical Council in Constantinople under Pope Agatho in AD680–81.

The chronicles seem confused as to what year the Council of Autun was held but the majority opinion favours the year AD670. This is the date I have also adopted as being more reasonable than the other dates suggested. Precise dating is sometimes confusing in chronicles and annals because they have survived only in copies written or compiled many centuries later. I make no apology for placing the arbitrary decisions on an agreed date. After all, I have no other pretensions for the Sister Fidelma stories other than that they *are* written as fiction.

For those who are sceptical about such events as the wives of clerics and other religious being sold into slavery with the sanction of Rome, I have to point out the following: during the time of Pope Leo IX (1049–54), the pontiff did sanction the rounding up of the wives of priests to become slaves in the Lateran Palace. Moreover, it was when Urban II (1088–99) was elected to the papacy that he reinforced celibacy not only by decree but also by force. While attending a council in Rheims he gave approval to the Archbishop of Rheims to order Robert, Count of Rheims, to abduct all the wives of priests and religious to be sold as slaves. Many of these women, driven to despair, committed suicide. Others fought back. While the Swabian Count of Veringen was away, hounding the clerical wives, his own wife was found poisoned in her bed as retribution.

It might also help readers to place locations by observing that the Gaulish River Liga, the Celtic name meaning silt or sediment and Latinised as Liger, is now the stately Loire; the Gaulish river name Aturavos is now the Arroux, and the Rhodanus is the Rhône. The town of Nebirnum is now Nevers, Divio is now Dijon and the Armorican port of Naoned is now the city of Nantes.

Chapter One

The two cowled figures were barely discernible in the dark shadows of the mausoleum. They stood silently by the large sarcophagus that occupied the centre of this small section of the musty catacombs, which seemed to stretch in every direction under the abbey. This was the ancient necropolis; old even before the abbey had been built. Since the site was sanctified, after the coming of the New Faith, it was where generations of abbots had been laid to rest.

There was silence here apart from the distant dripping of water. The atmosphere was dank and almost suffocating. A faint light permeated the underground caverns, giving a certain relief to the darkness, by which objects could be distinguished by their various differences in light and shade but without detail. The two figures stood without movement, almost as if they themselves were part of the stonework.

Then, in contrast to the faint dripping of water, there was a sudden soft shuffling noise, as leather came into contact with stone. One of the figures stiffened perceptibly as a glimmering light appeared across the cavern and caused shadows to dance this way and that in the gloom. A third figure, holding a candle, emerged between the tombs.

The figure also wore a hooded robe. It halted before the mausoleum.

'I come in the name of the Blessed Benignus,' its rasping voice intoned.

The waiting couple in the darkness visibly relaxed.

'You are welcome in the name of Benignus of sanctified name and thought,' said one, in a soft, female voice. The words were exchanged in Latin.

The newcomer hurried forward into the mausoleum and placed the candle on the side of the marble tomb.

'Well?' asked the second of the waiting figures. 'Does he still have it?'

The newcomer nodded quickly. 'He has placed it in his chamber.'

'Then we might easily take it. It will be a sign that God has blessed our endeavour,' replied the other.

'But we must act swiftly. The envoy from Rome has already spoken with him about it. If we are to use it as our symbol when the time comes, we must remove it now.'

'If this is to work in our favour and the people to be aroused, he must be prevented from spreading the truth of this great symbol. The people must believe in it without question.'

'Are we prepared for what we must do?' It was the woman's voice again.

'It is for the greater good,' intoned her companion.

'*Deus vult*!' the newcomer added solemnly. God wills it.

'It is agreed, then?' asked the woman with a catch of breath, as if caught by a cold air.

'The deed must be done tonight,' the newcomer said firmly.

The three looked at one another in the crepuscular light, and then with one voice they murmured: '*Virtutis fortuna comes*!' Good luck is the companion of courage.

Without another word, the three shadowy figures departed in different directions through the dark vaults of the catacombs.

'I will no longer tolerate the arrogance of that man!'

There was an astonished silence in the chapel as the voice echoed in the stone vaulted building. The abbots and bishops, who sat in the dark oak carved seats arranged before the high altar, turned almost as one to regard their grim-faced colleague. He was still seated but pointed an accusing finger towards the religieux seated further along the row.

'Calm yourself, Abbot Cadfan,' admonished Bishop Leodegar, who was presiding over the meeting. The chapel had been so arranged to serve the function of a council chamber. 'We are here to debate the future of our Churches, which are currently separated by language and rituals. Remember that blunt words may be spoken in seeking paths along which we might converge so that unity may be achieved. Such words should not be taken as personal insults.'

He spoke firmly in the Latin language that was common to them all.

Abbot Cadfan's scowl merely deepened.

'Forgive my bluntness, Leodegar of Autun,' he said, 'but I have the ability to recognise an insult from an opinion expressed in genuine debate. I will tolerate no insults from the enemies of my blood and my people.'

The elderly, grey-haired cleric seated at Abbot Cadfan's right side laid a gentle hand on his companion's arm. He was Abbot Dabhóc of Tulach Óc, who represented Bishop Ségéne of Ard Macha; the latter claimed episcopal primacy over all the five kingdoms of Éireann.

'I am sure Bishop Ordgar did not mean to sound arrogant,' he said diplomatically. 'While we speak in Latin, it is not the language of our mothers and thus we often lack the dexterity of expression with which we are comfortable. It may simply have been a matter of clumsy usage, or possibly different interpretation of emphasis?'

Bishop Ordgar, the subject of the initial angry outburst, had remained staring at Abbot Cadfan with sullen features. A sharp-featured, dark-haired individual with an unfortunate cast of the mouth that seemed to present a permanent sneer, he now turned his belligerent gaze on Abbot Dabhóc.

'Are you accusing me of not knowing good Latin?' he growled. 'What would you, a barbaric outlander, know of the refinements of the tongue?'

Abbot Dabhóc flushed. Before he had a chance to respond, Abbot Cadfan gave a short bark of laughter.

'Arrogance again – and from one whose people have not yet emerged from pagan savagery. Did we Britons not warn our neighbours of Hibernia that they should not attempt to convert these Saxons from their pagan ways, to teach them the ways of Christ and of literacy and learning? They are not yet sufficiently civilised to know what to do with it.'

Abbot Cadfan used the Latin name of Hibernia to refer to the five kingdoms of Éireann.

Bishop Ordgar thumped his fist on the armrest of his wooden seat. 'I am an Angle, you *Welisc* barbarian!'

Abbot Cadfan shrugged indifferently. 'Angle or Saxon, it is both the same, the same rasping language and the same ignorance. At least I call you by a proper name, but you, in your arrogance, call me *Welisc*. I am told this means "foreigner". Yet it is you who are foreigners in the land of Britain. I am a Briton, whose people were in that land at the beginning of time, while your barbaric hordes came but two centuries ago. You entered our land by stealth and guile, and then by invasions, bringing slaughter and death to my people. You seek no more than the wholesale eradication of the Britons. I tell you this, barbarian, you will not succeed. We *Welisc* – as you sneeringly call us – will survive and may one day drive you from the land you are now calling Angle-land that was once our peaceful land of Britain.'

Brows drawn together, Bishop Ordgar had sprung to his feet, knocking his seat over backwards, one hand apparently searching for a non-existent sword at his side.

Abbot Cadfan sat back and gave another bark of laughter and glanced round at the serious-faced prelates at the table.

'You see how the barbarian reacts? He would resort to primitive violence, if he had a weapon. He is not fit to call himself a man of peace, a representative of the Christ, and sit in discussion with those of civilised degree. He is just as savage as the rest of the petty chieftains of his people who, when they do not make war on us Britons, are at war with each other.'

A sudden noise interrupted the scene. A tall, swarthy-skinned man, seated beside Bishop Leodegar and wearing rich robes and a silver cross on a chain around his neck – which denoted he was of high rank among them – had risen to his feet and rapped loudly on the floor with a staff of office.

'*Tacet!* Be silent!' he thundered. 'Brethren, you both forget yourselves. You are gathered in council under the eye of God and the bishop of this place. As the envoy from the Holy Father in Rome, I am ashamed to witness such an outburst among the chosen of the Faith.'

That the envoy of Rome, Nuntius Peregrinus, had felt forced to intervene was a rebuke to the lack of authority displayed by Bishop Leodegar in controlling the delegates to the council.

Bishop Leodegar now raised a hand and gestured to the envoy to reseat himself. Then he said firmly: 'Brethren, you do, indeed, shame yourself before our distinguished envoy. This is a council of the senior abbots and bishops of the western churches, here to decide the fundamental ways of promoting our unity. It is true that this is supposed to be an informal opening, without the attendance of all our scribes and advisers, so that we could come to know one another before our main debates, but it is *not* a marketplace where we brethren can brawl and fight among ourselves.'

There was a muttering from the twenty or so men who were seated around the table.

Bishop Leodegar now turned to Bishop Ordgar.

'Ordgar, you are here as the personal representative of Theodore, who has been newly appointed by our Holy Father Vitalian in Rome as Archbishop at Canterbury. Would Theodore truly utter the words that you have used to a prelate of the church of the Britons?'

Ordgar was about to respond when Bishop Leodegar's stern look caused him to sink back in his chair with a sour expression.

'Cadfan,' continued Bishop Leodegar, 'you have come here representing the churches of your people, the Britons. Do you truly represent your people when you preach war and the elimination of the kingdoms of the Angles and Saxons?'

Abbot Cadfan refused to accept this censure silently.

'We did not ask the Angles and Saxons to invade our lands and seek our eradication,' he snapped. 'Is there a man among you who has not read the Blessed Gildas' *De Excidio et Conquesta Britanniae – The Ruin and Conquest of Britain*? Have you not heard how my people were massacred or forced to flee from their homes to other lands when the Angles and Saxons arrived? We are still being pushed to the west; others have fled to Armorica, to Galicia, to Hibernia and even to the land of the Franks, to seek respite from the ravening hordes.'

'That surely was in the past,' replied Bishop Leodegar. 'We have to live in the present.'

'Was Benchoer in the past?' demanded Abbot Cadfan.

Bishop Leodegar looked puzzled. 'Benchoer? I have noted that Drostó, the abbot of Benchoer, had not arrived here. What is it that you say about Benchoer?'

'Well may you ask why Drostó of Benchoer is not here,' went on Abbot Cadfan. 'Benchoer is one of our oldest abbeys that housed three thousand brethren dedicated to Christ. I know that Drostó was meant to be the senior representative of our churches here, not I. Is the Saxon who sits before me afraid to tell you why Drostó does not sit in this place?'

Bishop Ordgar scowled. 'The *Welisc* are always causing trouble,' he replied tartly. 'Their leader, whose outlandish name I can't pronounce, has been particularly boastful of what he intends to do to my people.'

'The King of Gwynedd is Cadwaladar ap Cadwallon,' replied Abbot Cadfan angrily. 'He descends from a line of great kings, great when your ancestors were scrabbling about in the mud!'

This time it was Bishop Leodegar who rapped on the floor for order.

'We will disband this council immediately if this continues,' he threatened.

Abbot Goelo of Bro Waroc'h, which lay in Armorica, cleared his throat. 'With respect, Leodegar, I think the council needs to hear the answer to the question posed by our distinguished brother from Gwynedd.'

'It is true that we had expected that the Venerable Drostó would represent your church at this council, Abbot Cadfan,' Bishop Leodegar said. 'What is it you imply about Benchoer?'

Abbot Cadfan turned his hard blue eyes directly on the tightlipped Bishop Ordgar.

'The Abbey of Benchoer is no more and Drostó sleeps with the few survivors in the woods of Gwynedd, moving each night in fear of their lives. A months ago, the leader of the Saxons of Mercia . . .'

'Angles,' corrected Bishop Ordgar loudly.

'. . . a barbarian called Wulfhere, led his hordes into Gwynedd and burned and destroyed our abbey at Benchoer, putting to the sword over a thousand of our religious. Is this the act of a Christian ruler?'

'A thousand brethren?' gasped one of the Gaulish delegates, in a shocked tone.

Abbot Ségdae of Imleach had been sitting listening to the argument in silence. He was chief bishop of the kingdom of Muman, the largest of the five kingdoms of Éireann. Now he stirred and gazed thoughtfully at Bishop Ordgar.

'Is this true, Bishop Ordgar?' he asked softly.

'Wulfhere is Bretwalda and—'

'Bretwalda? What is that?' queried Abbot Ségdae.

'It is a title which acknowledges that Wulfhere is overlord of the *Welisc* just as much as the kingdoms of the Angles and Saxons.'

'Acknowledged by whom?' Abbot Cadfan laughed sardonically. 'Not by the Britons. It is a title without meaning. We would have no "lord of the Britons", for that is what the title means, unless it be a Briton. We acknowledge no Saxon . . .' he paused '. . . nor Angle,' he added with emphasis, 'as lord over us. Certainly, we would not accept that a barbarian has such a right. Anyway, we are told that Wulfhere is not even acknowledged as lord by the other Saxon kings.'

Bishop Ordgar glowered across the table. 'Eorcenbehrt of Kent, the kingdom in which the primacy of Canterbury is placed, recognises him as such and gave him his daughter's hand in marriage.'

'Are you implying that Theodore, your archbishop at Canterbury, approves of that office?' demanded Abbot Goelo.

'Theodore has come to us from Rome and Vitalian has placed him as chief bishop of all the western islands.'

'He has no right to claim that position in any of the five kingdoms of Éireann,' Abbot Dabhóc immediately said.

Abbot Ségdae nodded in agreement and then looked at Bishop Leodegar, but addressed them all.

'I have come here to this ancient town of Autun in order to speak on the propositions that Rome has asked us to debate. It was a long and arduous trip with many dangers attending it. I represent the churches of Muman while my colleague, the Abbot Dabhóc, is here on behalf of Bishop Ségéne of Ard Macha. This argument is not germane to the propositions we have come here to discuss. The matters that are being argued, while horrendous and needing arbitration among the Britons and the Saxons, are not relevant to those matters which we have to decide.'

Abbot Dabhóc was shaking his head. 'I disagree. Are these not matters that reflect on the suitability of Bishop Ordgar to sit among us at this council? Does he approve of the massacre of religious by his people? He appears to give that approval. I think we should discuss this further. Let us hear from the representatives of the churches of the Franks, of the Gauls, of the land of Kernow and the kingdoms of Armorica.'

'It is right that we should have a say,' agreed an elderly bishop. 'I am Herenal of Bro Erech in the land of Armorica. I say that what I have heard from Bishop Ordgar does not reflect well on his calling as a man of peace.'

'Pah!' The sound was almost a spitting noise and it came from Bishop Ordgar. 'These Armoricans, Gauls, *Kern-welisc*, they are all the same people! They stick together. Let us waste no time in listening to them. I am here at the invitation of my brother Franks to discuss the Faith, not to hear the whining of barbarians.'

At once there was a chorus of angry voices. Bishop Leodegar was shaking his head sternly.

'Brothers in Christ! I beg of you to reflect on the matters that brought us hither from our various lands, from the peoples we represent. We have been instructed by His Holiness Vitalian to consider the statement of our fundamental faith in the Christ and of the Rule that we should all adhere to in every religious house in our lands. His Holiness has sent Nuntius Peregrinus to listen to our debates. These are the issues that should occupy our attention. These and no others.'

Abbot Dabhóc rose from his seat. 'Brethren, it is clear the atmosphere is stifled with the heat of anger and accusation. I propose that we delay the opening of this council for a day and a night. We have no scribes, nor advisers in attendance, so none of these contentious matters will be recorded. Let us go away and reflect on what has been said.'

Bishop Leodegar looked slightly relieved. 'An excellent suggestion,' he said.

'An insulting suggestion,' came the acid tones of Bishop Ordgar. 'You, Leodegar, as a Frank should be ashamed to be giving your support to these *Welisc*. They are as much enemies of your people as of mine.'

There were many cries of, 'Shame!'

'We are all one in Christ,' pointed out Abbot Dabhóc, 'or can it be that Bishop Ordgar would deny that? If it is so, then you have proven the point that Abbot Cadfan argues. You cannot be part of this council.'

'My authority is from Theodore of Canterbury who, in turn, was directly appointed by the Holy Father in Rome. What is *your* authority, barbarian?' Bishop Ordgar's brows came together threateningly.

'My authority is the church I serve,' began the abbot. 'And—'

Again Bishop Leodegar was rapping on the floor with his staff of office. He exchanged a questioning glance with Nuntius Peregrinus who shrugged and then nodded his head in answer. Bishop Leodegar took this as an affirmative to his unasked question and rose to face the delegates.

'I am closing this session. We shall pray and contemplate the purpose of our gathering for a day and a night. When we return here, which will be with our scribes and advisers, we will have no more of such arguments. There are more pressing matters to consider and discuss. Should anyone here attempt to continue this argument, then they will be expelled from the deliberations of the council no matter from what corner of the world they come. My brothers, let me urge this advice on you: *in medio tutissimus ibis* – you shall go safely into the middle course. Now depart and go in peace, in the name of the Most Holy, under Whose stern and watchful eye we gather to do homage.'

The abbots and bishops now rose in their seats and received the blessing from Bishop Leodegar almost reluctantly – and with not a little resentment from the chief antagonists.

As the gathering began to disperse, Abbot Ségdae moved across to Abbot Dabhóc.

'It is a long journey just to listen to the Briton arguing with the Saxon,' he said heavily.

Abbot Dabhóc shrugged. 'I have sympathy with the Britons. What Cadfan says is the truth. Both Angles and Saxons are constantly attacking the kingdoms of the Britons.'

'But I would have thought that Cadfan and Ordgar, as men of the Church, would employ diplomacy and turn their minds to what we came here to discuss.'

The two men had moved out of the chapel and into a courtyard with its central gushing fountain surrounded by scented gardens and tall buildings with Roman columns.

Abbot Dabhóc paused and looked upon the scene appreciatively.

'The long journey is worth it when we see wonders like this, Ségdae,' he observed. 'The cities built by the Romans are so unlike those of Éireann.'

It was true that outside the abbey, the city of Autun was a sprawl of Romanesque buildings which had originally been built many centuries before, when the Romans had marched into Gaul and defeated the Gaulish armies of Vercingetorix. They had built the city by a river and called it Augustodunum, but as the Gauls and the Romans had receded and merged with the invading Burgunds, it had become known as Autun, one of the earliest Christian centres in the part of Gaul now called Burgundia. The abbey retained many of its ancient Roman buildings, palaces and temples now re-dedicated to the Christian Faith. To Abbot Ségdae it seemed like a miniature Rome with its towering manmade constructions, a totally alien place to the small urban complexes of his native land.

There was a sudden shouting in the courtyard.

Abbot Ségdae started from his contemplation and glanced in astonishment across to where several of the prelates were engaged in a scuffle. Among them was Ordgar, who was grasping another cleric by the neck. It was Cadfan. The two men were shouting and hitting each other like a pair of quarrelling children. The others began dragging them apart. Cadfan's robe was torn while there was blood on Ordgar's face. It took no great linguist to understand the profanities they hurled at one another.

Bishop Leodegar hurried across, Nuntius Peregrinus at his side.

The other clerics were holding each man back, for if set loose they would doubtless have physically engaged with one another again.

'Brethren! Are you brothers in Christ or wild animals that you behave so?' came Bishop Leodegar's thunderous tone.

Abbot Cadfan blinked and seemed to come to his senses.

'The Saxon attacked me,' he said sullenly.

'The *Welisc* insulted me,' snapped Bishop Ordgar but he, too, was beginning to regain control of himself.

Bishop Leodegar was shaking his head with sadness.

'Shame on you both. Return to your quarters and pray forgiveness for your transgressions against the teachings of Our Lord. Shame is your portion until you have made atonement for your actions. I will give both of you a last chance to participate in our deliberations, not because of who you are but because of who you represent. Messengers will be sent to Theodore of Canterbury and to Drostó of Gwynedd informing them of how you carry out your sacred duties. If, when we next foregather, there is still enmity between you, then I shall dismiss you both from this council and will proceed without your representation. Do I make myself clear?'

There was a silence and then, like sullen children, first Abbot Cadfan and then Bishop Ordgar muttered agreement.

Bishop Leodegar gave a deep sigh. 'Now disperse,' he ordered. He glanced around at everyone. 'All of you, disperse.'

In ones and twos the men began to leave the luxurious courtyard, moving towards the main buildings of the abbey.

Abbot Dabhóc grinned at his companion. 'I tell you, Ségdae, this is the most hotblooded council that I have attended. I thought the arguments among our people, debating matters of the Faith, were fierce enough, but I have never seen clerics come to physical blows before.'

'I fear that our host is much too sanguine in hoping those two will declare a truce between them during the rest of this council,' Ségdae replied. 'And it will not just be the wars between Briton and Saxon but these ideas coming from Rome that will fuel the arguments. The Franks and Saxons support them – and we now have to argue against them. Such debate is bound to give rise to new animosities.'

'It is of no concern to us what the Franks and Saxons do in their own land.' Abbot Dabhóc grimaced sourly. 'We have our Faith and our own liturgy. Whatever decisions are made at this council cannot affect us any more than the decision made at Whitby.'

Abbot Ségdae shook his head in disagreement. 'First Whitby and now this council here in Autun. Where next? This erosion of our beliefs and cultures emanates from the new thinking at Rome, and I have no liking for it. Over the years, councils such as this have changed or amended the original concepts of the Faith until we can no longer be sure of the original teachings of the Founding Fathers.'

Abbot Dabhóc looked shocked but Ségdae continued, 'It is true, I tell you so. This is not the first time we have had to argue with Rome over the way they have altered even the very date on which Our Lord was martyred. Did not our own Columbanus argue with the Bishop of Rome over the date?'

'True enough, although at Ard Macha we begin to think it would be better for all Christendom to worship on the same day.'

'Better to worship in truth than in myth,' muttered Abbot Ségdae.

'Well, at least this council is not concerned with calendars and dates of ceremonies but in what we believe and how we should conduct ourselves in the religious houses,' Abbot Dabhóc concluded. 'I, for one, am looking forward to the debates.'

For the first time Abbot Ségdae allowed a brief smile to flit across his sombre features.

'At least, judging by the action of our brothers, those debates will be lively,' he joked.

They had halted in the corridor of the *hospitia* or guest quarters where individual chambers had been set aside for the accommodation of the senior delegates during the course of the council.

'I hear that your advisers have not arrived as yet?' Abbot Dabhóc suddenly remarked.

A worried expression returned to Abbot Ségdae's features. 'They were travelling separately and should have been here some days ago.'

'The seas can be tempestuous and it is a long voyage, even before coming to this land. Then there is a long river journey. Who are they? You have many good scholars in Muman.'

'Fidelma of Cashel has agreed to come to advise on the legal aspects of what we may agree – as it applies to the laws of the Fénechus, that is.'

Abbot Dabhóc's eyes widened. 'Fidelma? Her name is a by-word anywhere in the five kingdoms, especially since her investigation into the murder of the High King earlier this year. But murder is one thing; advising on how the decisions of this council may affect the laws and practices in the five kingdoms is another entirely.' He laughed suddenly. 'Perhaps, if our Briton and Saxon friends continue as they have done so far, we may be able to provide her with a new murder to investigate.'

Abbot Ségdae was disapproving.

'One should not be flippant about such matters, my brother. I simply wish, having found the circumstances that prevail in this abbey, that I had never asked her to come here in the first place. Anyway, the hour grows late. There is barely time to bathe before the evening meal.'

* * *

Someone was shaking him. He was aware of a voice calling urgently. Abbot Ségdae awoke, blinking against the light of the candle enclosed in a lantern that was held above him.

'Bishop Leodegar says you must come at once!'

Abbot Ségdae focused on the shadowy figure of the religieux who had been trying to rouse him from a deep slumber. He realised it was still dark and the room felt cold.

'What is it?' he demanded.

'Bishop Leodegar says—' began the other.

'I heard you,' replied the abbot, struggling to sit up. 'What has happened?'

The religieux seemed agitated. 'I cannot say . . . you must come.'

With a sigh, Abbot Ségdae swung from the bed and began pulling on his robe. Within a few minutes he was following the religieux along the darken corridor.

'Where are we going, or can't you tell me that, Brother . . . Brother . . . ?'

'I am Brother Sigeric.'

'So where are we going?'

'To the quarters of the Saxon bishop. Bishop Ordgar.'

'Why?'

'I am told only to bring you there at the urgent request of Bishop Leodegar.'

Abbot Ségdae sighed irritably. It was clear that he would get no further information.

However, it did not take long to reach a chamber where the door was open. Brother Sigeric motioned him inside. The sight that met his eyes caused Abbot Ségdae to pause on the threshold.

The first thing he saw was a religieux bending over a figure on the floor. He recognised the body immediately as that of Abbot Cadfan. A groan came from the man and Abbot Ségdae realised that Cadfan was semi-conscious – alive, Thank God! Then he saw Bishop Leodegar standing by a second body that lay beyond Cadfan. That body was also clothed in religious robes.

'Bishop Ordgar?' he asked tersely. 'Has Cadfan killed him then?'

There was a groan from the bed behind the door.

Abbot Ségdae swung round. Bishop Ordgar of Canterbury was lying on the bed barely conscious. Bewildered, the abbot turned back to Bishop Leodegar and the second body.

'I am afraid that it is your colleague, Abbot Dabhóc of Tulach Óc,' said Bishop Leodegar heavily. 'That is why I sent for you, brother. Abbot Dabhóc has been murdered.'

Chapter Two

'There it is!'

Clodio, the elderly but muscular boatman, took one hand from the tiller and pointed to the left bank as the craft swung round the bend of the broad river, among trees and short limestone reaches. The two religious seated in the well of the craft turned in their seats towards him and then followed his outstretched arm towards the embankment.

'Is that Nebirnum?' asked the female religieuse. Her robes identified her as being from the land of Hibernia. She was tall, well proportioned and her eyes were bright, though Clodio the boatman had difficulty discerning whether they were blue or green. They seemed to change with her moods. Rebellious strands of red hair escaped from her *caille*, or headdress. Not for the first time Clodio reflected that she was attractive. When she conversed with her companion, a Saxon religieux about the same age, a thickset man with dark brown eyes and hair, Clodio had been surprised at the easy intimacy of their relationship. Their names were Fidelma and Eadulf, and it was not long before the boatman realised that they were also man and wife, for he had overheard them speaking of a child they had left behind to come on this journey.

Fidelma was gazing up at the high sloping hill on which the buildings straggled around an imposing structure that proclaimed, by its very features, that it was an abbey of some importance. The boatman nodded. His Latin, the only language that they had in common, was fairly poor but understandable.

'That is the abbey of Nebirnum,' Clodio confirmed. 'There you may acquire horses for the last part of your journey.'

Eadulf, sitting beside Fidelma, winced slightly.

'A horse ride?' he asked in a painful tone. 'How far is it then to Autun from this place?'

Clodio, who worked the boat with his two hardy sons, was regarding Eadulf's lamentation with undisguised amusement.

'From Nebirnum to the great city of Autun is but two to three days' comfortable ride, no more. There is a good road due east.'

They had been in the riverboat for seven days. It seemed an eternity since they had landed at the Armorican port of Naoned and then commenced their journey upriver, along this majestic green waterway called the Liger. It was cramped in the small craft for, although they were the only passengers, the boatman was a trader along the river and transported bulky bales of materials and sometimes even live animals which had to be shipped from town to town along the banks of the winding thoroughfare. All the time, the craft been making its way against the flow of the river which rose, so they were told, over a thousand kilometres away in the mountains. Sometimes its flow was imperceptible and the boatman could even use a sail to progress; sometimes oars were necessary, long poles by which the craft was pushed. And, more often than not, mules were harnessed and pulled the boat, especially where the clear green water ran faster over the shallows through stretches of golden gravel that lined the banks. Fidelma had been duly impressed with the knowledge and skill in which the journey, first east and then south, along the broad waterway, had been conducted by Clodio and his sons. The craft was always on the move, in spite of the mighty strength of the river which occasionally ran around islands in the centre of the water, places of wild desolation. One lasting memory was of the women washing clothes along the banks, sometimes appearing in groups and sometimes as solitary figures, beating the wet clothing on rocks.

Now Fidelma sighed, but not at the prospect of exchanging the comfort of the boat for the saddle of a horse for she was a good horsewoman and had been at ease on a horse almost before she could walk.

'Where would we find horses? Horses cost money,' she pointed out.

'Is there anything in this world that is free?' Clodio replied philosophically. 'Ah, but wandering religious expect all things to be given freely to them, in exchange for a muttered blessing. It would be an ideal life if all were so simple, my friends, but I have a wife and sons to keep.'

Fidelma frowned at the implication that he feared they might not pay for the journey.

'Boatman,' she said sternly, 'did we not negotiate a fee for you to bring us from the port of Naoned to this place? Was it not a fair fee? If so, as we approach this place, now is the time for the fee to be paid.'

'I did not mean . . .' Clodio began, abashed, but Fidelma had already reached into her marsupium and counted out the coins that she thrust towards him.

'Remember, boatman, that a wandering religious may not always be a beggar,' she said stiffly.

Eadulf looked nervously at his companion and hoped that she would not boast of her relationship to the Kings of Muman.

'*Redime te captium quam minimo*,' he muttered, using the ancient Latin prescription for soldiers who were captured: if taken prisoner, pay as little as possible to buy your freedom. In other words, make sure you give the enemy as little information as you can. If Clodio thought that they were rich, greed might entice him to consider holding them for ransom. Eadulf had heard plenty of stories of pilgrims travelling in distant lands who were captured and held for ransom and sometimes never heard of again.

Fidelma gave him a look of understanding before turning back to the boatman.

'We promised to pay you and, even though it makes the rest of our journey difficult, for we cannot afford horses, we will do so,' she said quietly.

Clodio, who had not understood the Latin saying, merely nodded as his hands closed over the coins and dropped them into the leather purse at his belt.

'Bishop Arigius, at the abbey, will take care of you,' he told them. 'He is a man of good reputation.'

Turning to his two sons, he ordered them to take out the oars while he cried a warning and jerked on a rope to lower the single sail of the craft. Then he moved quickly back to the tiller and, with dextrous smoothness, drew the craft alongside one of the several wooden piers that jutted into the river at this point. In a few moments they were tied up and the sons of the boatmen helped first Fidelma and Eadulf ashore.

Clodio nodded to them both. 'Good luck on your travels, my friends,' he said. 'Follow that road up to the town and it will bring you to the doors of the abbey. Remember, it is the Bishop Arigius whom you wish to see.'

They said farewell to the man and his sons who now began to offload their goods. Merchants and onlookers were already moving down to the pier to examine what cargo they had brought as Fidelma and Eadulf set off up the road towards the main town. Eadulf had felt the heat of the early summer sun while he was in the boat but now on land it struck on his face and shoulders with a force that caused sweat to form on his brow.

'I swear, Fidelma,' began Eadulf, but his sandal struck a stone that stood prouder than the rest and caused him to trip, almost sending him headlong. He just recovered himself at the last moment with a muttered oath. 'I swear, Fidelma, that I am sick of travelling.'

Fidelma glanced at him without humour. 'Do you think I am not?' she said shortly. 'Since the birth of little Alchú, how much time have I spent with our son? Too little, that is for certain. When we returned from Tara a few months ago, I fully expected that we would be able to remain at Cashel for . . . well, for the foreseeable future.'

'We could have refused this journey,' Eadulf pointed out.

'Duty must come first,' Fidelma replied in a heavy tone. 'If my brother, the King, requests me to come here as aide and adviser to his bishop, Ségdae of Imleach, then this is where I must come. But you were not obliged to accompany me.'

'My place is wherever you are,' replied Eadulf simply.

Fidelma laid a free hand on his arm. 'I make no demands on you, Eadulf,' she said softly.

'Did you not say that duty must come first?' he replied with a raised eyebrow. 'And what greater duty is there than the moral code of the bonds that are between us? So do not question where my duty lies. It is just that I cannot see why some council of church leaders held in Gaul . . .'

'The Gauls are almost gone now,' corrected Fidelma. 'The Franks have overrun and settled this territory and call these lands the kingdoms of Austrasia and Neustria. Two brothers rule them, I am told.'

'Wherever we are,' Eadulf went on, 'I still cannot see why some council of church leaders in this remote spot has any influence on the five kingdoms of Éireann, or even on the Britons or Saxon kingdoms.'

'Perhaps not now but someday hence the influence of the decisions made here might be felt. That is why, when Vitalian, the Bishop of Rome, called representatives of the western churches to this place, Bishop Ségdae had to attend. You know that the practices we follow in Éireann are under threat from the new ideas springing up in Rome which are alien to our laws and to our way of life.'

'But Autun is such a long way from Cashel!'

'Thoughts and ideas travel faster than a man,' replied Fidelma firmly.

Eadulf sighed and shifted the weight of the bag that he carried on his shoulder. He cast an envious glance at Fidelma's light linen robes and wished he had something more cooling than the brown woollen homespun he wore as a Brother of the Faith.

But they were moving on easier ground now among the buildings, and the gates of the abbey were within easy access. There were plenty of people about but no one paid them much interest. It was clear that Nebirnum was a busy trading town filled with strangers, and many wagons loaded with goods were moving here and there.

At the gates of the abbey they encountered a Brother who seemed more of a sentinel than a welcoming religieux.

'*Pax tecum*,' Fidelma greeted the dark, sun-tanned man.

'*Pax vobiscum*,' replied the man indifferently.

'We have come from the distant land of Hibernia. We are on our way to the Council at Autun and were told that Bishop Arigius might facilitate our journey there.'

The man pointed through the gates. 'You may enquire for the bishop inside,' he said carelessly, and turned to continue to gaze at the passers-by.

'Not exactly an enthusiastic greeting for us *peregrinatio pro Christo*,' Eadulf muttered wryly.

Fidelma did not reply. A youthful religieux was passing through the quadrangle in which they found themselves, and she hailed him.

'Where can we find Bishop Arigius?' she asked.

The young man stopped and frowned. 'I am his steward. You are strangers in this place.' It was a statement rather than a question.

'We are on our way to Autun to attend the council there. We are from the land of Hibernia.'

The young man's eyes seemed to widen slightly at the latter statement. Then he said: 'Follow me.'

He led them to a door in a corner of the quadrangle, which gave entrance into a square tower that seemed to be opposite to what was obviously a chapel. They followed him up the dark, oak stairs to a door of similar hue. Here the young steward turned to them and asked them to wait. He knocked upon the door and, without pausing for an answer, opened it and passed inside, closing it behind him. They could hear the mumble of voices and then the door re-opened and the young man beckoned them inside.

Bishop Arigius was a tall thin man with sharp features, piercing dark eyes and thin red lips. His hair was sparse and silver grey. He had risen from a chair and crossed the room to greet them, a smile of welcome revealing yellowing teeth.

'*Pax vobiscum.*' He intoned the greeting solemnly. 'My steward tells me that you are bound for Autun, to the council, and that you come from the land of Hibernia?'

'He tells you no lie,' replied Eadulf, shifting the weight of his bag on his shoulder.

The motion was not lost on the bishop.

'Then come and be seated, put down your bags and join me in refreshment. A glass of white wine cooled in our cellars . . . ?' He nodded to the steward who hurried away to obtain the beverage.

'I am Bishop Arigius, the second of that name to hold office here in this ancient abbey.'

'An impressive building and an impressive town, from the little I have seen,' Eadulf replied politely after they had introduced themselves.

Bishop Arigius gave a smile of pride.

'Indeed. When the great Julius Caesar marched the Roman legions into this land, he chose this spot as a military depot for his legions. The Aedui, the Gauls who lived here, had a hill fort on this very spot, which Caesar refortified; hence the name of this place, which was Noviodunum – *novus*, the Latin for new, and *dunum*, the Gaulish word for a fort. So it was "new fort" and since then, changing accents have brought about its current name. It was one of the earliest places in which the Faith was established in this land, and for a while it became known as Gallia Christiana. The bishops here were renowned.'

'You have great knowledge of this town,' Fidelma said solemnly.

'*Scientia est potentia*,' smiled the bishop.

'Knowledge is power,' repeated Fidelma softly. It was a philosophy she had often expounded.

The young steward returned with a jug and beakers, which he filled with a golden-coloured wine. It was cold and refreshing.

'We make it from our own vineyards,' explained the young man in answer to their expressions of praise.

'Now,' Bishop Arigius said briskly, 'I presume that you have heard the news from Autun?'

Fidelma exchanged a puzzled look with Eadulf. 'The news?' she repeated.

'We only heard it ourselves yesterday afternoon.' The bishop looked from one to another expectantly as if all was explained.

'We are still at a loss,' Fidelma said. 'What news from Autun?'

Bishop Arigius sighed and sat back. 'Forgive me. Foolishly, my steward thought you might have been on your way to Autun because of the news.'

Fidelma tried to be patient. 'We have been travelling along the river for many days. We have heard no news for all that time.'

'One of the abbots from your land of Hibernia was murdered there.'

Fidelma was shocked.

Eadulf immediately asked: 'Do you know the name of this abbot? It was not Abbot Ségdae?'

Bishop Arigius shook his head. 'I know only that he was of your land.'

'What else can you tell us of what has happened?' Eadulf pressed.

'Nothing beyond that simple fact,' replied the bishop promptly. 'A passing merchant brought us the news yesterday.'

'No name was mentioned?' queried Fidelma.

'No name was mentioned,' affirmed the bishop.

There was a silence. Then Fidelma said: 'It is imperative that we should continue on to Autun as soon as possible. But the boatman who brought us hither said that it is a two- or three-day journey by horse from here.'

Bishop Arigius glanced out of the window. 'It is no use continuing on now, for the best part of the day is gone,' he declared. 'Stay and feast with us this evening and continue in the morning.'

Fidelma smiled sadly. 'Alas, we have no horses, and . . .'

The bishop waved his hand deprecatingly.

'One of our brethren leaves tomorrow at dawn with a wagon carrying goods destined for the brethren in Autun. You may ride on that and welcome. The road is good, especially at this time of year, being dry and hard, and it will take no more than four days to reach the town.'

'We accept,' Eadulf said hastily. The prospect of racing along strange roads on an equally strange steed had not been a pleasant one. Being seated comfortably on a wagon was a much better prospect.

'Excellent.' Bishop Arigius stood and they followed his example. 'My steward will show you to our *hospitia*, our guests' quarters, where you may rest and refresh yourselves. We gather shortly in the refectory; my steward will guide you there. The bell will toll for the services in the chapel. We rise at the tolling of the bell, just before dawn. I will instruct our brother to await you in the quadrangle to commence your journey tomorrow.'

'And the name of this brother?' asked Fidelma.

'Brother Budnouen. He is a Gaul.'

Brother Budnouen was rotund, with a podgy red face seemingly lacking a neck, for folds of flesh seemed to flop straight down on to his chest. Middle aged, short in stature and tanned, he had pale eyes, almost sea-green, and long brown hair, which they immediately saw was cut in the manner of the tonsure of St John rather than in the *corona spina* favoured by Rome. In spite of his heavy breathing, caused by his girth and weight, the brother's forearms seemed quite muscular from hard work, and his hands were callused. They later learned that this was due to his being a wagonman; the leather reins caused the hardening of the skin on the palms. It came as no surprise when he told them that he had spent his youth as a seaman, sailing along the ports of Armorica to Britain and Hibernia, whose languages he spoke with great fluency. He was an excellent companion; his eyes had a twinkle, his face a ready smile and his attitude was to look for the best that life had to offer. In fact, he was a very loquacious fellow and the moment they left the abbey at Nebirnum, Brother Budnouen kept up a steady commentary as he guided the wagon, pulled by four powerful mules, along the road which headed due east.

'I am originally of the Aeudi,' he told them. 'This was once Aeudi country, but then many years ago, the Burgunds came and drove us out. Some of us fled to Armorica. Some, like me, stayed to make the best of things. Now the Burgunds, in their turn, are made vassals by the Franks who call this land Austrasia.'

'The Aeudi were Gauls?' queried Eadulf, who was always determined to add to his knowledge. He and Fidelma were seated beside Brother Budnouen on the driving seat of the wagon as their guide and driver expertly directed the team of mules by a flick of the long leather reins now and again.

Brother Budnouen laughed pleasantly and there was pride in his voice.

'They were indeed the Gauls, my friend. I am descended from the great Vercingetorix – king of the world – who nearly destroyed Caesar and the Romans until he was forced to surrender in order to save the lives of the women and children that Caesar would have sacrificed by the thousands to ensure his victory. Caesar was so scared of that great man that he had him taken in chains to Rome, kept for years in a dungeon and then ritually strangled to celebrate his final victory.'

Eadulf pursed his lips. 'War is not a pleasant thing.'

'That was something the Romans found out. If they thought that the death of Vercingetorix would cowe us into submission, they were wrong. We rose many times against them but it seemed that when one legion was defeated, three more took its place. We were still fighting the Roman legions nearly a hundred years after Caesar departed. Eventually Gaul became a Roman province and peaceful, until a few more centuries when the Burgunds and Franks came flooding across the Rhine to destroy us.'

'What do you know of this city of Autun?' asked Fidelma, trying to change the conversation to the subject that was continuing to trouble her.

'Autun?' Brother Budnouen shrugged. 'There was nothing there but a few huts until the Emperor Augustus designated it as the new central city of the Aeudi. He called it Augustodunum, the fort of Augustus – that's where the Burgunds derived the name Autun. The Romans had made our own capital and fortress Bibracte uninhabitable as a punishment for Vercingetorix's near-defeat of them. They created Augustodunum into a great Roman city to impress the Gauls.'

He paused to negotiate a difficult bend of the road.

'The Faith reached the town very early. They say that it became an episcopal see in the time of the blessed Irenaeus, just over a century after the crucifixion of Our Lord. It is told that the son of Senator Faustus of Autun, a young man named Symphorian, converted to the Faith and destroyed a statue of the Roman goddess Cybele as a protest. He was arrested and flogged, but when he continued to refuse to deny the Faith he was beheaded in front of his mother, Augusta. They built the abbey over his grave, which was the ancient necropolis.'

Brother Budnouen chuckled and nudged Eadulf. 'They say if you pray by the grave, you will get a cure for the pox!' He paused, glanced in embarrassment at Fidelma and added: 'Begging your pardon, Sister.'

'I was trying to discover what the town is like today and why it was deemed the best place for this council,' Fidelma replied coldly.

'Who knows why?' replied the Gaul. 'Isn't Vitalian, the Holy Father, a Roman and perhaps he remembers that Autun was Augustodunum. The Romans have long memories. They never forgave our people for defeating their legions and occupying Rome itself, and that was so many generations before the birth of Our Saviour that they are almost beyond counting.'

Eadulf was about to ask him to explain but Fidelma, sensing that the question would bring forth another long discourse, nudged Eadulf discreetly and said: 'So who is the bishop of Autun now?'

'Leodegar,' replied the man at once. 'He is elderly but still has a sharp mind, and is renowned for his learning and virtue. The son of Frankish nobles, he grew up at the court of King Clotaire. He even helped in the government of the kingdom until he was named as bishop. He's a strong leader, they say, but too fond of reforms. What's more, he seems intent on repairing the old Roman walls of the city and restoring the Roman public buildings. I reckon that is probably why Rome has given him the opportunity to preside over this important council.'

'And do you know anything about the happening in Autun?'

'You mean the murder there? No, I'm afraid I cannot help you. I heard the merchants gossip, that is all. Some abbot at the council was found slain. There was talk of arguments and fighting among the clerics. But that is all I can say.'

If it was all he could say, Brother Budnouen certainly had a way of expanding such a little into long discourses, and by the end of the first day's travel Fidelma and Eadulf were as much exhausted by his constant prattle as by the exigencies of the journey. Nevertheless, they agreed that it did help to pass the time, and the Gaul was able to point out interesting aspects of the rolling countryside through which they travelled. In the evenings he knew places to stop where good food and beds were available, and with rivers or springs where it was safe to bathe. Fidelma longed for the rituals of the Irish baths and for hot water and soap, but she made the best that she could of it.

On the morning of the third day they passed an imposing hill rising out of a magnificent surrounding forest. To their surprise, Brother Budnouen halted his team of mules, climbed down and knelt in its direction as if in prayer. When he climbed back on the wagon, he explained: 'Bibracte – that was the capital of the Aedui, the very spot where Vercingetorix was proclaimed head of all the tribes of Gaul to confront Julius Caesar.' He pointed to the hill. 'It was there that Caesar defeated him and finished writing his account of how he conquered my people.'

'So how far to Autun now?' asked Eadulf wearily.

'We shall be there tomorrow morning. It is twenty-five kilometres more. Tonight we rest at a place outside the town so that we do not arrive at night time. As I say, Leodegar with Lord Guntram, the ruler of the province, has restored and maintains the old Roman walls and employs guards who do not like the approach of strangers during the hours of darkness.'

Fidelma was surprised. 'Is it so dangerous to be abroad in these parts then?'

'There is always danger, Sister,' the Gaul stated. 'The richer the towns, the more that thieves and robbers are attracted to them. Bands of robbers often prowl the roads.'

'Should we not have waited for warriors to guard *us*?' asked Eadulf, not disguising his nervousness. They had entered a countryside that was heavily wooded and could harbour vagabonds.

Brother Budnouen chuckled. 'Why would you want warriors to guard you? Do you carry treasure with you?'

'Of course not,' snapped Eadulf. 'It is just that our lives are precious to us.'

'Listen, my friend,' the Gaul was still smiling, 'your life is safer when you do not surround yourself with bodyguards, for bodyguards proclaim to bandits that you have something worth guarding. If you have nought but your life, then better not to let them think otherwise. Often I have passed along these highways and only once or twice was I stopped. But these days thieves are not interested in the goods I transport to the brethren in Autun, nor those I return with from Autun to Nebirnum. They want gold, silver, jewels and suchlike. Things for easy profit.'

'We will have to take your word for that,' Fidelma replied easily. 'But we will rest easier when we reach Autun.'

'You'll see it tomorrow,' Brother Budnouen assured her. 'Once we traverse this area which still retains its old Gaulish name of Morven – that means the country of black mountains because of the darkness of the green hills and forests here – once through here you will see the city of Autun.'

He was right. They approached the city about midday from the north-west, coming across the shoulder of a small hill. Enclosed by ancient grey walls, it seemed large to them since, although they had seen Rome, they had little to compare it with. That it was big and impressive was their immediate reaction. Moreover, rising above the red-tiled roofs of the buildings, on the far side of the city, was a massive complex like a castle – the great abbey itself. Part of it rose many storeys high and a massive tower stood at one end.

They turned their attention to the city ramparts, ancient walls that here and there showed signs of reconstruction. There was no denying that it was a beautiful location, sited among a lush green terrain with vineyards to be seen flourishing here and there around the city walls.

Brother Budnouen smiled in satisfaction as he glanced at their expressions. People from the western islands were always impressed with the cities of Gaul. As the wagon trundled down the roadway towards the river, he saw that his passengers were examining large square-shaped stone building to the right of the roadside.

'That was originally the Roman Temple of Janus,' he offered. 'It is used for other things now, of course. They do say that the Romans built it on one of the sacred sites of the Aeudi so that their god's power would negate the power of the old Gaulish god. A strange and fearful people, those Romans.' He chuckled and pointed to the river that they had to cross to enter the walled city. 'This is the Aturavos. Strange how, in spite of the Romans and then the Burgunds who have settled here, the old rivers, forests and hills retain their original Gaulish names. While our people have been forced to give way, our names survive.'

'Does the name mean anything?' enquired Eadulf.

'A shame on you for asking, Brother,' admonished Brother Budnouen. 'All names mean something. It means "the little river".'

The wagon rumbled across a wide wooden bridge towards an imposing stone gateway with a high circular arch and a further construction above it reaching heavenwards. Many people were passing to and fro beneath while armed guards were keeping watch on them.

'This is the main gate of the city on this north side. There are, of course, three other gates,' Brother Budnouen informed them. 'That is the style of the Romans. But one of the gates is in bad repair. That's the one that would have given more easy access to the abbey.'

'The walls are impressive,' Eadulf observed. 'I have not seen the like, other than in Rome.'

'The locals call Autun the rival city of Rome,' agreed the Gaul. 'The walls stretch all around it. We head south through the city to the far side where the abbey is situated.'

Once through the impressive gates, the odours of the city impinged on their senses. Fidelma and Eadulf were used to the countryside, and the towns of their own lands were little more than well-spaced villages without protective walls. Now the smells reawakened memories of Rome: the stench of sewerage, of rotting vegetables and unattended animal waste and offal in the streets, combined with the sweat of people crowded into confined spaces.

Fidelma shuddered, wondering how anyone could actually live in such a place.

Brother Budnouen glanced at her and grinned. 'It takes some getting used to, if you are country bred,' he remarked.

She did not respond, fearing the atmosphere would cause her to be nauseous. As they proceeded south along what seemed a principal street, women, whose dress announced them to be of some rank and wealth, passed by them, holding little bunches of flowers before their nostrils. It brought a faint smile to Fidelma's lips. At least she was not the only one to react to the stink of what some called civilisation. She could not remember seeing such things in Rome but then, of course, the thoroughfares of Rome were much wider. This street was lined with little shops, even blacksmiths and all manner of vendors of goods. The cacophony of noise – the shouting of the traders, vying with one another to attract customers, and the haggling of customers over prices – oppressed her ears in a solid wall of sound.

As they passed through a square, the crack of a whip nearby caused Fidelma to start nervously and peer around. In a corner of the square, she spotted a small platform on which were huddled half a dozen tiny figures. They were difficult to see, as a number of people were crowded before the platform. A tall man stood behind the figures, holding a whip. He was shouting but Fidelma had no idea what he was saying. Then her eyes widened as she saw that they were children, and that each child wore an iron collar about his or her neck. She drew a quick breath in horror.

Brother Budnouen followed her gaze. 'A slave auction,' he explained nonchalantly. 'There is quite a business done in the city. Many foreign merchants pass this way.'

'It's disgusting,' Fidelma muttered.

Brother Budnouen looked amused. 'What – slavery? How would the world function without slaves?'

'Easily enough,' she replied spiritedly.

The Gaul chuckled. 'Come, do not try to tell me that your people have no slaves.'

'Not in the sense you have them here,' she replied.

'In what sense then?' he asked, raising his eyebrows.

'We do have a class whom you could call non-free, the *fudir*,' she admitted.

'And how are they bought and sold?'

'They are not commodities bought and sold for profit like sacks of flour. They are usually captives in battle or those criminals who have lost their rights to be part of the clan, the basis of our society. We call them *daer-fudir* – they have to serve the clan until they have atoned for their transgressions or done sufficient to gain freedom. They do not suffer the hopelessness of slaves that we see in other lands. The law of our land favours the eventual emancipation of the *fudir* class.'

Brother Budnouen sniffed in disbelief. 'I have heard that some merchants of the Angles and Saxons sell children to the Irish as *servus* and what is that but a slave?'

'It is true that there is slavery among my people,' Eadulf intervened, 'especially among poor people who will sell their children or some other relative to merchants to raise money. I have seen these same merchants selling them in the ports of Hibernia and I hope the fashion will cease, for the Irish take them in innocence, not because of wanting slaves but thinking they are helping to rehabilitate *dear-fudir*, for the very word *fudir*, as I have heard it, means a remnant or someone who is superfluous. It is true, my friend, that the concept of one person being able to own another, as one would a piece of cloth or a sword, is beyond comprehension to the Hibernians.'

Brother Budnouen pulled a face. '*De gustibus non est disputandum*,' he shrugged, dismissing the argument. About tastes there is no disputing. 'But the Faith accepts the institution of slavery. Slaves who flee from their masters are condemned and are refused Eucharistic communion. Scripture supports this. Does not Peter say, "Slaves, submit yourselves to your masters with all respect, not only to those who are good and considerate, but also to those who are harsh". To claim it is wrong to have slaves is heresy.'

Fidelma was angry. 'Didn't Paul of Tarsus tell the Corinthians: "If you can gain your freedom, do so . . . do not become slaves of human beings".'

Brother Budnouen was enjoying the exchange.

'In the text from Titus, does not scripture instruct us, "Teach slaves to be subject to their masters in everything, to try to please them, not to talk back to them, and not to steal from them, but to show that they can be fully trusted so that in every way they will make the teaching about God our Saviour attractive"? You seem to be preaching rebellion, Sister. We are here to spread the Faith, not to preach the overthrow of the system and of kings and emperors.'

'I am not here to conduct a moral argument,' snapped Fidelma.

'*Quando hic sum, non ieiuno Sabbato – quando Romae sum, ieiuno Sabbato*,' Eadulf quoted, watching her expression.

Fidelma pouted in annoyance. It was the thought of the Blessed Ambrose: when I am here, I do not fast on Saturday. When I am in Rome, I fast on Saturday. It was an admonition to obey local customs and not to try to impose your own.

Nevertheless, the slave market and the sight of children being sold left a bad taste in her mouth. They passed through the square with Fidelma trying to avert her gaze from the forlorn-looking children waiting to be purchased. The sights and smells of the city, the noise that arose on all sides as their wagon trundled along the narrow streets, suddenly depressed her.

'Don't worry,' Brother Budnouen said, as if reading her thoughts. 'Not all streets are like this. This is the main road of commerce. Once we leave this, there are quieter streets which lead up to the ecclesiastical quarters.'

Again he was right.

They turned out of the bedlam, still moving southward. Almost at once, even from the roadway, they could see the imposing structure of the abbey rising over the other buildings. Even the smells were less dominant here, for the houses appeared as more spacious villas, just as Fidelma remembered them in Rome. It was another world from the crowded hovels that were clustered around the gate by which they had entered.

'Are all the entrances into the city as noisome?' demanded Eadulf, apparently sharing the same idea.

Brother Budnouen shrugged. 'The city gate areas are where trade is carried out. Where trade is done you have the most noise and waste,' he pointed out philosophically.

They came into a large stone-flagged square, reasonably empty of people. On one side, the buildings of the abbey rose skywards. Close up they were ugly and forbidding, and Fidelma viewed them without enthusiasm. From afar they had looked impressive. Now the high walls seemed to intimidate the surrounding buildings, as well as the people passing under their shadows.

'Well, this is the abbey of Autun and the end of our journey,' the Gaul said, as he swung the wagon round towards a low gateway and halted the mule team before it. 'That is where I deliver my goods. It is the entrance to the storehouses. But if you go across towards that building.' he indicated with his hand, 'you will find the office of the steward of the abbey. You may enquire there as to where you should go.'

Eadulf was already climbing thankfully down, removing the bags, before turning to help Fidelma alight.

'We thank you for the journey, Brother,' he said. 'And the pleasantness of your company, as well as the knowledge and advice that you have imparted.'

Brother Budnouen responded with his almost perpetual smile.

'I shall be in Autun for a week or so. Doubtless our paths will cross before I depart. Should you wish to journey back to Nebirnum with me, just ask the steward here and he will find me. I wish you luck in your stay, although you may not find the attitude of the religious here to your liking . . .' He shrugged. '"What went you out into the wilderness for to see? A reed shaken with the wind . . . a man clothed in soft raiment?"'

'We are well aware of scripture, my friend,' Fidelma replied, without humour. 'We have come to this country with no preconceptions. However, we are much indebted to you, Brother.'

Brother Budnouen raised a hand in parting and edged his cart closer through the large wagonway between the buildings. Eadulf, shouldering the bags, began to move off over the stone-paved square towards the door that the Gaul had indicated. Fidelma fell in step alongside.

'I am not impressed,' Eadulf remarked quietly to her, glancing round. 'Preconception or no.'

She gave him an amused sideways look. 'What – not impressed with one of the great cities of Christendom?'

He shook his head firmly. 'Give me the mountains, rivers and forests any day in preference to the confines of a city. It is like a prison with walls all around. And these grey, grim heights . . .' he indicated the abbey with a jerk of his head. 'There is something forbidding about the place.'

'The buildings are quite intimidating, I agree,' Fidelma replied, glancing upwards. 'I am not a city dweller. I also hate the idea of being confined. But we have to admit that such buildings have a curiously impressive quality of their own. So absorb the experience even if you cannot enjoy it. Now let us face the next ordeal . . . we must find out who has been killed here. Pray God it is not our old friend, Ségdae.'

They were some way off the steward's office when the door opened and a religieux exited. Eadulf hailed him and asked if this was where the steward of the abbey was to be found.

The man examined him for a moment and then frowned at Fidelma.

'Women go to the *Domus Femini*, the house of women,' he said in accented and guttural Latin, pointing along the side of the building. 'You are not welcome here.'

Eadulf stared at him in bewilderment. 'This is the abbey of Autun, isn't it?' he asked. 'We seek the steward here.'

A scowl settled on the man's dark features.

'Women are not welcome here,' he repeated. 'Go!'

Fidelma's lips thinned and her eyes grew dangerously bright.

'We *demand* to see the steward! she said, her words slow and clear. 'Where do we find him?'

The man was about to respond further when a familiar figure suddenly appeared in the doorway behind him. It was Abbot Ségdae. He looked grey and ill but he came swiftly towards them, hands outstretched in welcome.

'Fidelma! Eadulf! Thank God you have come at last!'

Chapter Three

'It is good to see you well, Ségdae,' Fidelma said warmly. The Abbot of Imleach had drawn them into the *anticum*, the antechamber of the abbey, but not before a sharp exchange with the religieux who had tried to prevent their entrance. The man finally shrugged and moved off. Now they were seated on wooden benches in a large hall with vaulted roof. There was no one else about.

'It is a relief that you have arrived.' The abbot was clearly in a state of agitation.

'It is obvious something disturbs you, Ségdae,' Fidelma observed.

'We heard that an abbot of the five kingdoms had been killed,' Eadulf went on. 'We were at Nebirnum and hastened here. Who was it?'

'Dabhóc, a kindly man who was attending here on behalf of the bishop of Ard Macha.'

'I do not know him,' Fidelma said.

'He was abbot of Tulach Óc, in the northern kingdom.'

Fidelma shook her head, for the name and place meant nothing to her.

'What happened, exactly?' asked Eadulf. 'Who killed him?'

Abbot Ségdae's face remained drawn. 'That is the precisely the problem which is being argued over. The body of Abbot Dabhóc was found in the chamber of Bishop Ordgar . . .'

'Not Bishop Ordgar of Kent!' Eadulf exclaimed.

'You know him?' Abbot Ségdae asked.

'I have heard much of him. I know that Theodore, who was appointed archbishop at Canterbury, is kindly disposed towards him. He believes firmly in the rules of Rome and has little sympathy towards the people or the churches of the west.'

'Ordgar is here as Theodore's representative,' Abbot Ségdae said gloomily, 'and I can vouch for his attitudes towards the representatives of the churches of the Britons. Alas, his manner is all too arrogant.'

'So it was Ordgar who slew Dabhóc?' interposed Fidelma.

'That is what has not been decided. There is unquiet in this abbey and the council has not been able to meet in formal session yet. There has been nothing but rumour and whisperings during the last week.'

'Was that why I was not welcome here?' asked Fidelma. 'That religieux who greeted us muttered something to that effect, and also something about my going to a *Domus Femini*. I do not understand.'

'No,' replied Abbot Ségdae. 'The bishop was disinclined to admit you here because this abbey, alas, is not a *conhospitae*, a mixed house. There is a separate house for the females under an *abbatissa*. The males remain here under the bishop and abbot of this place. He is a Frank called Leodegar – an intelligent man, but of that party which believes in the segregation of the sexes and the idea of celibacy among those serving the New Faith.'

'Then that makes our position awkward,' Eadulf pointed out.

Abbot Ségdae was contrite. 'I did not know that this situation prevailed here, otherwise I would not have requested that your brother, Colgú, send you here as my adviser.'

'Are there no female delegates to this council?' asked Fidelma. 'No male delegates who have brought wives or female advisers?'

'A few, but Leodegar has instructed that they cannot participate in the proceedings. He claims his authority is from the Bishop of Rome, Vitalian. Bishop Leodegar seems a complex person. He is given to strange moods. The women have been sent either to the *Domus Femini* or found accommodation in the city.'

Fidelma showed her irritation. 'Then it seems that our long journey here has been a waste of time. We shall also seek some accommodation within the city. I presume that there are some inns or hostels here – or do Bishop Leodegar's edicts run throughout the city?'

'Wait, I have not explained fully,' the abbot said rapidly. 'Your journey here was no waste of time, I assure you. I have had a long talk with

Leodegar and he has been persuaded that his need of your special talent outweighs his rules and restrictions.'

'How so?' she asked, still put out.

'Leodegar boasts his authority is from Vitalian in Rome – but he is also under pressure from Rome to make this council a success. Decisions need to be made on the future of the churches in the west. However, the killing of Abbot Dabhóc has caused things to come to a halt. No one knows what to do and the delegates may simply decide to return to their own lands with nothing achieved. Unless . . .' He glanced at Fidelma and Eadulf and made an awkward gesture with his hand.

Fidelma did not change expression.

'So, this Bishop Leodegar would like someone to investigate the circumstances of the murder?' she asked coldly.

'Exactly,' the abbot replied.

There was a long silence while Fidelma examined Abbot Ségdae's troubled features.

'Well, it is not a decision Eadulf or I can make without brushing the dust from our sandals,' she said at last. 'It has been a long journey and we would like a room to rest in and somewhere to bathe, if such a thing is possible in this city. So that brings me back to the problem of where we can stay. I don't suppose you have noticed a nearby inn?'

'Forgive me.' Abbot Ségdae was at once apologetic. 'In my distraction, I neglected to tell you that I had long talks with Leodegar and told him who you were . . . who *both* of you were. I spoke of the reputation you have each garnered in the five kingdoms, even being known in Rome when you resolved the mystery of the death of the previous archbishop of Canterbury there. Leodegar was most impressed and desires your advice. In return he has agreed that you and Eadulf can have a chamber in the *hospitia*, the guestrooms of the abbey. He also agrees that you may have free movement within this abbey. Bishop Leodegar needs your talent . . . as do I.'

There was a long pause while Fidelma considered the matter.

'Where is this *Domus Femini*, this house of women?' she suddenly asked.

Abbot Ségdae pointed through a window behind him. 'It adjoins the abbey. It is part of the same buildings but the doors and passages are sealed off and the entrance is separate. The abbess is one Audofleda, who is the superior of their order.'

'So they have no connection with this abbey?'

'The women do join the brethren in the chapel for the morning and evening prayers. They come to the chapel here but are seated in a separate area, behind wooden screens, so there is no communication between the sexes.'

'Is this separation the decision of all the religious? I have not come across such extremes before.'

'I think it was the Rule imposed by Bishop Leodegar. He is one of the group that is pressing Rome to declare that no one entering the religious should be married because they say worldly distractions prevent them from doing the work of God.'

Fidelma sniffed in disapproval. 'And they seek to enforce their views on others. It is a wonder this Bishop Leodegar has allowed Eadulf and myself into this place at all.'

Abbot Ségdae grinned ruefully. 'Above all else, Bishop Leodegar is a wily politician. He saw immediately the advantage of having a renowned advocate from Abbot Dabhóc's own land conducting an investigation in the company of someone who is from the land of Bishop Ordgar.'

Eadulf whistled softly.

'A means to show an unbiased judgement, eh? I hope the good bishop has not already proceeded to judgement and merely wants us to endorse it.'

'We must also wait until the outcome of this matter before according motives to Bishop Leodegar that he may or may not possess,' replied Abbot Ségdae in slight rebuke.

'But the warning is well taken,' asserted Fidelma. 'We will watch the proceedings of Bishop Leodegar very carefully.'

'Will you undertake the task?' Abbot Ségdae prompted dolefully as a silence fell. 'The murder weighs heavily upon me, Fidelma. Dabhóc was one of our own.'

'As Fidelma has said, we cannot answer until we have bathed and rested,' Eadulf replied firmly. 'Then we would have to discuss the matter both with you and Bishop Leodegar. So we will accept the hospitality of this abbey *pro tempore* until we decide.'

Abbot Ségdae suddenly looked hopeful. They had been speaking in the language of the five kingdoms as their common tongue, but now he looked up and called in Latin across the *anticum* to where a religieux was crossing the stone-flagged floor.

'Brother Chilperic!'

The man came towards them with a puzzled look on his handsome features as he saw Fidelma. He had fair hair, blue eyes and was about their own age.

'This is Bishop Leodegar's steward, Brother Chilperic.' The abbot made the introductions. On learning their names, Brother Chilperic was politeness itself to Fidelma.

'Forgive any surprise, Sister, but the abbot has probably explained that we have certain rules stating that women are not allowed here. However, I am told they have been put in abeyance so far as you are concerned. The bishop has been awaiting your arrival with some impatience. Chambers have been set aside for you in our *hospitia* and you have only to tell me any other requirement you may have.' He turned to Abbot Ségdae. 'Bishop Leodegar will obviously want to be informed of the arrival of your compatriots. Would you do so while I conduct them to their quarters?' Receiving assent, he turned back to Fidelma and Eadulf. 'Come with me.'

They followed him, having made an arrangement to meet with the abbot after they had rested.

Brother Chilperic led them up several flights of wooden stairs. The abbey seemed as cold and grey on the inside as it had appeared on the outside. But now and then, through the windows they passed, they caught the sunlit vista of green fields and forests and the winding blue strip of the river. They had obviously been taken to the side of the abbey that overlooked the southern walls of the city, on the opposite side to the sprawl of the city itself. Fidelma estimated that the rooms of the *hospitia* must be on the third level of the abbey – a fact confirmed by the steward. He showed them to a comfortable chamber with walls clad in yew and polished birchwood. It was spacious and there was even an adjoining room prepared for ablutions and toilet requisites.

Brother Chilperic caught Fidelma glancing around with an air of appreciative surprise.

'This chamber was originally set aside for visiting nobles; kings have stayed here, such as the noble Dagobert and Judicael of Domnonia,' he said.

Fidelma bowed her head. 'Then we are truly honoured, Brother Chilperic. We did not expect such comfort.'

'It is you who honour our abbey, for I am told you are sister to the king of your own land. I shall order water to be heated and some food to be brought to you, and if there is anything else that you require . . .'

'Then we shall ask,' Fidelma finished solemnly.

When the door closed, she turned to Eadulf and grinned. 'Well, things seem to have improved slightly.'

'Why is it that I get the feeling that our hosts are a little over-indulgent to us?' he replied. 'Altering the Rule of the abbey, providing us with a chamber and service better suited to a king . . . Can it be that there is something more that they are not telling us about the death of Abbot Dabhóc?'

'It is no use thinking about that until we have seen Ségdae again and Bishop Leodegar,' reproved Fidelma. 'Now, who shall bathe first?' she asked brightly, knowing that Eadulf had never really taken to the Irish custom of a full body wash once a day.

Some time later, when the eastern sky grew dark, Fidelma and Eadulf were seated in Abbot Ségdae's chamber, which was but a short distance along the same corridor. One of several set aside for the delegates to the council, it was nowhere near so well presented as their own chamber. It was sparsely furnished and with an economy in fittings, which doubtless meant that the religious visitors to the abbey were expected to share the same frugality of life as the brethren. By comparison, they were being treated as royal guests and Fidelma presumed that Abbot Ségdae had emphasised her status as sister to the King of Cashel. Ordinarily, she would have objected, but had decided to withhold her condemnation until she observed whether such emphasis was help or hindrance.

'Perhaps you should tell us first of the facts relating to this death?'

Fidelma invited, relaxing back in her chair and feeling more comfortable after her bath.

'As I have told you,' began the abbot, 'a week ago, Dabhóc was found with his skull smashed on the floor of Bishop Ordgar's chamber here. Lying unconscious by his side, having received a blow to his head, was Abbot Cadfan from the kingdom of Gwynedd. Also in the chamber was Ordgar himself, who seemed in a semi-conscious state.'

'A semi-conscious state?' interrupted Eadulf. 'What does that mean?'

'He claimed he was drugged.'

'And what did Cadfan and Ordgar say about this situation?' asked Fidelma.

'Ordgar claimed that he had no knowledge at all of what had taken place. He said that he had drunk wine last thing at night, as was his custom, and fell into a dreamless sleep. He now claims his drink was drugged. The physician confirmed Ordgar's condition. At least, his condition fitted the facts that he claimed.'

'And Cadfan?'

'Cadfan says that a note – which he no longer has, incidentally – summoned him to Bishop Ordgar's chamber on urgent business.'

'When was this scene uncovered – the finding of the body of Dabhóc?'

'Well after midnight but certainly before dawn,' Abbot Ségdae replied.

'So when was this note delivered to Cadfan?'

'He says he was awoken in his chamber by a knock and the note placed under the door. He went to Ordgar's chamber, knocked and a voice bade him enter. He did so – and immediately received a blow to the head. He knew nothing else until he came to, having been carried unconscious back to his own chamber. He swears that he saw neither Dabhóc's body nor Ordgar. When he entered the chamber it was in darkness.'

'A curious tale,' Fidelma observed.

Abbot Ségdae nodded glumly. 'And one which will end this council, unless it is explained. There is already much friction here. At the opening of the council last week, Ordgar and Cadfan came to physical blows.'

Fidelma's eyes widened. 'Really?'

'That was on the evening just before the murder,' confirmed the abbot.

'Was Dabhóc concerned in this fight?'

'He had intervened in the debate as peacemaker, no more. Many others did as well.'

'Is it felt that Dabhóc was slain because of his attempt to act as peacemaker between the two?' asked Eadulf.

'No one knows what to think. Both Ordgar and Cadfan are confined to their chambers while Bishop Leodegar has been contemplating what to do. In a few days' time the ruler of this kingdom, Clotaire, is due to arrive to give his approval to the findings of this council, but there has been no formal meeting, let alone debate on the motions that Rome has sent for consideration. As I say, many of the delegates are talking about returning to their lands.'

'Leodegar has a tough decision to make,' Fidelma observed.

'He must either pronounce the guilt of one or the innocence of both,' agreed the abbot. 'Both men have proclaimed their innocence and both have proclaimed their hatred of one another – and so accusations are made with venomous conviction.'

'And what do you say? You are the senior representative of Éireann.'

The abbot raised his shoulders and let them fall in a hopeless gesture.

'That is my dilemma, Fidelma. You know the rivalry between my own abbey of Imleach and that of Ard Macha. In recent years Ard Macha has been claiming to be the senior bishopric of the five kingdoms, and now claims authority even over Imleach – yet Imleach existed before Ard Macha was established.'

'How does this affect your thoughts on this matter?' asked Fidelma, a little impatiently.

'I am, as you say, now the senior representative. If I do not demand that a pronouncement of guilt and reparation be made following Dabhóc's death, Ségéne, the abbot and bishop of Ard Macha, could accuse me and Imleach of not caring because Dabhóc was representing Ard Macha. If I do make the demand, then I am demanding that Bishop Leodegar make a decision that is a choice between the guilt of Ordgar or Cadfan. If nothing at all is done, then the council disbands and Leodegar has to answer to the Bishop of Rome.'

'In other words, there is a political decision that weighs on your mind over and above the moral decision of what is right, what is truthful?' Fidelma summed up.

Abbot Ségdae smiled tiredly. 'I wish I saw it as so clear cut, Fidelma. But just consider this – the conflict between Ard Macha and Imleach and the conflict between the Britons and the Saxons balance on this matter. Whatever decision is made will result in resentment and conflict. I need advice in making that decision.'

Fidelma pursed her lips, as if in a soundless whistle, and glanced at Eadulf.

Abbot Ségdae meanwhile had suddenly noticed the lateness of the day. He rose.

'Bishop Leodegar will be waiting for us. Let us not keep him further.'

Bishop Leodegar settled himself in his chair and regarded both Fidelma and Eadulf with a searching scrutiny. He was elderly; his black hair was streaked with grey and his eyes were dark and fathomless. His features were pale and lean, the skin tightly stretched across the bones, the Adam's apple prominent. The way he sat, tensed and leaning slightly forward, put Fidelma in mind of a hungry wolf waiting to pounce.

'You are both very welcome at the Abbey of Autun,' he said finally, as if making up his mind about something. 'Abbot Ségdae', he glanced to where the abbot was seated alongside Brother Chilperic at the side of the chamber, 'has told me much about you both, and it is good that you have arrived safely in this place.'

They were seated before him in chairs provided by Brother Chilperic.

Bishop Leodegar hesitated a moment, before continuing, 'I understand that you have been told that this abbey consists of a house for the males and one for the females. We are not a mixed house, although both sexes come together in the abbey chapel for the morning and evening prayers. Here, we follow the idea that celibacy should be the Rule – and in celibacy we come closer to the divinity.'

Fidelma and Eadulf remained silent.

'I realise that you follow those who do not agree with this Rule,' went on Leodegar. 'For the sake of the matter before us, we are prepared to overlook some of our Rule. The only condition I must stipulate is that you proceed with circumspection in this abbey.' He paused, and when neither

Fidelma nor Eadulf commented, he went on: 'From what Abbot Ségdae has told me, it seems that you both have a talent for considering puzzles and finding solutions to problems. We stand in great need of such talent at this moment.'

Fidelma stirred slightly. 'Abbot Ségdae has told us briefly of the facts,' she said.

Bishop Leodegar nodded quickly. 'Much hangs on the success of this council. The future of the western churches will be decided here.'

Eadulf raised a cynical eyebrow. 'The future?' he queried. 'Surely that is an excessive claim?'

'I do not speak such words lightly,' Bishop Leodegar replied defensively. 'The Holy Father has decreed that we should consider two matters very carefully and our decision on them will affect the churches here, in the west. The first and fundamental matter is the central doctrine of our Faith: which declaration of our beliefs are we to adhere to? Do we declare for the Credo of Hippolytus, or do we declare for the *Quicunque* – the faith of the Blessed Athanasius – or, indeed, should we keep to the words as expressed at the Council of Nicea? It is fundamental. We must ask ourselves what is our belief as followers of the Christ.'

'*Credo in Deum Patrem omnipotentem; Creatorem coeli et terrae . . .*' muttered Eadulf.

'Indeed, Brother,' responded Bishop Leodegar, 'but should we not say *ut unum Deum in Trinitate, et Trinitatem un unitate veneremur*?'

Eadulf smiled briefly at the exchange. Was there much difference in expressing a belief in God as Father, Son and Holy Spirit, and a belief in one God in Trinity, and Trinity in unity? Different words that meant the same thing.

'And is that what this council is about? Simply the form of the words of the Creed, our declaration of Faith?'

Bishop Leodegar's brows drew together. 'You should be aware, Brother Eadulf, that among the churches of Gaul, and even among the Franks, the teaching of monothelitism has been developing, contrary to the orthodox interpretation of the Faith. It is therefore important that we have a universal creed, the Rule of our belief.'

'Monothelitism?' Fidelma tried to analyse the word from its roots.

'The teaching of how the divine and human relate in the person of the Christ,' explained Eadulf. 'It teaches that Christ had two natures – divine and human – but only one will.'

Bishop Leodegar nodded approvingly. 'The orthodox interpretation is that Christ had two wills, human and divine, which corresponded to His two natures. But monothelitism has gained favour both in the east and in the west. Honorius, the first of his name to be Holy Father in Rome, has favoured it and so it has spread.'

'And the council is just to condemn that and agree on a creed?' Fidelma realised that her knowledge was lacking in the constant arguments and decisions of the various councils of bishops that frequently met to decide what their flocks should or should not believe. She was more concerned with the law of her own country, and she had often questioned her entry into the religious life. It had only been a means to an end for it was the fashion of the five kingdoms for most of those following the professions to enter the religious.

'It is also for the purpose of agreeing that there should be one Rule for all the religious houses in western Christendom,' the bishop told her. 'One set of laws as to how each community should conduct themselves.'

'One Rule for all communities?' queried Fidelma, with surprise. 'But all our religious houses draw up their own Rule according to their individual needs and purposes.'

'The Holy Father believes such matters should be made uniform through the Faith.'

'And what standard does he suggest?' she asked dubiously.

'It has been suggested that the Rule of the Blessed Benedict, composed over one hundred years ago, should come to define how those in the abbeys and religious houses should govern themselves in their everyday life.'

'I have heard of the Rule,' Eadulf said, 'but Benedict was from a place called Latina. His Rule was fitted for those of the community that he founded there, and it was shaped by his views and culture. Why should his Rule be applied to communities of other lands whose manner of living and culture are so very different?'

'That is precisely the point of this council, my young Brother in Christ.

I am well aware that the Gauls, Armoricans, Britons and the people of Hibernia have their own particular rituals and manners. Indeed, until a few years ago, those rites were also practised among the majority of the Saxons and the Franks. But now we must strive for some uniformity in our beliefs and practices. This, therefore, is an important council. Yet it now stands in danger of disbanding before it has even commenced its deliberations.'

Fidelma was thoughtful. 'So what is it that you are proposing?'

Bishop Leodegar looked uncomfortable and then he tried to smile.

'You are direct, Sister,' he said.

'It saves time,' she replied gravely.

'Very well. What I propose is that you and Brother Eadulf, not being here when the murder was committed and therefore not involved, will have the confidence of the council to investigate this matter and make recommendations as to who is responsible.'

'How will that save the council?' Fidelma asked.

'You, Fidelma, are of the land from where the murdered abbot comes and therefore a good advocate for his rights. Eadulf is a Saxon and as such will not ignore the rights of Bishop Ordgar. You are acceptable to the Hibernians, and Eadulf is acceptable to the Angles and Saxons.'

'And what about the Britons who are also involved?' Fidelma queried.

'I am told that your reputation is known even among them due to some service you performed for the King of Dyfed and the church of the Britons. I am sure that they, too, will accept you as a just advocate.'

Fidelma glanced across to Abbot Ségdae who had remained silent during this time.

'And this is what you also wish?' she asked him.

Abbot Ségdae bowed his head in agreement.

'It is the only just way that I can think of in order to end the dissension which has held up the council during this last week. I think that your brother, the King, would support me in this for, as you know, the matter has repercussions between his kingdom and that of the north.'

Eadulf did not look happy.

'There are many uncertainties in this matter,' he pointed out.

'Which are?' demanded Bishop Leodegar.

'Firstly, this matter is over a week old. Doubtless, Abbot Dabhóc has been buried . . . ?'

'Of course, as is custom,' replied the bishop.

'So we are unable to see for ourselves what the wound was, how it could have been delivered, how the body lay on the floor and so on.'

Bishop Leodegar looked surprised. 'Why is that necessary?'

'Perhaps not necessary but helpful,' interposed Fidelma. 'What we are hearing is that, when everything is pared away and we get down to the basic facts, you have two men, bitter enemies to one another, and we must judge which one of them is telling the truth.'

'Or which one is telling the lies,' added Eadulf.

Bishop Leodegar sat back, eyes narrowed. 'Are you saying that this is impossible to judge?'

'*Impossibilium nulla obligatio est*,' Fidelma replied philosophically. 'If I thought it impossible I would not even be discussing it. We are merely pointing out the difficulties.'

'So you will undertake it?' pressed Bishop Leodegar.

'We will do so,' she replied after a slight pause.

The man seemed to relax in relief. 'Then it is agreed?'

'Do we have freedom to question all those whom we deem it necessary to question?' asked Fidelma. 'Do I have that authority from you?'

The bishop looked puzzled. 'But you only need to question Ordgar and Cadfan.'

Fidelma shook her head. 'You sound as though you have prejudged matters, Bishop Leodegar. We will not prejudge – not even when it appears a simple choice between one or another. If you want us to proceed then it will be under the conditions that I stipulate or not at all.'

A slight look of annoyance crossed the bishop's face.

Abbot Ségdae cleared his throat noisily.

'We realise that you do things differently here, Bishop Leodegar,' he said hastily. 'However, in our lands we have a legal system which allows our advocates certain freedoms when they investigate.'

Bishop Leodegar regarded him thoughtfully for a few moments.

'I have already said that I am prepared to waive the Rule of this abbey to allow Fidelma access to where no women are allowed.'

'And I have agreed to be circumspect,' replied Fidelma firmly, 'but it is the authority to investigate as I would do in my own country under my own law system that I need. I know no other way of undertaking this task.'

'I have heard of your laws and methods from travelling religious from your lands,' the bishop said after some thought. Then, as if making up his mind, he squared his shoulders and said, 'Very well. I see no reason to restrain you in this matter. I give you those freedoms.'

'*And* to Brother Eadulf,' added Fidelma brightly. 'Remember, Eadulf is a *gerefa* of his own people, a magistrate of the Saxon laws.'

'That I understand, which is why I said that Eadulf will be seen as unbiased in the matter of Bishop Ordgar. These facts should be made known to the community because it will enforce the authority of your findings. I give you full and free permission to question whom you wish on this matter. I will announce this at evening prayers. I only ask that your resolution be quick so that the delegates may be satisfied. Clotaire, who is our King, will be arriving here soon to give this council his royal approval. It would benefit all of us if the matter were resolved by the time of his arrival.'

'There are no guarantees in life, save only one – that we are all going to die at some time,' responded Fidelma. 'We will do our best to solve this matter, but we cannot guarantee a resolution by a certain time. Is it agreed?'

Bishop Leodegar raised his hands as if the matter were now beyond him.

'Very well,' Fidelma rejoined. 'Let us begin with a few questions to you.'

The bishop looked at her in surprise. 'Questions to *me*?'

'Of course,' went on Fidelma, unperturbed at his astonishment. The Frankish bishop was obviously not used to being questioned. 'Who was it who discovered the body and the state of affairs that existed in Bishop Ordgar's chamber?'

'It was Brother Sigeric,' volunteered the steward Brother Chilperic, who had sat in silence until that moment.

'Ah, Brother Sigeric. And who is he?'

'One of the scribes.'

'We shall need to speak with him, of course. Is he available?'

Brother Chilperic nodded briefly.

'Excellent. What was the name of the physician who examined the body – and was it the same person who checked the wound of Abbot Cadfan and also examined Bishop Ordgar?'

'Brother Gebicca is the physician,' replied Brother Chilperic.

'And now,' Fidelma turned back to Bishop Leodegar, 'tell us about your role in this matter?'

'*My* role?' Bishop Leodegar was puzzled.

'Perhaps I have chosen the wrong word. I am told that Abbot Ségdae was awoken by a request to attend in Ordgar's chamber. When he arrived, he found that you were already there. How did that come to be?'

'Brother Sigeric roused me first,' explained the bishop. 'He told me there had been an accident and I was to come immediately.'

'In what circumstances did this Brother Sigeric rouse you?'

'It would be best to tell the story as fully as you can,' intervened Eadulf. 'Presumably, you were asleep in your quarters?'

'I had meant to retire after the midnight prayers,' Bishop Leodegar began. 'That is my custom. I was particularly tired that night as I had dined with a local nobleman who was visiting the abbey and he had been much the worse for our local wine. However, just as I was retiring, Bishop Ordgar came to my chambers. He wished to complain further about Abbot Cadfan. He was with me some time before I could get rid of him. He was very angry about the behaviour of the Briton that evening. I told him that this was a council in which all representatives must be treated with latitude. After he left me, I fell asleep until I became aware of Brother Sigeric shaking me. It was not then dawn. However, it was that point of darkness just before dawn when you can hear the birds stirring and crying to one another as they sense the approach of light.'

He paused and Eadulf prompted: 'Go on.'

'It is as I said. Brother Sigeric urged me to put on my robe and come to Bishop Ordgar's chamber. He said there had been a bad accident.'

'Did he describe what sort of accident or how he had discovered it?'

'Not at that time, but later he said . . .'

Fidelma raised a hand. 'We will speak to Brother Sigeric himself on that matter. Let us concentrate on what you did at the time.'

Bishop Leodegar hesitated a moment and then continued, 'I followed him as he asked me to. Brother Sigeric was in an agitated state and so I did not pursue him with questions at that time. I entered Ordgar's chamber . . .'

'Was there a light it in?' Fidelma asked quickly.

Bishop Leodegar nodded. 'A candle was burning.'

'So you could see the interior quite plainly?'

'I could see that there appeared to be two bodies there and that Bishop Ordgar was slumped on his bed, groaning.'

'Did he say anything as you entered?

'He seemed to be in pain, and mumbling. He was clearly not himself.'

'And you saw the body?'

'I immediately noticed Abbot Cadfan who lay stretched on the floor beside the bed. There was light enough to see blood on the back of his skull.'

'You could see blood by the candlelight?' queried Eadulf.

Brother Leodegar frowned. 'Yes . . .' He realised what Eadulf was asking. 'Well, I could see some dark, sticky stuff – and, of course, it turned out to be blood.'

Eadulf smiled in approval. 'Was he conscious?'

'No, and he did not revive until he was carried back to his own chamber.' He paused, then realising that more was expected of him, went on, 'I was about to bend down to him when I saw the body of Abbot Dabhóc. I called to Brother Sigeric to rouse my steward. I also told Sigeric to fetch our physician, Brother Gebicca. I went to Bishop Ordgar to see if I could administer to him, but it was as if he was intoxicated. He was mumbling nonsensical things.'

'Did he smell of wine or beer?' asked Fidelma.

'There was an aura of stale wine about him,' admitted the bishop.

'And then?'

'Then Brother Gebicca arrived and soon after, Brother Chilperic. When Gebicca pronounced that Abbot Dabhóc was dead, that a blow from behind had crushed his skull, I knew that I should advise Abbot Ségdae, as the senior cleric from your land. I sent Brother Sigeric to rouse him.'

'And all the time Cadfan lay unconscious while Ordgar was in a state of intoxication?' put in Fidelma.

'We did not neglect Cadfan,' he replied. 'Brother Gebicca examined him and it was decided to take him back to his chamber where it took a day or so for him to recover fully. We also removed Ordgar to a nearby chamber. When I finally questioned Ordgar, he said he had taken wine as was his custom before retiring and knew no more until he awoke sick and dizzy. He was aware of the people in his chamber but could not say what was happening until he recovered. He thought, at first, that he had been made ill by bad wine – but when I told him what had occurred in his chamber, he believed that Cadfan had tried to poison him.'

'So, according to Ordgar, why had Dabhóc been killed by Cadfan?' asked Eadulf.

'Ordgar claimed that Dabhóc must have interrupted Cadfan's attempt to kill him and paid with his life.'

'And Cadfan's wound? How did he explain that?'

'Ordgar believed it was either administered by Dabhóc before Cadfan killed him or even by Cadfan himself.'

'A self-inflicted wound that rendered Cadfan unconscious for a day?' Eadulf looked cynical. 'That is hardly a self-administered blow, and if inflicted by another person, would not have allowed the killing of that person before unconsciousness.'

Fidelma shot him a look of disapproval for being so open with his thoughts.

'We may pursue such matters when we question Ordgar and Cadfan,' she said. 'I presume that you also questioned Cadfan? What was *his* version of this story?'

'He told me that someone had slipped a note under his door, knocked and run off before he could open it. The note told him to go to Ordgar's chamber at once as there was some urgency. He came to the chamber, found the door ajar, knocked and a voice bade him enter. He recalled nothing except a sharp pain on the back of the head until he recovered consciousness a day or so later.'

For a while Fidelma said nothing, sitting head slightly forward with her eyes focused on the middle distance.

'A strange tale indeed,' she said at last. 'Abbot Ségdae has informed us that Ordgar and Cadfan are confined to their chambers until the matter of the responsibility is resolved.'

'That is true.'

'And presumably both are outraged by their confinement?'

'As you can imagine,' conceded Bishop Leodegar. 'But what other course of action can I take?'

'And how is this suspicion and confinement received by the delegates to this council?' asked Eadulf. 'You have spoken of the tensions. Is anyone taking sides?'

Bishop Leodegar gave a bark of cynical laughter.

'They would not be human if they did not. The Saxons and some of our Franks support Ordgar. The Britons, Gauls and Armoricans denounce Ordgar and demand the release of Cadfan. Those clerics from Hibernia call down a plague on both houses and demand reparation for the death of the representative of the bishop of Ard Macha. So what am I to do?'

Fidelma stood up abruptly, so abruptly that she caused some surprise. She glanced though the tall windows at the darkening day.

'You are following the right path,' she declared. 'You may announce what we are doing at evening prayers. Tomorrow morning we will start in earnest upon this quest and begin by speaking with Brother Sigeric. I presume the chamber where it happened is now empty?'

Bishop Leodegar nodded. 'As I said, we removed Ordgar to a more secure room.'

'Then we will visit the original chamber after we have seen Brother Sigeric.'

'I will ensure that all is ready for you.' Bishop Leodegar became more assertive. 'I only hope that you are both as clever at solving conundrums as Abbot Ségdae has assured me that you are.'

'That will be for you to judge, Leodegar of Autun,' Fidelma replied quietly. 'Eadulf and I can only do what is in our power to do, and trust the riddle is one that can be solved.'

Chapter Four

Fidelma and Eadulf were awakened just before dawn by the sound of singing. Eadulf lay for a while trying to adjust to the unfamiliar music. It was Fidelma who recognised it.

'It must be the *matutinae laude* – the gathering for morning praise. I have heard that in Rome. It seems some of these abbeys sing Psalms to greet the dawn.'

Eadulf groaned. 'I hope we are not expected to adopt these ways while we are staying here. I am often told that I am tone deaf.'

'You will recall that our arrival, after so long a journey, has excused us from attending this morning's prayers,' Fidelma replied cheerfully. 'Nonetheless, it is dawn and perhaps we should wash and be ready for the day.'

It was wise advice, for no sooner had they finished than Brother Chilperic knocked at their door carrying a tray of fruit, bread and cheese with which to break their fast. He seemed to read the question in Fidelma's eyes as he set the tray on the small table.

'The bishop thought it might save some embarrassment on this first day to allow you to break your fast here in the *hospitia*. Abbot Ségdae will speak with you about meals in the refectory. You will appreciate that our refectory is not used to the presence of women.'

'You do not have to explain,' Eadulf said, helping himself to a piece of fruit. 'But I wonder who would be embarrassed if Fidelma walked in?' he added mischievously as he bit into the fruit with relish. His eyes widened appreciatively as he munched on the juicy pulpy mass. 'I have not tasted the like of this for a while. What is it?'

'*Malum Persica*, Brother Eadulf,' replied Brother Chilperic. Then he added: 'The bishop thought I could wait and, after you have breakfasted, conduct you to the chamber where the killing took place.'

'We are ready to commence the day's task once we have done so,' Fidelma replied, as she took a similar piece of fruit to that which Eadulf was enjoying. 'What was it that you called this – a Persian apple?' she asked, as she tasted it gingerly.

'Yes, that is correct,' confirmed the steward.

'It is very soft and sweet. Do you buy them from Persian merchants?'

Brother Chilperic shook his head. 'Some centuries ago, when the Romans conquered this land, they brought with them seeds of this fruit and planted them. The abbey gardens grow a fine crop. Thank you, but I have eaten,' he added when Eadulf pushed the bowl of fruit in his direction.

'Well,' Eadulf smiled as he finished and wiped his mouth, 'the earth did not tremble last night when Bishop Leodegar announced that a woman would be stalking the corridor and halls of this abbey?'

Brother Chilperic was uncertain how to take his humour.

'The Rule of the bishop has only been in force a year,' he explained. 'We were not always segregated from women but, like many another religious community, this was a mixed house. Many here still have wives and even children in the adjoining *Domus Femini* – wives we had to put from us if we wished to continue as religious here.'

Fidelma raised an eyebrow. '*Put* from you?' she queried.

'Declare before God and the bishop that we no longer recognised our marriage vows because God had the greater calling on us,' confirmed Brother Chilperic.

'And what would have happened had you not done so?'

'We would have had to leave and seek another place. But many communities in Burgundia . . . in Austrasia and Neustria are rejecting mixed houses, so where could we go? This is our land.'

'Would going further west have been so bad?'

Brother Chilperic seemed suddenly gloomy. 'Many of us, men and women, are of this city. This is where we have been born, brought up and belong. Many of us in this community, that is. We are the sons and daughters of former brothers and sisters of the community. There is no option but to obey this order.'

Fidelma was shocked. 'No option? How is that?'

'Bishops are all-powerful. Many are temporal princes, not just men of God. They have to be obeyed.'

'Bishops such as Leodegar?'

Brother Chilperic seemed reluctant to admit it.

'Has this been reported to Rome?' asked Eadulf, aghast.

'I fear that Rome would care little about it. Rome now sees itself as a temporal power set up to govern not just the morality of the princes of the former empire but to demand tribute from them. That is why Rome does not like the western churches. The constant arguments between your own churches and Rome have gone on for some time now.'

Fidelma regarded him with interest. 'And did you put your own wife away from you?' she asked unexpectedly, using his phraseology.

The young man flushed. 'I . . . I have no wife,' he muttered. He rose. 'Perhaps it is time to start the examination?'

Eadulf glanced at Fidelma with an expression that indicated he felt it best to avoid further conversation in that area.

'Before we start, I think we should like to be shown something of the abbey,' Fidelma said. 'It would help us.'

Brother Chilperic looked uneasy. 'I do not know,' he said hesitantly.

Fidelma's brows came together. 'Come, come, Brother Chilperic. It is useless our being here if we do not know where we are exactly.'

The tour was a cursory one, but at least it helped Fidelma and Eadulf to orientate themselves. The abbey was larger than they had expected and was bounded on two sides by the tall city walls. There appeared to be one main building, then a large chapel and several smaller structures interspersed with little courtyards and gardens. From the *anticum*, in the main building, they exited into a large courtyard with its entrance to the great chapel on the opposite side. To the south side of the courtyard was a small building entirely on its own which housed the apartments of Bishop Leodegar. Trees of apple, pear, plum and quince surrounded it. Separate to this was the house of the physician, with an infirmary and the physician's garden for herbs and healing plants.

The main building contained the work rooms of the community – the bakehouse, brewery and kitchens next to the refectory – and beyond that, the *latrina* were housed at ground level. There was also a common room for the brethren called the *calefactorium* which, in winter, was heated by flues under the floor fed from the kitchen fires, and next to this was a *scriptorium* or library. There was also a *vestiarium* for the storing of clothes, because the warmth of the *calefactorium* helped preserve them and also kept the manuscript books of the *scriptorium* at a reasonable temperature.

Above this main building were the *dormitoria* for the brethren. The individual chambers were for the more senior members of the community. Then there was a second storey with other chambers and the *hospitia*, which were more ostentatiously furnished for guests of importance.

Brother Chilperic had paused in the main courtyard to point out some of the focal points of the abbey. He spoke with some enthusiasm.

'We are in a corner of the old city, bounded on two sides by the ancient walls. The western wall runs behind the chapel and the southern wall is beyond the bishop's house. Beyond the southern wall, through which we have access by means of a gateway into a tunnel made though the wall, we have our farmstead. There are cow sheds, goat sheds, pigsties, sheep, hen and duck houses and another garden for our vegetables – such as garlic, onions, cabbages, lettuce and celery.'

'And do the brethren take turns in looking after the animals and produce?' Fidelma asked.

Brother Chilperic shook his head. 'The farmwork is done by the slaves and supervised by the brethren.'

'Slaves?' Her eyes widened.

'We don't allow slaves in the abbey,' went on Brother Chilperic, as if he had not noticed her shocked expression. 'They only work on the farm. We have twenty field slaves who belong to the abbey.'

'The chapel is quite spectacular,' Eadulf remarked, trying to give Fidelma a warning glance not to pursue the matter of slaves again.

Brother Chilperic turned to him with pride and said, 'It was once a temple of the Romans before being consecrated to the use of the true Faith.'

Attending prayers on the previous evening, they had already observed its large interior. It was a tall building, with a semicircular apse at the southern end in which stood a high altar. It was unlike the churches that Fidelma and Eadulf were used to. To the west of the altar was a smaller one dedicated to Apostle Peter and, on the opposite side, another dedicated to Apostle Paul. The congregation stood before the altar while the officiating priest performed the rituals. There were wooden screens, which they had noticed separated the women from the men. The women from the *Domus Femini* entered the chapel, apparently by some underground route through the vaults that stretched as far as the *Domus Femini*, and took their places unseen behind these screens.

Brother Chilperic told them that the *Domus Femini* stood to the east side of the abbey, separated by a large courtyard and a wagonway. It was up that wagonway that Brother Budnouen had taken his cart to unload his goods when they had arrived on the previous day. These women's quarters had once been part of the main abbey buildings, but now all other entrances had apparently been blocked off so they were isolated from the brethren of the abbey, apart from the underground passage to the chapel.

Fidelma and Eadulf were certainly impressed by the size of the complex of the abbey. It was like a small town in itself and almost self-sufficient. One could lose oneself quite easily in the numerous halls, chambers and corridors.

A bell started to toll and Brother Chilperic started nervously.

'I think we should begin your work, for the day is passing rapidly,' he ventured.

'We have already begun our work,' Fidelma said mildly. 'But let us now see where Abbot Dabhóc met his death.'

Looking relieved, Brother Chilperic set off up the stairs of the main building to the *hospitia*, but led them to chambers on the far side of the building from where their own were situated. Their guide paused before a door and announced: 'This was the chamber where Abbot Dabhóc was killed.'

'And it was Bishop Ordgar's chamber?' queried Eadulf.

'It was,' replied the steward. He opened the door. There was a single window facing them that lit the room well in spite of the fact that it was facing north across the sprawl of the city. It was not a bright day but the light was enough to reveal a scene that caused them to halt in surprise on the threshold.

'This room has been ransacked.' Eadulf stated the obvious.

Bedding was strewn on the floor, blankets and bits of broken furniture were scattered here and there, two cupboard doors hung off their hinges while loose bricks had even been prised out of the wall.

'Destructive but thorough,' muttered Fidelma. 'Someone appears to have been looking for something.'

Brother Chilperic was in a state of shock.

'It was not done last evening,' he said.

Fidelma turned to him with a frown. 'So you looked in this room last evening?'

The steward appeared suddenly awkward.

'I just . . . I wanted . . . wanted to see if it was ready for your inspection.'

Fidelma replied patiently, 'My inspection was to see if anything had been previously missed. I did not want the room made ready or tidied before it.'

'Well, you certainly got your wish,' Eadulf said ruefully, indicating the mess.

A thought struck Fidelma.

'When exactly did you come here and observe that there was nothing amiss?'

'When?'

'You said that this had not happened last evening. What time were you here?'

'After the evening prayers.'

'After Bishop Leodegar announced in the chapel that we would be investigating the matter of Dabhóc's killing?'

'After that,' agreed the steward.

Eadulf was nodding thoughtfully. 'So someone was scared that something might be found . . .' he began.

Fidelma silenced him with a sharp look.

'There is nothing to be gained here,' she said. 'If you would be good enough to indicate Brother Sigeric's chamber or tell us where we might find him? Then I think, as steward, your duty would be to inform the bishop about this matter.'

The young man replied, 'At this hour Brother Sigeric will be in the *scriptorium*, Sister. I will take you there.'

'One moment.' Fidelma was looking at the doors to the individual chambers in the corridor. 'If this was Bishop Ordgar's original chamber, tell me who occupied the rooms on either side.'

'His steward, Brother Benevolentia, is in the chamber to your left,' Brother Chilperic indicated. 'Bishop Ordgar has now been moved to the chamber on *his* left.'

'Whose chamber is that, on the other side to Ordgar's original chamber – to the right?'

'That is now unoccupied,' replied Brother Chilperic.

'And unoccupied on the night of the murder?'

The man shook his head. 'No, that was occupied by Lord Guntram.'

'Lord Guntram? The local governor?'

'He had come to the abbey to see the bishop and stayed late so that he was in no condition to ride back to his fortress.'

'Ah, he was the visiting nobleman of whom Bishop Leodegar spoke. How do you mean – he was in no condition?'

Brother Chilperic looked uncomfortable. 'He is a rather profligate young man, I am afraid, and the bishop keeps a good wine cellar.'

Fidelma was quiet as they followed the steward to the *scriptorium*. Leaving them at the door, he hurried off to convey the latest development to the bishop, his leather sandals slapping on the flags of the corridor.

Fidelma and Eadulf watched him go. Then Eadulf said in a whisper, 'You think that someone in the chapel, on hearing we were investigating the matter, hurried to the chamber to search it?'

'And why would that be?' countered Fidelma. 'If there was something incriminating in that chamber, why not retrieve it during the week that has passed since the killing of Dabhóc?'

Eadulf looked disappointed. 'It is a mystery,' he admitted.

Fidelma chuckled. 'We are here to solve such mysteries,' she reminded him, before reaching forward to turn the handle of the door into the *scriptorium*.

There was only one person inside – a young man poring over a scroll that was spread on the wooden table before him. He looked up as they entered and nervously started to rise in his seat. When Fidelma began to introduce herself, the young man made a motion of his hand.

'I know who you both are. I saw you in the chapel last night.'

'Be at ease, Brother Sigeric,' invited Fidelma. 'I understand that you were first on the scene in Bishop Ordgar's chamber. You are a scribe in this abbey, I believe?'

The young man sank back into his chair and carefully laid his quill down on the desk before him.

'I write a fair hand,' he said, almost defensively. 'I have good Latin, passable Greek and some Hebrew. Therefore, in kindness, I am scribe to the bishop.'

'And are you a Frank?'

'I am a Burgund. I was born and raised in this city.'

'Have you served long in this abbey?'

'Since I was fifteen years old.'

'So that would be . . . ?'

'I have seen four and twenty summers.'

'Nine years,' reflected Fidelma. 'You must know this abbey well.'

The young man shrugged but said nothing.

'I would imagine that there has never been a mysterious death at the abbey before,' she continued.

'None that I am aware of.'

'And now you have played a central role in the matter.'

Brother Sigeric looked alarmed. 'I don't know what you mean.'

'You are a key witness.'

'I saw nothing,' replied the young man.

'On the contrary, you saw a great deal by discovering the scene of the murder.'

The young man's jaw came up. 'I was not there when the Hibernian abbot was killed.'

'We did not say that you were. But we would like to find out exactly how you came to Bishop Ordgar's chamber that night. It was in the hour before dawn, I am told.'

Brother Sigeric sniffed slightly. 'I explained everything to Bishop Leodegar.'

'And now you will explain to me.'

'I was just passing . . .'

'In the middle of the night?' intervened Fidelma. 'Tell me, where is your chamber in relationship to Bishop Ordgar's?'

The young man seemed unwilling to speak for a moment.

'The rooms of the *hospitia* are on the second floor of this building,' Fidelma prompted him. 'Surely the *dormitoria* are on the first floor?'

'As scribe I have my own chamber. It is on the second floor . . .'

'Where exactly?' she pressed.

'It is on the eastern side of the building overlooking the courtyard between this building and the *Domus Femini*.'

'Then it still does not explain why you were just passing Bishop Ordgar's chamber in the middle of the night.'

The young man sighed deeply as if suddenly resigned. 'The women here live separately to the men,' he muttered.

The sentence surprised Fidelma. 'I do not see the connection.'

'When the Blessed Reticulus became the first bishop here, or the first we know of, as many claimed Amator preceded him, this was a mixed house. But Bishop Leodegar is of the faction that believe men and women should be separated and, indeed, that the clerics should adopt the code of celibacy if they wish to serve the New Faith. Yet we still have free choice on the matter. Rome has not decreed it as the Rule.'

'So you do not agree with Bishop Leodegar's Rule? There is no need to be defensive on this matter,' Fidelma assured him. 'Eadulf and I share not only a union in our Faith but a union in marriage. There is no Rule of celibacy in our churches either.'

The young man was nervous. 'You will understand, then,' he said, almost pleading.

'We can only understand when we know what it is that you are trying to say, Sigeric. Now, explain why you were abroad that night before dawn.'

Brother Sigeric bit his lip. 'I went to meet a girl.'

He paused and Fidelma had to prompt him to continue.

'Who was this girl?'

'Her name is Valretrade. She is one of the religieuse who serve in the *Domus Femini* beyond the wall. We became friends when this was still a mixed community. She also had a talent for copying the old texts and so we met here. After the bishop separated the communities, we contrived to meet regularly.'

'And that night you were on your way to an assignation with Valretrade?'

'I had received a message from her urging me to meet her.'

'How did you receive such a message?'

'It was a crude method. My room, as I said, looks across the courtyard that separates us from the *Domus Femini*. Almost exactly opposite to my window is the chamber occupied by Valretrade. We arranged that when either one of us needed to see the other urgently, we would place a lighted candle in the windows.'

'And that night you saw the candle?'

Brother Sigeric nodded quickly. 'I was not sleeping comfortably and I awoke. That was when I saw the candle. I lit an answering one in my window. Once it was seen, the arrangement was that Valretrade raised her candle and moved it from side to side three times. I then did the same. If she then extinguished the candle, it meant that she was on the way to our meeting place. This happened that night and so I left to go to our prearranged meeting point, having also extinguished my candle.'

'What if you had not awoken and seen the candle? It was not a guaranteed way of communication.'

'I grant you that,' the young man said. 'But it was the best we could do in the circumstances. Usually, there was never urgency in the meetings. We knew, more or less, on which nights we would meet. That night was different. The signal meant it was urgent.'

'And where did you meet?'

'The pre-arranged meeting spot is by a certain tomb in the catacombs beneath the abbey. It is an old necropolis and where all the old bishops of this abbey are buried.'

'So you went and met Valretrade?'

'I never reached there. I was passing by Bishop Ordgar's chamber when I noticed the door partly opened and saw what lay inside: the Hibernian and the Briton, lying in blood on the floor, and the Saxon unconscious on the bed. I struggled for a moment between loyalty to the abbey and concern for Valretrade, then I realised that I should rouse the bishop – and that is what I did. After that, it was an hour or more before I could get away. I finally proceeded to the catacombs, but Valretrade was not there.'

'What did you do?'

'I returned to my chamber and re-lit the candle, but although I waited until dawn there was no answer to my efforts. I was puzzled until I remembered that while, after the signal, her candle seemed to be extinguished, the light had actually moved away from the window as if the candle was placed elsewhere. At the time, I just thought that she needed the light. By dawn I thought perhaps the signal had not been fully observed and she had changed her mind.'

'So a week has passed since then. What has Valretrade told you about her urgent desire to see you that night? And, of course, your candle mystery?'

Brother Sigeric turned a woebegone expression to them.

'She has told me nothing, for I have not seen her.'

Eadulf was frowning. 'Are you saying she made no attempt to contact you again through your rather cumbersome method?'

'None.'

'Have you not contacted her?'

'I tried on the subsequent night without success.'

'Well, we can surely get a message to Valretrade on your behalf. I presume she was angry that you did not turn up at the meeting place.'

Brother Sigeric shook his head sadly. 'On the fourth day I summoned up the courage to go to Abbess Audofleda and request to see Valretrade. I saw her stewardess, who turned me from the door.'

'What did this stewardess tell you?'

'She told me that she could not help me even if she wanted to, and claimed that Valretrade had left the abbey and run away.'

'Run away? Did you know of any cause why she would do so?'

Brother Sigeric looked as if he were in physical pain. 'She would never have run away before she had spoken to me.'

'But she tried to contact you and you did not turn up.'

He hung his head and made a sound like a sob. 'If things were so desperate, she would have waited. I know her. She would have sent a note to me, some message.'

Fidelma leaned forward and patted the young man comfortingly on the shoulder.

'We will do our best to find out more for you, Sigeric. We will have a word with this Abbess Audofleda and if there is a mystery there, we shall uncover it. In the meantime, try not to worry and—'

Just then, the library door opened and Brother Chilperic entered.

'I have informed the bishop,' he said, without preamble. 'He will await your findings on the matter as soon as you are ready.'

'We have finished here,' she replied, with a smile to Brother Sigeric as she moved towards the door. 'Thank you for your assistance, Brother. We shall not forget and will doubtless see you again soon.'

Brother Sigeric smiled sadly in response.

'Do you need to look at Ordgar's chamber again?' asked Brother Chilperic, 'or should I give orders for it to be cleaned and tidied?'

'I have done with it. However, you may indicate where we will find Abbot Cadfan.'

'He will be found on the third level. You recall where I showed you the chamber of Bishop Ordgar? Good. Along that corridor to the right, you find a small corridor leading off it, and Abbot Cadfan will be found there.'

'In that case we will speak with Bishop Ordgar first and Abbot Cadfan afterwards. We will not need your services in that for we can find our way.'

Brother Chilperic seemed reluctant to be dismissed but Fidelma and Eadulf were already moving off. He shrugged and turned away.

Chapter Five

Bishop Ordgar did not stand as Fidelma and Eadulf entered his chamber, but remained seated, the scowl on his saturnine features giving the impression of an angry and forbidding personality. Behind him stood a young man with black curly hair who watched their entrance with pale blue eyes. He made a step forward as if to greet them, then halted and glanced nervously at the seated bishop before drawing his tongue across his lips as if to moisten them.

'You are Brother Eadulf of Seaxmund's Ham?' The young man directed his question at Eadulf. 'You are the *gerefa* that Bishop Leodegar has told us of?'

'I am he,' Eadulf confirmed, replying in Saxon, for the question had been asked in that language albeit accented in the way of someone who spoke it as a foreign tongue. Then he switched to Latin. 'This is Fidelma of Cashel, sister to King Colgú, King of Muman – an advocate of the courts of the five kingdoms of Éireann – my wife.'

Eadulf knew that Fidelma did not like to announce herself in such a grandiose manner but, from what he had heard of Bishop Ordgar, he knew that they had to impress him from the outset. Eadulf had heard stories of the Saxon bishop's arrogance and was aware that if it was not challenged from the start, it would be impossible to conduct any form of interrogation with him. Eadulf spoke with his eyes focused unswervingly on the gimlet gaze of the bishop.

'I was told the woman's name was *Sister* Fidelma,' the bishop replied, still speaking in Saxon, his thin mouth twisting in a sneer.

'The Faith encompasses people of many backgrounds,' Eadulf responded evenly, 'but, of course, you are right. We are all equals in serving the Faith, bishops or abbots. And "the woman" *is* my wife.'

Again he chose his words carefully and with emphasis to bring Bishop Ordgar away from any mistaken sense of importance.

Eadulf then turned to the young man who had greeted him. 'And who are you?'

'I am Brother Benevolentia, steward to my lord, Bishop Ordgar.'

'But you are not a Saxon?'

'That is true, Brother. I am a Burgund.'

Fidelma had struggled to follow the conversation; although she had a rudimentary knowledge of Saxon, she was uncomfortable in that language when it came to nuances and complicated subjects.

'May we speak in Latin?' she asked, speaking for the first time.

Both Bishop Ordgar and Brother Benevolentia looked surprised and the bishop shrugged. Fidelma took it as an affirmative.

'Good, since we need to seek answers to some questions.'

'I was told it was Brother Eadulf who was to represent me,' Bishop Ordgar said. 'You know that I have a position of some importance? I represent Theodore, archbishop of Canterbury. As soon as this council is ended, I am to continue my journey to Rome to consult with His Holiness Vitalian.'

'Then you have not been accurately informed of my role,' Eadulf said.

'But we are told that you are of the kingdom of the East Angles and a *gerefa*,' intervened Brother Benevolentia. 'My lord, Bishop Ordgar, has naturally presumed that you would want to support one of your own kin in this matter.'

Eadulf nearly smiled at the arrogance of the presumption.

'Sister Fidelma and I have been asked by Bishop Leodegar to investigate the matter of the death of Abbot Dabhóc and report to him. That is all. There is no question of representing the interests of anyone except the interests of the dead abbot in the discovery of who killed him.'

Bishop Ordgar did not look happy.

'Then let us hope you have not forgotten your duty to your own people,' he snapped. 'I understand that you have been many years among the people of that western island. I trust you know where loyalty and duty lie.'

'My duty to my own people is a duty to *truth* – where ever that truth might be,' Eadulf snapped back. 'And until we obtain some answers from you, Ordgar of Kent, the truth will not be known.'

'You forget to whom you speak, Brother.' Brother Benevolentia sounded aghast at Eadulf's tone.

'I am well aware that I speak to a witness to a murder. Our purpose here is that we require answers to questions,' replied Eadulf, unperturbed. 'Can we now proceed to obtain them? And let us return to speaking in Latin!'

In the angry exchange they had lapsed into Saxon.

Bishop Ordgar opened his mouth to respond but suddenly checked himself. He breathed out slowly and composed his thin autocratic features.

'Ask your questions then, Eadulf of Seaxmund's Ham,' he commanded.

Eadulf glanced at Fidelma, who nodded with amused approval to indicate that the bishop might respond better if Eadulf, not she, continued to put the questions.

'Describe what happened on the night that Abbot Dabhóc was found in your chamber.'

Bishop Ordgar was dismissive. 'Since I was drugged, I cannot say.'

'Tell us, then, what exactly you remember of that night. You remember going to your chamber, I suppose?' Eadulf could not help the sarcasm in his voice.

'Of course. After evening prayers in the chapel, I went to see Bishop Leodegar to register a complaint about the behaviour of Cadfan who had been discourteous to me earlier. Then I returned to my chamber. I composed myself for sleep having taken, as was my custom, wine. I came awake feeling ill, with an oppressive headache and unsure of my surroundings. I think I remember someone shaking me and raised voices all round. I become unconscious again, and when I awoke for the second time I was in this chamber with the physician tending me. The headache and nausea lasted for some time. It was only after I recovered that I was told that Abbot Dabhóc had been discovered dead in my chamber, with Abbot Cadfan nearby on the floor. When I was found, I was told that I had been regaining some degree of consciousness on the bed but I cannot be sure. That is all.'

'It gives rise to several questions,' Eadulf asserted.

Bishop Ordgar sat back with eyes narrowed. 'Then ask them,' he said.

'Let us start with the wine. You imply it was drugged?'

'I *state* it was drugged,' the man corrected. 'Nothing but drugged wine would have such an effect on me.'

'Where did this wine come from?'

'I don't understand.' Bishop Ordgar seemed confused. 'Do you mean what vineyard supplied it?'

'Who gave you this wine?'

Brother Benevolentia coughed nervously and stepped forward to say, 'It was I who placed the wine by the bed of the bishop. I do so every night, since it is his custom to take a drink before retiring. It helps to induce sleep and . . . and . . .'

Eadulf saw a look of annoyance form on the bishop's features as if he felt the steward was revealing flaws in his nature that he would best like to keep hidden.

'And this wine was bought from where?' pressed Eadulf.

'I purchased a small amphora in the local market.'

'And where was this amphora kept?'

'In the chamber of the bishop. It was a small amphora of red wine so there was no need to take it to the cooler cellars.'

'So wine had already been drunk from it before? It was not newly bought wine?'

'The bishop had been served from the same amphora during the preceding three or four days.'

'And, that night, you poured the cup with your own hand,' Eadulf went on.

'I did.'

'Where is the amphora now?'

'It was thrown away as it had been emptied that night.'

'I suppose the cup was also thrown away?' Eadulf remarked dryly.

'It was washed and cleaned the next day,' replied Brother Benevolentia complacently.

'So we have only Ordgar's word that the wine was drugged.'

'Since when is my word to be doubted?' Ordgar demanded in a threatening tone.

Eadulf was unabashed. 'It is not a question of doubt but a question of confirmation. Tell me, if you are used to drinking wine, how did that wine taste that night?'

'Taste?' Brother Ordgar frowned. 'How do you mean – taste?'

'Was there anything unusual about it?'

'No.' Then he suddenly paused. 'Except . . .'

'Yes?' Eadulf prompted hopefully.

'I thought there was a sweeter taste than usual to it. But it was not disagreeable,' the bishop admitted.

'Very well. Now, Brother Benevolentia, at what stage in the evening did you pour the wine?'

'The bell rang in the chapel at the end of prayers. Thinking that the bishop would return straightway, I hurried to his chamber and poured the wine.'

'Except that I did *not* return straightway,' pointed out Ordgar. 'I went to see Bishop Leodegar to complain about the conduct of the Briton at the council.'

'Did you wait in the bishop's chamber until he returned?' Eadulf asked Brother Benevolentia.

The young man shook his head. 'I left the wine by the bedside as usual and then returned to my own chamber, where I fell asleep immediately.'

'And your own chamber is where?'

'Next to the bishop's, so that he could call me in the night if I am needed.'

'Was the door of the bishop's chamber locked?'

'Locked? No door is locked in the abbey.'

'Then anyone could enter the room and have access to the wine at any time?'

'Yes. The empty amphora was stored in a cupboard out of sight but after I had poured the wine, the cup was left at the bishop's bedside.'

'And you were asleep very quickly? You said that you did not hear the bishop return to his chamber.'

'I did not.'

'Did you hear the arrival of Abbot Dabhóc or Abbot Cadfan during the night?'

Brother Benevolentia made a negative gesture. 'As I say, I am a sound sleeper.'

'When did you wake?'

'Not until the physician of this abbey, Brother Gebicca, knocked upon my door and told me the bishop had been taken ill; he said he needed my help to remove him to a new chamber where he could be nursed. It was when I entered the room that I saw the body of the Hibernian and the blood and also the unconscious form of the Briton.'

'And the next morning, was it you who cleared away the remains of the wine and washed the cup?'

Brother Benevolentia shook his head. 'I think it was Brother Gebicca. He cleared up when the body was taken away.'

'How long have you been steward to Bishop Ordgar?' Eadulf asked suddenly.

It was the bishop himself who answered.

'My last steward died from fever on the voyage. It was while I was visiting the abbey of Divio, on my way here, that I met with Brother Benevolentia and offered him the post.'

'Divio?'

'It is a city of the Burgunds which lies north of here,' supplied Brother Benevolentia. 'I served in that abbey there as a scribe so have been with Bishop Ordgar for only three weeks.'

Fidelma had stood silently listening in approval to Eadulf's questioning. Now she felt compelled to ask the bishop a question of her own.

'How well did you know Abbot Dabhóc?'

'I knew him not at all. We met formally before the council opened but barely exchanged a few words.'

'You did not express a difference of opinion in debate?'

'There have been no debates.'

'I was told there was an opening session at which acrimonious remarks were passed.'

'It was not a debate but an assembly where delegates could meet before the start of the working sessions. My quarrel was with Cadfan the Briton,' asserted the bishop.

'So you have no idea why Abbot Dabhóc would call at your chamber in the middle of the night?'

'None whatsoever, unless he was inveigled there by the *Welisc* who killed him, to lay the blame on me. That is my belief.'

'You dislike Abbot Cadfan very much, I hear?'

'They are all the same, these *Welisc*. They are enemies of my blood. Whining and ungrateful.'

'Isn't that understandable?' asked Fidelma.

Bishop Ordgar jerked his head towards her and his eyes narrowed angrily. 'What do you mean?'

'It is not so many years ago that your people crossed the seas and began to drive out the Britons, whom you call "foreigners" – *Welisc* in your language – from their lands and began to settle on the farms and the villages from which they had been dispossessed. Even now you continue to drive them westward. Do you expect gratitude and kindness from them?'

Bishop Ordgar's lip curled arrogantly. 'God showed us the way to the island of the Britons and gave it to us to inhabit.'

'But it was inhabited already.'

'Inhabited only by sheep. God would not have made the *Welisc* sheep if He did not expect them to be shorn.'

'They have not been shorn so easily,' Fidelma observed. 'They still fight for the possession of their lands.' It was clear that she had no liking for the bishop. 'If it was God Who showed your people the way, Ordgar of Kent,' she continued, 'then He came in a strange disguise. At the time, it was Woden, Tyr, Thurnor and Freya whom you worshipped. You see, I know of your gods, for many of your people worship them still. A generation or two ago, none of the Angles and Saxons knew or cared of the Christ until the missionaries from my people raised you from your idols. Do not blame God nor Christ as the reason why you continue to persecute and dispossess the Christian Britons.'

Brother Ordgar swallowed hard. He was trying to think of some suitable retort when Fidelma turned to Eadulf. Out of courtesy she continued to speak in Latin.

'We need not trouble Bishop Ordgar nor Brother Benevolentia further . . . at this time.'

Eadulf was confused. His mind was actually turning over the truth of what Fidelma had said because he himself had worshipped Woden into his teenage years before a wandering missionary from the land of Hibernia converted him to the New Faith. He realised Fidelma was turning for the door and glanced quickly back.

'We have finished for the moment,' he said hastily.

'Wait!' Bishop Ordgar called, as Eadulf was about to follow Fidelma. 'I need to be cleared of these foul accusations at once. When am I to be allowed to resume my seat at the council?'

It was Fidelma, in the doorway, who turned back to him.

'When we have finished our enquiry, Bishop Ordgar of Kent,' she replied curtly. 'You will be informed when that is, have no fear.'

Eadulf followed her as she paced rapidly down the corridor. They found themselves in a tiny hallway at the end where there was a large window. It overlooked a small courtyard with a little flower garden and splashing fountain. There she paused, leaning on the windowledge and slowly breathing in the fresh air.

'I am sorry, Eadulf,' she said, feeling him standing behind her and knowing he would be looking at her with a reproachful gaze. 'Something about that man and his arrogance causes my ire to rise. I should not have spoken so harshly about your people and their history.'

'I am not oblivious to their faults,' acknowledged Eadulf. 'There are no people on the face of this earth who are possessed of all the virtues. Our storytellers say that our forefathers were being driven from their own lands by hostile tribes, and that is why they crossed the sea to Britain and fought the natives for the right to settle there.'

'Good for your people, but hard for the Britons who were dispossessed.'

Eadulf sought to change the subject. 'So you think Bishop Ordgar might be guilty of this crime?'

'It is certainly a weak story that he has to tell. But in its very weakness the truth might lie. Overall, it is too curious a story to be made up.'

'What of the young man, Brother Benevolentia?'

'He seems in awe of Bishop Ordgar and will do what his master tells him.' Fidelma straightened up from the windowledge and saw that Eadulf was looking gloomy. 'It is early days yet,' she smiled.

Brother Chilperic's directions were easy to follow.

When they entered Abbot Cadfan's chamber, in response to his invitation, the Briton came forward with an outstretched hand and clasped first that of Fidelma and then that of Eadulf. He was short, with dark hair, and his black eyes seemed devoid of pupils, for the colours appeared to merge together, making one large orb in each socket.

'I know of you, Fidelma of Cashel,' he said animatedly. 'I was at the court of Gwlyddien of Dyfed when you and Brother Eadulf came there and solved the mystery of what happened at Pen Caer. I am glad that you are here. If there is any who can solve this matter, then it is you.'

'Pen Caer was some time ago.' Fidelma gave a deprecating smile. 'I only hope that we can fulfil your expectations.'

'What happened in the kingdom of Dyfed has often been told at the feasting fires even in the northern kingdom of Gwynedd. But come, be seated, let me offer you refreshment.'

It was certainly a better reception than that given them by Bishop Ordgar. The pair seated themselves and accepted his wine. It was white, cool and refreshing.

'Now,' the Briton began in businesslike fashion, 'I know that I am accused by Ordgar of killing poor Abbot Dabhóc. So please ask your questions and I will tell you what I know as facts.'

Fidelma felt comfortable with Cadfan's easy manners and recalled that the Britons had a similar law system to those that the Brehons used. She reminded herself that among the Britons there was an office called a *Barnwr* that was their equivalent of a Brehon.

'Let us start off by asking you when you first met Bishop Ordgar. It would be useless asking you if you disliked him.'

Abbot Cadfan chuckled in genuine amusement.

'Dislike would be too mild a term.' He paused reflectively. 'Though that admission will do me no good in an investigation such as this. Anyway, the truth is the truth. If he were lying in need of help on the far side of a road, I could not bring myself to emulate the story of the Good Samaritan. Perhaps I do not have sufficient faith in the Christ. But to answer your question, I had no idea of Bishop Ordgar's existence until I arrived here in Autun. We first encountered each other outside the council chamber and I told him that when the council met, I was going to raise a proposition that they should begin by censuring the Saxon kingdoms for the wanton destruction of Benchoer.'

Seeing that Fidelma and Eadulf looked blank he continued: 'Benchoer is the largest and greatest of our religious houses in Gwynedd. Drostó, the abbot, was invited to this council; I was to come along as his assistant. Just before we commenced our journey, the Saxons of Mercia attacked and burned Benchoer and slaughtered nearly a thousand of our brethren there. I was not present at the time, thanks be to God, for I had gone to consult with the bishop of Dewi Sant in Menevia about matters that needed to be raised at this council. We heard that Drostó and a few survivors had fled into the forests and were being pursued by the Saxons. Then we had a message from Drostó himself, saying that he could not desert his people at such a time. So it was agreed that I should come here as representative because this council was too important to ignore. The proposals being debated here might greatly affect our churches and abbeys.'

He paused. Eadulf was looking uncomfortable.

Fidelma regarded Abbot Cadfan in sympathy.

'Over a thousand of your brethren killed, you say?'

'Of religious brothers and sisters,' confirmed Cadfan. 'It was an unprovoked attack by the Saxons.'

'The ambition of Wulfhere to rule over all the Saxon kingdoms is well known,' Eadulf observed slowly. 'He also claims to be Bretwalda, that is lord over the Britons. He persuaded the authority of the archbishop at Canterbury to recognise that title. His alliances and conquests now hem in my own people, those of the kingdoms of the East Angles. He controls the kingdom of the East Saxons and also the kingdom of Lindsey to the north of us.'

'You'll forgive me if I am more concerned with my own people,' Abbot Cadfan replied dryly. 'It is Wulfhere's attempts to destroy us that are on my mind. I asked Ordgar, as a man of Christ, representing the new bishop sent by Rome to administer to the Saxon kingdoms, if he would join me in condemning this sacrilege and unprovoked attack on a religious house. The man laughed in my face and said he rejoiced to hear of the success of Wulfhere's exploits.'

Eadulf dropped his gaze to the floor and was now clearly embarrassed.

'There has been continual warfare between your people and mine,' he offered, feeling he should make some comment.

Abbot Cadfan's expression was controlled. 'Why is that, Brother Eadulf? Did we invade your lands or did you invade our lands? Surely, you are too intelligent to blindly side with your people when they are in the wrong?'

'So,' interrupted Fidelma hastily, 'Bishop Ordgar refused to condemn the destruction of Benchoer. What happened then?'

'We went into the council and before I had a chance to raise the matter, Ordgar began to insult me; this led to an argument and the council was adjourned. As we were leaving, Ordgar insulted me once again. Alas, it is my great fault that I am cursed with a quick temper. Losing it, I struck Ordgar and he struck back – and the next thing I knew, we were wrestling on the floor. It was unforgivable and undignified. Then the brethren were pulling us apart.'

'When was this?' asked Fidelma. 'I mean, when was it in relationship to the events in Ordgar's chamber?'

'It was the very same afternoon.'

'So tell me what happened after you and Ordgar were forcibly split up?'

'I decided to avoid him and went with one of the Gaulish brethren to see that ancient Roman theatre which is not far from this abbey. It is an amazing place and—'

'We have seen Roman theatres,' Eadulf pointed out, observing the enthusiasm in the man's eyes and wishing to keep to the matter in hand.

'Not an amphitheatre like this, that seats fifteen hundred people. It is—'

'Did anything of relevance happen at the theatre?' interrupted Fidelma quickly. 'Is this why you mention it?'

'No.' Realising that he should stick to the important facts, the abbot went on, 'We returned here for evening prayers. I saw Ordgar in the chapel but again, avoided him, then came here to my chamber and retired for the night. I was awoken by a tapping on the door. I called out, but there was no answer. It was still dark but I felt it was not long before dawn. I lit a candle, but when I went to the door, the corridor was empty. However, there was a note on the threshold. A scrap of parchment.'

'What was on it?' asked Eadulf.

'It bore the name of Ordgar and said that he was at great fault and wished to see me at once. That he would be waiting in his chamber for me.'

'We were told that you no longer have this note,' Fidelma said.

'I had it on me when I went to Ordgar's chamber, but when I recovered consciousness it was gone,' explained Abbot Cadfan.

'I see. It said nothing else?'

'Nothing.'

'Did you not think it was strange – to receive such a note at such an hour?'

Abbot Cadfan glanced at him with a frown. 'In what way strange?'

'That Bishop Ordgar, after the encounters you had had with him, should suddenly send you an apology and invitation at such an hour?'

The Briton shrugged. 'Paul encountered a blinding light on the road to Damascus,' he replied. 'Why not Ordgar in the middle of the night?'

'I doubt whether even Paul had the disposition of Ordgar,' observed Fidelma softly.

Abbot Cadfan thought for a while and then said: 'When I consider it in hindsight, then perhaps it *was* strange. I suppose that I was concerned with letting Christendom know of the crime at Benchoer. So I went eagerly to his chamber. I thought he had truly changed his mind. And now the note has vanished, which makes me appear a storyteller.'

'What then?'

'I tapped on the door and it swung open so I went inside. It was dark and I called out. Then there was a split second of pain. I think I knew that I had been struck from behind. The next thing, I was back here on my own bed. Someone had bandaged my head, which was painful and bloodied.' He raised a hand to his head. 'There is no bandage now, but you may still see the scar and the faint bruise that still exists.'

'Were you told of what had happened?'

'I was told that Abbot Dabhóc was dead, that I had been found unconscious and that Ordgar was claiming that he had been drugged. I was also told that the physician Brother Gebicca had brought me back to my chamber and tended me. Then the next day, Bishop Leodegar informed me that Ordgar was accusing me of contriving this murder in order to put the blame on him. It therefore seemed obvious to me who the culprit was.

I say it was Ordgar who was waiting behind the door to strike me down as I entered.'

Fidelma was puzzled and said so.

'I do not follow your logic here, Abbot Cadfan. How do you reach this conclusion?'

'Easy enough. I met Abbot Dabhóc at the council. Why would I kill him? He was sympathetic to me, and the people of Iwerddon, as we call your country, share many of our rites and rituals. Whereas Saxons do not. I had no reason to argue with Abbot Dabhóc. The accusation Ordgar levels at me is false. He disliked Abbot Dabhóc as much as he disliked me. I say that Ordgar arranged the whole thing to put the blame on *me*. It is as simple as that.'

There was silence for a moment. Then Abbot Cadfan regarded Eadulf as if a sudden thought had occurred to him.

'Didn't I hear that you, Brother Eadulf, went to one of those schools for physicians that are renowned in Iwerddon?'

'I went to Tuam Brecain,' Eadulf acknowledged.

'Excellent. Now, please, examine my head. Look at the wound on my scalp and the bruises.'

Eadulf rose and went to examine the abbot's head.

'I can see a jagged cut running from a line just above the left ear,' he reported. 'It is healing well but was fairly deep, I would say. There is still bruising all around. I would guess that it was inflicted by a blunt instrument.'

Abbot Cadfan gave him an approving look.

'You have a discerning eye, Brother Eadulf. I will not argue with your finding. So tell me, how did I, having drugged Ordgar and killed Abbot Dabhóc, then inflict this wound on myself? A wound on the back of my head that knocked me unconscious for many hours.'

'It would be difficult,' Eadulf conceded, rubbing his chin thoughtfully. 'But perhaps Dabhóc inflicted the blow just as you killed him, or else you had an accomplice?'

'You disappoint me,' Abbot Cadfan replied, still cheerful, 'I would say it was impossible to exert that much power with the one hand I would have had free to use. Can you imagine me picking up a piece of wood and attempting to strike myself on the back of the head?' He laughed. 'As for Dabhóc inflicting the blow, that is out of the question. Don't take my word for it – ask Brother Gebicca. And once struck, I would be incapable of summoning enough strength to kill him. As for an accomplice – who would be my accomplice?'

'Has the physician, Brother Gebicca, remarked on this matter?' asked Fidelma.

'I pointed out the facts to him and he conceded the logic. It is a matter that I shall maintain in my defence,' replied Abbot Cadfan firmly.

'Defence?' Fidelma repeated the word with mild reproach. 'No one has been formally accused as yet.'

'It will happen, I am sure of it,' Abbot Cadfan sighed. 'Bishop Leodegar is a Frank. Aren't they first cousins of the Saxons? The language is similar. I believe that he has already made up his mind what course to take and that does not involve causing upset to the Saxons or to Rome. Isn't Ordgar the emissary of Theodore of Canterbury, sent to minister to the Saxon kingdoms by none other than Pope Vitalian in Rome? I cannot see Bishop Leodegar upsetting such powerful authorities. He will sacrifice me, there is no doubt.'

'Bishop Leodegar is going to abide by the truth,' Fidelma assured Cadfan. 'That is why we have been commissioned to investigate this matter.'

Abbot Cadfan suddenly burst out laughing.

'Forgive me, forgive me, Sister Fidelma,' he said, wiping his eyes on his sleeve. 'I mean no insult. But Leodegar will do what is best for Leodegar and his Frankish Church. He will not censure the likes of Ordgar for fear of displeasing Rome. What does he care for the plight of us Britons?'

'I trust you are wrong, Abbot Cadfan, for truth must prevail in the end,' observed Fidelma, rising and moving to the door.

'Truth can prevail – but let us hope that it does so while I still live,' replied Abbot Cadfan. 'Keep me informed of your search for it.'

Fidelma paused at the door. Her face was serious.

'Truth *will* prevail, Abbot Cadfan. I will see to it.'

Chapter Six

'Well, one of them must be lying as there seems no common ground,' Eadulf remarked after they had left Abbot Cadfan. 'Their stories are totally at odds with one another.'

'On the contrary, the facts of the story are the same,' Fidelma argued. 'Neither one is disputing the facts, only who is responsible.'

'One says he was drugged. The other says he was asked to go to Ordgar's chamber and then hit on the head. They can't both be telling the truth.'

'Perhaps they can,' Fidelma said quietly.

Eadulf shook his head. 'In the end it will be a matter of who we are to believe – Ordgar or Cadfan. It is like throwing up a coin and choosing which side it falls in order to make a decision.'

'Truth is never found through a game of chance. Our resolution must be based on other factors.'

'But what other factors are there?' demanded Eadulf. 'All I see is two people making two different claims.'

'We have scarce begun to investigate.'

'You think the physician, Brother Gebicca, might have something to say? We could go to see him now.'

A bell started to ring.

'I think that means it is time for the midday meal,' Fidelma said. 'Afterwards, let us find the apothecary of Brother Gebicca and see what he has to tell us.'

They made their way downstairs and saw an orderly line of brethren, hands folded before them, heads bowed, waiting to file through the doors into the refectory. The men cast surreptitious glances at Fidelma as she and Eadulf joined the line. At that moment, Abbot Ségdae appeared.

'Ah, Fidelma, I hoped to find you. You and Eadulf are to eat with us at the table reserved for the delegates from the five kingdoms.'

'We were just wondering about it,' she said with some relief as the abbot guided them past the line and into the refectory.

'You can tell me how much progress you are making over the meal,' the abbot said, as he led the way through the great refectory hall past the long benches and tables at which the brethren were gathering. Half-a-dozen religieux were already seated at the table to which he showed them. Abbot Ségdae called their names one by one in introduction. The names flowed over Eadulf's head but he understood they represented the leading clerics of all five kingdoms. It was obvious that Abbot Ségdae was regarded as the senior ecclesiastic among them.

A single bell rang and everyone in the refectory rose. At that moment, Bishop Leodegar entered with Brother Chilperic at his side and joined those at the table at the far end of the hall. Everyone had remained standing as the bishop took his place and spread his arms.

'*Gloria in excelesis Deo et in terra pax hominibus bonae voluntatis*,' he intoned.

'*Laudamus te*,' mumbled the gathered brethren.

'*Benedicimus te, Gratias agimus te . . .*' the bishop continued with the Latin ritual.

After the *gratias* and blessing they could thankfully sit and break bread and partake of cold meats and cooked vegetables.

'So, have you seen all those you wished to see?' asked Abbot Ségdae brightly, as he passed a plate of meat to Fidelma.

'We have only spoken with Ordgar, Cadfan and Sigeric,' she replied.

'And have you reached any conclusions?'

'You know my methods, Ségdae,' she said. 'We have not spoken as yet to everyone that we need to question.'

The abbot did not look happy. 'It would be good if we could clear up this matter quickly.'

'Yes, it would be good. However, we are not possessed of second sight and can only do our best in finding out the culprit.'

The abbot concentrated on helping himself to some vegetables.

'Bishop Leodegar keeps reminding me that King Clotaire himself is expected in a few days,' he said.

'Someone mentioned that Leodegar was raised at Clotaire's court,' observed Fidelma absently. She had noticed that a young man seated at the end of the table kept looking at her, but when he saw her gaze upon him he dropped his eyes and pretended to concentrate on the plate before him. She tried to remember the name by which Ségdae had introduced him. A northerner? Ah, Brother Gillucán was the name.

'Clotaire is a young man,' the abbot was explaining. 'He is the third to bear his name as King, so I am told. So Leodegar must have been raised by one of his forebears. This Clotaire is only seventeen years old; he was ten years old when he succeeded his father, Clovis, to the throne.'

She turned in surprise. 'Ten years old? That is surely below the age of inheritance?'

'It is the custom here. The eldest son succeeds the father, and if he is under age there is a guardian appointed to govern in his place.'

'A curious and unstable method of governing,' she commented.

'Clotaire should be here shortly to officially sanction the council's findings and recommendations. The papal envoy is already here. He is seated next to Leodegar. Can you see him?'

Fidelma glanced over her shoulder but there were too many of the brethren in the way to see the man's features.

'So?' she asked, holding her cup out for Eadulf to pour some of the cool water from the jug that stood on the table.

'Leodegar takes every opportunity to inform me that the council cannot make progress unless this matter is cleared up,' sighed Ségdae. 'If it has not been resolved by the time Clotaire arrives, then how can the King make his public support for the decisions of the council?'

Fidelma turned to the abbot. 'I suspect Leodegar has already decided what decisions the council should make, especially when the council has been set up by Rome which does not like our rites and practices. Let us hope he has not also decided who is guilty of the murder.'

'You are discerning as always, Fidelma,' the abbot remarked. 'If the

Bishop of Rome instructs a council to make a decision and indicates what decision he wants made, then I would say that it is a foregone conclusion. I do not like it, but I fear we are here simply to give authenticity to a decision already reached in Rome.'

Fidelma returned his gaze levelly. 'If I thought that, and I had the authority to give my vote in the council, I would not give that authority. I would not even attend.'

'Exactly so. We are invited here merely to register our protest when the decision is announced,' said the abbot glumly. 'You may have noticed that we who follow the church of Ailbe, Patrick and Colmcille are in a minority.'

'If Rome wants to go down that path, why follow them?' Fidelma asked. 'Those churches in the east have not done so.'

Abbot Ségdae was unhappy with her choice of words.

'Careful, Fidelma, lest you be accused of uttering heresy,' he warned. 'Rome should still be our centre, for was it not the great apostle Peter who chose Rome as the place where the church of Christ would be founded? Did not Christ tell him that he was the person who would form His church?'

'So why argue with Rome?' interrupted Eadulf. 'Why not accept their dictum and make life easier?'

Abbot Ségdae turned to him with a frown. 'Rome is but an erring parent, Eadulf. We follow the original precepts of the Founding Fathers of the Faith, the rites and rituals, the dating of our celebrations. It was not we who changed, but Rome who started to alter her ways and follow other paths.'

'Isn't that exactly what the churches in the east claim? They say that the churches there follow the orthodox rites that Rome rejected.'

'Their split was over politics, not theology.'

'How so?' demanded Eadulf.

'The eastern churches split when the Roman Empire itself split; when the Emperor made his capital at Byzantium and called it after his own name Constantinople. The separation between Rome and Constantinople caused the two adherents of the Faith to move apart.'

Fidelma nodded in agreement. 'Just as these new ideas of Rome are moving it apart from us in the west. Rome rejected the teachings of Pelagius, it expelled Arian and now it is at odds with monothelitism. One day this movement for segregation of the sexes and celibacy will probably be accepted as Rome's teaching. Where will Rome's constant revision of the Faith and its rites end? One day, we may find no connection at all with the original creed of the Founding Fathers of the Faith.'

'I had no idea that you thought so deeply on such matters, Fidelma,' the abbot said.

'I do not wear my ideas on the sleeve of my robe, Ségdae,' she replied softly. 'But that is not to say that I do not have them. I believe the Faith is for the individual to accept or reject; it is not for someone else to tell them what they should believe or how to do so. My public concern is for the law; for truth and justice.'

Eadulf coughed nervously. Fidelma glanced up, realising that many of the brethren were now filing out of the hall.

'You will forgive us now, Ségdae, for we must continue our task,' she said, rising.

After they left the refectory, Eadulf whispered: 'Is it wise to be so outspoken?'

'Perhaps not,' she replied. 'Yet I cannot repress my thoughts entirely. It is not my nature.'

'Of all the places in the world, I do not think this is the one for an open discussion on theology.'

She looked at him and then started to chuckle.

Eadulf was about to open his mouth to protest when she explained: 'I do not laugh at you, Eadulf. It is the thought that this great abbey, with its council on the future of the Church, is not a place for a discussion on theology. If not here, then where?'

'It can only be in a place where minds are free to receive ideas so that they can be discussed,' Eadulf said grumpily. 'Where minds are already made up, no discussion and exchange of ideas can thrive.'

Fidelma reached out to touch his arm. 'Sometimes I forget how wise you can be, Eadulf,' she smiled. 'I will be more attentive as to how I express my thoughts in future. Now, let us find Brother Gebicca.'

Brother Gebicca was typical of all the physicians and apothecaries that Fidelma and Eadulf had ever known. He was elderly, but moved with a swift decisive energy as he bent his spare frame over the pestles and jars arrayed on his workbench in the malodorous rooms that he inhabited. He glanced up as they entered and his face registered surprise as he saw Fidelma followed by Eadulf.

'You are a woman!' he frowned.

'You are very observant, Brother Gebicca,' she replied with humour. 'That is essential in an apothecary.'

The physician made a cutting motion with his hand.

'This abbey has been forbidden to women,' he said.

'You were not at evening prayers in the chapel last night?' she asked.

The apothecary was still irritable. 'Why should I be? I have plenty to occupy my time and a dispensation from the bishop to concentrate on the health of the brethren. What are you doing here?'

'Had you attended then you might have heard the bishop announce our presence and purpose here. We are investigating the death of Abbot Dabhóc.'

Brother Gebicca's eyes narrowed slightly for a moment. Then his expression eased.

'Ah. Brother Chilepric did say something about your coming.' He rose from the stool before his workbench and went to splash his hands in a bowl of water before wiping them on a linen cloth.

'Now, what is it that you want of me?'

'To tell us what you know of the death of Abbot Dabhóc.'

Brother Gebicca glanced from Fidelma to Eadulf and back again, then gestured for them to follow him through a door that led out into the herb gardens behind the apothecary. There were a couple of low stone bench-like seats, where they sat. The area was bathed in the early afternoon summer sunshine, which was full of the different scents from the herbs and flowers in the garden. It was comforting, almost soporific to sit in the natural warmth after the cold interior of the abbey.

'On the night of the killing of Abbot Dabhóc, we understand that you were summoned to Bishop Ordgar's apartment by Brother Sigeric?' Eadulf opened the questions.

'Brother Sigeric was acting on the instructions of Bishop Leodegar who was already attending the scene,' Brother Gebicca confirmed pedantically.

'On reaching Ordgar's chamber, who did you attend to first?'

'I first confirmed that the Hibernian abbot, Dabhóc, was beyond help. That was easy enough. The back of his skull had been smashed in with a heavy force. Then I turned to the unconscious Briton, Abbot Cadfan. He, too, had been struck on the head but I saw that, although there was a cut and abrasion and the swelling had already started, he still lived. So then I moved on to Bishop Ordgar.'

'And what did you find?' encouraged Fidelma.

'He was lying on his bed, semi-conscious. He was mumbling a great deal and incoherent. His breath smelled strongly of alcohol.'

'You mean that he was drunk?' asked Eadulf.

'I believed so at first, but then I came to the conclusion that he had been drugged.'

'Why was that?'

'The state of the eyes, the tongue and lips. I have practised the healing arts for many years and know the difference between an over-indulgence in alcohol and the effects of certain herbs that can produce a similar stupor.'

'So what did you do?'

'I told Bishop Leodegar that he would get no sense from either Cadfan or Ordgar for a while. My estimation was that it would take at least a day for both men to recover sufficiently to explain what had happened. Bishop Leodegar, at my suggestion, had Abbot Cadfan carried back to his own chamber where I washed and dressed his wound, applying a poultice to defuse the swelling and heal the cut. Then I left someone to watch him. I was pleased with his progress; he is a strong man and has healed well.'

'And Bishop Ordgar?' asked Eadulf.

'As for Ordgar, he was removed to another chamber – in the same corridor. He could not, of course, remain in his own chamber with the blood and the fact that someone had died violently there. Ordgar's steward, Brother Benevolentia, was roused and we carried the bishop to the new chamber. I instructed his steward to remain with him for the rest of the night and try to get him to swallow as much water as was possible at regular intervals in order to flush the system.'

'And the body of Abbot Dabhóc?'

'The body was removed to the mortuary where I later prepared it for burial. There were no other wounds than the blow that had splintered his skull. Obviously, it was a blow that was delivered from behind and with considerable force.'

'And what about Bishop Ordgar's chamber?' asked Fidelma.

The physician looked at her questioningly.

'I am told that you cleaned it,' she explained. 'You also washed the cup in which it was thought the wine had been drugged. Is that so?'

'Should I have left a cup of drugged wine standing there for anyone to take or contaminate their drink from?' retorted Brother Gebicca with some irritation. 'That would have been dangerous.'

Eadulf bent forward quickly. 'There was still wine in the cup?'

'It was half full.'

'Then Bishop Ordgar had not entirely drained it?'

'Had he done so, he might have been dead.'

'Are you sure?' asked Fidelma in surprise.

Brother Gebicca looked pained. 'I would not state anything that I know to be false. Of course I am sure.'

'You did not keep nor analyse this wine?'

'I ensured that it was disposed of, both the cup and the amphora. By chance it seemed that the amphora was empty anyway.'

'So there is no evidence of what this wine was, nor how the drug came to be in the wine? I mean, whether the drug was put in the cup first or into the amphora.'

The physician made a negative gesture with one hand.

'The fact that it was in the cup was cause enough for me to ensure no one else would drink from it and suffer illness or death,' he replied.

'We each have our tasks to fulfil, Brother Gebicca,' replied Fidelma softly. 'Your task is to save life but mine is to discover why life is lost.'

Eadulf had been thoughtful for a few moments and now he said: 'Let me ask you a question, Brother Gebicca. It needs must be a hypothetical one. Would it have been possible for Bishop Ordgar to have killed Abbot Dabhóc, struck Abbot Cadfan and then take the poison himself, swallowing only a mouthful or so to give him the effects you saw but not enough to kill himself?'

Brother Gebicca considered. 'Anything is possible, but Bishop Ordgar would have to be a man with fine judgement to know how much of that noxious brew to swallow in safety.'

'But he could have done so?' pressed Eadulf.

The physician spread his arms in a helpless gesture. 'Yes, he could have done so. But as a physician, I would say it was most unlikely, unless he was practised in the ways of poison.'

'When you were tending to both Abbot Cadfan and Bishop Ordgar, did you question them about what had taken place?' Fidelma asked next.

'In fact, both men, when returning to consciousness, asked me what had happened. They said that they had no memories of it.'

'They claimed they recalled nothing?'

'Bishop Ordgar said he remembered taking wine, as was his custom before retiring and falling asleep. Abbot Cadfan said he entered Bishop Ordgar's chamber, having been summoned there in the middle of the night, and was struck from behind and knew nothing else. I would say that the suspicion is more strongly connected with Ordgar, were it not for the fact that Cadfan claimed he had received a note from Ordgar asking him to attend him. No such note was found.'

'Let me ask you another question,' said Eadulf. 'Speaking as a medical man, could Cadfan's injury have been self administered?'

'Absolutely not.'

'Then, what you are saying, in fact, is that suspicion rests equally on both men.'

The physician shrugged as Fidelma rose slowly from her seat.

'I don't suppose that you knew any of these three clerics before they arrived here at the abbey?' she added as an afterthought.

'Most of the learned bishops and abbots who are attending this council are strangers to this city. I have practised my arts only in Divio and here in Autun. I am under the impression that most of those attending the council are unknown to each other.'

'Thank you for your time, Brother Gebicca,' Fidelma said.

'It is of little service, I'm afraid,' the physician said, standing up and conducting them back through his apothecary to the door. 'If I would venture an opinion, I would say that it comes down to which person you believe. Both of them cannot be telling the truth. A man is dead and there were only two others in the room. If the choice were mine, I would toss a coin.'

Chapter Seven

They left Brother Gebicca in his apothecary and walked slowly across the great courtyard to the main abbey building in silence.

'It seems the physician agrees with me,' Eadulf ventured after a while. 'It does come down to a matter of choice.'

'I am not prepared to make that judgement at the moment, Eadulf,' Fidelma said stubbornly. 'I do not feel that we have enough information.'

'We have all the information that we are likely to get,' Eadulf pointed out. 'There are no other witnesses.'

'Then we need to give this more thought.'

'If only the cup and amphora had not been destroyed. A good apothecary might have been able to identify any poison and so confirm Ordgar's story.'

'The destruction of the cup is regrettable,' replied Fidelma. 'The amphora does not matter.'

'How so?'

'Because the poison would have been mixed in the cup, not in the amphora, which was empty after the wine was poured. It is logical that it was too late that night to throw the amphora away. It was not the next day but it would have told us nothing so we need not concern ourselves with it. However, the cup . . . that's a pity.'

They had not reached the door of the building when Brother Chilperic came out and walked towards them.

'I am off to our herb garden,' he greeted them. 'Are you seeking anything in particular?'

'For the moment we are just exercising,' replied Fidelma. 'The late-afternoon sun is very inviting, Brother Chilperic. Where is your herb garden?'

'It is a separate one to that which the apothecary cultivates for he has his own needs. It is this way, if you wish to see it.'

They fell in step with him. He guided them alongside the abbey wall and through a small courtyard at the back of the main building into a large open space which surprised them. It was full of aromatic herbs and spices being tended by two elderly members of the brethren.

'It looks a beautiful garden,' Fidelma acknowledged.

'It is, indeed, and I'm afraid that it invites us to be lazy and sit in contemplation when we should be about God's work in tending the garden. Would you like to see our herbs and spices? We grow a great variety for the consumption of our brethren.'

'I would not like to encourage indolence, Brother Chilperic, and stop you working.'

'The sun is encouragement enough. But perhaps you need to get on about your own work. How is the investigation? Do you need anything? Have you made a decision yet?'

Eadulf pursed his lips as he began to say, 'We are faced with . . .'

Fidelma knew that he was about to say 'a blank wall' and it suddenly gave her an idea.

'Faced with a small problem,' she ended quickly for him 'But you, Brother Chilperic, are the very person who can help us with it.'

'I am?'

She inclined her head towards the high wall that separated the abbey from what was called the *Domus Femini*.

'We would like to have a word with the *abbatissa*.'

'Abbess Audofleda?' queried the steward in astonishment.

'That is her name, I believe,' agreed Fidelma. 'Can you arrange it?'

'Abbess Audofleda sees no one from the abbey without the bishop's express permission,' muttered Brother Chilperic. 'Anyway, I do not see why your investigation should take you to the *Domus Femini*.'

'Knowledge of the relevance is surely mine and not to be shared with anyone during an investigation.'

The steward looked worried. 'In such a matter I must first consult Bishop Leodegar.'

Fidelma was about to protest when she realised that the young man was clearly incapable of making the decision without the approval of Leodegar. She knew she must not underestimate the power of the bishop. Instead she said: 'Consult him then. We would not wish to upset the bishop. But if you can seek his permission straight away . . . ?'

Brother Chilperic hesitated. 'The bishop is visiting in the city. He will not return to the abbey until the evening meal.'

Fidelma glanced at the sky. The afternoon was well progressed but there would have been plenty of time to visit the *Domus Femini*. Presumably it would not be until the morning that they would now receive permission to meet Abbess Audofleda. That would be a waste of many hours. Fidelma felt a compulsion to finish this task as soon as possible and set out for home again, for she had felt uncomfortable ever since their arrival at the abbey.

'I cannot see why you need to visit the *Domus Femini*,' the steward repeated. 'The murder was done here, we have the people involved, so why do you need to speak with Abbess Audofleda?'

Eadulf noticed that Fidelma's eyes had become bright and her jaw muscles were tightening.

'My friend,' he said, taking Brother Chilperic by the arm, 'you must understand that it is our task to conduct our investigation in our own way. Bishop Leodegar gave us full permission to do so. So what we do is our own concern, with due respect to your position as steward of this abbey.'

'I will still have to seek the permission of Bishop Leodegar,' the man said mulishly.

Fidelma had recovered her good humour.

'In that case, we can do no more for this day.' She turned to Eadulf. 'While we are here we may as well see something of this city.'

As Eadulf voiced his assent Brother Chiperic looked shocked.

'Are you intending to leave the abbey?' he asked in surprise.

Fidelma frowned. 'Is there an objection to that too?'

The steward gestured helplessly. 'The bishop left no instructions.'

'Why would he?'

'Because the general rule is that no one leaves the abbey without permission of the bishop. If they are strangers, like you, they need someone to guide them. It is a matter of protecting our delegates.'

'I scarcely think that such rules apply to us. Are not all the delegates free to come and go? After all, there was no concern for our security before we came to the abbey.'

'I can only abide by the bishop's Rule.'

Fidelma was astonished and said so.

'I have no other instructions,' muttered Brother Chilperic.

'Are we allowed to return to our own chamber without being accompanied?' snapped Fidelma.

The young man looked unhappy, torn between his duty to the bishop and Fidelma's displeasure. However, Fidelma had already turned and walked away, her lips compressed tightly. Eadulf paused only a moment before following her. He fell in step as she stormed across the stone-paved courtyard; the smack of her shoes on the stones created an angry timbre.

'I hate being restricted,' she said at last, slowing to a more reasonable pace.

'I don't think it is the young man's fault,' Eadulf said, referring to Brother Chilperic. 'He's scared of making a decision which would displease the bishop.'

'Of course it is not his fault. It is the bishop who is trying to control what people do and where they go. I wonder what Leodegar is scared of?'

'Perhaps it is just that he is so used to dictating rules and having them obeyed that everyone is now in a position where they cannot think for themselves,' offered Eadulf.

Fidelma suddenly halted. 'Go and find Abbot Ségdae, Eadulf. I am sure *he* is not a man to be bound by the constraints of this abbey. Ask him for permission for us to leave and for his support if we are forbidden.'

Eadulf hesitated and then shrugged, and as he moved away, Fidelma called: 'I'll wait in the *hospitia*!'

Eadulf raised a hand without breaking stride to acknowledge her.

Deep in thought, Fidelma returned to the *hospitia*. She hoped that Bishop Leodegar was not going to press her as to why she needed to visit the *Domus Femini*. She wanted to see if Brother Sigeric's tale connected in any deeper way with the events of Abbot Dabhóc's death. But she felt frustrated that she was being so hampered by the segregation that Bishop Leodegar imposed on his brethren. She longed for the logic and attitudes of her own land.

Fidelma entered the chamber, and as she closed the door she heard a slight movement behind her. Heart beating fast, she wheeled round and saw the figure of a man in the shadows.

'Who are you?' she demanded, trying to suppress the fear in her voice.

'I did not mean to frighten you, Sister.' The voice spoke in her own language. It was that of a nervous young man.

She recognised the young religieux as the one whom she had observed watching her from the end of the table in the refectory.

'You are Brother Gillucán, aren't you?'

'I am – I was – Abbot Dabhóc's steward and companion on this pilgrimage.'

Fidelma moved across the room and sat on the edge of the bed, gesturing to the chair.

'You have a strange way of introducing yourself, Brother Gillucán.'

The young man seated himself, saying in a low voice, 'Everywhere in this abbey, there is a feeling of being watched. One needs to be cautious.'

'Why would you be watched?' Fidelma asked.

The young man shuddered. 'I do not know. I long for my own country.'

'You are from Ulaidh?'

'I am of the Uí Nadsluaig although I served at Tulach Óc.'

'You do not like this place?'

The young man gave a curious gesture with his hands that Fidelma was not sure how to interpret.

'It is cursed. Souls are in torment – I have heard them.' He sighed. 'There is something in this abbey that is evil, Sister. In truth, I am scared.'

She raised an eyebrow. 'You speak with emotion, Brother Gillucán. You had best explain yourself.'

'I am not sure where to start.'

'The beginning is the best place to start,' she encouraged him. 'You are, or were, steward to the abbot of Tulach Óc?'

He nodded. 'Yes. I served Abbot Dabhóc for five years as his chief scribe and steward.'

'So that is why he chose you to accompany him to this council?'

'It was. It is a great honour to be chosen to travel abroad and come to an important council such as this. We came, of course, in the name of Ségéne, the Bishop of Ard Macha.'

'Of course. And how long have you been here?'

'We arrived at this abbey ten days ago. After a few days, when all the major delegates had arrived, the Bishop of Autun opened the council. Only the main delegates were invited to attend that session. All the scribes and advisers were excluded so I did not witness the conflict which I heard about afterwards.'

'The conflict?'

'When Abbot Dabhóc returned, he was not happy. He told me that there had been great animosity between Abbot Cadfan of Gwynedd and Bishop Ordgar of Kent. It had even turned to physical violence between them. He lamented that it would be impossible for any agreements to be made while the two of them took such positions.'

Fidelma was frowning. 'So he told you the details?'

'I was also his *anam chara*, his soul friend.'

In the Faith of the five kingdoms, each person found an *anam chara* with whom they could discuss their problems. It was an ancient custom going back to the time when the old religion was followed. Elsewhere in Christendom, people had to confess in public or in private to the priests and then accept penance. That was not the purpose of a soul friend, who would discuss and advise on matters of spiritual conflict. There was no guilt and no penance with the *anam chara*, just a way forward when dealing with problems.

'You said that you were frightened. Was it these animosities that made you so?'

The young man seemed to consider his words carefully before responding, 'Not exactly. That evening, after that first meeting, Abbot Dahbóc was worried about the situation and resolved to see Bishop Leodegar the next morning. He wanted to find out if there was some way of compromise. Of course, it was the next morning that I learned that he had been killed in Ordgar's chamber.' He paused, upset.

'So you think that he went to Bishop Ordgar's chamber, that there was a row and he was killed in the course of that altercation?' Fidelma asked gently.

'It is a plausible explanation. Yet Bishop Ordgar says that he was drugged and I hear he did not recover for a full day. And Abbot Cadfan says he was called to Ordgar's chamber and then knocked out.' The young man rubbed his brow. 'There is one thing that I cannot understand, and it is this that creates anxiety in my mind. That morning, when I heard what had happened to Abbot Dabhóc, I went to his chamber to pack his belongings and found that his room had been ransacked.'

'Ransacked?' Fidelma leaned forward. 'Was this not the abbey authorities merely searching for any relevant material related to Abbot Dabhóc's killing?'

'It was not,' asserted Brother Gillucán. 'The abbey steward, Brother Chilperic, who made some initial enquiries, had not been to Abbot Dabhóc's chamber by the time I went there. Moreover, all the abbot's belongings had been removed. In fact, Brother Chilperic accused *me* of removing them, and demanded to see my hands.'

'Your hands – why?' Fidelma demanded.

Gillucán shrugged. 'He said something about the person who had searched the chamber having cut himself while taking things, for there was some blood in evidence. Anyway, Brother Chilperic assured himself that it was not me, but he searched my chamber to ensure that what I said was true.'

Fidelma considered the matter for a moment. Dabhóc's chamber had been ransacked on the very morning that the chamber in which he had been murdered had also been searched. What was the connection? There must be one.

'He made no mention of this to me. Where is your chamber in relationship to the abbot's? Did you hear anything of this search?'

'I am in the adjoining corridor, Sister. So I heard nothing.'

'Was anything further said about this matter? Was a search made for the missing belongings? Perhaps some enterprising but misled brother, thinking the abbot had no need for the clothes, had appropriated them?' She knew there was a custom of sharing the clothes of a dead religious among the poor.

Brother Gillucán shook his head. 'It was not just clothing that was taken. Everything was gone.'

'What is your definition of everything?'

'Money carried by the abbot, funds to cover our journey, letters from the Bishop of Ard Macha to various dignitaries which were kept in a book satchel, the abbot's missal and some gifts – one in particular . . .' His mouth snapped shut suddenly and he looked about with an almost exaggerated conspiratorial glance.

Fidelma examined him with interest. 'And this particular gift . . . what was that?'

The young man lowered his voice. 'Abbot Dabhóc had been entrusted by Bishop Ségéne with a precious gift to be handed to His Holiness.'

'To the Bishop of Rome?' asked Fidelma in surprise.

'An emissary of Vitalian is attending this council to give the Holy Father's personal blessing to it.'

'I know. And so there was a gift brought from Ard Macha for this envoy to take to Rome?'

'There was.'

'Are you suggesting that Abbot Dabhóc had not passed that gift to the emissary before it was stolen?'

'Just so. There was to be a ceremony of presentation at the end of the council.'

'And the nature of the gift?'

'I did not know exactly.'

'So what – exactly – *did* you know?'

'The gift was housed in a reliquary. Abbot Dabhóc carried it in a special sack and never let it out of his sight on the journey here. I caught a glimpse of it once. It was a box of wood and metal, inlaid and encrusted with many precious and semi-precious jewels.'

'I have often seen the like,' Fidelma admitted. 'Our metalworkers are famous for such fine works of art. A reliquary box would obviously indicate that it contained some holy relics.'

Brother Gillucán shrugged. 'I presume so, but I cannot swear to it. Abbot Dabhóc never spoke to me of the box nor of its contents.'

'I still cannot see why you are fearful.'

'I'll come to that. But about this box: as I say, someone had doubtless carried it away on the night that the abbot was killed. Then the night afterwards, my own room was also searched.'

'Yes, you have said that Brother Chilperic insisted on searching your room.'

'No, it was searched again.'

'What was taken?'

'Nothing.'

'Nothing at all?'

The steward shook his head.

'So it was not Brother Chilperic, searching again to ensure that he had not missed anything?'

'I asked him. It was not.'

'And you had not been entrusted with anything from the abbot that might warrant a search?'

'Nothing.'

'Curious,' mused Fidelma. 'Why would they go through your room then? It seemed they already had the money and the reliquary box.'

'I do not know, Sister. I only feel that there are eyes in all the dark corners of this abbey – watching, waiting!'

'And you have became fearful in consequence?'

'There is more.'

'Then tell me all, for I cannot make judgements on half-stories.'

'I only became fearful two nights later. You see, I awoke in my chamber. It was dark and I was aware of someone bending over me; a hand was on my mouth and a sharp blade at my throat.'

Fidelma sat up a little straighter. 'Go on.'

'A voice said: "Where is it?" and the hand was removed so that I could answer.'

'Where is it?' she repeated.

'Exactly so. I replied that I did not know what they meant.' Brother Gillucán carefully turned his head sideways and pointed to a thin red line across his neck. It was not deep and already healing, but significant enough. Certainly, a blade had been held there. 'That was the reply. And so I cried out, "Do not kill me for my ignorance. Tell me what you want and I will try to help." The voice said: "Did your master give it to you?" And I—'

'Master? What language did the intruder address you in?'

'It was in Latin, Sister. That is the language we have to use in common here.'

'And what did you reply?'

'Having assumed it was Abbot Dabhóc of whom he spoke, I responded that he had given me nothing. Nor could I help them, for his room had been emptied.'

'What then?'

'The knife's pressure increased and I cried out once more that I could not help them and for the sake of pity to spare my life. I am sure the man holding me down on the bed would have cut my throat. Then another voice, a voice in the darkness behind him, said, "Leave him. He obviously knows nothing." The person holding me said: "Say nothing of this for if you do, we will return when you least expect it." I heard them exit my chamber and lay for a long time not knowing what to do.'

'And what language was this exchange conducted in?'

'Still in Latin.'

'Did you report the matter?'

Brother Gillucán shook his head dejectedly. 'I want to live and return to Tulach Óc. However, I have heard of you and Brother Eadulf, and I knew that I should tell you what I know. That is why I have done so, but with discretion. I want no one to know that I have seen you.'

'I understand. How will you return home to Tulach Óc?'

'There are some pilgrims from Mágh Bhíle who are on their way back from Rome. They stayed in this city last night, and leave tomorrow. I shall go with them, and be thankful to do so.'

'And you cannot describe these missing belongings of Abbot Dabhóc further?'

Brother Gillucán hesitated. 'As I said, I caught sight of the reliquary box only once.'

'And?' encouraged Fidelma.

The young man screwed up his eyes as if to conjure the image before him.

'It was of copper, some tin, enamel and a wood base. It was in the shape of a hexagonal house, with a pitched roof and gable ends, as is typical of the reliquary boxes made by our craftsmen.'

'You mentioned jewels?'

'There are decorative mouldings, mounts with red enamel and settings in which emeralds are cast. I do not think they were coloured glass settings. No, I think they were precious and semi-precious stones.'

'And the size?'

'Perhaps fourteen centimetres at the base, perhaps ten centimetres deep and five in width.'

Fidelma nodded, for most reliquary boxes from the five kingdoms were made roughly to those dimensions.

'Oh, and I forgot – there were words engraved on the lid.'

'Which were?'

'One name was Benén.'

'Just that name?' queried Fidelma, for it was a popular name used among certain of her people.

'That is all I remember. But there was another name inscribed on it. I can't recall it.'

'Well, little things can mount up,' said Fidelma. 'I think you have been very wise in telling me what you know, Brother Gillucán. However, we are dealing with beings in corporeal from and not the legions of the cursed as you have described them. "Souls in torment", I think you said.'

The young man shook his head gloomily. 'Truly, Sister, there *are* souls in torment in this abbey. Voices crying out in pain and agony. I have heard them,' he added with emphasis.

Fidelma wanted to smile but kept her features controlled, for the young man was in earnest.

'Perhaps you could tell me what you heard and in what circumstances.'

But Brother Gillucán seemed nervous and was having difficulty in making up his mind to speak further. Eventually he said: 'I went to the *necessarium*,' and flushed a little.

Fidelma was puzzled, not having come across the word before.

'*Necessarium*?' she repeated.

'The *latrina*. It was before dawn and I . . . the call of nature . . .'

'Go on,' Fidelma said impatiently. 'I am not so sheltered from life that I need protection from natural functions of the body.'

'I was sitting in the *necessarium* when I heard a low wailing sound.

The cries of souls in torment – that is the only way I can describe the sound. Then cries of terror, wailing in fear and anguish. It was terrible to listen to. I have to admit, I fled from the room and did not stir until well after first light.'

It was clear that the young man had truly heard something that had frightened the wits out of him.

'Where did these sounds come from?' Fidelma probed. 'You say that you were in the *necessarium* – so were the sounds in the same room?'

Brother Gillucán stared at her for a moment.

'They seemed to come from the walls,' he said. 'That is it! They came from the walls. The voices of the cursed.'

'Where is this *necessarium*?'

'On the ground floor, beyond the refectory.' He swallowed nervously. 'I feel that this place is cursed, Sister. I cannot wait for dawn tomorrow, when I will start back for the kingdom of Ulaidh.'

Fidelma regarded the frightened young man with sympathy.

'If you wish, you could accompany Brother Eadulf and myself back to the five kingdoms, or even go with Abbot Ségdae and his steward.'

'After what has happened to my abbot and then to me, the quicker I leave this city, the better I shall like it,' he said. 'No, I shall leave in the morning with the pilgrims for Mágh Bhíle, as I have said.'

'Then God be on every road that you travel,' Fidelma replied gravely.

Brother Gillucán rose quickly. 'If you do find the abbot's reliquary box, please remember it was a gift from Ard Macha to Rome.'

'I will remember it, Brother Gillucán.'

'Then may God protect you in this evil place, Sister.' He moved to the door, halted before it and looked back apologetically.

'Sister, would you mind checking that the corridor is empty?'

She rose without a word and went to the door to open it. A swift glance up and down the corridor ensured that no one was within sight.

She stood back and he slipped out.

'*Slán abhaile*,' she whispered, feeling sorry for the frightened young man. Safe home.

Chapter Eight

Eadulf had returned frustrated, not having found Abbot Ségdae. The latter and some other delegates were apparently holding a meeting on some of the proposals that would have to be discussed by the council when it was finally convened. The abbot had given orders that they were not to be disturbed. Fidelma was philosophical and decided that they would wait until the next day before going to see the Abbess Audofleda. She took the opportunity to tell Eadulf about her visitor.

'So now we are told that the abbey is haunted?' he said, his tone sceptical.

'The young man heard something. It doesn't mean that his interpretation is the correct one.'

'Perhaps I should examine this *necessarium*,' mused Eadulf. The *hospitia* had its own *latrina* so he had not seen the one that was for general use. He had not expected to be taken seriously, but Fidelma agreed.

'Find out its location and make a visit there later tonight when all is quiet. With luck, you may stumble across some reasonable explanation for what young Gillucán thought he heard.'

Eadulf groaned inwardly. Truth to tell, he retained some of the superstitions of his pagan upbringing and still believed in malignant spirits. Fidelma pretended not to notice his woebegone expression.

'What is of more concern to me is the fact that Abbot Dabhóc was carrying a valuable gift for the Bishop of Rome – this reliquary box. Did whoever killed him steal it?'

Eadulf sprawled into the chair that had been earlier vacated by the young man.

'Well, if they did, they were certainly not the two men who later visited Gillucán and threatened him with a knife,' he commented.

'How do you reach that conclusion?' Fidelma asked.

'Simple enough. If they already had the box, having ransacked Dabhóc's chamber, why would they search Gillucán's room and then return a second time in the middle of the night to threaten him with a knife, asking the question, "Where is it?"'

'The "it" in question being a reference to the reliquary box?'

'I think that is a logical deduction,' Eadulf agreed.

'But that brings up another question,' Fidelma said. 'Who, then, did take this mysterious box?'

'Or did Abbot Dabhóc hide it somewhere safe before his death and now no one can find it?' Eadulf said. 'Should we not have another examination of his chamber?'

'We will, but we must also consider whether this matter is relevant to his murder, or simply a coincidence. And, of course, if either Ordgar or Cadfan were involved in the murder – why would they want this reliquary box?'

'It would not be the first time members of the Faith have been tempted by temporal wealth or by some religious icon,' Eadulf commented.

Fidelma had to acknowledge he was right but did not feel satisfied that this was the answer.

'We don't know if it was valuable. That would depend on whose relics were in the box. From the name Gillucán gave me, I cannot think that it is anyone well venerated.'

'What was the name again?'

'Benén was the name on the box, according to Gillucán.'

Eadulf frowned. 'Benén. There are many who have entered the religious who call themselves by that name. They think it makes them of a more holy disposition. When I was a student at Tuam Brecain, I knew a few of that name. And—' He suddenly sat up straight. 'Do you mean Benén mac Sesenén of Midhe?'

Fidelma stared at him. 'The successor of Patrick?' she asked.

'The same,' Eadulf agreed. 'You should know his work well, for he was one of the three representatives of the Church who sat on the nine-man commission who edited the laws of the Fénechus and produced the *Senchus Mór* – the great law book by which you Brehons set such great store.'

'Benén,' she echoed. He had been the favourite disciple of Patrick, his co-adjutor at Ard Macha, and he also wrote Patrick's biography. 'Of course, Benén!'

They were silent for a few moments.

'Why would the bishop of Ard Macha send the relics of Benén to Rome?' Fidelma wondered, almost to herself. 'He never left Ulaidh or Midhe during his temporal life, so why send them there? There seems no connection.'

Eadulf shrugged. 'That is a question beyond my answering.'

There came a tap on the door. It was Abbot Ségdae.

'I am told that you were looking for me, Brother Eadulf? I was in a meeting with some of the Armorican abbots.'

It was Fidelma who told him of the problems that they were facing.

'I thought this had all been clearly agreed by Bishop Leodegar,' the abbot said peevishly. 'Perhaps you are right. He wields such a strong hand with his community here that it could well be that no one, not even his steward, will do anything without his direct approval.' He sighed deeply. 'I will have another word with him on his return and *insist* that he makes clear that you can question whoever you want, whenever you want and wherever you want.' He added heavily, 'Some of the delegates are speaking of withdrawing from this council. Already there is talk that the council is cursed.'

Fidelma examined the abbot with surprise. 'Cursed? It is unlike clerics to use such strong language, Ségdae.'

The Abbot of Imleach nodded moodily. 'Even if this council goes ahead, I do fear the outcome. I have spoken to many, as I have said before, and the Gauls, Britons and the people of our own five kingdoms will not accept these new ideas from Rome easily.'

'When you were with Abbot Dabhóc, did he ever speak to you of a gift he was bringing here for the Nuntius to take back to Rome?' Fidelma asked, changing the subject.

Abbot Ségdae looked bemused. 'What sort of gift?' he asked. 'He never mentioned anything to me.'

'Then please speak of this to no one,' Fidelma replied. 'We think it was a reliquary box – the relics of the Blessed Benén who was Patrick's helper and disciple.'

'At Imleach we have long known that Ard Macha has been attempting to claim that it is the primacy of all the five kingdoms and we have long fought against it,' said Abbot Ségdae. 'We know that the bishops of Ard Macha have already written to the bishops of Rome to enlist their support. Perhaps this is another means of trying to solicit the backing of Rome.' He tutted to himself. 'It is sad that even in the Faith, man resorts to politics . . . !' He suddenly looked hard at Fidelma. 'Are you saying there is some connection with the death of Dabhóc and this matter?'

'I am not saying that . . . yet,' she responded. 'I would appreciate it that nothing is said.'

'You have my word. Have you spoken to Dabhóc's steward? I forget his name but he might know something.'

'I *have* spoken to him – but again, I would appreciate it if no more was said.'

'Very well.'

There came the distant ringing of a bell.

Abbot Ségdae glanced up in surprise. '*Tempus fugit*. It is the bell to end the day's toil in the abbey and prepare for the evening meal.'

For people from the five kingdoms it was a signal for their daily bath, which always occurred before the evening meal.

The abbot hurriedly made his excuses and left them.

They joined him when the bell tolled again to announce the evening meal. Brother Gillucán was at the table in the refectory looking withdrawn and nervous, and while Fidelma glanced encouragingly at the young man she did not refer to their earlier meeting, nor did he. Abbot Ségdae waited until after the ritual of the *gratias*, the meal and the dismissal were over before approaching Bishop Leodegar. After a hurried conversation, the bishop accompanied the abbot back to where Fidelma was waiting with Eadulf.

'I apologise, Sister Fidelma, if my intentions were misinterpreted. I will make sure that my instructions are followed more carefully. Of course you have the freedom to come and go, as you will. Only please respect my wish that you are circumspect.'

'That was my understanding of our agreement,' said Fidelma solemnly. 'I was sure that Brother Chilperic was simply being a little over-zealous.'

Bishop Leodegar looked a little uncomfortable. 'Just so. Just so. Though I must confess that I cannot understand why you need to consult with Abbess Audofleda.'

'It is difficult to explain where one's path will lead in an investigation,' Fidelma said smoothly. 'Perhaps into a blind alley, perhaps down a side turning, perhaps nowhere at all. One has to follow one's instincts.'

'Very well, I shall send a message to Abbess Audofleda telling her to expect you. Tomorrow morning, perhaps?' But his voice betrayed both reluctance and curiosity.

Fidelma bowed her head in acknowledgement.

The bishop waited a moment more before, with a jerk of his head towards both of them, he turned and moved off.

Later that night, Fidelma woke Eadulf. He blinked in the candlelight.

'It's still dark!' he protested sleepily.

'And time to do some investigation – remember?'

Eadulf groaned. 'So I must go seeking the ghosts of Brother Gillucán's imagination?'

'As you suggested yourself. Find the *necessarium* and see what there is to be seen. I do not think there will be anything, but one needs to be thorough.'

Still grumbling Eadulf climbed out of the bed and pulled on his robe.

'*Auroa Musis amica*,' chuckled Fidelma as she watched him.

'We have a similar saying,' replied Eadulf without humour. 'The early bird catches the worm.'

'So I suppose you know where to go?' she asked, as he took the candle and made his way to the door.

He turned back with some of his old spirit.

'I am not so slow,' he chided. 'You may have noticed that after the evening meal, I followed a couple of the brethren who were almost running along the corridor. They led me to the *necessarium*.'

Fidelma was puzzled. 'How did you know they were going there?'

'When you see men hurrying in such a manner after having imbibed, then it is logical enough.' He allowed himself a grin before adding: 'I'll be back soon.'

The *necessarium* for the brethren was along a corridor that led to the far side of the abbey, against what Eadulf judged to be the southern wall of the city. He moved quietly along the corridors, holding the tallow candle before him to light his way. There were few lanterns in this section of the abbey; the guest quarters were, of course, among those areas that were well lit.

Eadulf suppressed a shiver as he crept down the narrow stairwell to the lower floor. He paused to listen at the bottom before making his way along the final darkened corridor to the room which the brethren used as the communal *necessarium*. He entered it, closed the door behind him and, holding up his candle, peered around.

It was a large square room with a stone trough in the middle in which water lay reflecting the candlelight with curious sparkles and ripples. This was for washing. The floor itself was tiled, and around the walls was a continuous line of marble seats with no partitions between them. In each seat was a hole that dropped into darkness but from which Eadulf could hear the trickle and splash of a watercourse – a stream that ran underneath. Each person could go to a chosen seat and perform their natural functions before moving to the central pool to wash. There was little privacy here when one came to perform one's ablutions. A memory returned to Eadulf; it was like one of the communal *necessaria* that he had seen in Rome when he was there.

An objectionable odour rose from the open seating. He sniffed in disapproval, wondering which poor member of the brethren was sent down to clear the water channel when it became blocked with the excrement of his fellows. Eadulf screwed up his face into an expression of distaste, trying to push the unwelcome thought from his mind.

He moved to stand near the centre of the room by the water trough and listened, but there was no sound apart from the trickling of the water channel beneath the seats. He waited a few moments and then slowly walked around the walls by the seats, pausing now and then to listen. A sudden hooting sound caused him to stop in his tracks with heart pounding, until he realised it was the mournful cry of an owl. There were two windows, high up and open to the sky, and the bird must have flown by. He crept on again. No, there were no cries of souls in torment.

Eadulf even climbed to the back of the stone seating and placed his ear against the wall to listen. Nothing. No demonic cries or whispering through the stonework. Sighing, he climbed down again. He next looked at the windows and then the door, trying to place the room in the context of the whole abbey complex. Turning back to the wall on whose seats he had climbed to listen, he realised that this must be a dividing wall between the male quarters and the *Domus Femini*, the house of women.

Giving a final glance around, and holding his candle high, he went to the door and opened it.

A figure loomed large before him.

'Brother Eadulf!'

Eadulf took a step backward and stifled his cry of surprise.

'What are you doing here?' demanded the voice.

The figure held up a lantern and Eadulf recognised the steward of the abbey, Brother Chilperic.

He recovered himself quickly. 'A curious question, Brother,' he replied in a dignified tone. 'What would anyone be doing in a *necessarium*?'

'At this hour? But there is a *latrina* in the *hospitia*.'

'We are not all blessed with bodily control and when drink is taken . . .' Eadulf shrugged. 'I had no wish to disturb Sister Fidelma. That is why, having seen the brethren coming here, I crept out of the chamber to emulate them without waking her. Actually, I had forgotten it was such a long way down here.' He grinned. 'Your wine is potent on the system.'

Brother Chilperic looked unconvinced.

Eadulf decided to take a chance on the spur of the moment and added: 'What is beyond the wall, Brother Chilperic? As I was sitting there, I thought I heard someone crying.'

The steward looked sceptical. 'Nothing is beyond there except the work-rooms of the *Domus Femini*. No one would be there at this time, unless it was some animal you heard. A cat, perhaps?'

'Of course, that would be it. Well, it is chilly here. Let me pass and return to my interrupted sleep.'

The young man hesitated and then stood aside.

'May your sleep not be troubled further, Brother.'

Eadulf could not help but wonder if the steward was being sarcastic.

'And may you also have some rest this night,' he replied stiffly. Hurrying back to the *hospitia*, he found Fidelma awaiting his return with some impatience.

'Did you discover anything?' she demanded.

'I did not, but I was myself discovered,' he replied, throwing off his robe and collapsing on the bed. He told her of his encounter with Brother Chilperic before describing what he had seen.

She was thoughtful for a while but not concerned about the steward of the abbey.

'If Brother Gillucán heard anything untoward while he was sitting in the *necessarium*, it most likely came from the water channel that takes the effluence from the *necessarium* out to wherever it flows.'

Eadulf had his eyes shut. 'I suppose so,' he muttered sleepily.

'It is possible that sounds echo along the water channel,' went on Fidelma.

'Possible,' yawned Eadulf again.

'And the wall there . . . you say that it borders on to the women's house of the abbey?'

Eadulf let out a faint snore. He was asleep.

Fidelma frowned in annoyance. Then she smiled softly at his sleeping form and, reaching over, blew out the candle.

Eadulf felt he had barely fallen asleep when the sunlight streaming in through the window caught his face and caused him to blink. Fidelma had already washed and was sitting breaking her fast with some fruit.

'Come, get ready. I let you sleep through morning prayers and there is much to be done today,' she called, seeing he was awake.

He rolled out of bed still feeling exhausted.

'Can't we do it later?' he protested.

'We cannot.'

They were walking down the stairs to the *anticum* of the abbey when Brother Chilperic appeared, hurrying up the stairs, his forehead wrinkled into a frown. He came to an abrupt halt and gave Eadulf a close scrutiny.

'I am looking for Abbot Ségdae,' he said. 'Is he still in the *hospitia*? Have you seen him?'

'We have not,' replied Fidelma. 'You look agitated, Brother. Is something wrong?'

The steward shrugged. 'I simply needed to report a matter to him now that he is the senior delegate from your country.'

Fidelma was intrigued. 'Is there anything I can help with?'

'Alas, no. You probably knew Brother Gillucán, who was the companion of Abbot Dabhóc. He intended to set out to return to his home this morning.'

Fidelma nearly made the mistake of admitting knowledge but, remembering what Brother Gillucán had asked, that she should say nothing, she simply asked, 'Does he need some assistance, then?'

'No longer.'

A cold feeling suddenly seized Fidelma. 'No longer? Please explain,' she asked.

'It seems that he set out alone in the early hours without informing anyone. He was found floating in the Aturavos . . . that's the river that runs to the north side of the city. It looks as though he was attacked by robbers, for they stripped him naked. He should have waited to return with a group of pilgrims who were setting out later today.'

'Are you sure he left the abbey on his homeward journey?' Fidelma could not help asking the question.

'What else would he be doing, outside the abbey at that time? Also, when I heard, I went to his chamber to check. All his belongings were gone. The conclusion is obvious.'

'And you say he was travelling alone?' asked Fidelma, remembering that Brother Gillucán had told her that he was going to travel in company that day.

Brother Chilperic nodded moodily. 'His body was found alone. No one else was with him. Again, the conclusion is obvious. To travel alone is unwise in these troubled times,' he commented. 'They left him with nothing and cut his throat.'

'No one saw anything?' queried Eadulf.

'The river is, as you must have seen, outside the city walls,' the man said. 'It is wrong to leave the city at night. Indeed, wrong to leave the abbey at night.'

'Are you certain that is what happened?' Fidelma pressed. 'That he left the abbey at night to set off on his homeward journey? You have guards at the city gates. Did they see him go?'

'He left the abbey before dawn. No one saw him,' Brother Chilperic replied impatiently. 'The body was discovered by a fisherman a little downriver not long after sun-up.'

'If we see Abbot Ségdae, we will inform him of this tragedy and say that you are looking for him,' Fidelma said, realising they were showing too much interest. 'In the meantime, can you tell us which of the rooms Abbot Dabhóc occupied?'

'It is empty,' replied the steward, his mind clearly elsewhere. 'There is nothing there now.'

'But where is it located?'

'It is back in the *hospitia*, in the same corridor as Bishop Ordgar's chamber – the third along from where he is.'

She thanked him but Brother Chilperic was already on his way. Once out of the steward's earshot Fidelma spoke her thoughts.

'Brother Gillucán feared for his life and now he is dead,' she said quietly.

'Do you think there is some connection with the death of Abbot Dabhóc?' Eadulf asked.

'Let's keep an open mind. You noticed the look that Brother Chilperic cast in your direction?'

'He is probably still suspicious at finding me in the *necessarium*, especially as it was probably near the hour when this Brother Gillucán was making his way out of the abbey. But I thought Gillucán said he was joining a group of pilgrims for the journey?'

'He did. We'd best keep our own counsel on this, Eadulf,' Fidelma replied, keeping her voice low, 'until we find out whether it is in some way connected with the matter here or just a coincidence, There is no use putting ourselves in harm's way. If Gillucán felt fearful enough to leave the abbey before dawn on his own, then the very thing he feared befell him.'

'But why? I cannot see any logic in this matter.'

'Perhaps there is something more to the killing of Abbot Dabhóc, and now his steward, than merely the argument between Ordgar and Cadfan. What was it that those who ransacked Dabhóc's chamber were looking for – the reliquary box? If so, why didn't they find it? Who has it? And was this what Gillucán was being asked about when his room was searched? There are too many questions, Eadulf. Too many questions and not enough facts.'

'For once, I agree,' Eadulf said. 'So where do we turn next? Should we see what else we can find out about Brother Gillucán's death?'

'Not at the moment. If it is connected with Dabhóc's death then we do not want to alert our adversary that we suspect anything.'

'So what now?'

'Let us have a brief glance at the chamber occupied by Abbot Dabhóc before we return to our initial plan to speak with Abbess Audofleda. Now we know that Dabhóc did not have far to go to meet his death. His room was in the same corridor as Ordgar's room.'

The chamber that had been occupied by Abbot Dabhóc was empty and had been cleaned thoroughly. There was certainly nowhere to hide such an object as a reliquary box. Fidelma gazed around.

'Well, this room is not going to tell us anything,' she sighed.

There was a hollow cough behind them at the doorway. The saturnine figure of Brother Benevolentia stood regarding them,

'Were you looking for me?' he asked. 'My chamber is just along here.'

Fidelma turned to greet him. 'As a matter of fact, no. We were looking at the chamber Abbot Dabhóc occupied.'

'Is there anything I can help with?'

'We were told that this chamber was ransacked on that same night as he was killed. I don't suppose you heard anything?'

'As I mentioned before, I did not hear even what was happening in poor Bishop Ordgar's chamber, since I sleep so very soundly. I knew nothing until Bishop Leodegar and his steward roused me,' Brother Benevolentia said.

'Do you know Abbot Dabhóc's steward?' asked Fidelma.

Brother Benevolentia shook his head.

'So you have no idea where his chamber is located?'

'I do not know him but his chamber is on the left, down that corridor,' he indicated. 'The first door you come to. I don't think he is there right now, although I saw Brother Chilperic leave it earlier. Have you knocked upon his door?'

'No, he is—' began Eadulf, then fell silent with a glance from Fidelma.

'No, you are right. He is not there,' she added. 'But if his chamber was there, then you must surely have known him?'

'Ah, I see what you mean. The word you used implied that he was a person I knew well. He was familiar to me only as one of the foreign delegation, and I certainly did not know him, other than to exchange a courteous greeting when passing.'

'Then thank you for your help, Brother Benevolentia.'

The religieux nodded to them and retired into his own chamber.

Fidelma moved to the chamber that he had indicated and opened the door. It had been left tidy, the blanket folded on the bed. As Brother Chilperic had said, it was empty but with no sign of a hurried departure. It would reveal nothing more than the abbot's chamber had revealed.

Behind her, Eadulf remarked: 'A bit of a pedantic character.'

Fidelma shrugged absently. 'Who – Benevolentia? Perhaps he is right. Language should be used precisely, especially in legal matters.' She gestured to the tiny room before her. 'This won't tell us much, either.' She turned and left, closing the door behind her.

'At least we now know the location of these chambers,' she observed, as she led the way back down to the main hall of the abbey.

'Is that important?' asked Eadulf.

'It is always good to know the precise layout of where the crime is committed and the surrounding area. Have you noticed that Abbot Cadfan's chamber was the furthest away from Ordgar's chamber and along another corridor? Everyone else was in the same corridor or adjacent, like Gillucán.'

Eadulf supposed that he had registered the fact but could not see that there was any relevance.

'As I say, it is good to know the layout,' she repeated.

They were crossing the *anticum*, having ascertained that the only way to gain entrance to the *Domus Femini* was to leave the main door and walk along the north side of the square, then go up the wagonway into the central courtyard. The main door to the women's community was on the far side of this courtyard.

A voice suddenly called Fidelma's name and they saw a figure hurrying towards them across the marble flagged hallway. It was a tall, dark man with a pale olive complexion, wearing the robes and tonsure of Rome, and his attire was not of some poor cleric but someone of rank.

'Sister Fidelma! I thought I recognised you. It is good to see you again.' He was holding his hand out in greeting to her.

Fidelma took it, her brow furrowed as she tried to place the man from distant memory.

'You do not recognise me? No matter. It has been a few years since you were in Rome.'

Memory suddenly came to her. 'You were a scribe in the Lateran Palace . . .'

'I was scribe to the Venerable Gelasius, *nomenclator* to His Holiness. I saw you several times in his office when you were investigating the death of the Archbishop Wighard. The Venerable Gelasius has frequently wondered how life was treating you since you left Rome. We have heard many things about you and of Brother Eadulf.' He turned to Eadulf and smiled, reaching out to take his hand. 'And you, I believe, are Brother Eadulf? I cannot recall meeting with you, though I know you were assisting Sister Fidelma in Rome.'

Eadulf's greeting was restrained, as he could not place the man at all.

'You are Brother Peregrinus,' Fidelma suddenly said.

The man chuckled. 'I am honoured to be remembered. I am Nuntius Peregrinus now.'

'And you are the emissary from Rome?'

'I am indeed envoy to the council. I brought the instructions from His Holiness, Vitalian, to Bishop Leodegar, concerning the council and giving it blessing and authority. I have to await the outcome of the debates and take those decisions back to Rome again. I am sure the Venerable Gelasius will be delighted to hear the news. It was only yesterday that the bishop told me of your presence here. I have been visiting some of the outlying churches near this city. But I am glad that matters have entered safe hands. What has transpired here is sad. It was a wise decision of Bishop Leodegar, to seek out your talents to resolve the matter.'

Fidelma was deprecating.

'We can only do what we are able, Nuntius. I trust that the Venerable Gelasius is well and presumably still in his position in Rome?'

'He is, indeed, and thinks of you with kindly thoughts. You performed a great service for Rome, which he does not forget.'

'He flatters me.'

'Not so. Since Vitalian was elected to the throne of the Blessed Peter, the Church has been taking great strides forward. The schisms that Christendom has suffered are slowly mending, thanks to His Holiness. He has sought to repair the connection between Constantinople and Rome by friendly advances, and sent envoys and gifts to Patriach Peter of Constantinople. In that he has been successful, and now his name, as a Bishop of Rome, has been entered in the diptychs of those eastern churches for the first time in many a generation.'

'Diptychs?' frowned Eadulf.

'The lists of those regarded as worthy and in communion with the teachings of the Faith and elevation to high office,' explained Fidelma in a swift aside.

'Exactly so,' Nuntius Peregrinus confirmed. 'Vitalian has also tried to heal the rift between the Saxons and the Britons, as you know, by sending Theodore to minister to them. And he is trying to deal with the heresy of monothelitism and bring all the churches into a one-ness with Rome. Hence the importance of this council.'

Fidelma sighed softly. 'He is obviously ambitious for Rome.'

'Ambitious for the furtherance of the Faith.'

'As I say, we will do our best to resolve the matters that have created a postponement to the coming together of that council. Tell me, Nuntius, did you inform Bishop Leodegar that you knew me?'

'No. I wanted to see you first, to make sure that you were the same Fidelma whom I saw in Rome. Would you prefer I did mention you?'

'You may do so freely,' she replied.

'Well, if there is ever help required, you may count on it that you have an influential friend at the Lateran Palace, Sister,' the Nuntius assured her.

'And if there is anything I can do here, let me know. Perhaps we can meet later and talk about the passing of the years. The Venerable Gelasius will be eager to hear all that has befallen you.'

'Then let us meet in the *calefactorium* before the evening meal,' suggested Fidelma.

'Excellent. I shall be there.'

With a wave of his hand, Nuntius Peregrinus turned and hurried away. Behind him, his silent shadow, an armed member of the *custodes* of the Lateran Palace, reinforcing Peregrinus' rank as envoy of Vitalian, emerged from a corner and followed him.

'A small world,' muttered Eadulf as they continued on to the door.

'It might be beneficial that the Nuntius remembers us,' Fidelma remarked. 'I have a feeling that we might need his help in dealing with Bishop Leodegar.'

Chapter Nine

Fidelma and Eadulf emerged into the great square before the abbey. They walked slowly along the flags to the broad wagonway that led up to the large central courtyard. On one side was the huge wooden door that was the entrance to the *Domus Femini*. The courtyard itself was pretty enough. There was the inevitable fountain in the centre. It was a marble statue of a strange beast from whose mouth the water gushed. The entrance opposite to that of the *Domus Femini* had been blocked up, as this obviously led into the male quarters of the abbey. There was one dark arched recess further down off the wagonway, which Eadulf initially thought might lead to a doorway providing a shortcut into the abbey, but he saw that even that was blocked.

They approached the large oak door, which was studded with iron. A rope hung to one side and Fidelma tugged on it. They heard the distant clang of the bell and waited. After a short while, a small hatch in the centre of the door was drawn aside and two pale eyes stared out.

'I am Sister Fidelma and this is Brother Eadulf. We are here to see the *abbatissa*, Abbess Audofleda. She is expecting us.'

This received a curt response: 'Wait!' Then the hatch was slammed shut.

Fidelma turned and smiled wryly at Eadulf.

'Not overly welcoming,' he muttered in response.

Suddenly bolts were drawn noisily back and the big door swung slowly inwards.

A religieuse stood framed in the doorway. She gave the impression of tallness, of an austere face, a large nose, dark, almost black eyebrows and bright blue eyes. Her hands were folded in front of her, hidden within the folds of her black robe.

'Enter,' she commanded, taking a step backward to allow them to do so.

They became aware of another religieuse, who was obviously the door-keeper, pushing shut the heavy door behind them. Once again, the sound of the bolts being pushed home was like the blow of a hammer falling on an anvil.

'Are you Abbess Audofleda?' asked Fidelma.

The woman sniffed in disapproval. 'I am Sister Radegund,' she replied curtly. 'I serve the *abbatissa*. You will follow me.' Her manner was as sharp as her features.

Without further ado, she turned and walked swiftly along an arched corridor into a small quadrangle, veered right and followed another short corridor to a circular stone stairwell. Taking the stairs with surprising speed, without once glancing behind to see if they were following, she then set off along another passageway. Eadulf had seen many religious houses but none with such an air of gloom. The male section of the abbey was grey and brooding enough, but the *Domus Femini* was infinitely worse. He felt quite depressed as he looked around the grey stone walls hoping for some relief – some flowers, icons, wall paintings – anything to relieve the drabness that reminded him of a fortress rather than a house devoted to the worship of God.

Sister Radegund halted abruptly outside a door.

She finally turned and glanced at Fidelma and Eadulf for a moment, almost as if ensuring that they were presentable enough to be shown into the presence. Then she rapped upon the door. A voice came faintly bidding them enter.

They were shown into the study of Abbess Audofleda. Although the *abbatissa* and her sisters had attended the morning and evening services, they had been invisible to Fidelma and Eadulf because they entered the chapel by a separate route and were shielded from the brethren by wooden screens. Abbess Audofleda was seated behind her table and wore a head-dress which was drawn back so that her face was fully visible, but covering her hair. A woman of middle age, she could never have been described as attractive, thanks to the bony forehead, jutting jawline and large nose with a prominent bump that could almost be described as hooked. The eyes were pale and without compassion. The lips were thin, and the skin ashen where it was not blotched upon the cheeks.

'This is Sister Fidelma and Brother Eadulf, *abbatissa*,' intoned Sister Radegund, who stood deferentially before them with hands still folded and eyes downcast.

Abbess Audofleda sat back, her own hands placed firmly on the table in front of her. She stared in disapproval, firstly at Eadulf and then at Fidelma.

'I am asked by Bishop Leodegar to see you. He says that you have requested to speak with me. For what purpose?' Her voice was harsh and she spoke Latin badly.

'We are . . .' began Fidelma. She was waved to silence by an imperious gesture of a pale thin hand.

'I know who you are, Sister. That much was explained when Bishop Leodegar addressed the community in the chapel the other night. You have been allowed to investigate the death of one of the delegates to the council. I disapprove. That is not a woman's place, especially one who purports to be a religious. However, the bishop has made this curious decision. I was not consulted. My question is, why do you come here?'

Fidelma exchanged a quick glance with Eadulf. Abbess Audofleda was as unfriendly as her looks portended.

'We have come to address a few questions to you,' she replied coolly.

'I see no reason why,' replied Abbess Audofleda. 'Our sisterhood is separate from the brothers of the abbey and there is no connection between us and the deaths that have occurred. We know nothing of them nor do we wish to know anything of them.'

Eadulf saw the warning sign as Fidelma's eyes narrowed.

'You'll forgive our impertinence, *abbatissa*,' he said hastily, in a conciliatory voice. 'We have not come here without a good reason, for we believe there is a connection between your sisterhood and the events that took place surrounding the death of Abbot Dabhóc.'

The thin eyebrows of Abbess Audofleda arched.

'Do you call me a liar?' she snapped. 'I said that there are none.'

Eadulf was dismayed by the overt antagonism of the woman.

This time Fidelma had recovered herself sufficiently to attempt to follow Eadulf's displomatic path.

'We would not suggest that you have spoken anything but the truth, as you know it. We would only point out that perhaps we have some information that you might not know about.'

'Which is?' There was a sneer in Abbess Audofleda's tone.

'Sister Valretrade.'

They heard the audible gasp from Sister Radegund. Fidelma saw the warning glance that Abbess Audofleda gave her.

'What do you know of Sister Valretrade?' The *abbatissa*'s eyes were glinting suspiciously.

'We know that on the night of the killing, she had sent a signal to one of the brethren to meet her, and it was that action which set off the events leading to the discovery of the scene in Bishop Ordgar's chambers. We need to question her about this as being pertinent to our investigation.'

For a moment Abbess Audofleda looked uncertain.

'Contact between the sisterhood and the brethren is forbidden,' she said woodenly.

'Nevertheless, it happened,' Fidelma assured her. 'By the way, when did this Rule of segregation of the sexes and the ideas of celibacy come into force in this abbey?'

The *abbatissa* looked surprised at the sudden change of subject. She answered defensively.

'One year ago, not long after Leodegar became bishop and brought his teachings here.'

'And you were already abbess here?'

'I was invited to take charge here by the bishop after the decision had been made. He could not find a suitable superior among the sisterhood, so he asked me to come from Divio to take over. It is the duty of the community to obey their bishop and the Rule was made clear. Our people should not question the Rule. But these questions are irrelevant to . . .'

'To the matter of Sister Valretrade,' Fidelma said brightly. 'I am sorry. I have let natural curiosity overcome me. Now, I would like to speak with her.'

Abbess Audofleda's thin lips twitched. 'That is impossible.'

'I have been assured by Bishop Leodegar that the entire community will co-operate with my enquiry,' Fidelma cautioned.

'It is neither a matter of co-operation nor lack of it. Sister Valretrade is no longer part of this community. She is not here.'

'Not here?'

'Not here,' affirmed the abbess.

'Then perhaps you can inform us where she is?'

'I cannot be specific.'

'Try,' Fidelma pressed a little sarcastically.

'Then she might well be anywhere. A week ago she left here, saying that she could no longer accept the Rule.'

Fidelma tried to hide her disappointment. 'When did you say she left?'

'A week ago.'

'Was she sent away in punishment for contacting Brother Sigeric?'

'Punishment? I do not know this Brother Sigeric.'

Fidelma raised an eyebrow slightly. 'You did not know that she was in love with a young man in the abbey?'

'I only knew that she was distracted from her duties here. Had I known, I would have reported the matter to the bishop so that he could discipline the young man for enticing Valretrade from her bond to the Faith.'

'You say you do not know Brother Sigeric. Are you denying that he came to the *Domus Femini* a few days ago to find out where Sister Valretrade was?'

A crimson hue spread over Abbess Audofleda's features.

'Excuse me, *abbatissa*.' It was Sister Radegund who spoke nervously from the door before she could say anything. 'I did not wish to bring the matter to your attention, as you have been so busy, but a young man did come to our door – a young religieux. He demanded to know where Sister Valretrade was. When I told him to go away, he grew insistent, and I informed him that she had left the *Domus Femini* and was no longer in our charge. He was very insistent and I had to close the door on him. I was reluctant to bother you at the time, and until the matter was mentioned just now I had forgotten all about it.'

'Did the young man mention his name to you?' demanded the abbess of her steward.

'I do not think so, *abbatissa*.'

The woman turned back to Fidelma with a triumphant expression. 'So, you see, we have *not* heard of this Brother Sigeric.'

'Why do you think Valretrade left the *Domus Femini*?' Fidelma asked coldly. 'And given that she was so "distracted", in your words, by this young man, did she not tell him that she was leaving?'

'I am not here to speculate about the workings of a young girl's mind. Perhaps she is with this young man of whom you speak. Find him and you may find her.'

'If he was with her, he would hardly have come to the abbey seeking her,' Fidelma pointed out.

'So maybe she had come to her senses and realised she should leave him,' the other woman retorted.

'So you offer no reason why she left?'

'Reason? I am afraid that you do not understand the Rule by which I govern this community. She left because she could not abide that Rule.'

'So she left, and did not even tell the person who seemed to matter most to her that she was leaving.' Eadulf's tone was reflective.

'The person who mattered most?' The pale face that turned to him was full of disdain. '*I* am the person who matters most in this community.'

Fidelma pointed to the crucifix that hung on the wall behind the Abbess Audofleda.

'I thought that there was a more important Being in a religious house before Whom everyone was equal,' she said.

Abbess Audofleda's cheeks coloured again, this time with anger.

'The girl disobeyed the Rule! Had she remained here, she would have been chastised for her transgressions. It was her self-interest that caused her flight!'

'"Whatever you do to the least of My brethren, you do to Me",' Eadulf muttered audibly.

'I have wasted enough time.' Abbess Audofleda rose and looked across to Sister Radegund. 'Show these . . . these visitors out. We have finished.'

Eadulf followed Fidelma who had said nothing further but turned to leave. He had reached the door when the abbess, unable to restrain herself, shouted after them: 'And I will see that Bishop Leodegar knows of your insults. He has had men flogged for less.'

Fidelma hesitated, and then shook her head quickly in Eadulf's direction, indicating that he should say nothing further.

Once outside the oak doors of the women's community, the couple breathed deeply to release their sense of frustration. They then began to walk slowly across the courtyard towards the wagonway.

'And this woman is the *abbatissa* of the community?' Eadulf marvelled. 'I pity the poor girls in her charge.'

'I pity Sister Valretrade. With such a superior, I think I too would also leave,' Fidelma replied. 'By the way, we must tread carefully. I don't think we should take her threats lightly.'

'Threats? About my being flogged?' Eadulf was unconvinced.

'Remember that we are in a different country with different customs,' urged Fidelma. 'While we have dispensation to conduct this investigation, it is only because it is of a political use to Bishop Leodegar. We are without real authority and we are vulnerable.'

'Leodegar would not dare,' asserted Eadulf.

'He might well. By throwing that threat at us, Audofleda has revealed that Bishop Leodegar has used this power before.'

'But to take a religious and have them flogged for no reason . . .'

'Oh, they would find a reason. I think we should make sure that Brother Sigeric is warned as well. I would not put it past Audofleda to report the matter to Leodegar.'

They halted by the blocked-up entrance halfway down the wagonway and Eadulf glanced up at the grey walls behind them.

'I have never known a place that exudes such deep melancholy. I was thinking about what Brother Gillucán told you that he heard.'

'What made you think of that?'

'The fact that he was in the *necessarium*, one wall of which backs on to this *Domus Femini*. That was where he claimed he heard the sound of souls in torment. I can well believe that he heard sounds of lamentation from the poor women enclosed in that place.'

Fidelma realised that Eadulf was being darkly humourous, but her eyes suddenly widened.

'Children!' she exclaimed. 'Of course!'

Eadulf looked at her in surprise.

'Were we not told that the wives of the brethren here, and their children, were taken to live in the *Domus Femini*? Wives and children that the brethren were forced to put from them – that was the phrase.'

Eadulf nodded slowly.

'Don't you see?' Fidelma went on. 'If Audofleda governs so badly, perhaps Gillucán did hear those children wailing in anguish.'

'You mean she is ill treating the children?'

Under the law of the Brehons, ill treatment of children was not merely condemned but punishable. Until the age of their maturity, the honour price of children was placed, under the laws, as the honour price of a chieftain or a bishop no matter who their parents were – that was seven *cumals*, the value of twenty-one cows. So such a thing seemed impossible.

'As I have said, Eadulf, we are in a different culture here, but nonetheless I indeed to pursue this and discover the truth, even though I have recourse to no local law or authority.'

'I can't see how you are going to do that,' he rejoined. 'There is no returning through *that* door.'

'Then I will have to find another way inside,' Fidelma replied calmly.

'You are not going back on your own.'

Fidelma was amused. 'I hardly think you will be able to fade into the background in a house of women, Eadulf.'

He suddenly stiffened and drew her back into the shadow of the arched recess.

'What . . . ?' she began to protest.

He leaned forward and whispered in her ear, 'Sister Radegund has just left the *Domus Femini*. Look . . . but carefully!'

The tall woman was moving rapidly across the courtyard, heading towards the main square. In fact, she was moving so quickly that she was almost running, with her head-dress and robes flowing out behind her. The two watchers pressed back in the shadows, waiting until she had passed them. She had already crossed the square by the time they had emerged, and they saw her disappearing down a street towards the city buildings.

'Where is she off to in such a hurry?' murmured Eadulf.

'Let's find out,' replied Fidelma. 'Come on. We must not lose her.'

Before he could protest, she had set off across the square, almost trotting to keep up with the woman. There were plenty of people about, but no one seemed interested in them, so Fidelma and Eadulf hurried on down the darkened streets without challenge.

Sister Radegund seemed so intent upon her errand that she did not pause or glance backward once. That was just as well for her followers. She moved through several streets, each one a little more narrow than the last, and soon the odours that had assailed them when they first arrived in the city began to rise around them. Sewerage ran here and there, and thin feral cats and slavering dogs fought over the refuse in the gutters.

Sister Radegund suddenly ducked into a broad street. Along this street were several premises of traders. It was clearly a major thoroughfare. They saw her enter a building where clothes were hanging outside as if on display, as well as a number of animal skins.

'It looks like a . . .' Fidelma paused, trying to find the right word '. . . a place where a seamstress does her work.'

They moved cautiously towards the building and Fidelma took a quick glance through the open door. Sister Radegund was standing with her back to the door and an elderly woman was bending over a bundle of cloth. The old woman's eyes luckily were not focused on the door. Fidelma gestured to Eadulf to follow her back a few yards to where there was a dark space between the buildings; here they could pause without being seen in the open street.

'It seems that Sister Radegund is simply on a mission to buy some cloth,' Fidelma said in disappointment. 'I have obviously become too suspicious.' Just then, she heard someone saying something along the street and then the clatter of wooden-soled shoes followed. She chanced another quick look round the corner of the building.

'Radegund is off again. Her journey is not yet over,' she said to Eadulf. 'Let us stay with her.'

Head still slightly downward, Sister Radegund was continuing her journey with the same intensity as when she had left the *Domus Femini*. They followed at a reasonable distance but there seemed little chance of the stewardess looking back towards them. When she disappeared around the next corner, they followed and found that the broad thoroughfare had opened into a large square. In the centre was yet another ornate fountain, gushing and splashing. A few dogs were lapping around the base.

Fidelma and Eadulf halted at the entrance to the square, sheltering in the corner of a building.

Sister Radegund had hurried across the cobbles straight to the gates in a high wall that fronted a building on the far side. A giant of a man, a warrior armed with sword and spear, stood outside. While he had breast armour, he wore no hat and his head was a tousled mess of blond, almost white, curls that merged into a heavy beard which came to his chest. He nodded pleasantly to Sister Radegund as if he knew her and without a word turned and tapped upon the wooden gate with his free hand. They heard three distinct blows followed by two more rapid ones. The gate opened almost at once and Sister Radegund slipped inside. The gate closed immediately.

There was a rattle of wheels behind them and a man came along the thoroughfare pushing a handcart loaded with various iron goods. He was a heavily built fellow, and by his dress he was a tradesman of sorts. As they stood hesitantly on the corner, unsure of what to do next, he greeted them in a friendly fashion.

'Are you lost?' He spoke in the local language that, to Eadulf's ear, sounded strangely akin to his own Saxon speech, for he seemed to understand the sense of it. He tried a response in Saxon and, to his surprise, the man replied.

'I spent time among your people. My father was a ship's captain. Now – are you lost?'

'We are unsure of where we are,' Eadulf told him. 'What is this square?'

'This is called the Square of Benignus.'

'Benignus?' queried Eadulf, thinking he had misheard. 'You mean "the Square of the Benign"?'

The man set down his cart and flexed his hands as if to help the circulation.

'No, my friend. *Of* Benignus,' he said. 'You are obviously strangers here. Benignus was a holy martyr who was born in this city before going to spread the word of the Faith in the old city of Divio many centuries ago. The square was named after him for it is said it was on this very square that he lived.'

'Ask him who that big house belongs to – the one guarded by the warrior,' Fidelma said to Eadulf.

'Whose fine villa is that then?' Eadulf asked the carter. 'And why is it guarded by a warrior?'

'That is the villa of the Lady Beretrude, mother of the lord of this territory. She is benefactor to the city and the most powerful person in these parts.'

'Eadulf!' interrupted Fidelma with a soft warning. She had just noticed a man exit from the very house they were talking about. He was clad in religious robes and raised a hand in familiar farewell to the warrior. Then he was striding across the square towards them.

It was too late to move. He had seen them.

'Sister Fidelma! Brother Eadulf!' he hailed. 'What are you doing here?' Brother Budnouen halted before them, smiling broadly.

'We were lost and this man was giving us directions,' Eadulf explained hastily.

'You must be lost, indeed, to be in this area of the city,' replied the jovial Gaul.

The man with the cart had touched his forehead in salute.

'I am glad that you have found your friend,' he said pleasantly. 'You will be able to get to where you wanted now.' He heaved his cart up and moved on his way.

'And where was it you wanted to get to?' asked Brother Budnouen.

'Back to the abbey,' Fidelma said hastily. 'We had gone for a walk to explore the city and must have taken a wrong turning somewhere.'

'I forget that you are unused to large towns in your lands. Well, have no concerns for I am going back to the abbey myself.'

'We don't want to take you out of your way at all,' Eadulf said. 'We looked for you in the abbey but have not seen you there.'

Brother Budnouen shook his head. 'You will not. For I do not stay with Bishop Leodegar's community. I stay with a friend in the city, just off the square before the abbey.'

'Speaking of squares, that is a curious one,' Eadulf said slyly, turning back to the square behind them. 'That man with the cart thought we were looking for the villa of some lady or other. What was her name? Bertrude . . . no – Beretrude.' He pointed at the villa from which Brother Budnouen had just emerged and hoped the Gaul had not realised that they had noticed him coming from there. 'He told us that she lived there. Why would he assume we were looking for her?' He looked innocently at the Gaul.

Brother Budnouen seemed thoughtful.

'I suppose it is a logical mistake, since Lady Beretrude is the most prominent person here in the city,' he said. 'She is mother of the lord of this territory – Lord Guntram – and is a very influential lady. Perhaps the man thought strangers wandering in this part of the city would naturally be seeking her out.'

He volunteered no further information and Eadulf realised that for some reason he was not going to admit any connection with either the woman or the villa.

'The man was telling us that the square has a connection with a holy martyr.'

Brother Budnouen raised an eyebrow. 'He was a loquacious fellow, that fellow with the cart,' he observed softly. Eadulf wondered if there was a hint of suspicion in his voice.

Fidelma said hurriedly: 'He was quite helpful, although we had to rely on interpretation through Eadulf's own tongue. The man seemed quite proud of this local martyr.' She mentally forgave herself the lie.

'It is certainly a matter of great local controversy,' said Brother Budnouen. 'You refer to Benignus, of course.'

'Controversy?'

'Some say that Polycarp of Smyrna sent this saintly man called Benignus to Divio . . .'

'Divio?' Fidelma frowned. 'This place has been mentioned before.'

'It's about seventy kilometres to the north east of here. The city is in the old territory of the Lingones, once a great people of Gaul. Benignus was sent to teach them the Faith. Now the Burgunds claim Benignus as one of their own. The story is that he was martyred and the common people worshipped at his grave. Then Bishop Gregory of Lingonum, who disliked Benignus, tried to stop this worship. But Autun and two other towns have equal claim on this blessed martyr, with each insisting that they hold his true grave and his relics. An argument began over who had the prior claim. One hundred years ago, accounts called *De Gloria Martyrum* started to be circulated in which all these claims were put forward and argued. Each town called the other's claims falsifications and lies. In this city, he is supposed to be buried in the necropolis under the abbey, but in Lingonum an entire basilica building has been erected over a tomb that is claimed as Benignus' last resting-place.' Brother Budnouen chuckled suddenly. 'The place was actually built by the same Bishop Gregory who had first claimed that the tomb was that of a heathen and not the martyr. They say he changed his mind when he saw how much money was to be made from the pilgrims who flocked to pray there.'

Fidelma sniffed in disapproval. 'So the argument continues between these towns?'

'And probably will as long as no one can offer proof. However, it is a subject that is best avoided among most of the Burgunds, and especially in the Lady Beretrude's presence.'

'Why is that?'

'Lady Beretrude claims that Benignus was among her ancestors some four centuries ago. Most of the Burgunds seem to have adopted him as a patron of their people, their saviour who will one day free them from the rule of the Franks.'

'This square we just left was named after him, we were told.'

'The Square of Benignus?' Brother Budnouen shook his head. 'It was Lady Beretrude who had it named such, and in recent memory. I suppose its claim to the name is as good as any other.'

'Why is there no memorial to Benignus in the abbey?' asked Fidelma. 'I have not seen one.'

'Franks now run the abbey,' said Eadulf. 'Even if his last resting place were there, they would ignore such a Burgund worthy.'

'Bishop Leodegar is a hard taskmaster, my Saxon friend,' Budnouen agreed. 'He would not recognise a Burgund as in any way influential. I am glad that I am not of his community.'

'What community do you belong to? To the abbey in Nebirnum, I suppose,' asked Fidelma.

'Not so. I am my own man, for all the communities of Gauls are almost drowned in the sea of Burgunds and Franks. Our people have been swept westward. As you already know from our journey here, I earn my daily crust by running goods from the merchants on the river by Nebirnum to Autun, and sometimes I have been known to go as far as Divio.'

'Do you know Abbess Audofleda?'

The jovial Gaul looked at her. 'Have you encountered Abbess Audofleda? Ah yes, you would do so, of course.' It was clear that, knowing the segregation Rule, he would assume that Fidelma was staying in the house of women. 'Yes, I have had dealings with her.'

'There is no enthusiasm in your voice?'

'Enthusiasm, Sister?' mused the Gaul. 'My life has not been made richer by my contact with Audofleda. I admit to a dislike of her. She seems typical of her people, arrogant and overbearing in proclaiming her piety and all without reason.'

'What do you mean by that?' asked Eadulf.

Brother Budnouen paused for a moment. Then: 'Let me put it this way, I knew of Audofleda in a past life.'

'In that case, you cannot let your story end there before you have begun it.' Fidelma looked at him in curiosity.

The Gaul looked surreptitiously around him as if to ensure there were no eavesdroppers, before saying, 'I told you that my journeying took me sometimes as far afield as Divio.'

'Which is where Abbess Audofleda comes from,' Fidelma put in, remembering what the *abbatissa* had said.

'Except that she was certainly no abbess then,' agreed Brother Budnouen.

'Go on.'

'To be truthful, Audofleda was a woman of the streets. Until a few years ago, she was known in certain parts of Divio as such.'

Fidelma was surprised but not shocked. 'She is not to be condemned for that, but rather pitied that she had no recourse to a happy life other than sell her body to men.' She was thinking of her friend Della in Cashel who had once been a prostitute and whom she had helped.

'True enough, true enough,' sighed Brother Budnouen. 'However, I do not think she wallowed in self-pity for her fate but many said she chose the life out of her hatred for men. And when I heard of this sudden conversion to the religious life, not just conversion but her appointment by Leodegar to be the *abbatissa* of the *Domus Femini* here, I had pause to think.'

They waited a moment and then Fidelma asked: 'And what was the outcome of your thoughts?'

Brother Budnouen shrugged. 'I do not believe in such a rapid conversion, and if I had a daughter who said she wanted to pursue the religious life in Audofleda's *Domus Femini*, I would rather kill her with my own hands than allow her to go into that house of suffering.'

'That is an interesting choice of words, Budnouen,' said Fidelma. '"House of suffering". Why do you use that term?'

'There is no happiness there,' the Gaul said simply. 'It's true that I only deliver goods to the main door and am not allowed in, but when I deliver these goods I see the suffering on the faces of the girls who take charge of them . . .'

'Such as?' Fidelma pressed.

'There was a Sister Inginde and Sister Valretrade . . .'

'Valretrade?' She echoed the name.

'You know her?' Her tone had not been lost on the astute Gaul.

'*Of* her,' corrected Fidelma. 'I am told that she left the community a week ago.'

'Ah, that is why this time I looked for her in vain. A nice girl. So, I am pleased.'

'Pleased?'

'Pleased that she left Audofleda's community, for it means she now has freedom to search for a place where she can fulfil her life. Doubtless, she has left with Brother Sigeric. I was their go-between whenever I could be so.'

'In what way?'

'I knew that Valretrade was deeply in love with Sigeric and messages were hard to send between the two communities. Therefore, whenever I was in Autun I was able to pass messages between them. I am happy to hear that they have gone.'

Fidelma shook her head. 'Sigeric is here and knew nothing of her going. He finally went to see Audofleda, who told him that the girl had gone and gave him no other information. He asked us to intercede on his behalf to discover more. Audofleda told me not a short time since that Valretrade had left because she disagreed with the Rule.'

'She would not have left without Sigeric knowing,' asserted Brother Budnouen. 'You don't know the depth of feeling between those young folks.'

'How long are you staying in Autun?' asked Fidelma, after a thoughtful pause. 'Do you have any more trade to do?'

'Well, within a few days I am taking goods to the fortress of Lord Guntram, and—'

'I meant, do you have more business with the *Domus Femini*?'

'I have already done my trade there. The goods were taken, checked and paid for by Sister Radegund. I cannot go again without arousing suspicion. Sister Radegund runs the place like a fortress. No one is allowed in or out without scrutiny – and certainly no male is allowed in.'

They had passed up the broad thoroughfare from the Square of Benignus and drawn level with the building where Sister Radegund had gone in to see the seamstress. Brother Budnouen pointed to it.

'That is the shop of the mother of one of the members of the *Domus Femini*. She makes dresses and sells clothes here. I sometimes trade with her. But even she is not allowed into the *Domus Femini* to see her daughter.'

'Do you know the name of her daughter?' asked Fidelma. 'It's not the stewardess of the community, is it?' She glanced at the place where cloth and animal skins hung outside. Inside, she could see the elderly woman now sewing.

'Sister Radegund?' Brother Budnouen's eyebrows went up in surprise. 'Good Lord, no. What makes you ask? Oh, because you know Sister Radegund is the only one allowed to have dealings with the outside world for purposes of commerce?'

'So I had heard,' Fidelma said as they moved on. 'Is there no one else who has free access to and from the *Domus Femini*?'

'No one,' the Gaul assured her. Then a thought struck him. 'But I was forgetting – *you* must surely have free access to the *Domus Femini*, Sister?

Or can it be that you are staying among the other wives and advisers of the delegates to the council in the city? I heard that some of the delegates who did not know the Rule of Leodegar's abbey had brought their wives or female advisers with them. They had to find accommodation not far from the abbey.'

Fidelma did not respond for a moment, then admitted, 'No, Eadulf and I are staying together at the abbey.'

She was amused by the Gaul's look of utter astonishment.

CHAPTER TEN

On reaching the abbey, they bade farewell to Brother Budnouen as he hurried off on his business, and made their way through the *anticum* of the abbey to their chamber in the *hospitia*. As they reached it, a door further along the corridor opened and a grim-faced Abbot Ségdae emerged.

'Have you heard the news?' he greeted them without preamble.

'About Brother Gillucán, Abbot Dabhóc's steward?' enquired Fidelma, guessing the subject of his anxiety. 'Brother Chilperic told us earlier this morning. Has there been a further development?'

Abbot Ségdae motioned to their chamber. They took the hint and led the way inside.

As Eadulf closed the door behind them, the abbot sank into a chair and heaved a deep breath.

'Abbot Dabhóc murdered and now his steward. I am coming to agree with some of the delegates that this place is cursed.'

Fidelma sat down on the bed while Eadulf went to a jug and poured some water. His mouth was dry after the morning's excursion.

'It is not the place that is cursed, Ségdae; people create their own curses,' replied Fidelma gravely.

'Brother Gillucán was sitting calmly at our table last night,' the abbot reflected sadly. 'Now he is dead, killed by robbers while leaving the city this morning, his body stripped and dumped in the river after his throat was cut. How can such things happen?'

'I meant to ask Brother Chilperic how Gillucán was recognised as belonging to the abbey when it was his naked body that was discovered in the river?' asked Eadulf, sipping his water.

'Apparently by his tonsure. Some boatmen brought the body to the abbey to be identified.' The abbot looked troubled. 'As a senior member of our delegation, I asked Brother Gebicca to examine the body so that I could make a proper report to the bishop of Ard Macha.' He hesitated. 'When he did so, there was one thing which he found curious.'

Immediately Fidelma's head rose a little. 'Go on,' she said.

'They cut poor Brother Gillucán's throat and threw him in the river . . . but in spite of that, faeces were clinging to parts of his body, under his fingernails and smeared on his flesh. I had to order that his body should be completely washed and ritually cleansed before burial. It was as if the poor boy had crawled through a sewer before his death. It was rather disgusting.'

Fidelma was thoughtful. 'The river where he was found . . . do the city's sewers empty into it?'

'I suppose so,' admitted Abbot Ségdae.

'Were the sewers at the spot where he was found?'

'Not really. But even with the sewerage in the water, well . . . that would not account for the smearing on his legs and arms. The current of the river is quite strong as it passes by the city walls and the effluence is carried along rapidly. I would not have thought it would have covered his body in the way it did if he had simply been immersed in it as it flowed down the river. It seemed to me, as I have said, that he had crawled through it or had been flung in it.'

The abbot was clearly distressed at the idea of the mistreatment of the young religieux.

'It does seem curious,' Fidelma admitted quietly. 'And no witnesses have come forward? I mean, no one who saw Brother Gillucán leave the abbey, pass through the city gates or noticed if anyone was following him? I thought guards were at the city gates all the time.'

'I am told by Brother Chilperic that the guards saw no one. No one at all. Tell me, Fidelma, do you think that there is some connection between the deaths of Dabhóc and Gillucán?'

'I wish I could give you an answer, Ségdae. On face value, there seems none, and yet I do not entirely believe in coincidences.'

'So you have come to no conclusions as yet?'

'Not yet.'

'So sad, so sad,' muttered the abbot. 'Brother Gillucán was leaving for home this morning. He told me that there were some pilgrims going back to the five kingdoms who were staying in the city. He was supposed to be travelling with them.'

'It would have been better to have joined their party,' agreed Fidelma, glad that the question was raised, as she could not have mentioned that Gillucán himself had told her as much. 'What made him change his mind?'

'I don't know,' replied the abbot. 'He seemed strangely frightened last night. The first I knew that he had left on his own was when Brother Chilperic announced the finding of the body.'

'Who were the pilgrims?'

'Three members of the community of Mágh Bhíle in the north. They had been staying as guests of a wealthy lady in this city. Beretrude is her name.'

Fidelma did not allow herself to show any recognition of the name and hoped Eadulf would not say anything.

'Do we know whether he contacted these three pilgrims before he left?'

'We don't. I am told they left this morning.'

'Are many religious attacked by robbers in such a fashion in these parts?' asked Eadulf.

'According to Brother Chilperic, it is unusual for a religious to be killed by robbers. They are usually interested only in money or goods, not in taking a life.'

'Yet poor Brother Gillucán was stripped and robbed and, although we cannot be sure, his naked body was defiled by being thrown into excrement,' Fidelma observed thoughtfully. 'The circumstances sound unusual at the least.'

Abbot Segdae regarded her unhappily. 'This council is turning into a nightmare. If it were not for the important decisions that have to be made, I would suggest that our delegation withdraw.'

'That would not be good politics,' Fidelma pointed out.

'You are right, of course. We must stay focused on the issues before us.' The abbot rose abruptly. 'I will leave you now, but if you come across any information which may help me with my report to Ségéne of Ard Macha . . .' He did not finish but left them.

'Brother Sigeric will be anxious to hear what we have discovered about Sister Valretrade,' Eadulf told her when they were left alone.

'Then we'd better tell him,' Fidelma agreed. It was clear that her mind was elsewhere for the moment and they left the *hospitia* in silence.

They found Brother Sigeric at work in the library, sitting quietly in a corner transcribing some manuscript. He looked up and an expression of hope quickly flitted across his face. Fidelma's demeanour told him there was none, however, and his features resumed their wistfulness.

'We saw Abbess Audofleda, but she simply confirmed what Sister Radegund had told you – that Sister Valretrade left her community about a week ago, having refused to obey the Rule.'

'Lies!' snapped Sigeric hotly.

'Why would you say they were lying?' asked Fidelma.

'Because she would not leave here without me,' the young man replied simply.

Fidelma nodded sympathetically. 'I have heard similar comment from Brother Budnouen.'

'Budnouen used to take messages between us,' Brother Sigeric acknowledged. 'I had heard that he had returned to Autun but have not seen him yet. He is a merchant and . . .'

'We travelled here with him the other day,' Eadulf informed him. 'The thing is, Sigeric, if Abbess Audofleda and Sister Radegund are telling lies, what is their purpose and where is Valretrade?'

Brother Sigeric scowled. 'I'll wager that she is imprisoned somewhere in the *Domus Femini* as a punishment for her relationship with me,' he said, answering the second question first. 'I will break in and find her.'

He half rose as if that was his immediate intention but Fidelma reached out a hand to stay him.

'That will serve no purpose, my young friend,' she said. 'Calm yourself. Let us try to work out a better strategy. Meanwhile, you must have a care. If you are right about what has happened to Valretrade, then Audofleda might surmise you would take that action. I think that the *abbatissa* is one who will hold a grudge. She even threatened us with punishment.'

Brother Sigeric sank glumly back on his seat. 'In the early days, Bishop Leodegar punished those who were reluctant to divorce their wives. He had some flogged.'

'Do you mean that they were not given a free choice to leave if they did not agree with his Rule on celibacy?' Fidelma was horrified.

The young scribe shrugged to show she was right.

'It is hard to believe,' observed Eadulf.

'Yet believe it you must. I know it is unusual to you. From what I have heard, there are few places among the Gauls and Franks and even in your western islands, where abbots, bishops and the religious are not married. But these celibates are a small band of fanatics who can only impose their views by force.'

'Can you give any reason why Abbess Audofleda would deny that Valretrade was in the *Domus Femini*?'

'Only to keep us apart,' was the young man's immediate reply.

'She claims that she knew nothing of your relationship. Sister Radegund supported her in that, saying that she had not mentioned your visit to the abbess.'

'Then I say she lies again.'

'Valretrade disappeared on the night Abbot Dabhóc was slain,' Fidelma said. 'I think it is important that we find someone who is willing to talk about her.'

'Such as?'

'Budnouen mentioned someone who knew Valrctrade . . . what was her name?'

It was Eadulf who remembered it: 'He mentioned a Sister Inginde.'

The young man's eyes widened. 'She was Valretrade's closest friend in the community! They worked together.'

'Then we need a method of trying to contact her,' Fidelma said.

'There is one easy way of sneaking into the *Domus Femini*, but if one is caught . . .' Brother Sigeric ended with a shrug.

'Perhaps that is a risk that should be taken for the sake of truth.' Fidelma's expression was grim.

Brother Sigeric looked at her closely. 'Would you be willing to chance this? After all, being a woman you would have a better chance of escaping detection than a man would have.'

Eadulf protested immediately. 'There is only one way into the house of women, and that is through the main gate. I doubt whether Sister Radegund would allow Fidelma to walk in again, especially to speak with any member of the sisterhood.'

'But there is another easy way in or out of the *Domus Femini*, isn't there, Sigeric?' Fidelma was looking at the young man expectantly. 'The passage through the vaults under the abbey.'

'That is so, but I would need to show you the way. In fact, it is the same passage through which the sisters of the *Domus Femini* come each morning and evening to attend service in the chapel.'

Eadulf raised another objection to the plan.

'So you enter the *Domus Femini* – but what then? You would also need to be able to find Sister Inginde. How would you do that?'

Brother Sigeric was enthusiastic.

'She shared the chamber with Valretrade. I can draw you a plan that would show you how to get there, if you could follow it.'

'I can follow it,' replied Fidelma firmly. 'So long as it is accurate.'

Eadulf was still not convinced. 'I think it foolhardy. What if you were discovered?' he protested.

'I will ensure that I am not discovered,' Fidelma replied simply. 'We must find out about Valretrade. I believe that some of the answers to all this mystery might be resolved when we know why she disappeared.' She turned to Sigeric. 'So when would be the best time to undertake this underground route?'

His answer was immediate. 'This very night.'

'Excellent,' Fidelma said. 'The best time is when the sleep period is at its deepest.'

'You must give yourself sufficient time to enter the *Domus Femini*, find the chamber of Sister Inginde and then question her. Then you will have to retrace your steps,' pointed out Brother Sigeric.

'And all without being observed,' muttered Eadulf.

'Show me the way into the *Domus Femini* and your plan of how I might find the chamber of this Sister Inginde, and I will do the rest,' Fidelma said confidently.

'That is good,' replied Brother Sigeric. 'I will wait for you here, in the library, after the midnight bell has sounded and the last prayers have been said. Then the brethren go to their slumbers. We will wait a while and then go to the vaults.'

Fidelma and Eadulf left the young scribe in an excited frame of mind and returned to the *hospitia*.

As they entered their room they heard the distant toll of a bell.

'Time for the evening bathe,' Fidelma sighed. 'But I suppose it must be in cold water again. I can never get used to these foreign customs where people do not heat water for an evening bath. In fact, I have noticed that these people hardly ever bathe, just have a wash with cold water in the morning and perhaps take a swim in the river every so often. They do not even use soap. How can people exist like this, Eadulf?'

Eadulf controlled his expression for a moment. He had grown up in such a fashion and even now he could not get used to the bathing customs of the people of the five kingdoms of Éireann.

Each morning it was the custom to rise and wash their hands and face but then in the evening, before the evening meal, they bathed, a full body wash, with hot water. And this was the daily custom! Eadulf shivered. When he was growing up, he swam in the river near his home once a week and that was his bath. But the rituals of Fidelma's people continued to amaze him. The soap they used called *sléic* and linen towels and the sweet scented herbs and oils that were used for the bath took some getting used to.

When the toiletry demands had been met and they had changed into clean robes, Fidelma and Eadulf went down to keep their appointment with Nuntius Peregrinus.

The envoy from the Bishop of Rome was already waiting in the *calefactorium* and rose to greet them when they entered. He had been talking to his ever-present *custodes*, the Lateran Palace bodyguard. The warrior discreetly removed himself to another corner.

'More bad news, I hear,' Nuntius Peregrinus said sombrely as they seated themselves.

'You mean about Brother Gillucán?'

'The young Irish Brother,' he agreed. 'He was the servant of Abbot Dabhóc. That is sad.'

'Not only sad but a mystery,' replied Fidelma softly.

The envoy's eyes widened a little. 'I do not understand.'

'That death strikes down both the abbot and then his steward in different circumstances but so close to one another: is there some connection?'

'But this young Brother was attacked by robbers after leaving the abbey. That has nothing to do with the abbot's murder, surely? It is a sad fact of life that there are robbers in our world, those who waylay and attack strangers, to steal whatever wealth they think they have on them. Those of the religious are not immune to such evil people.'

'Odd that no one saw him leave – and not even the vigilant guards at the city gate saw him pass through,' mused Fidelma.

'And what items of worth would a young religieux have on him? I understand the young man was not possessed of wealth, unlike someone of substance – such as yourself,' Eadulf added with a touch of malicious humour.

The Nuntius did not appreciate Eadulf's jocularity.

'Robbers will rob even for a good pair of leather sandals these days.' He hesitated and repeated, 'You surely do not think there is a connection between this young man's death and the murder of his abbot?'

'My task is to come to no conclusion until I am in possession of all the facts,' Fidelma replied.

'Did you know Brother Gillucán?' Eadulf asked.

'No. I met all the delegates but not their stewards or advisers,' said the Nuntius. 'I was present at the opening of the session and saw the enmity between some of the delegates.'

'The argument between Ordgar and Cadfan, you mean?'

The Nuntius nodded briefly. 'That prelates of the Church can be so antagonistic to each other is a cause of sadness when we should be united in Faith. I had to intervene in order to help Bishop Leodegar bring them under control.'

'The more vehement the proclamation of the Faith, the more vicious the denunciation of others who deviate from that person's vision,' interposed Fidelma. 'The Faith can breed great hatreds.'

'You surprise me, Sister!' The Nuntius was scandalised.

'Surely you cannot be surprised by reality, Peregrinus?' Fidelma replied. 'We must accept that we are all frail creatures. I have not studied my country's law and pursued its practice these many years without a realisation that humans are not perfect and rational beings. They can be sly and oft-times evil, whatever their calling in life.'

'We of the Faith must aspire to higher codes of behaviour.'

'Aspire, yes,' she agreed, 'but I am afraid there is often a gap between aspiration and achievement. What was your opinion of Abbot Dabhóc?' Fidelma swung back to the original subject.

Nuntius Peregrinus thought for a moment.

'He seemed a most moderate man. He tried to make peace between the Briton and the Saxon on that first day when they had the argument. I noticed that.'

'Is it your opinion that he was killed because he intervened between them?' asked Eadulf.

'It would seem so.'

'Yet his room was ransacked the same night. Robbery seems so prevalent these days. Could that be a possibility in this matter?'

'But the abbot was murdered in the chamber of Ordgar . . . are you saying that Ordgar killed him in the course of a robbery?'

'I did not say that. I simply said that his chamber was ransacked and some things have gone missing.'

The Nuntius did not respond.

'Did you meet Abbot Dabhóc apart from that opening session?'

'Yes. I went to look at the old Roman amphitheatre, which is not far away from here. Several of the delegates to the council had gone there. Abbot Leodegar wanted to show them some of the beauties of this city. I met Abbot Dabhóc there.'

'Ah!' Fidelma exclaimed. 'And his steward was not with him?'

'Now that you mention it, the young man *was* accompanying the abbot. We exchanged a few words – incidentals, that is all. He removed himself from our company immediately after that.' The words were spoken almost defensively.

'And when you were alone with Abbot Dabhóc, wasn't there talk of a gift?' The sharp tone in Fidelma's voice caused the Nuntius to blink.

'You seem to know a great deal, Fidelma. Yes, there was such talk.'

'And what was said?'

'The abbot advised me that he had brought a special gift from Hibernia. It was a reliquary that he wanted me to take as a present to His Holiness on behalf of the bishop of Ard Macha.'

'But, presumably, this gift was not handed over?'

The Nuntius Peregrinus shook his head.

'Did you know what the gift was?'

'Holy relics, that is all,' the Nuntius replied at once. 'They were the relics of a disciple of Patrick who took the Faith to the Hibernians.'

'The relics of Benén mac Sesenén?'

'No name was mentioned that I recall. We were to wait until the end of the council. There was to be a closing ceremony and it was thought fitting to make the presentation there so that all might witness Ard Macha's tribute to Rome.'

'Whose suggestion was that?'

'The abbot's, naturally. I think he was quite proud of the gift and wanted the other delegates to see what Ard Macha was sending to His Holiness.' He frowned suddenly. 'You would doubtless know that the bishop of Ard Macha is seeking His Holiness's blessing and recognition to be the primate of your land of Hibernia.'

Fidelma pursed her lips in disfavour.

'We have long been aware that the *comarb* of Patrick, as we call the bishops of Ard Macha, make the claim that they are the senior bishops in the five kingdoms. It is not a claim that is supported by the other bishops. Least of all those in my brother's kingdom of Muman.'

'*Comarb*?' The Nunfius hesitated over the word.

'Successor,' explained Fidelma. 'Abbot Ségdae, who is now the senior delegate of Hibernia here, is recognised as *comarb* of the Blessed Ailbe who came to our kingdom before Patrick arrived in the island. It was Ailbe who brought the Faith to our southern kingdom. According to our scholars, he has more right to be recognised as senior bishop. Ségdae is both abbot and bishop of Imleach, the abbey founded by Ailbe. Most people do not acknowledge that the bishop of Ard Macha has a right to this title of *archiepiscopus* – it is not the way in which our churches are organised.'

The Nuntius Peregrinus gave a deep sigh.

'Ecclesiastical politics, then? This gift would not have pleased Abbot Ségdae. It seems that you should be thinking along those lines as the gift has disappeared.'

Fidelma caught the suspicious tone in his voice.

'Do you imply that Abbot Ségdae might be involved in this matter?' she asked.

The Nuntius spread his hands.

'If, as you suggest, the theft of the reliquary box was somehow a motive for the murder of Dabhóc, then Abbot Ségdae is a prime suspect because of the very reason that you have now pointed out.'

'Who, apart from you, knew the nature of the gift? I mean, knew that it was not only a reliquary box but the nature of the relics inside?' Eadulf asked.

'I had thought only Abbot Dabhóc and perhaps his servant, young Brother Gillucán, knew. All I knew was it contained the relics of the Blessed Patrick's disciple and his successor.'

Fidelma was silent for a moment. As the Nuntius pointed out, she had given the very reason why Abbot Ségdae could be regarded as a prime suspect. Yet he was her brother's friend and adviser and, indeed, had performed her wedding ceremony. But such a bribe as Ard Macha was offering to Rome was certainly not in Imleach's nor Ségdae's best interests.

'When did you learn that the reliquary box had been stolen?' Eadulf was asking.

'When?' The Nuntius screwed up his face as if to help his memory. 'I think it was just after the murder, but I can't be sure. Someone was talking about the abbot's chamber being searched.'

'Who was that?'

'I don't recall . . . no, wait! It must have been Brother Chilperic, the steward.'

There came the toll of a bell. The Nuntius rose quickly.

'Ah, we are called for the evening meal.'

Fidelma could not help noticing that he looked slightly relieved.

'Surely, Peregrinus, if the reliquary box was not in Abbot Dabhóc's room, the logical thing would be that it was being taken care of by his steward – Brother Gillucán?'

'Oh yes, that was the first idea.' The Nuntius coughed. 'Brother Gillucán was questioned about that – but he denied knowledge.'

'By whom was he questioned?'

'I presume that Brother Chilperic spoke with him.'

Fidelma and Eadulf now rose from their seats.

'You've been most helpful, Nuntius Peregrinus,' Fidelma said. 'I hope we may continue to have your full support to resolve this matter, and that before long you will be able to take our findings to our friend, the Venerable Gelasius, in Rome.'

'As I said previously, I am sure he will be delighted to know that you have been instrumental in investigating this matter. My prime task is to ensure that, in spite of these setbacks, this council meets and discusses the matters that the Holy Father has placed before them.' He added: 'It is good to talk with you again, Fidelma, although I was hoping that we would be able to reminisce about the times in Rome.'

He nodded to Brother Eadulf then turned to join his silent *custodes* and those moving in the direction of the refectory.

Fidelma and Eadulf followed at a more leisurely pace.

'What do we do now?' Eadulf asked. 'Do we confront Abbot Ségdae with the claim that he had a good reason to kill Dabhóc and steal this reliquary box?'

Fidelma shook her head.

'We will leave Abbot Ségdae alone for a while – at least so far as that matter is concerned. I can't help feeling that Ségdae, even if he were capable of such a crime, would not commit it in such a complicated way. He does not possess such a devious mind. Anyway, first let us enjoy the evening meal.'

Chapter Eleven

They entered the *scriptorium* to find Brother Sigeric ready and waiting for them in the darkness. They stood together without speaking for a long while, listening until they were assured that slumber had overtaken the brethren of the abbey and all was quiet. Then Brother Sigeric lit a lantern.

'Do you have the plan of the *Domus Femini*?' Fidelma asked, keeping her voice to a whisper.

The young scribe nodded and produced the piece of papyrus, which he spread on the table. He quickly explained to Fidelma how to follow the route to what had been Sister Valretrade's quarters.

'The plan is as accurate as I can make it,' Brother Sigeric went on. 'I told you that Valretrade's chamber was across the courtyard almost opposite mine and we used to signal one another by candlelight. In order to help you, I have left a candle alight in my window. You can check that, and when you are directly opposite then you should be in Valretrade's chamber. Now, come with me and I will show you the entrance to the *Domus Femini*.'

'A moment, Brother,' intervened Eadulf as a thought occurred to him. 'You say this passage is used by the members of the women's community to come to the chapel?'

'Don't worry.' Brother Sigeric understood what was on his mind. 'No one will be about now. Anyway, it is not really a passage, as you shall see. It is a way through a maze of underground vaults. There are plenty of areas where one could hide if anyone did come along unexpectedly.'

'It is too late to start worrying about discovery now,' Fidelma told Eadulf. 'Let us go.'

Brother Sigeric extinguished his lantern. From the *scriptorium* they went out into the moonlit courtyard which separated the main abbey building from the chapel. Crossing the courtyard, the moon was bright enough to guide them. It was obvious that Brother Sigeric knew the way and at one stage Fidelma whispered to him not to proceed so quickly. Inside the chapel, he paused. There was a small light burning by the door which was always left alight as a symbol of the eternal spirit. Brother Sigeric simply took the candle from his lantern and lit it again before proceeding to a door at the rear of the chapel. He pulled back a bolt, swiftly and silently. The door opened onto a flight of wooden steps, which plunged into utter blackness below. Here he bade Fidelma and Eadulf halt while he moved down into the darkness. They could hear him descend until they saw only a wisp of light. A few moments later, he returned with the comforting glow of the lantern.

'All is clear – come on.' Holding the lantern high, Brother Sigeric motioned them to follow him downwards but not before asking Eadulf to draw the door closed behind him.

At the foot of the stairs they paused.

The smell was of that curious mixture of earth and decay that Fidelma associated with the catacombs of Rome where she had been lucky to survive. It was very cold and damp.

'They say that before the abbey was built, this was an old necropolis of Augustodunum, the burial place of the Romans,' explained Brother Sigeric in a whisper.

The area was not completely dark. In the gloom they could see arches and pillars spreading every few metres, supporting the vaulted roof above them. Among these were tombs, some made of marble and others of stone.

'How far does this underground world spread?' asked Eadulf with a shiver.

'It seems to spread under the whole abbey,' replied Brother Sigeric. 'Come, follow me.'

He set off through the maze of arches and tombs, moving with confidence, having trodden the path many times, and appeared unconcerned at the various deceptive side turns and byways. Fidelma quickly realised that if they did not have a guide, they would be hopelessly lost in moments.

'Are there only two entrances and exits from this dark maze?' she asked. 'I have never seen the like of this outside the catacombs of Rome.'

'There is a third exit, but that is all,' Brother Sigeric said.

'Where does that lead? Is it still part of the abbey?'

'It leads to a small tunnel under the walls of the city itself; an exit to the south west. In the old days, when all the nobles lived in the city, it used to be an escape route south to the great forests if the city was under attack.'

'Is it still used?'

'Not since I have been in the abbey. I have seen it, of course. All the bolts are on the inner side of the doors so that no one can enter without having someone with foreknowledge on this side of the door.'

Eadulf looked apprehensively around into the gloom. There seemed a faint light emanating from somewhere but he could not locate it. Brother Sigeric saw his wandering gaze and realised what he was looking for.

'There is a faint light that issues through the vaults. It seems to come from some of the rocks that were in the roof of the original caverns. A sort of phosphorus, I think.'

'And was Sister Valretrade ever concerned about coming alone to a place such as this to meet with you?' Eadulf demanded, awe-struck at the magnitude of the vast vaults.

'She knew the route well, so she was not worried. However, it was simpler for me to meet with her on the far side, which I will show you shortly.'

'I was thinking,' begun Eadulf, 'as you were not there to meet her, that night when Dabhóc was killed, was there a possibility that she could have set off to come into the chapel, but that her candle blew out and she lost her way in the darkness?'

It was a grim thought but he felt it had to be voiced. However, Brother Sigeric dismissed it immediately.

'There is no way. She knew the place too well. Also, we met by a special spot. If either of us went to that spot and the other did not turn up, then we moved a particular stone ornament so that the other might know we had been there. Then we returned to our chambers to rearrange our meeting. We had agreed never to go beyond that point.'

They had reached an area in which there seemed a series of small side rooms; in each of them was some sort of very ornate sarcophagus: Brother Sigeric halted before one of the rooms and motioned them inside.

'This is where we met, and you see that little statuette there?' He pointed to a miniature statuette of a little man with the legs of a goat and horns on his head, holding a set of pipes. Fidelma thought she had seen something similar before in Rome. 'We used to place that on one side of the sarcophagus or the other to indicate that we had come here but not found the other. Of course, that did not happen often.'

He led them from the mausoleum and a short distance to where another flight of stone stairs ascended.

'The doorway at the top leads directly into the *Domus Femini*,' he told Fidelma, taking from his pocket a candle, which he handed to her. 'You should not need this but if you do, use it only in an emergency. Valretrade told me that Abbess Audofleda allows the corridors to be lit with lanterns here and there. That can be a good thing or a bad thing. If you meet anyone . . . well, let us hope that they are all asleep.'

Fidelma silently admitted that she shared that hope.

'I wish you'd let me come with you,' Eadulf urged.

She shook her head immediately. 'Don't be silly. If I did run into anyone, it would be hopeless to disguise you as one of the Sisters. I will try to bluff them and hope that that works.'

Eadulf did not look convinced.

Fidelma drew out Brother Sigeric's plan and studied it again.

'The door above is not locked?'

'Never to my knowledge,' Brother Sigeric replied.

'And it enters at this point, between the storeroom and the kitchen of the *Domus Femini*?'

'It does.'

'Then I shall delay no longer.'

'We will wait for you here,' Eadulf assured her.

Brother Sigeric pointed back to the meeting place that he had shown them.

'We will make ourselves comfortable there until your return. It should not take you long to find the chamber of Inginde and Valretrade.'

Without another word, Fidelma climbed the stairs to the door. It was closed but she felt for the latch, and it opened easily. She glanced down to where the men were waiting, Brother Sigeric holding the lantern high to give her as much light as possible, then she raised her hand to them before stepping through the doorway and closing the door behind her.

She stood for a while, back against the door, waiting for her eyes to adjust to the gloom. She was determined to follow Brother Sigeric's advice and not use the candle that she had now placed in her *marsupium* unless there was a need.

In fact, moonlight was filtering through a window somewhere, giving a strange soft blue light in the stone corridor before her. She moved forward determinedly, keeping the image of Brother Sigeric's plan in her mind. The plan was, indeed, accurate for there were no surprises to confront her and, thankfully, all the corridors appeared to be deserted.

She had no problems traversing the large hall that appeared to be the women's *calefactorium*. Then she had to choose the right-hand passageway, which led to a stairway going up to the next level. There Fidelma paused to examine the plan by the light of a lantern hanging from a metal arm on the corner and which lit the divergence in the passageway. According to Brother Sigeric's directions she must bear to the right and then climb up another circular stone stairwell to the next level, before turning left. Three doors along would land her at the chamber that Sister Valretrade had shared with Sister Inginde.

Folding the map, she thrust it back into her *marsupium* and moved cautiously forward. The only thing that worried her was, if Sister Valretrade had truly been moved, would Sister Inginde have a new companion in her chamber? But it was a risk that she felt was worth the taking.

She reached the circular stairwell easily enough and had her foot on the bottom step when she heard a sound above her. Someone was coming down. Thankfully they were moving slowly, but the light from their candle was casting its glow downwards. Fidelma froze, her mind racing, and then she retreated, searching desperately for some place to hide from the oncoming figure. There was none – and no time to get back to the entrance of this corridor before the person reached the bottom step.

Pulling her hood over her head, she drew her robe around her and turned, pretending to be walking towards the stairwell just as the figure emerged.

The figure halted and raised the candle carried before it.

From beneath her hood Fidelma saw that it was an old woman, an elderly member of the community. The candle was held in a skeletal and shaking hand. The eyes were wide and vacant-looking, and the mouth was slack. Fidelma took a quick decision.

'*Bene vobis*,' she intoned hollowly as she moved past the old woman.

'Blessings on you, Sister,' the elderly woman mumbled in reply as she stood aside.

Heaving a deep sigh, Fidelma ascended the spiral stairs quickly and moved up into the darkness. She paused at the next floor, listening, and heard the sounds of the old woman shuffling along the corridor. There was no cry of alarm nor quickening of pace which could have meant that she had been recognised as an interloper. Fidelma waited a moment more and then peered in the gloom along the row of doors, counting them until she identified the right one.

This would now be the most dangerous moment, in her estimation.

If it was the wrong door, if Sister Inginde had been moved or if someone else had been moved in with her . . . If! What was the saying that she had heard once? 'With an "if" one could place Rome in a bottle.' No time for an 'if' now. Pushing back her hood, she moved quickly to the door. Pausing, she listened for a moment. All was quiet.

Reaching for the handle, she turned it slowly, scarcely daring to breathe. It opened noiselessly and she slipped inside, closing the door behind her.

The chamber was not dark; there was the soft moonlight by which she could make out distinct forms. That she must be in the right chamber was evidenced by the fact that through the window directly opposite she could see, across the courtyard, a flame flickering in a window. Brother Sigeric's candle, lit to guide her!

She briefly glanced around. There were two beds and, thankfully, only one was occupied. There was no other person in the room.

Leaning forward, she shook the sleeping form gently by the shoulder. The girl started awake and as her mouth opened, Fidelma reached forward and placed her hand over it to stop any cry of alarm. She hoped that Brother Sigeric was right, for he had told her that the girl spoke a good Latin.

'Quiet! I mean you no harm,' she hissed. 'Are you Inginde?'

The frightened girl, eyes wide above Fidelma's hand, nodded.

'Then I need your help. My name is Fidelma – I am a friend of Sigeric. Do you know his name?'

The girl nodded briefly again.

'Then I am about to release my hand. Do not cry out.' She removed her hand and went on quietly: 'I have come to help Sigeric find Valretrade. She used to share this chamber with you, but we are told that she has decided to leave this abbey and the city.'

'That is what is said,' replied Sister Inginde cautiously.

'Sigeric does not believe it.'

'May I sit up?' asked the girl.

Fidelma moved back and sat on the wooden bed opposite to the girl. Sister Inginde swung out of her bed and reached for a robe, which she draped round her shoulders.

'I cannot see you well,' she said. 'What did you say your name was? Fidelia?'

'No, Fidelma.'

'An unusual name.'

'Not in my country. You would call it Hibernia, a land to the west.'

'Then you are not of this community?'

'I am attending the council.'

The girl shook her head. 'No women are allowed to attend the council . . .' she began and then paused. 'Oh, so you are the person that the bishop mentioned during evening prayers the other day. You are investigating the death of the Hibernian abbot. How is that possible?'

'In my land I am a lawyer. Bishop Leodegar has given authority to me to investigate.'

The girl, Inginde, still seemed suspicious. 'But if you have the bishop's approval, what are you doing creeping into the chambers of the Sisters in the middle of the night like a thief?'

Fidelma chuckled dryly. 'Perhaps this is the only way I can seek the truth without being thwarted by your *abbatissa* – Audofleda.' The girl suddenly shivered. 'It is she who says that Valretrade has left the *Domus Femini*,' Fidelma added. 'Is it true?'

'Valretrade has not been here for nearly a week,' confirmed the girl.

'And she left of her own free will?'

'So Abbess Audofleda tells us.'

Fidelma leaned forward, hearing caution in her tone. 'Do you believe it?'

The girl stirred uneasily. 'Why would I not believe it?' she replied guardedly.

'Let us be honest with each other,' Fidelma urged. 'Tell me what you know about Sister Valretrade and her disappearance from this abbey.'

Sister Inginde hesitated and then said: 'I knew she was having an affair with Brother Sigeric.'

'Only an affair?' pressed Fidelma.

'A figure of speech. They were meeting regularly, but that was no business of mine. They were discreet, but because I am sharing this cell, I could not help but observe her signal to Sigeric and his signal to her. Valretrade confessed to me about her relationship.'

'Did anyone else in the community know of it?'

'I don't think so.'

'So tell me how she came to disappear. Was it on the night Abbot Dabhóc was killed? Or did you see her afterwards?'

'We were told at morning prayers about the abbot. And I was told that Valretrade had left while we were on our way to morning prayers.'

'Tell me what happened.'

'Well, there is not much to it, really. That night, Valretrade put a candle on the windowledge there,' she indicated with her head, 'which was what she did whenever she arranged to meet Brother Sigeric. When she saw the answering candle in his chamber window, across the courtyard . . .' The girl paused and frowned as she glanced out of the window. 'Why, there is a candle burning across there now – in Brother Sigeric's cell. What does that mean?'

'That is to guide me to the right room,' explained Fidelma. 'Go on.'

'I saw his candle alight that night,' continued the girl. 'Valretrade put on her robe and left to meet him.'

'She didn't return?'

Sister Inginde shook her head.

'She left her clothes and belongings here?'

'That was a curious thing. They were here when I went down to the wash house first thing in that morning. I was wondering why she was so late back. When I returned – they were gone. I presumed that she had come back while I was at my ablutions and had taken them.'

'And she departed from the *Domus Femini* without saying goodbye to you but finding time to write a note to the abbess?' Fidelma spoke in a tone of disbelief.

Sister Inginde shrugged. 'What else could I think?'

'When were you told that she had left the community for good?'

'At the midday meal. That was when Sister Radegund told me that Valretrade had left a note and gone.'

'How long had you known Valretrade?'

'Since I came here a year ago.'

'And you had always shared this chamber with her?'

'Since my arrival,' confirmed the other.

'Therefore, you must have thought it odd that she had left without a word to you. Also, didn't you think it strange that it was at the same time as the abbot was killed?'

'From what we were told, the abbot's death had nothing to do with Valretrade.'

'Did Sister Radegund show you this note that Valretrade had written?'

Again came the shake of the head.

'Did you *ask* to see it?'

Sister Inginde chuckled softly. 'You don't ask questions of Sister Radegund and certainly not of Abbess Audofleda.'

Fidelma could agree with the girl's statement.

'Did she give any indication of why she wanted to see Sigeric that night?'

'Surely that much is obvious, Sister? They were lovers.'

'Nothing else? There was no other concern?' She noticed the slight hesitation. 'Go on,' she urged. 'There was something then?'

'It was just her attitude,' replied the other. 'I think there was some air of excitement when she came to the chamber that evening, something on her mind. I am sure that she had heard or seen something that had . . . I suppose "upset" is the word I am looking for. Yes, that had upset her. I asked her what the matter was but she refused to say.'

'Would you agree that if she was leaving the abbey of her own free will, she would have mentioned it to you or spoken to Sigeric?'

'So far as I suspected, she had met up with Sigeric and they had run off together. I did not know that she hadn't until Sigeric came to the community a few days later to enquire where she was.'

Fidelma frowned. 'I thought Sister Radegund was the only one who knew that?'

'I was near the doors and overheard him speaking to her.'

'Didn't it make you suspicious?'

The girl shrugged. 'Valretrade was from Autun. She had a blood sister living here. I thought she might have gone there and waited for a time when she could have contacted Sigeric. I know nothing else.'

Fidelma sat silently for a while, turning the information over in her mind. She felt that there was nothing more to be gathered from Sister Inginde. It was disappointing. There seemed no obvious link between the death and disappearance that she could see.

'Thank you, Sister Inginde,' Fidelma said, rising. 'There is no need to tell you that this matter must be kept strictly between ourselves.'

'Are you going to try to find Valretrade?' asked the girl softly.

'Yes, I shall try,' Fidelma replied grimly. 'I promised Sigeric that I would do what I could.'

'I hope you may be successful. Remember, Abbess Audofleda is powerful. I would be careful of her.'

'I intend to be,' Fidelma replied as she moved towards the door. 'If you need to contact me urgently, the only way I can think of is by the same method that Valretrade used – the candle in the window.'

'I shall remember. But only if it is urgent.'

'Thank you, Sister Inginde. You have been very helpful.'

Fidelma turned out of the chamber and moved back to the stairwell. The *Domus Femini* was silent. Nothing stirred. She returned to the door to the vaults without incident. As soon as she came down the stairs and entered the vaults, Eadulf and Brother Sigeric came forward anxiously.

'Did you see her? Did you see Sister Inginde?' demanded Brother Sigeric immediately.

'She confirms that Valretrade vanished last week,' Fidelma said. 'She says that she did not return that night, having set off to meet you.'

'Did not return?' Brother Sigeric was aghast. 'But the signal was made that she had been at our meeting place and was returning to her chamber.'

'I think we should return to the *scriptorium* where we may discuss things more comfortably,' Fidelma advised. 'It is better than discussing it here.'

Brother Sigeric reluctantly picked up the lantern and led the way back out of the abbey's catacombs.

Once in the *scriptorium* they seated themselves in a corner while Fidelma recounted the conversation she had had with Sister Inginde.

'So, according to what Sister Inginde was told by Sister Radegund, Valretrade was supposed to have left a note with Abbess Audofleda explaining that she was leaving Autun,' she concluded.

Brother Sigeric's reaction was immediate.

'Lies!' he snapped. 'I swear she must be a prisoner in the *Domus Femini*. It is some fiendish punishment of that woman Audofleda.'

'We can ask to see this note,' Eadulf suggested. 'I suppose Valretrade had the capability of writing it?'

Brother Sigeric frowned. 'Of course she could write.'

'Ah yes.' Eadulf suddenly remembered. 'I am sorry. You told us that she had worked in the *scriptorium* with you. So, would we recognise her handwriting?'

'All scribes write with their own peculiarities,' Sigeric said. 'She wrote with a distinctive hand, and with the letters "b" and "d" she had a tendency to put a short diagonal line across their stem.'

'Very well,' said Fidelma, 'we must remember that and see if we can have sight of this letter.'

'Letter or not, she would not leave without communicating with me. I insist that she did not leave of her own accord.'

'Are you saying that she was abducted?' Eadulf asked.

'That is precisely what I am saying. There are rumours . . . about other women and their children . . .'

'Rumours?' demanded Fidelma. 'What do you mean?'

'They say that wives and children have disappeared from the *Domus Femini*.'

'You mean the wives and children of some of the brethren here?'

Brother Sigeric nodded and Fidelma exhaled in irritation.

'Why was I not told before? Never mind! When did you hear such rumours?' she asked.

Brother Sigeric ran the fingers of one hand through his hair as if the motion would spark off memory.

'I am not sure. They began during the last two or three weeks. Some of the brethren were speaking of it. Valretrade once mentioned that some of the married women had decided to leave.'

'Can you remember her precise words?'

Brother Sigeric thought for a moment. 'Not really – I'm sorry.'

'Did she know of any reasons for their leaving? What did these women say?'

'They were gone before any of the community knew they were leaving so she never spoke to any of them.'

Fidelma's eyes narrowed. 'Do you mean that they disappeared from the *Domus Femini* in the same manner as Valretrade?'

The young scribe stared at her, trying to read a meaning in the question.

'Disappeared?' he echoed.

'How many married women and children are, or were, in the community?'

'Brother Chilperic would know the correct number,' began the scribe.

'An estimate,' snapped Fidelma. 'You can surely give us that.'

'I suppose about thirty or more of the brethren had liaisons or were married, and there were about a dozen children.'

'And these brethren – have they left here?'

He shook his head. 'No, the brethren are still here in the abbey. They were mainly the ones who decided to obey Bishop Leodegar and divorce their wives – like Brother Chilperic.'

'So, how many of their wives and children were still left in the *Domus Femini*? Fidelma's jaw had tightened and she banged her fist on the nearby table, startling them both. 'Information! *Sine scientia ars nihil est*!' Without knowledge, skill is nothing.

'I don't understand,' ventured Brother Sigeric.

'I cannot conduct an investigation without information. Had I known about these stories of wives and children being missing, then I could have asked relevant questions.'

'But it was just rumours,' protested Brother Sigeric. 'Except . . .'

'Except what?' demanded Fidelma.

'One of the brethren was speaking to a merchant from the city. The man was buying some of our surplus farm produce. He said that he saw three of the female religious with a foreign man. He was surprised because he knew them to be from the *Domus Femini* and formerly married to some of the brethren before . . .' He ended with a gesture.

'And when were they seen?'

'Just over a week ago.'

'Where? In the city?'

'They were seen entering Lady Beretrude's villa.'

Fidelma did not comment for a while and then she said: 'I should have known this so that I could verify it. If stories of the disappearances are truc . . .' she blinked tiredly, 'then there are many questions to be asked.'

Chapter Twelve

The next morning, after prayers and the breaking of the fast, Fidelma and Eadulf found Brother Chilperic waiting for them outside the refectory. He seemed anxious.

'Bishop Leodegar requests that you attend him in his chambers as soon as possible.' The steward's tone matched the tense expression on his features.

'Abbess Audofleda has protested,' muttered Eadulf.

They found the bishop in an angry mood.

'I have received a complaint from Abbess Audofleda.'

Fidelma was unperturbed by his belligerent manner and, in fact, assumed a sad expression, shaking her head as if in sorrow.

'Indeed, I wanted a word with you about that woman before we send our report to Rome.'

'She tells me,' Bishop Leodegar fumed, 'that you have been insulting and forget your—' He halted and frowned. 'Send to Rome? Explain yourself.'

'I wanted to discuss the matter with you immediately, but it so happened that I encountered an old friend of mine, the Bishop of Rome's emissary to the council.'

'The Nuntius Peregrinus?' Bishop Leodegar's demeanour changed slightly. 'Do you know him? He did not tell me.'

'Of course. I was going to discuss the *abbatissa* with you, but after speaking with him, I felt it was a matter that I should bring to his attention and forward my complaint to Rome.'

Bishop Leodegar was bewildered. 'Complaint? Complaint? But it is Abbess Audofleda who complains of *you*.'

Fidelma shrugged with a tired expression. 'Well, she would, I suppose. It seems a good defence to do so. But I feel that I cannot overlook this matter.'

'*You* cannot overlook . . . ? What are you saying?'

'I believe you have mentioned that this abbey – that both communities, in fact – have already adopted the Rule of Benedict?'

Bishop Leodegar nodded slowly.

'Then I suggest you instruct Abbess Audofleda as to that Rule, for does it not say that *abbatissa* ought always to remember that they are representatives of the Christ and must be mindful of the tremendous judgement that awaits them if they do not carry out their work in the manner of a poor and unworthy toiler in the field? From the start, her arrogance surpassed my imagination. And when I told her that we spoke in your name, for you have conceded authority to us to investigate and come to some conclusion on the unnatural death of Abbot Dabhóc, she refused utterly to co-operate. I asked myself, who is in charge of this community? Is it you, or is it Abbess Audofleda?'

Bishop Leodegar flushed. 'Abbess Audofleda is in charge of the *Domus Femini* but under my jurisdiction,' he said defensively. 'This is not what she told me.'

'Of course not,' Fidelma said. 'I suggest that her position and the Rule are carefully explained to her, for she has shown disrespect to you as her superior.'

'Abbess Audofleda said—' began Bishop Leodegar, trying to salvage his original complaint.

'I am not interested in what she said,' interrupted Fidelma. 'It is annoying that she should so far forget her position and duties as head of the female community that she feels able to disobey the authority you gave us. Is it wise that a woman of her background, without any formal training or previous life in the religious, should be put in charge of the *Domus Femini*?'

Fidelma normally would never have mentioned the background of a woman in such a manner, but she did nothing without a purpose.

Bishop Leodegar was flustered now, trying to cope with an unexpected situation.

'Abbess Audofleda,' he began again, 'says—'

'And *I* said that I am not concerned with Abbess Audofleda's protests! But I am most irritated by her actions, and have decided that she is in grave error. When the Nuntius Peregrinus leaves for Rome, I shall ask him to report the situation here to my good friend, the *nomenclator* to His Holiness.'

Bishop Leodegar's mouth slackened. He ran his tongue over his lips.

'The *nomenclator*?' he croaked.

'The Venerable Gelasius. When I was in Rome, I conducted an enquiry for him. I thought that you knew that? I shall be asking the Nuntius Peregrinus to take a letter to the Venerable Gelasius to inform him of the conditions that I found here and which I feel should be considered.'

Bishop Leodegar's features showed his concern.

'Venerable Gelasius?' he muttered. He clearly knew of the reputation of the *nomenclator* of the Lateran Palace.

'I presume that you know him?' pressed Fidelma.

Bishop Leodegar shook his head. 'I have received instructions from him on the running of this council . . . letters he sent on behalf of the Holy Father.'

'As *nomenclator*, he receives all complaints and petitions and advises the Bishop of Rome how to act upon them. I felt that the Venerable Gelasius should know how the head of one of the communities acts, especially when that community is currently the centre of an important debate on the future of the western churches. Were these facts known, it could well be that the authority of this council would be called into question.'

Bishop Leodegar spread his hands plaintively. His voice was unnaturally subdued.

'I am sure there is some misunderstanding, Sister. Perhaps you have misinterpreted Abbess Audofleda's attitude?'

Fidelma appeared surprised. 'On the contrary, I thought Abbess Audofleda expressed herself very concisely.'

'She may have been under a misapprehension,' the bishop coughed. 'I had not personally told her of your authority. My steward, Brother Chilperic, may not have set out the situation clearly to her.'

Fidelma was not mollified.

'I thought that she was most forceful on the subject. After all, you also explained our position at evening prayers on the day we arrived here.'

Like most autocratic people, as Fidelma had already surmised, the bishop was in awe of those with greater powers and autocracy.

'Perhaps if I explained again to Abbess Audofleda?' he said persuasively. 'This time, I will do so in person. Can we not rescind the idea of this letter to the Venerable Gelasius? It would be untimely in view of Rome's interests in the outcome of this council. I know – let us wait on a decision on the matter until the time is ready for the Nuntius to commence his journey to Rome. What do you say to that?'

At this point, Eadulf, inwardly smiling, decided to play his part: 'Perhaps Bishop Leodegar is correct,' he said heavily. 'Perhaps the Abbess Audofleda behaved wrongly due to ignorance but there is no need to bring down censure on the entire community here. I am sure we can leave it to the bishop to point out the error of her ways.'

Bishop Leodegar began to look hopeful.

'I think I will be able to persuade Abbess Audofleda to be more co-operative and will certainly censure her on your behalf.'

'And allow Brother Eadulf and myself the freedom of the *Domus Femini* to pursue our investigation?'

Bishop Leodegar inclined his head in submission.

Fidelma still seemed relcutant. Then she sighed.

'Very well. For the time being, I shall put this letter of complaint aside. We will review the matter when the time comes to make reports to Rome about this council. By the way, one of the witnesses that I have consulted is the scribe Brother Sigeric. He has been most helpful. I would not like anything to happen to him.'

Bishop Leodegar's eyes narrowed. '"Happen" to him?' he asked carefully.

Fidelma gestured indifferently. 'Perhaps I have expressed myself crudely. I merely meant to say that his well-being is essential to my final report.'

Their eyes met and it was clear that the bishop understood what she was saying. He dropped his gaze first.

'You have no reason to suppose any harm will befall Brother Sigeric,' he said tightly. 'I will ensure that.'

'That is good. Very well – then we are agreed.'

She turned to go but Bishop Leodegar said: 'A moment, Fidelma. There is another matter. Lady Beretrude has invited all the delegates to the council to a reception at her villa, which is but a short walk from here. Lady Beretrude is the mother of the ruler of this province, Lord Guntram. Of course, the reception should have been given to all the foreign prelates by Guntram, but . . .' He shrugged. 'Lord Guntram is not enthusiastic about fulfilling such functions and his mother often receives distinguished visitors on his behalf. You and Brother Eadulf are invited to attend.'

'We would be delighted to accept. When would this reception be?'

'Late this afternoon. I have asked the delegates to gather in the *anticum* when they hear the continuous toll of the bell.'

'Then we would like to see Abbess Audofleda before that.'

Bishop Leodegar immediately looked unhappy.

'I would need to see Abbess Audofleda first to explain what has happened, and she will not be available until this evening as there are other matters that need her attention. Perhaps the meeting could be postponed until tomorrow morning? I assure you that all will be well then.'

Fidelma felt she had no choice other than to accept the delay.

'I will make the arrangements,' the bishop promised. 'And I am sure Lady Beretrude will be delighted to welcome you today. Hearing of your arrival in Autun, and of your investigation, she has especially requested your presence. And she has extended her invitation to all the women accompanying the delegates. She understands that different people have different customs and she is a lady of great liberal attitudes.'

'Then we will not disappoint her.'

Outside the bishop's chamber, Eadulf was smiling.

'That was a skilful piece of diplomacy,' he said approvingly.

Fidelma shrugged. '*Cain cach sái, discir cach dái*,' she said, expressing an old proverb of her people.

Eadulf was unsure of the meaning.

'Every wise man is courteous, every idiot is a bully.'

Eadulf pulled a face. 'So you think the bishop is an idiot?'

'Idiot enough not to realise that his pretentiousness can be spotted by the intelligent. That makes me pause . . .'

'Pause?'

'I had been thinking that the bishop himself was behaving in a highly suspicious manner in this affair. However, I've had second thoughts.'

'How do you mean?'

'Because if he were involved, he would go out of his way not to bring about my suspicions in the manner he does. Therefore, he is either an idiot or perhaps he is . . .' she tried to think of the right word '. . . *aneladnach*.'

'Untrained? Without art?' Eadulf tried to hazard a translation in Latin. 'Ah, without guile. Well, that's not the same as an idiot.'

'Perhaps, in some people's interpretation,' replied Fidelma. 'I mean that maybe he really doesn't know that what he is doing is wrong. Perhaps it is part of his culture?'

Eadulf sniffed deprecatingly because the Frankish culture was similar to his own.

They were walking through the *anticum* when Eadulf spotted the steward, Brother Chilperic, attending to some placing of furniture.

'There is a man who would know about Leodegar's culture,' he said.

Brother Chilperic had spotted them and looked surprised. Doubtless he had been thinking that the bishop's wrath had been about to fall on them. And so he looked disconcerted for a moment.

'Is all well?' he asked as they came up to him.

'Why wouldn't it be?' asked Fidelma innocently.

'I thought the bishop looked angry about something, that is all,' replied the steward, taken off guard.

'In fact, it was we who had a complaint to make,' Eadulf replied. 'We had the feeling that our investigation was not being taken seriously.'

'Oh, not so, not so,' Brother Chilperic said at once. 'There is much tension in the community. The brethren await your conclusions with some anxiety. Bishop Ordgar paces his room like a caged lion, while Abbot Cadfan possesses an amazing vocabulary in several languages which, I thank God, there are no females present to hear . . . oh, I crave your indulgence, Sister.'

Fidelma actually chuckled. 'I can imagine what Abbot Cadfan's choice of words must be in any language. It is difficult to be confined all this time and under suspicion. If I could work this matter any other way, I would. However, what would happen if both of these prelates were able to freely wander about? They would soon encounter one another and, after what has passed between them, that would not be politic, would it?'

Brother Chilperic thought for a moment and then nodded.

'They would probably attack one another and there would be another death on our hands! Bishop Ordgar, however, is outraged that he has been refused permission to attend Lady Beretrude's reception.'

'Until the investigation is finished, it would not be wise to invite them into the same room. And to invite one without the other would be to imply guilt of the one who was not invited,' Fidelma pointed out. 'However, is this reception of such importance?'

Eadulf knew she was seeking information.

'Lady Beretrude, as the mother of the lord of this province, feels that a civic welcome is due those gathering in this territory to debate matters affecting the Faith.'

'And will Lord Guntram be at this welcoming ceremony?'

For a moment the steward looked embarrassed.

'The Lord Guntram is a young man who, I am afraid, does not see his civic duties as a matter of priority yet. You must make allowances for his absence. In years he is mature, but he prefers hunting, wine and . . .' He said in a low voice, 'I am afraid he is not a good representative of the Burgunds.'

'How long has Burgundia been under the rule of the Franks?' Eadulf asked. 'We seem to find resentment continuing between the Burgunds and Franks.'

'It is only a few generations ago since we lost our independence.'

'Ah, so you call yourself a Burgund then?' asked Fidelma.

Brother Chilperic straightened himself. 'I am proud to be of the blood of Gundahar who founded our nation,' he replied with dignity.

'But now you are ruled by the Franks.'

'The Frankish army overcame our last king, Gudomar, and our armies. Yet we have retained our name and our identity. We are Burgunds.'

Fidelma was thoughtful. 'Are you saying that you – the Burgunds – would wish to be independent of the Frankish rulers?'

'*Vita non est vivere sed valere vita est*!' declared Brother Chilperic firmly. Life is not only to live, but to be strong, to be vigorous.

'And you feel that the Burgunds cannot live or be vigorous under the rule of the Franks?'

'It is not only my feeling but that of most of my people,' he assured her. 'Our problem is that Burgundia has been so long under the yoke of the Frankish kings, we have almost forgotten to be Burgunds. The people need some symbol to stir them to manhood again.'

'And will that happen?' asked Eadulf.

Brother Chilperic shrugged. 'Who knows? There is a rumour . . .' He glanced round surreptitiously. 'You will forget I spoke thus, for Bishop Leodegar is a Frank and close to the royal family of the Franks.'

'We wish only to learn,' Fidelma replied. 'Leodegar will hear nothing of what you say. So what is this rumour?'

Brother Chilperic dropped his voice to a whisper.

'You may have heard stories that it was a holy man called Benignus who brought the Faith here and died a martyr. I began to hear some months ago that it was being said among the peasants that the true king of the Burgunds would one day re-emerge with the symbol of Benignus to raise the people into regaining their freedom.'

'Was this a recent rumour?' Fidelma tried not to show her sudden interest.

'One of many. Peasants are always dreaming.' Brother Chilperic gave a harsh laugh. 'It is left to us to deal with the reality.'

'Which is?'

'The reality is that we are a small people. The Franks are many – Austrasia and Neustria spread around us like an engulfing sea. We have to accept the heavy hand of history.'

'I think you told us that you have served in this abbey before Bishop Leodegar came here?'

'I was born in this city and entered the abbey when I was fifteen years old. I met my . . .' He paused and a faint flush came to his cheeks.

'No need to be reticent, Brother Chilperic,' Fidelma said gently. 'It is no crime to have married. Only Bishop Leodegar's new Rule makes it so in his eyes. So, you were about to say that you met your wife in this abbey?'

The steward nodded slowly.

'And you were content as man and wife, serving the Faith in this community until Bishop Leodegar arrived?'

'We were content because we had not seen the error of our ways.'

'And who told you the error of your ways?' asked Fidelma.

The young man looked startled for a moment. 'Why, Bishop Leodegar instructed us on the Rule, of course.'

'The Rule is one thing, but who told you it was the only path of the Faith?'

Brother Chilperic hesitated again. 'You must know that it was the bishop who called us together and instructed us on the true path and segregated us, and we were told to divorce our wives so that they could go into the *Domus Femini*.'

Eadulf muttered, 'And God said: "Who told you that you were naked?"'

Brother Chilperic frowned. 'What?'

'I was just thinking of a line from the Scriptures,' Eadulf said. 'It is no matter.'

'So when this was done,' continued Fidelma, 'you and your wife decided to divorce?'

'It was the logical decision.'

'And your wife went to the *Domus Femini*?'

'She did.'

'And has remained there?'

'Oh yes.'

'But you have never seen her since, even though she is but a short distance from you.'

'Oh yes, I have seen her now and then for our positions make it necessary for us to meet occasionally.'

Fidelma was surprised. 'I thought no one had intercourse with the opposite community?'

'I am steward here.'

'And your wife is . . . ?'

'Stewardess of the *Domus Femini*.'

'You mean your wife is Sister Radegund?' Fidelma could not keep the surprise from her reply.

Brother Chilperic bowed his head. 'Radegund is her name but I must point out that she is no longer my wife and that I have, as instructed by the bishop, put her from me.'

Fidelma let out a long sighing breath.

'Tell me, Brother Chilperic, you mentioned that Bishop Leodegar is a Frank. Do you not resent him?'

Brother Chilperic looked startled.

'He is a Frank and, as I say, closely connected with the royal family. He spent a long time at court before he was given Autun as his bishopric. He is a powerful man.'

'And you are happy to serve him?'

'I am his steward.'

'That is not what I asked. Surely, as a Burgund and feeling as you do about the Franks, you must resent Leodegar being placed in charge and of the way he has so drastically changed the abbey from what you knew?'

Brother Chilperic looked uncomfortable.

'I am in service to this abbey, Sister. There is a Rule here and I have sworn to obey it. And now, you must excuse me.' He turned on his heel and walked off.

Eadulf shook his head at Fidelma. 'What are you trying to do? Stir up alarms and enmity?'

'Sometimes a little prompting can bring surprising results.'

'Oh come, you don't think that the problems here are to do with enmity between Burgunds and Franks?'

Fidelma stared at him for a moment and then sighed.

'There are many problems here, as you say, Eadulf. To be honest, I think this entire community is festering underneath this exterior of obedience. Why this abbey should be chosen by Rome as the place to hold a council on the future of the Faith, I do not know. I begin to think that the death of poor Dabhóc was just a superficial event on the surface of something that goes very much deeper.'

'But what?' demanded Eadulf.

'I don't believe in a sixth sense but if I did, I would say it was that. I have a feeling – that is all.'

'Look,' Eadulf said quietly, 'here comes Bishop Ordgar's steward. He's seen us and is coming over.'

The tall figure of young Brother Benevolentia was crossing the *anticum* with the clear intention of joining them.

'Bishop Ordgar said that if I saw you, I was to ask you how much longer your enquiry is going to take,' he greeted them.

'I would wager those were not the terms in which he couched the question,' muttered Eadulf in an amused tone.

Brother Benevolentia looked embarrassed.

'His language was a little more forthright than that, Brother,' he admitted.

'I must reply to him that it will take as long as it takes,' replied Fidelma firmly.

Brother Benevolentia shrugged indifferently. 'Well, it is little concern of mine.'

'How so, Brother?' asked Eadulf, interested by the comment. 'You are his steward.'

'Bishop Ordgar told you that his own steward died on his journey to Divio. Because I was in service there and knew something of your Saxon tongue, I replaced the steward, but only temporarily. I do not intend to give my services for any longer than is necessary. I am determined to remain in my native city and as soon as the bishop returns to his kingdom of Kent, I can settle here.'

'Providing the bishop is free to return to Kent,' pointed out Eadulf.

Brother Benevolentia merely nodded.

'It certainly looks black for him,' he agreed. 'So you think that he killed Abbot Dabhóc?'

'He is one of the suspects,' cut in Fidelma before Eadulf could reply. 'However, we are some way from establishing the truth of the matter.'

'Well,' Brother Benevolentia said, 'I have delivered the message that Bishop Ordgar has entrusted to me. He is even now appealing to the Nuntius Peregrinus for his freedom and asking him to overturn the decision of Abbot Leodegar and yourself.'

'I appreciate your honesty, Brother. Do you like serving Bishop Ordgar?'

'I neither like nor dislike him,' Benevolentia told Fidelma. 'My stewardship to Ordgar has only been of a few weeks' duration. It will continue only so long as this council lasts.'

'Then you will return to Divio?'

'I was a scribe there and write a good hand in Greek and Latin.'

'You are young. Where did you pick up such knowledge?'

'My family . . .' He paused.

'Your family?' prompted Fidelma.

'My family in the abbey of Divio taught me, for I was taken there as a young boy for my education and trained as a copyist in the library.'

'Then you are fortunate indeed, for the ability to read and write in several languages is an excellent security for the future,' Fidelma said kindly. 'Even outside the religious houses, many great families employ their own scribes.'

'Indeed,' Eadulf agreed, then added, 'if the Rule of Bishop Leodegar is not to your liking, Brother, I am sure there are local lords who would welcome such abilities.'

Brother Benevolentia stared at him for a moment.

'Local lords?' he said tightly.

'Lord Guntram might stand in need of a good scribe.'

'Guntram is the ruler of this province.'

'So you have heard of him?'

'Of course. I am a Burgund. His mother is Lady Beretrude of a noble Burgund family. They are of the line of Gundahar, the first great king of the Burgunds. Every one in Burgundia knows the family.'

'Lady Beretrude is quite a powerful lady, then?'

'She is beneficent and kindly to her people,' replied Brother Benevolentia enthusiastically. 'At least, according to the stories that I have heard.'

'Do you know much about Lord Guntram, her son?'

Brother Benevolentia shrugged. 'He is not as great as . . .'

'As his mother?' supplied Eadulf.

'Just so,' the steward answered.

'Is it not said that children often have to walk in the shadow of their parents?' remarked Eadulf.

Brother Benvolentia smiled without humour. 'Yet it may also be said that every great man overshadows his parents.'

'That is so.'

The steward bowed his head for a moment. 'And now I have duties to perform, if you will excuse me?'

They watched him stride off.

'The trouble is,' volunteered Eadulf, 'he is right, you know.'

'Right? About what?'

'We cannot insist that Bishop Ordgar or, indeed, Abbot Cadfan, be confined for ever.'

'We are not confining them for ever, only until we have a solution.'

'But how long can we continue to restrain them?'

'Let us go and find the Nuntius Peregrinus. If Ordgar is appealing to him, we'd better make sure the appeal ends in conditions suitable for our purposes.'

Puzzled, Eadulf turned after her as she strode off.

'One thing that surprises me,' he confided as they walked together, 'is that Brother Chilperic was married to Sister Radegund. She looks older than him and is not an attractive person.'

'You surprise me.' Fidelma cast him a disapproving look. 'You forget *sua cuique voluptae* – everyone has their own pleasures.'

They found the Nuntius in the *calefactorium*. The Nuntius rose as Fidelma strode across to him.

'I need your help,' she said without preamble.

Nuntius Peregrinus gestured with his hand. 'You have only to ask.'

'Have you seen Bishop Ordgar yet?'

'I was just about to do so, having heard that he wanted to see me.'

'As you know, I initially thought it advisable to keep Bishop Ordgar and Abbot Cadfan confined to their quarters until my enquiries into this crime are ended. Bishop Leodegar agreed with this course of action.'

'A wise precaution,' agreed the Nuntius.

'Yet there is still much to do and I am unsure when the conclusion will be reached.'

'So?'

'Bishop Ordgar wants you to overrule us. Now, I am cognisant of the office held by both Ordgar and Cadfan. Both could be released if they give their word of honour to keep separate from one another until the matter has been resolved.'

'If they agree?'

'They should give their parole to you and you will enforce their obedience as a senior representative of the Church.'

'I will put it to them, and if they are willing, then I will instruct them to take an oath by the sign of the Holy Cross,' the Nuntius said after some thought.

'Excellent. That will solve their complaints and stop them from distracting us until we have finished the investigation.'

'Does that mean they are allowed or not allowed to attend the Lady Beretrude's reception for delegates?'

Fidelma shook her head. 'They must confine themselves inside the abbey until the matter is resolved.'

'Do you expect the guilty one of them to attempt to escape? Is this why you give them freedom from their chambers?' the Nuntius asked with interest.

'No. I wanted them to be confined for their own safety as much as anything else,' Fidelma revealed. 'Please, make it a further condition of their freedom outside their chambers that they should have their stewards with them at all times.' Then to Eadulf's surprise, she added quietly, 'Either one of them could be the next victim.'

CHAPTER THIRTEEN

The villa of Lady Beretrude was larger than Fidelma had imagined it, having seen only the entrance in the Square of Benignus. Once through the warrior-guarded portals, the villa and its surrounding gardens seemed to cover an enormous amount of ground. The small building at the entrance had only been a gatehouse. On either side of the wooden gates was a stone pillar with a carving on it. It was a curious letter 'X' enclosed in a circle. Fidelma presumed it had some meaning. Then, beyond the gates, one entered into a fragrant garden of flowers with a fountain positioned as its focal point. They were growing used to the fact that fountains predominated in the buildings of Autun. This one reminded Fidelma of the fountains that she had seen when she had been in Rome. Crafted from marble, it consisted of little statues of chubby cupids holding bows and arrows, with water spewing from their mouths.

The afternoon was warm, although the sun was already lowering above the tops of the buildings to the west and its rays caused the white walls to be splashed in shades of pink. The perfume from the many flowers, enhanced by the warmth, was almost overpowering to the senses. Among them, Fidelma was able to identify the pungent smell of rosemary. She had encountered the unusual fragrance in Rome and had especially asked what it was, with its trailing green foliage and purple, pink or blue flowers. She had been told it was called 'dew of the sea' – *rosmarinus* – and had discovered that apothecaries used it to help improve the memory.

The council delegates, the grim-faced abbots and bishops, stood in uneasy groups around the central fountain. The splash of the water was a curiously comforting background but could not dispel the tensions evident among those gathered there. A few of the wives of the clerics had come from their lodging house to join their husbands but they, too, appeared uncomfortable. The Rule of Bishop Leodegar seemed to have taken the natural ease and composure out of their relationships, as the married couples knew that they were disapproved of. It seemed to Fidelma that they were trying to pass unnoticed, and they moved into corners of the garden where they thought they might pass unobserved.

Fidelma was well aware of the hopeful glances that were cast towards her and Eadulf as they entered. It was as if no one wanted to be there, and was looking for someone to take the lead in expressing this fact. Fidelma had decided that it was a good moment to assert some of her authority. She had forewarned Eadulf that she would make an affirmation of her rank and culture at this gathering. It was only the third time that Eadulf had seen her discard her simple and practical form of dress for this magnificent outfit.

She now wore a gown of deep blue satin with intricate gold thread patterning. It fitted snugly into her waist before flowing out into a full skirt, which came to her ankles. The sleeves were of a style called *lam-fhoss*, tight on the upper arms but spilling out just below the elbow and around the wrists in imitation of the lower part of her dress. Over this was a sleeveless tunic called an *inar*, tight fitting and covering the top of the dress but ending at the waist. From her shoulders hung a short *lummon*, a cape of contrasting red satin edged with badger's fur. The cape was fastened on the left shoulder by a round brooch of silver and semi-precious stones. On her feet were specially decorated sandals, sewn with pieces of multi-coloured glass, and called *mael-assa*.

Round her wrists were bracelets of complementary-coloured glass, and at her neck was a simple golden torc, indicating not only her royal position but that she was of the élite Nasc Niadh, bodyguards to the kings of Muman. Around her fiery red hair was a band of silver with three semi-precious stones at the front, two of them emeralds from the country of the Corco Duibhne and the third a fiery red stone which reflected the stones used in the silver brooch that held her cape. This headband served to keep in place a piece of silk that covered her hair but left her face bare.

It was called a *conniul* and indicated her married status, for it was the custom of the married women of Hibernia to cover their heads to show their position.

Eadulf wore his woollen homespun russet-brown robes but, as a concession to Fidelma, he also wore the golden torc of the Nasc Niadh which her brother King Colgú had inaugurated him with following their success in identifying the assassins of the High King the previous winter.

Even Abbot Ségdae had smiled with approval when he, and the other delegates of Hibernia, greeted them in the *anticum* of the abbey. They had walked down to the Square of Benignus together, guided by one of the abbey community. Warriors met them at the gates and scrutinised the party. Fidelma noticed they affected to wear the same manner of apparel, armour and weapons, as the Roman legionaries of old. They were all clearly professional and were Lady Beretrude's personal guard.

There were several diverse groups in the garden, even some nationalities that neither Fidelma nor Eadulf could identify. Courtesies were exchanged as several delegates recognised one another. The Nuntius Peregrinus, the Papal envoy, immediately came forward to greet Fidelma and Eadulf. The Nuntius noticed her inquisitive gaze at the other delegates.

'They are not here. As you suggested, I put it to Ordgar and Cadfan that it was not politic to make any appearance here until you have finished your enquiry. I also put the idea of parole to them, which they begrudgingly accepted, especially the condition that they should only move outside their rooms in the company of their stewards. So their stewards remain in the abbey as well.'

Fidelma nodded absently. 'I see no sign of Abbess Audofleda or anyone from the women's community,' she remarked.

'Neither Abbess Audofleda nor any of her community is invited here. Only the bishop and one or two of his helpers are here from the abbey. The reception is for the delegates to the council and those whom the delegates have brought with them.'

'Their wives and any female advisers?'

The Nuntius moved uncomfortably. 'Just so.' He turned to greet some other guests.

Men and women in simple attire were now moving between the guests bearing trays with cups of wine and dishes of olives and bread.

It was not until Fidelma was taking a proffered cup of wine that she realised that the woman who was bearing the tray had an iron collar about her neck. She glanced quickly round at the other servers and saw that they all wore this distinctive badge. She drew Eadulf aside.

'These poor creatures, they are slaves.'

Eadulf was sanguine about it. 'Remember the lines Brother Budnouen quoted? "What did you go out into the wilderness to see . . . a man dressed in fine clothes?"'

'That seems to be a favourite saying to excuse things that one finds abhorrent in other lands. I don't need lectures in scripture,' she replied irritably. 'You know my views. To keep these poor folk with iron collars on their necks, women as well as men, is not the sign of a good woman of the Faith. Even in Rome they do not shackle house servants in this manner. I thought this Lady Beretrude was supposed to be known for her goodness?'

Eadulf knew that slavery was a way of life to most peoples he had encountered, but it was not the time nor place to have a philosophical argument with his wife on the subject.

'We do not know much about Lady Beretrude. Perhaps she is neither good nor truly of the Faith. One thing we must not do and that is judge people by our own standards.'

Fidelma was about to speak when the sharp blast of a trumpet cut through the summer air. Everyone turned in the direction of the sound.

Several people had emerged from the villa and positioned themselves on the steps of the veranda overlooking the garden where the guests were gathered.

A man was lowering a trumpet from his lips and standing to one side. Two fully armed warriors had placed themselves on the bottom steps. Two more well-dressed men of youthful appearance also stood aside to allow Bishop Leodegar to come forward escorting a tall, middle-aged woman. The couple paused for a moment at the top of the steps that led down into the gardens.

'Delegates, welcome the Lady Beretrude,' cried the trumpeter.

The woman stepped regally forward a pace and gazed down on the assembly. Those gathered, politely applauded. Instantly Fidelma took a dislike to her. Perhaps it was the over-application of make-up on her pale features, the thick red on the lips and bright spots of red on the white cheeks, the black lines to accentuate her eyes and the eyes themselves – cold, pale blue and almost without pupils. The hair was black and curly. Its blackness seemed unnaturally so. The features were thin; the nose was long, giving emphasis to the look of arrogance on her features as she surveyed the guests.

Bishop Leodegar took a step that brought him by her side again and held out his left hand, slightly above waist level. Beretrude placed her right hand on it and allowed herself to be guided down the steps, and in this regal fashion they began to move around the groups in the garden with Leodegar introducing the woman to first one delegate and then to another.

'She's looking at you,' whispered Eadulf.

Fidelma was aware that Lady Beretrude had given some glances in her direction and then muttered something to Leodegar, who replied then began to guide Lady Beretrude towards her.

'This is Fidelma of Hibernia, sister to a king in that country,' he announced. 'A kingdom called Moo-awn, I believe.'

The pronunciation seemed close enough.

Lady Beretrude gave Fidelma a lengthy scrutiny, from the top of her head down to her feet, as if she were some exotic figure that she had never encountered before.

'The sister of the king of . . . I cannot repeat your outlandish names. But Hibernia, that I know of. I hear it is at the limit of the world, inhabited by a wild people who live a wretched existence on account of the cold.'

Eadulf's jaw tightened as he waited for Fidelma's explosive reaction.

'Neither so wild nor so wretched, my lady,' she replied, keeping a tight control of her features.

'Ah, but I hear the people in Hibernia are cannibals as well as gluttons. Do they not consider it honourable to eat their dead fathers and to openly have intercourse with their mothers and sisters as well?'

Eadulf gasped loudly at the insult, but Fidelma was perfectly controlled.

'Beretrude,' she said softly, dropping the courteous form of address, 'your ability to read Strabo does you credit. I did not think women in your culture read Greek, but your knowledge of it seems excellent. Mine, alas, must be of poor quality but, even so, I do recall that Strabo did point out that he made those observations never having been to my country, not having trustworthy witnesses to guide him. He admitted to basing his remarks solely on rumours that he heard about cannibalism among the Scythians.'

Lady Beretrude's eyes narrowed as she realised that Fidelma would not be so easily insulted.

'Of course, one shouldn't base knowledge on one source,' she said coldly, her expression full of venom. 'Pomponius Mela was not well disposed to your people either and considered them unrefined, ignorant of all the virtues and totally lacking all sense of duty.'

'I must congratulate you again on your knowledge of the Latin writers as well as the Greeks who served the old Roman Empire,' Fidelma replied, smiling. 'What is sad, however, is the fact that neither of those writers, as great as they were in their own time, which is now many centuries past, ever visited Hibernia, otherwise they would have seen the error of relying on gossip and rumour. It is good, Beretrude, that in this day and age, people of intelligence and learning no longer indulge in making judgements on information gained at secondhand.'

An angry flush had come to the Lady Berctrude's cheeks as she also realised that she was unable to assert authority over Fidelma.

She opened her mouth, hesitated and then spoke again.

'Bishop Leodegar informs me that you have some knowledge of law?'

'The law of my own land,' confirmed Fidelma.

'How quaint. He tells me that the Hibernian delegates have demanded that you choose which of the two foreign clerics killed the Hibernian delegate?'

'Bishop Leodegar,' Fidelma replied, glancing at him directly, 'has actually commissioned me to investigate the killing of Abbot Dabhóc of Ard Macha. In my office, as a minor judge of my own land, it is a task that I sometimes undertake.'

'Indeed?' There was still the underlying sneer in Lady Beretrude's voice. 'It seems to me to be a task most unsuited for women.'

'An unpleasant task for everyone, since murder is a very unnatural thing,' Fidelma responded stolidly. 'However, once done, then someone has to undertake the discovery of the culprit – male *or* female.'

It seemed to Eadulf that Fidelma had purposefully left the sentence in ambiguous form as to whether the murderer or the investigator was male or female.

Lady Beretrude was about to speak again when Bishop Leodegar, looking uneasy during this exchange, took her by the arm and moved her on to introduce her to someone else.

'Somehow, I do not think you have made a friend in Lady Beretrude,' Eadulf commented as he and Fidelma drew away. It was then he saw how angry the woman had made her. Her eyes were like pieces of sparkling ice.

'I swear, Eadulf, there are times when I would enjoy physical violence. That was one of them.'

'I thought that you handled her insults well.'

'Belligerence and ignorance are never handled well, especially when the person who delivers them revels in them as if they were a virtue.'

She looked around. The groups of delegates were still sipping wine and talking with one another. However, she noticed that each nationality tended to keep to itself, although her own people seemed to mix more freely with the Britons, Gauls and the Armoricans. They talked in excited groups with raised voices. The delegates from the Frankish kingdoms and from the Anglo-Saxon kingdoms seemed more subdued.

Lady Beretrude was continuing to move from group to group with Bishop Leodegar, who was still introducing the various officials.

'Well, as everyone is busy, perhaps it is a good time to explore a little,' Fidelma suggested. 'If it is true that some of the women from the *Domus Femini* have come here, we need to find out why. For the time being, I do not think asking Lady Beretrude will be of benefit. I'll go along that side of the villa, through the gardens towards the back,' she said, pointing to the western side, 'and you explore the other side. If any of the guards stop you, we can pretend that we were looking for . . . for . . .'

'The *necessarium*?' Eadulf said wryly.

'Just so.'

She turned and made her way slowly towards the area of garden that stretched along the western side of the villa, against which the sun was causing the white walls to reflect in a pink glow. Eadulf waited to ensure her departure had not been observed before he edged slowly to the side of the villa that was now fairly shadowy, being on the opposite side to the setting sun. He hesitated a moment and glanced quickly around before moving along the pathway out of sight of the main gathering. On his right-hand side was a high wall, and to his left was the villa wall itself. There seemed no windows on this side of the villa at ground level but there were several windows above, which obviously looked out over and beyond the high border wall.

He was unsure of what exactly Fidelma expected him to find. Did she think he would find a group of women or Valretrade in the villa? He would go as far as he could. If the passage ran around the back of the villa he could circumnavigate it, or if he found a door open, he could look inside with his ready excuse of seeking the *latrina*. The passageway was devoid of anything interesting except for a couple of tall wooden barrels. Some five metres beyond this he saw an iron gate that blocked the pathway. It was securely fastened. Just before this, to his left, there were some stone steps that led down to a door in the side of the villa below ground level. It was a plain, iron-studded wooden door. He was about to go down the steps to investigate when he heard a cry.

It was a child's cry. There came the sound of a harsh command. Footsteps were approaching.

For a moment Eadulf froze in indecision. It was shadowy here but there was only one spot that afforded any cover. Hastening to the barrels, he crouched down behind them. He heard the clang of bolts being drawn on the iron gate, a chain being unfastened and a rough voice giving orders. The footsteps halted and there was a faint moan of a child before a scuffling sound.

He chanced peering out around the barrel and saw the child first, a young boy no more than eight or nine years old. Following him were two religieuse, women in torn and dirty robes. Behind them was a warrior, with drawn weapon, a short sword, and then another man whose back was towards him.

Eadulf's eyes widened in surprise as he realised that the two women and the boy had their hands bound before them. The warrior was prodding them down the steps to the door. There he used the base of his sword-hilt to hammer on the door in a curious series of knocks. The door was opened and the trio were pushed through.

Then the man half turned. It was good that he did not turn fully, for had he done so then his gaze would surely have fallen on the astounded Eadulf.

Eadulf recognised the man, even in profile.

He had last seen him only a few months before and that was in An Uaimh on the banks of the great river that flowed through the High King's territory called the middle kingdom of Midhe. The man had been in the process of being banished from the kingdom under Fidelma's sharp tongue, and he had turned and said: 'I shall remember you, Fidelma of Cashel.' And he had not meant it as a kind thought.

Of all the people in the world, the fact that Verbas, the merchant of Peqini, was here in the villa of Lady Beretrude came as a complete shock to Eadulf.

Fidelma had found herself moving through a series of small, exquisitely fragrant gardens, each separated by trelliswork or other fencing, some with hanging plants. There were stone seats and little figurine fountains again, each one different, and they seemed to stretch along the side of the villa, all bathed in the warm glow of the lowering sun. Fidelma had seen such gardens before when she had been in Rome but none had been executed with such miniature precision. The plants and design were pleasing to the eye. She thought of the more natural and, perhaps, rugged gardens of her own land, and wondered whether such a form could be transferred to Cashel, although these plants might not thrive in a more rainswept and colder climate.

As she bent down to examine the plants more closely, there was a slight rustle behind her and she heard the sharp accented tone in Latin.

'Ah, the lady Fidelma.'

Fidelma swung round and found Lady Beretrude smiling at her from a mask-like face.

'I am sorry if I intrude in your private gardens,' Fidelma began. 'I was lured by the fragrance of your plants and herbs.'

To her surprise, Lady Beretrude showed no resentment.

'It is my indulgence to spend time in this garden,' she replied. 'I have many herbs here that are not to be found elsewhere. Friends have brought them from eastern countries and I do my poor best to cultivate them.'

'Indeed,' Fidelma replied politely.

'We grow olives here and crush them into oil.'

'I was admiring those trees. I have not seen their like before.'

'Ah, the cypresses.' The woman glanced across. 'As you know Greek' – was there a touch of bitterness in her tone? – 'you will know that the cypress is associated with Hades, the Greek God of the Dead and the subterranean kingdom of the dead.'

Fidelma pretended to be interested in the plants as she could think of no suitable reply.

'There are some curiosities in that corner which you may find of interest,' went on Lady Beretrude. 'Go, take a look; feel free to examine the plants.'

She waved her hand to a corner of the garden where a multitude of green flowering plants grew and whose fragrance was powerful.

'That is basil in the front – my cooks use it in the food. It is quite pleasant and comes from the east. It is named from the Greek *basileus* or "king" for it is said that it grew above the spot where Constantine and Helen discovered the remains of the True Cross.'

Under the watchful gaze of Beretrude, Fidelma bent and pretended to become absorbed in the flowers. In fact, it was not a total pretence because part of her mind was, indeed, fascinated by the plants here.

'If you go behind the basil you'll see an evergreen shrub with pink flowers,' instructed Beretrude. 'Step over the little fence and you can bend down to smell it.'

Fidelma had noticed that there was a border of wooden boards around this part of the garden, which separated the herbs from the row of evergreen bushes behind. It was only about sixty millimetres high.

'It is called oleander, the plant that grows in the south of the country,' continued the woman. 'Ah, excuse me . . . I am being called away. Stay and enjoy the fragrances.'

She moved away.

Fidelma pulled a face, wondering if Lady Beretrude was trying to make up for her previous lack of civility by this show of friendliness. She bent down to smell the strange pink flowers that hung in clusters from among the leathery, dark green leaves. She had one foot in the bordered shrubbery enclosure and the other outside when she became aware of something sliding by her foot. Her mind registered a grass snake.

'Fidelma?'

Eadulf had appeared in the garden and saw Fidelma standing near the shrubbery. She turned, with one foot still across the fence.

'I was just looking at the herb garden. What is it?' She noticed that he seemed excited.

'You will never guess who I have just seen here in the villa,' he began.

Fidelma gave a sudden yelp of pain. 'Something has bitten me,' she said.

Eadulf hurried forward, glanced down and swore in his own language. Then he reached forward and pulled her out of the shrubbery onto the path.

'An adder!' he cried. 'Quick.' He was undoing the belt at his waist. As she watched, puzzled, Fidelma began to experience numbness around her ankle. A pain was creeping up her leg. She felt her heart beginning to thump wildly and a sick and dizzy feeling overcame her.

Eadulf was strapping something around her leg and drawing it tight. Then she seemed to be falling to the ground. A moment later she was dimly aware that he had lifted her in his arms and was hurrying along the path. She tried to speak, and then all seemed to go black.

Abbot Ségdae saw Eadulf first as he came around the side of the villa into the main garden, carrying the inert form of Fidelma.

'What has happened?' he demanded, running forward. Several other Hibernian delegates came crowding round.

'We must get her to an apothecary!' cried Eadulf. 'She has been bitten by a poisonous snake. An adder.'

Bishop Leodegar, followed by Lady Beretrude, came elbowing his way through the throng. He had heard what Eadulf said.

'Bitten by an adder, you say?'

'Take her into my villa, and I will send for my apothecary,' instructed Lady Beretrude.

Eadulf shook his head. 'We'll take her back to the abbey to Brother Gebicca,' he said firmly.

'But that will take time,' protested Lady Beretrude. 'She'll be much better off here. I will personally look after her. If the poison isn't treated quickly it could be dangerous . . . fatal even.'

'I know that,' Eadulf snapped. 'I have some knowledge. Someone guide me back to the abbey. Quickly!'

At once several of the Hibernian delegation, including Ségdae, volunteered to accompany him. Eadulf managed, with their help, to hoist Fidelma on his back and he, without another word, began to hurry forward in a trot surrounded by the Hibernian clerics; those in front and either side seemed to clear the way. For a moment it looked as though the warriors of Beretrude would halt them at the gates but Lady Beretrude made a signal to indicate they should be allowed to pass. She stood, without emotion, watching their departure with Bishop Leodegar at her side.

Head down, with the weight of Fidelma on his back, Eadulf gritted his teeth and hurried as fast as his burden would allow him. He was exhausted and sweating by the time they came into the great square before the abbey. One of the clerics had run forward to alert the physician. Brother Chilperic appeared in the *anticum*.

'Let me take her, Brother,' he said, observing Eadulf's panting and fatigued features.

'Just lead me to Brother Gebicca,' grunted Eadulf.

He was bent forward now so that he could see only the lower part of Brother Chilperic's legs, the heels hurrying before him, guiding him through the *anticum* and out into the main interior courtyard, crossing to the apothecary's house. He was aware of doors opening and then hands were removing his burden and he straightened to see Fidelma being laid on a bed among the almost suffocating odours of the apothecary's room.

'What exactly happened?' asked Brother Gebicca.

'She was bitten on the ankle by an adder. A poisonous snake.'

'Are you sure?' demanded Brother Gebicca.

'It was a black snake. I've seen them before.'

The apothecary turned back to Fidelma who was breathing rapidly and with a shallow motion. She appeared in a comatose state.

'You did not try to cut the wound and suck out the poison?'

Eadulf shook his head.

'That is good. The venom is inserted into the blood directly under the skin and so it is useless to try any way of extracting poison after this time. I see you tried to restrict the flow of blood. That is not much good,' as he spoke he was removing Eadulf's tourniquet. 'What is good, however, is that you have kept the limb, where the wound is, at the lowest part of the body. Now go and let me do my work.' He turned to the clerics crowding in. 'Go! I will call you if there is a need.'

Reluctantly, Eadulf allowed himself to be dragged away from the apothecary by Abbot Ségdae and guided to the *calefactorium*. Someone brought in a jug of good strong *corma* and mugs were produced.

'How did it happen?' asked Abbot Ségdae.

'It was in the herb garden,' Eadulf said shakily. 'The viper was among the shrubbery and she was bitten by it.'

'Let us pray that Brother Gebicca knows how to treat the poison.'

At that moment, Bishop Leodegar entered the room, having followed them from Lady Beretrude's villa.

'How is she?' he asked.

'We are awaiting word from your apothecary,' replied Eadulf.

'The Lady Beretrude has offered to send healing herbs to our physician should he need them,' the bishop continued. 'She feels responsible, for she was showing the garden to Sister Fidelma just before it happened.'

'It is thoughtful of Lady Beretrude,' Abbot Ségdae acknowledged when Eadulf made no response.

'Is there anything I can do?' asked the bishop.

'Until Brother Gebicca informs us of the situation, there is nothing,' Eadulf replied.

An age passed by in which no one spoke, but the *corma* was handed silently around as they sat waiting. Then Brother Gebicca entered and peered around in search of Eadulf. The latter sprang to his feet and moved towards him.

'What news?'

'She has a strong heart and a good constitution. Her pulse is normal. She will have a painful swelling on the leg for a day or two but, after a good night's rest, she will start to mend.'

'The venom has dispersed?' demanded Eadulf, scarcely believing the news.

Brother Gebicca nodded affirmatively. 'I have seen worse cases. The effect in her case has been like a powerful bee-sting; painful and causing irritation. But in a strong adult, with a good constitution, the body recovers.'

'Can I see her?' Eadulf asked.

Brother Gebicca shook his head. 'She is sleeping now. Sleep is always a good curative in such matters. Let her rest and we will see how she is in the morning. I will sit up with her to ensure there are no complications during the night.'

He left with a nod that encompassed everyone in the room.

There were murmurs of congratulation from many while Abbot Ségdae clapped Eadulf wordlessly on the shoulder. Eadulf paused for a few moments before, as the abbey bell tolled, following the example of the others as they moved to the refectory for the evening meal.

The next day, after morning prayers and the ritual breaking of the fast, Eadulf went directly to Brother Gebicca's apothecary.

Fidelma was sitting up and sipping at a hot broth that Brother Gebicca had prepared from various herbs. That it was unpleasant in its taste was obvious from her expression. She looked up in relief as Eadulf entered.

Brother Gebicca turned to him with a look of satisfaction.

'All is as I said, Brother. She has a painful swelling on the leg but nothing worse.' He turned back to Fidelma. 'I was asking, how it was that you did not recognise the poisonous serpent to avoid it? They do not attack unless they feel threatened.'

'We do not have such serpents in Hibernia,' Fidelma answered simply. 'I have not seen such a poisonous reptile before.'

'It is true,' Eadulf confirmed, seeing Brother Gebicca's look of disbelief. 'There are no reptiles of that sort in the five kingdoms.'

'Yet I have heard that they exist in the island of Britain, so why not in Hibernia? Are they not in close proximity? Is the warning of hidden danger not international – *latet anguis in herba* – a snake lies concealed in the grass? How can it be a warning if there is a country without snakes?'

'That is a mystery,' Fidelma replied firmly. 'Yet it was told long ago that our people were destined to live in a land without snakes.'

Brother Gebicca sniffed cynically and it was clear that he did not believe it so Fidelma decided to explain.

'The progenitor of our race, Goidel Glas, son of Niul, in far-off times, served in the army of the Pharaoh Cingris in Egypt. A poisonous snake bit him but an Egyptian healer and holy man, who had been befriended by his father Niul, healed the boy. But the wound left a green mark on his skin. That is why he was called *glas*, which means green in our tongue. The healer then prophesied that he would eventually lead his people to an island at the edge of the world where no poisonous snakes would dwell. It was Goidel's descendants who brought our people to the island that you called Hibernia.'

'A pagan belief,' dismissed Brother Gebicca. 'Superstition.'

'Pagan or not,' Eadulf put in, 'it is now being said that this miracle was wrought by Patrick when he came to convert the island. It was he, we are told, who drove out all the poisonous serpents.'

Fidelma stirred restlessly. 'How long before the swelling disperses and the wound heals?' she asked.

The physician began to bind the wound again.

'There is no infection now. The wound is healing well and the swelling will go down in a day or two. I would advise rest, lest unnecessary movement causes the blood to circulate any residual venom through your body. Are you sure that you feel no ill-effects?'

'None.'

'The application of yellow snowdrop and vervain seems to have worked well. However, for a few days, drink a cup of the infusion of vervain and that will finish the attack of the poison.'

'But can I get up now, for there is much I must do.'

Brother Gebicca showed his disapproval.

'You must do as you think best,' he shrugged. 'I have done *my* best and you are healed of the immediate effects of the poison. My advice is that you go to your room and rest for at least today.'

Eadulf was in agreement. 'The apothecary is right, Fidelma. If there is anything that needs to be done, I can do it.'

'At the moment, you may help me to our chamber,' Fidelma replied grimly. It was clear that, in spite of her question, she was not able to move without help.

Supported by Eadulf, with her arm around his shoulder, Fidelma thanked the apothecary and, limping a little, made her way to the main building of the abbey. One or two of the delegates greeted her and asked after her health. Abbot Ségdae also met them and pressed his profound relief at seeing her in a better state than on the previous night. Finally, they reached their chamber and Fidelma collapsed on the bed, exhausted by the effort.

Eadulf went to get her some water and she sipped at it gratefully.

'I rather think the apothecary is right,' she admitted, after handing the mug back to Eadulf. 'I need more rest than I thought. That walk was quite tiring.' She noticed the basket of fruit and another of various herbs in the room. 'The abbey, at least, seems to be concerned for my health,' she said.

Eadulf glanced at the baskets.

'Bishop Leodegar brought those in. Apparently, the Lady Beretrude sent them, fruit and healing herbs, and with all good wishes for your recovery.'

Fidelma frowned suddenly. 'Lady Beretrude?' She remembered the moments in the garden with Beretrude encouraging her to look more closely at the shrubbery . . . at what was it – the oleander?

Eadulf saw her frown. 'What is it?'

'I just wondered if Beretrude knew there was a poisonous snake in the shrubbery.'

Eadulf was surprised at the question. 'Why would she know that?' he demanded.

'She was encouraging me to go near the shrubbery just before you came.'

'She could not have known a poisonous snake would be there.'

'There was a wooden border around those shrubs. It was of such a height that a snake would not be able to move over it. Perhaps the creature had been purposely placed there.'

Eadulf was dubious. 'Are you saying that she deliberately tried to kill you?' He looked unconvinced. 'The bite of a viper does not necessarily mean death. Even Brother Gebicca likened it to a bee-sting, affecting only the young and those with weak constitutions.'

'It is debilitating nonetheless for that,' replied Fidelma in annoyance at his argument. 'It might have been an attempt to prevent me from pursuing the investigation.'

It was then that Eadulf remembered what he had been about to tell her at the moment that the snake had bitten her.

'I think we were right to suspect that Beretrude might have some connection with the women from the *Domus Femini*,' he said slowly. 'Last night I saw something at the villa that shocked me, and that was when I came to find you in the garden.'

Fidelma turned an enquiring look at him.

'After we had agreed to part and look round,' Eadulf told her, 'I went along the eastern side of the villa. I had some idea of finding a back entrance and having a look inside.'

'Go on,' she said, when he paused.

'I came to an area where stone stairs led downwards into a cellar. At the foot of these stairs was a door – a solid wooden one with no grille in it and no handle or lock, so it seemed. I presumed it could only be opened from the inside.'

'And so?'

'I was about to go down the steps to examine it further when I heard the cry of a child.'

Fidelma's eyes widened a little. 'A child? This came from behind the door?'

'No, it came from beyond an iron gate in the wall. I heard a man's harsh commands so I hid behind some barrels. The gate opened and a child and two women were pushed through by a warrior. The women were clad in the robes of religieuses. They had their hands bound in front of them, even the child. As well as the warrior, who had his weapon drawn, there was someone else . . .'

Fidelma was irritated by Eadulf's dramatic pause.

'And who was this someone else?' she prompted.

'An old friend of ours.'

'Old friend? Stop speaking in riddles, Eadulf. Just tell me who it was.'

'Verbas of Peqini.'

Chapter Fourteen

Fidelma had lapsed into a thoughtful silence at the news of the presence of Verbas of Peqini at Lady Beretrude's villa. Eadulf sat and waited, not wishing to interrupt her thoughts as she considered the ramifications of his news. But it was not long before she told him, 'The fact that Verbas is here does not alter the basic mystery around the murder of Dabhóc, although it puts an interesting slant on matters.'

'He could not have known that we were here, surely?'

'I agree – it must be a bizarre coincidence although, as I have said before, I have never really believed in coincidences. However, he could not have known we were here before arriving. He must have arranged to trade with Lady Beretrude some time ago.'

'But to trade in what?' wondered Eadulf.

'You say that there were two religieuse and the child and they seemed to be prisoners?'

'Verbas and a warrior were taking them into an underground room at Beretrude's villa,' confirmed Eadulf.

'Then I fear this has something to do with the disappearance of the religieuse at the *Domus Femini*.'

'And the cries that Gillucán heard? Could they have been the cries of children?'

'Let us not leap too far ahead.' Fidelma swung off the bed and tried to stand but immediately sank back with a word that was unusual for her to utter.

'Brother Gebicca said that you should rest,' Eadulf admonished.

'I know what he said,' she replied coldly. 'The point is that the time is passing swiftly. There is much to be done, especially in view of this information. I want to have a further word with Abbess Audofleda.'

'I can do that,' offered Eadulf. 'I know what it is that I must look for.'

Fidelma was not persuaded.

'Oh, come,' protested Eadulf. 'I know enough about your methods and this matter. True, I am not as well versed in the law of the Brehons but I am an hereditary *gerefa* of my own people – and are not my people closely related to these Franks or Burgunds – closely enough that I might understand their way of thinking?'

Fidelma was slightly surprised at the vehemence in his tone. The thought occurred that perhaps she was being selfish. Eadulf had his pride as well. She knew that if she had a fault it was the belief that only she could gather the evidence and resolve a mystery. And even as that thought came to her, she remembered the many times that Eadulf had almost single-handedly resolved a case. There was the time in Gleann Geis, when he had had to argue on her behalf in front of Murgal the Brehon when Fidelma herself was charged with murder. It was Eadulf's arguments that had secured her release. Then, of course, there was the time they had arrived at Aldred's Abbey where she had fallen ill and was confined to her bed while Eadulf had done all the investigation so that together they had solved the mystery of Abbot Botulf's murder. She had, indeed, to remind herself that Eadulf was an hereditary *gerefa* or magistrate of his own people. His mind was just as sharp and penetrating as her own. Indeed, was that not part of the mutual attraction that had brought them together?

She sighed deeply and held out a hand to him.

'Eadulf, Eadulf,' she said softly, 'you have great patience with me. I tend to be a little selfish in these matters.'

Eadulf felt awkward. He was unused to Fidelma apologising.

'It's just that I can save time in this matter,' he said gruffly. 'It is best that you spend a day recovering and come to the matter fit and well tomorrow.'

'You are right. Just remember not to say anything to the abbess or to Sister Radegund that might compromise Sister Inginde. Let us keep her information to ourselves – and beware in your dealings with Sister Radegund.'

A frown started to gather on Eadulf's face. 'Why her particularly?'

'You saw Beretrude. Compare her features with Sister Radegund's. If there is not a likeness there, and a relationship, then I am no judge of such matters. Also, remember that we followed her to Beretrude's villa in the first place.'

Eadulf realised that Fidelma might be right. He had not thought about it before. There *was* a strong likeness between the older and the younger woman. He was about to comment when there was a tap on the door; in answer to Eadulf's response it opened and Brother Chilperic entered.

'I came to see if there is anything you require, Sister,' he said, with a nod of acknowledgement to Eadulf. 'We were all alarmed to hear the news of your accident.'

'I am told that I need to rest here today so that the swelling on my leg has time to disperse and heal.'

Brother Chilperic expressed his sympathy. 'Bishop Leodegar asks whether he can have a word with you if you are able.'

'Indeed, if he has time to spare now, I would appreciate it,' she replied with resignation.

When he had gone, Fidelma said: 'You had better wait to hear what Bishop Leodegar has to say before going to see Abbess Audofleda.'

'Are you sure that you should be left alone today?'

'I will ask Ségdae if he or one of his brethren can spare some time to sit with me,' she replied.

Eadulf was approving. Fidelma was never one to be nervous. However, he was anxious that she should have some protection in his absence after the incident in Beretrude's garden. While it could have been an accident, it was better to be cautious.

Bishop Leodegar entered with a worried frown.

'Ah, it is good to see you looking better, Fidelma.' He sounded thankful. 'Lady Beretrude was most concerned. Her servants searched the grounds and apparently found the viper and killed it.'

'I hope that you will assure Lady Beretrude that I am recovered. The physician says I should rest for today.'

'So Brother Chilperic tells me. He will ensure your meals are brought here. I merely wanted to express my pleasure that the snake has done no permanent harm to you.'

'I am told such venom can even kill?'

Bishop Leodegar nodded absently. 'It has been known to.'

'Then I was very lucky. I hope Lady Beretrude will ensure that there are no other poisonous reptiles in her villa.'

The bishop missed the double meaning. 'It was lucky that Brother Eadulf was with you and rushed you straight to Brother Gebicca's apothecary.'

'I trust the reception was not entirely ruined?' asked Fidelma.

Bishop Leodegar looked uncomfortable. 'After the delegates from Hibernia accompanied Eadulf back to the abbey, the reception broke up.'

He was about to leave when Fidelma said: 'I am told that Autun is a trading centre in this country.'

'It has been a centre of trade since the Romans built it.'

'And what does it trade in?'

'It produces wine, of course, and olives. We trade with livestock and cheese.'

'And slaves?'

Bishop Leodegar seemed to pause before he added: 'And slaves.'

'Are the traders all local, or do you attract foreign traders here?'

'The rivers are good highways. But, of course, we are a long way from the sea in most directions. Trade tends to be mainly local otherwise our goods would perish on the long journey. But sometimes foreign merchants call here.'

'Have you heard of Peqini?'

The bishop considered for a moment and shook his head. 'It sounds a strange name.'

'I understand it is a land in the east.'

'Then I have not heard of it.'

'There are no eastern traders passing through this city?'

'I cannot see why eastern traders would be interested in this place. They have their own wines and olives. I have heard their riches surpass ours. The foreign merchants who pass through our city are not usually from places of far distance.'

'Does Lady Beretrude trade much?'

The bishop looked horrified at the suggestion. 'Lady Beretrude is a noble. Merchants and farmers pay her tribute. What a curious question you ask.'

'I am merely interested in how things are governed, that is all. So she would not be interested in trading with eastern merchants?'

'If eastern merchants were interested in trade in Burgundia then they would go to Divio or to Nebirnum, both of which stand on great riverways where traffic is easier. They would also have a wider choice of goods. If they did come here, then they would usually be found in the market by the northern gates. Why are you so interested?'

'Just curiosity,' sighed Fidelma. 'Thank you. You have satisfied it. Now I feel rather tired and will rest.'

Bishop Leodegar excused himself and left.

'You were angling to see if he knew about Verbas of Peqini?' Eadulf regarded her with a serious expression.

'Either he does not, or he is a good liar. I wonder if he is as much a friend of Lady Beretrude as he maintains?' She sighed deeply. 'You had better be off on your quest. On your way, can you ask Abbot Ségdae to attend me?'

Eadulf was walking up the wagonway towards the courtyard that gave entrance to the *Domus Femini*, mentally rehearsing how to face the formidable Abbess Audofleda, when he noticed with surprise that the door was opening. A tall man emerged, followed by a young-looking woman. They were both clad in the robes of the religious. The man saw him and said something to his companion, who immediately withdrew inside and closed the door.

The man did not seem to be perturbed and walked on towards him with an easy stride. As he drew nearer, Eadulf saw that the religieux was young and quite handsome. He had dark brown hair, brown eyes, a swarthy skin and a firm chin. His teeth shone brightly each time he smiled. There was something, however, that Eadulf distrusted about his smile and his manner.

'Good day to you, Brother Eadulf,' he stated as they drew together. 'It *is* Brother Eadulf, is it not?'

Eadulf halted with a frown. 'That is my name. I do not know you.'

'Forgive me. I do not wish to appear to have the gift of second sight. I have seen you in the refectory and at prayers, of course. Bishop Leodegar announced your name to us in the chapel – your name and that of the Sister from Hibernia, Philomena . . . ?'

'Fidelma.' Eadulf was annoyed that the man thought he could not possibly work out how he knew his name and would ascribe it to some supernatural effect. 'Her name is Sister Fidelma.'

'Ah yes, such a curious Hibernian name. But you are a Saxon, are you not?'

'I am from the kingdom of the East Angles,' corrected Eadulf in a heavy tone. 'And you are?'

'Forgive me again. I do not mean to create mysteries. I am Brother Andica. There is no mystery about me. I am from Divio and I am a Burgund.'

'I thought the male community of the abbey were not allowed to visit the *Domus Femini*,' Eadulf remarked, indicating the building with a movement of his head.

'And neither are they – generally speaking,' Brother Andica said condescendingly. 'But here you are, presumably on your way to the *Domus Femini*.'

Eadulf reddened as the man turned his implied question into one directed at himself.

'As you have already remarked, Brother Andica, Bishop Leodegar has explained why I am here,' he replied.

'Your investigation? You seek information among the women? How interesting. How does the investigation go? Are we soon to hear who killed the Hibernian abbot?'

'You will hear no doubt when the investigation is concluded,' Eadulf replied. 'So why are you visiting the *Domus Femini*?'

Again came the flash of Brother Andicca's white teeth. He was, thought Eadulf, an extremely vain young man.

'Although our communities are separated, we do occupy the same abbey, and this necessitates some communication.' Eadulf could hear his patronising tone. 'I assure you, Brother, there is nothing sinister to my being there.'

Eadulf bridled. 'I did not suggest there was,' he snapped.

Again the flash of teeth.

'Of course not, Brother,' the man said in a pacifying tone which made Eadulf almost grind his own teeth. 'I heard that a poisonous snake had bitten the Sister from Hibernia. I hope it is nothing serious.'

'No, it is nothing serious,' replied Eadulf.

'That is good. At this time of year the vipers in this part of the world are active. They can cause fatalities.'

'She has been well treated.'

'Ah, by the excellent Brother Gebicca, no doubt? That is good. One should have a care of snakes.'

Eadulf stared at the annoying young man.

'I agree, Brother Andica. We shall have an especial care of snakes from now on. And now, if you will forgive me, I must be about my business.'

'*Vade in pace*,' replied the young man in a grave voice but he was smiling as if it were a jest.

With a brief nod, Eadulf strode on to the door of the *Domus Femini* and reached for the bell chain. He tugged on it, his ill humour somewhat increased. It was some time before the hatch swung back and the sharp eyes peered at him.

'Brother Eadulf to see the *abbatissa*,' he announced curtly.

The hatch slid shut and he heard the bolts rasping, metal against metal, before the door opened and he stepped inside without awaiting an invitation. The door shut behind him and he turned to see Sister Radegund sliding the bolts back into position.

'Who was the young Sister letting out Brother Andica a few moments ago?' he asked the stewardess brusquely.

Sister Radegund blinked. She seemed surprised at his question. 'Who? Brother who?'

Eadulf sighed impatiently. 'It is a simple question, surely?'

Sister Radegund coloured. 'I assure you, Brother Eadulf,' her tone was cold, 'only *I* have opened and closed this door this morning.'

'Are you telling me that Brother Andica did not pass through this door a few moments ago?'

'Brother Andica? I can assure you that no brother has been here.'

Eadulf opened his mouth and then snapped it shut. That such a barefaced lie could be told was beyond his capability to deal with. If Sister Radegund had argued that the blue sky was, in fact, red in colour, there was no means to discuss the matter. So it was with this denial.

'You wish to see Abbess Audofleda?' the stewardess asked. 'If so, come with me.'

Without waiting for his answer, she turned and hurried off. Eadulf, recalling the way to the abbess's chambers from the last visit, fell in step behind Sister Radegund who, as before, moved at a remarkably rapid pace.

Abbess Audofleda was standing in her chambers before the fireplace. It seemed chill in the dark stone rooms of the abbey in spite of it being a hot summer's day outside. She was dressed in black robes, her dark eyes sparkling with controlled anger and her mouth a thin slit. Her hands, clasped tightly together before her, revealed the tension that was evident in the very stance of her body.

'Brother Eadulf,' announced Sister Radegund, taking up her stand as she had previously done in front of the closed door.

'Well?' The word from the abbess was a hiss, as if he were intruding in a place he was not wanted.

'*Abbatissa*,' Eadulf responded in an equally sharp tone, 'I presume that you have spoken with Bishop Leodegar and you know why I have returned?'

Abbess Audofleda looked as if she was confronted by something distasteful.

'I know that in spite of my protest at the arrogance displayed in your previous visit here, the bishop has informed me that I must see you again and answer your questions. I have been told that the woman from Hibernia lies ill from a snake bite, perhaps a just punishment for her arrogance. So I presume that you are to ask further questions.'

Eadulf's face hardened. At least the attitude of the *abbatissa* did not soften his resolve to pursue the questions without making allowance for diplomacy.

'As a member of the Faith, you will be comforted to know that Sister Fidelma has improved and is now healing from the bite of the poisonous snake,' he replied, his voice heavy with sarcasm. 'However, I am, indeed, here to act in her place in the pursuit of truth and justice. There should be no difficulties – *veritas simplex oratio est* – the language of truth is simple.'

Abbess Audofleda was clearly annoyed. 'This matter is distasteful to me,' she said. 'So ask your questions, the quicker that this might be ended.'

'Let us return to the matter of Sister Valetrade,' began Eadulf.

'We have already told you about her. She decided to leave us – that is all.'

'Indeed,' replied Eadulf. 'You mentioned that she left you a note.'

The abbess sniffed. 'What of it? They all left notes. She could read and write.'

'I had assumed she could write,' Eadulf replied without humour. 'So she handed you this note?'

'Sister Radegund gave me the note.'

Eadulf was turning to the stewardess when he suddenly paused as he realised what the abbess had said.

'They *all* left notes?'

'The women who departed all left notes telling me that they were leaving, rather than confronting me in person.'

'And did they all hand these notes to Sister Radegund?'

Sister Radegund answered the question.

'They did *not* hand them to me,' she said sourly. 'The notes were always left in my chamber where I carry out the administration of the *Domus Femini*.'

'And you are saying that you had no discussions with any of those who chose to leave?' he pressed. 'Tell me, how many *have* left?'

'About twenty or so. They all preferred to leave the abbey before dawn without announcing their intentions to anyone. Like the cowards they were, they simply slipped out into the darkness . . .'

Eadulf turned back to the abbess. 'Did you not think this was strange behaviour?' he asked.

'I merely thought it cowardly behaviour and in keeping with their attitudes,' snapped Abbess Audofleda. 'They disagreed with the Rule.'

'I would like to see this note from Sister Valretrade.'

A frown crossed the abbess's features. 'You question its existence?' Her tone was challenging.

'I said, I would like to see it,' repeated Eadulf calmly.

The abbess opened a cupboard and took out a thin veneer-like tablet. Eadulf thought it was probably birch bark, which many still used to write upon. She handed it to him without a word. He took it and examined it. It was written in Latin. The characters were certainly well formed but he was looking for the cross lines on the stems of the b's and d's – the peculiarity of Valretrade's hand as Brother Sigeric had described it. There were none. He read the note quickly.

Abbatissa Audofleda – I can no longer agree with the Rule of the abbey. I am leaving to search for a community to which I will feel able to contribute and where I will be at ease. I have heard of such a community in the southern mountains founded by the Blessed Gall of Hibernia. In sorrow, Valretrade.

'You see?' Sister Radegund's voice showed her annoyance. 'You had no need to doubt our word.'

Eadulf did not reply; instead he put the piece of birchwood in the *marsupium* that he carried.

'With your permission, *abbatissa,* I will keep this for the time being.' His tone made it clear that he would keep it whether she gave permission or not. 'And the other notes, do you have them?'

This time she handed him a small bundle without protest. They were mostly the same, written on bitch bark, some bearing three or four names. All ascribed their leaving to their disagreement with the Rule of the *Domus Femini*. Only Valretrade's note mentioned the intention to go to the abbey of Gall.

'They all seem remarkably similar,' Eadulf pointed out. 'As if they were written by the same hand.'

'It is my belief that Valretrade wrote them all. She had been a scribe; her fellows doubtless paid her to write the notes.'

'And all these women objected to the segregation of the sexes in the abbey?'

'The Rule is clear,' the abbess said distantly. 'If they did not like it, then they were free to go.'

'Most of them were married. Some of them even had children. Separation must have been hard for them.'

'They had been given the choice by the bishop a year ago. That was to leave or accept the Rule.'

'Many felt they had to stay as this was the only place they knew. They had been born here and lived here all their lives.'

'The choice was their own,' replied the woman stubbornly.

'How many of your community are wives of the brethren?'

'None.'

The answer came back quickly from Sister Radegund and took Eadulf by surprise. His look prompted Abbess Audofleda to add: 'My stewardess means that Bishop Leodegar declared all the marriages of those who chose to stay invalid under the Rule.'

'But some had children?'

'The children were taken care of.'

'So how many of these women and children are now in the care of the abbey?'

Abbess Audofleda glanced at her stewardess.

'It has only been in the past few days that the last of them have departed from the *Domus Femini*,' Sister Radegund replied firmly. 'Most of these departures have happened in the last two weeks.'

This time Eadulf was unable control his surprise. 'In the last two weeks?'

'That is so.'

'Where did they go?'

'After they leave here, it is not our responsibility to know where they go. I presume one encouraged another and, like sheep, they all flocked together – eager to leave here for a more indolent life.'

Eadulf examined her keenly. 'Did their husbands . . . did their *former* husbands,' he emphasised as he saw the frown gather on her brow, 'know of their departure? Were they informed that their wives and children were leaving?'

'It is not our task to inform them or ensure that these women, who reject the religious life, inform those with whom they formerly consorted,' Abbess Audofleda said irritably.

Eadulf was thoughtful for a moment. 'How many women now pursue the religious life here under your Rule?'

It was Sister Radegund who answered.

'There are fifty in the *Domus Femini*.'

'And before?'

'Perhaps a hundred.'

'A sad decrease,' he commented.

'The chaff sometimes has to be blown away from the wheat,' replied Abbess Audofleda unctuously.

'That is true,' agreed Eadulf, sounding amiable. 'So those who are now left display the true vocation, according to your Rule?'

'I believe so.'

'Well, that is good. You must be proud of the good work you have done here. I believe you said that Bishop Leodegar invited you here especially for that purpose?'

'He did.'

'From Divio, I think you said.'

'I did not say.'

'Then I must have heard it from someone else. But you did come from Divio, didn't you?' Eadulf went on. 'You must have done good work there for the bishop to ask you to come here.'

'Bishop Leodegar has not complained of my work here,' the *abbatissa* said coldly.

'Of course,' agreed Eadulf easily. Then: 'Does this house have a good relationship with Lady Beretrude?'

The *abbatissa* glanced quickly at Sister Radegund before returning her gaze to him.

'Lady Beretrude? She is the mother of Lord Guntram who governs this province and is a benefactor to this house.'

'I am told that you Burgunds consider her a generous patron?'

Abbess Audofleda looked annoyed. 'I am a Frank. But it is true we have cause to thank her.'

'I apologise – but a Frank from Divio?' said Eadulf. 'I thought that it is a Burgund city.'

'I did not say that I was born or raised there, but that I was in charge of—'

'Another *Domus Femini*. I understand. But do you get on well with the Lady Beretrude? Does she approve of the changes made to this abbey?'

'Of course,' Abbess Audofleda replied at once.

'You frequently meet to discuss matters?'

'Not frequently. Sometimes my stewardess acts as my deputy in certain transactions.'

'Transactions?' Eadulf stared directly Sister Radegund.

The stewardess was staring at the floor.

'My stewardess and I discuss matters with the bishop and if there is anything of consequence that needs to be drawn immediately to the attention of Lady Beretrude or Lord Guntram, then my stewardess does so on my behalf.'

'So apart from Sister Radegund, none of your community should have cause to venture out to Lady Beretrude's villa?'

'Only in exceptional cases does anyone from the *Domus Femini* venture out from here,' replied the abbess crossly.

'What would constitute such an exceptional case?'

The *abbatissa* exhaled in impatience. 'Really, Brother Eadulf! I see no point to these questions.'

'You will oblige me, *abbatissa*,' Brother Eadulf stated firmly. 'I am trying to clarify something in my own mind.'

The woman went to protest again but then shrugged.

'For example, then, some of the delegates to the conference that the bishop is holding, not realising the Rule and custom here, brought wives and women with them. They were placed in a local inn for they could not stay in either part of the abbey – *unlike* the dispensation the bishop has now given to the Hibernian woman.' There was bitterness in her voice.

'And how did this constitute an exceptional case for members of your community to venture out?'

'The bishop asked if selected members of my community could advise and guide these foreign women during their stay in the city. There was a visit to the Roman amphitheatre that needed several of our Sisters to attend, in order to escort the visitors.'

'Was Sister Valretrade one of those?' asked Eadulf as the thought occurred to him.

'If we had realised then that she could not be trusted, we would . . .' cut in Sister Radegund and fell silent as Abbess Audofleda cast her a withering glance.

'Had we realised that she had commenced this . . . this affair,' the *abbatissa* went on, 'she would not have been given the task of escorting the wives of the foreigners.'

'When did you find out about this affair? Was it before she disappeared?'

Abbess Audofleda stamped her foot. 'This is too much! We have been patient. The questions are now ended.'

'Why do you not allow your stewardess to reply?' Eadulf demanded.

'Because I choose not to,' replied Abbess Audofleda. 'Now remove yourself from this place.' Her jaw was thrust out and her lips set in a thin line.

There were so many more questions Eadulf wanted to ask, but he saw that it was useless. He looked coldly at her.

'It is your choice, Abbess. Of course, we will mention your lack of co-operation in our report to the Venerable Gelasius in Rome.'

He turned to see Sister Radegund look anxiously at the abbess, who merely tossed her head.

He walked to the door.

'I am sure you will find your own way out,' called the abbess rudely.

Outside, Eadulf paused. He felt frustrated at having learned little more than what he had already suspected – that Sister Valretrade had *not* written the note and that she had *not* left of her own free will.

Striding off along the corridor to the stairs that led to the main doors of the building, he heard a soft voice call on him to wait a moment. Eadulf turned. An attractive young girl in religious robes stood in the shadows of a deep alcove. She gestured quickly towards him in a conspiratorial way.

'Stay a moment, Brother. I need to speak to you.'

Chapter Fifteen

The girl reached out a hand and pulled him into the alcove. Her expression was anxious.

'I saw you go to the *abbatissa*'s room. Are you the Saxon who is the companion of the Hibernian woman who is investigating the deaths in the abbey?'

'I am. Who are you?'

'My name is Inginde.'

'Ah, of course.' Eadulf glanced quickly round. 'Perhaps now is not a good time to speak. Sister Radegund might come after me at any moment to ensure I have left the building.'

'I just wanted to know if you had any news of Valretrade yet?'

'We are still looking,' he told her, 'but you can be assured that she did not leave this place of her own free will. The note she left was certainly not in her own hand.'

The girl's eyes widened. 'How could you know that?'

'A scribe will tell you that each person has their own style of forming letters. I have ascertained that she did not form the letters in her note.' He paused as a thought struck him. 'Is there any place in this building where she could be kept out of the sight of the community here?'

'You mean as a prisoner?' breathed Sister Inginde.

'As a prisoner,' confirmed Eadulf.

The girl shook her head immediately. 'There is nowhere that one can hide in this place. I know every corner of it. No, you must accept that poor Valretrade has left this abbey – and who knows where she has been taken.'

'I understand that other women and their children have also disappeared from this community recently.'

'It is so,' Sister Inginde conceded. 'We were told they no longer wished to live by the Rule of the *abbatissa*.'

'Has anyone mentioned the villa of Lady Beretrude in this connection?'

The girl looked shocked. 'Lady Beretrude? I don't understand.'

'Could those who have disappeared from here have been taken there?'

Sister Inginde regarded him curiously for a moment. 'Do you know that Sister Radegund is related to . . .' she began.

There was the noise of a chamber door opening.

'Don't worry. We are near a solution, I promise.' Eadulf felt reckless, trying to reassure this sweet-faced, anxious girl. 'We think the answer might lie at Beretrude's villa. I promise all will be revealed soon.'

The girl did not answer but sank back into the shadows as Eadulf turned and hurried off along the corridor.

The voice of Sister Radegund called suspiciously from behind him. 'You are slow in making your departure.'

'I think I took a wrong turning.' Eadulf turned and tried to look apologetic.

'Then I will show you the way.' Sister Radegund brushed by him with a purposeful stride. He followed her meekly.

'I was surprised that you and Abbess Audofleda were not at the reception given by Lady Beretrude yesterday,' he said, trying to open a conversation.

'It was only for the delegates to the council and their advisers,' Sister Radegund snapped.

Eadulf felt he could chance some boldness, remembering what Brother Budnouen had told them.

'I wondered whether Lady Beretrude had not invited the abbess because she had an objection to her previous life in Divio.'

Sister Radegund stopped and gasped. A red hue had come to her cheeks.

'My . . . Lady Beretrude is . . .' she began, and suddenly became confused.

'You were about to say . . . is your mother? You bear a close resemblance to her.' Eadulf felt he had nothing to lose by making the guess.

Sister Radegund recovered quickly.

'Lady Beretrude is my aunt. I am not ashamed of it. And you seem to know a great deal.'

'I need to know more,' Eadulf pressed, but she had turned swiftly and did not answer him. They came to the main door and Sister Radegund bent to draw back the bolts. Eadulf opened his mouth to speak again but she simply pointed through the open door.

'*Vade in pace*,' she said in dismissal.

Eadulf had no recourse but to leave.

Fidelma was dozing when Eadulf arrived back at the *hospitia* of the abbey. Outside the door sat a muscular young religieux from Imleach who had been placed on watch by Abbot Ségdae. Eadulf exchanged a few whispered words with him and decided to let Fidelma continue to sleep. Sleep was always a good healer. He would go instead to the library in search of Brother Sigeric.

Brother Sigeric was not in the *scriptorium* but he found the steward, Brother Chilperic, seated there looking over some columns of figures on a clay board. The steward glanced up with a rueful smile.

'The accounting of the abbey,' he said, laying down his stylus. 'It is a job I dislike. Running the affairs of the abbey is much like being a trader. The bishop is very particular that we do not enter into debt.' He paused. 'Can I help you, Brother?'

Eadulf was about to say, 'No,' when a thought occurred to him. 'Do you know Brother Andica?'

'Of course,' came the immediate response. 'Why do you ask?'

'I met him a short while ago.'

'He is one of our stonemasons. An excellent artisan.'

'Is he from these parts?'

'A Burgund? Yes, he is. Why?'

'I would have thought that a stonemason could demand good fees in a city like this and never be out of work. But I suppose he wanted to serve the Faith, a man with religious zeal?'

'Not really. He is not very devout. He is more concerned with pride in his city and his people. I fear that pride will one day get the better of him.'

Eadulf raised an eyebrow in silent question, and the steward grew confidential.

'Our bishop, as I have told you before, is a Frank and well connected with the ruling house. Brother Andica sometimes has difficulty in keeping his pride in check. Once or twice the bishop has had to remonstrate with him on his disrespectful tone towards our Frankish rulers.'

'Is Andica something of a fanatic in these matters?'

Brother Chilperic shook his head.

'We can all be proud of our peoples, but when serving in the religious we are supposed to serve the wider humanity. Christendom becomes our nation.'

'And yet overcoming a pride in one's people can be a hard aspiration as, indeed, Cadfan and Ordgar have already discovered.'

The steward was thoughtful.

'Now that they have been allowed freedom outside of their chambers, they pace the abbey like restless beasts. I was once in Rome and saw the caged lions – big cats – which had been brought there from some corner of the earth. That is how I see the abbot and bishop. However, they have avoided one another so far. I do hope that you and Sister Fidelma will make a decision as to which one is guilty before there is another killing.'

'Another killing?'

'I am sure that if they do meet, one of them will kill the other.'

'I am afraid it is not so easy as making a choice,' Eadulf sighed. 'It is a question of finding the truth.'

'Are you near that truth?'

'It takes time.'

'Ah, *tempus omnia revelat*,' intoned Brother Chilperic piously. 'Time reveals all things. It is a good thought, Brother Eadulf, but sometimes events as well as people cannot wait. I have advised you, Brother. There may come a moment when the bishop will say, "Take the advice that Horace gave in his *Epistles*".'

Eadulf searched his memory. 'I do not think that I am acquainted with that advice.'

Brother Chilperic's expression was a little malicious. '"You have played enough, eaten and drunk enough",' he quoted.

'You are saying that he plans to dismiss us?'

'*Verbum sat sapienti*,' the steward replied almost complacently. A word is enough for a wise man.

'Does he not care who the guilty person is?'

'He cares more that this council meets and makes the decisions required by Rome. Only the fact that you are known to the Nuntius Peregrinus keeps the bishop patient . . . for the present. But he believes that we cannot wait for ever.'

Eadulf was irritated. 'It will not be for ever. It will be when the truth is known.' He turned and left the *scriptorium* abruptly.

Outside he met Brother Sigeric about to enter.

'Brother Chilperic is working in there,' Eadulf warned Brother Sigeric when the scribe looked surprised as Eadulf closed the door firmly.

'Then by all means let us move to a place where we may talk freely,' Brother Sigeric replied. They entered the main courtyard of the abbey and went to stand by the fountain. 'I understand that you saw Abbess Audofleda again. Did she show you the letter from Valretrade?'

'The letters were not formed just as you told us,' Eadulf said, taking the birch bark from his *marsupium* and showing it to Brother Sigeric. 'In fact, the same hand wrote all the notes from those married women who quit the community.'

'I *was* right. Valretrade did not write it,' the young man said after one glance. 'I will swear to it.' His face was anguished. 'What could they have done with her? You are sure that she is not a prisoner of Audofleda?'

'She is not in the *Domus Femini*,' confirmed Eadulf. 'Nor are the other women and the children who have disappeared.'

'But you believe all the disappearances are connected?'

I believe so.' Then a thought occurred to Eadulf. 'Tell me, do you know Brother Andica?'

'The stonemason? Why do you ask?'

'Does he have reason to be in the *Domus Femini*?'

'As a master stonemason he has to ensure the good repair of both sections of the abbey.'

'Of course. I did not think.' Eadulf felt a little disappointed at the easy explanation.

'As a matter of fact, before the Rule of segregation was put in place by the bishop, there was a long gallery that linked the two sections of the building. It was Andica's task to seal it, but to do so he had to work on both sides of the wall that he had built. So that would be the reason why he has free access.'

'Do you mean that he is still working on this gallery?'

'I am sure he is.'

'And one can still pass between the two sections of the abbey? Then there is another way into the *Domus Femini*, apart from the underground method that you showed us?'

Immediately Brother Sigeric shook his head.

'I am not sure about that. It is now called the forbidden gallery. We are not allowed into it. It should be sealed.'

'Describe this gallery to me,' prompted Eadulf.

'It was a long passage that was said to be part of the original Roman building that stood on the site of the abbey. There are tall arches and an upper gallery on which some ancient statues stand. At the far end, the arched door leads into the *Domus Femini* but, as I say, I am sure that Brother Andica is supposed to have blocked it up. No one is allowed there any more, as it provides no useful function.'

Eadulf was contemplative.

Finally Brother Sigeric prompted: 'What are you going to do about finding Valretrade?'

'Once Fidelma has recovered . . .' Eadulf began vaguely. He laid a hand on Brother Sigeric's arm. 'Don't worry, we will find her,' he said, trying to sound reassuring. 'Leave it to us and say nothing further to anyone about this. We will keep you informed.'

Eadulf was still pondering gloomily on the subject the following morning when Fidelma rose, feeling her old self. The leg was tender but the swelling had receded and she was able to move freely. A good sign was that her appetite had returned and she made an excellent attempt at breaking her fast. Brother Gebicca came by soon afterwards, checked the wound and pronounced himself satisfied.

'The poison is dispersed and there are no signs of any residual matters. The tenderness should be entirely gone by tomorrow.'

After Brother Gebicca had left, Fidelma made Eadulf sit down and go through his encounter with Abbess Audofleda and its consequences again. He had done so the previous evening but her mind had still been hazy. Now she listened for the most part in silence, questioning only to amplify on a point here and there. Eadulf also told her of Brother Andica, of Sister Inginde, of Sister Radegund's relationship to Beretrude and, finally, of the warning that Brother Chilperic had given that Bishop Leodegar was ready to cancel their investigation.

'That must not happen,' Fidelma said forcefully. 'We know that there is more to this matter than Cadfan and Ordgar. Verbas of Peqini is lurking around the villa of Beretrude. Why? Sister Radegund is related to Beretrude and we now learn that all the married women and their children have left the community. Some have been seen entering Beretrude's villa. I think something very sinister is happening.'

She was silent in thought a moment before she said: 'I am intrigued with this gallery that Sigeric mentioned. When Brother Chilperic took us around the abbey to acquaint us with it, he neglected to show us this.'

'As it is sealed up and no one can pass between the abbey and the women's community, perhaps it was not considered important enough. I am told it is called the forbidden gallery.'

'Nevertheless, we must ensure that this is the truth of the matter rather than rely on hearsay. Do you know where it is?'

'I know roughly from Sigeric's description.'

'Then let us make that our first priority of the day.'

One thing that Fidelma knew Eadulf was good at was spatial concepts. He could look at a building and know its geography without having to spend time exploring it. He had correctly guessed where the abbey buildings were joined together, having observed the forbidding outside walls and then translated this into the internal geography. He was able to conduct Fidelma through the large and now empty refectory hall, beyond the kitchens and through the storerooms. Everywhere seemed deserted. He paused, examining some passages, and then moved into a hall that was filled with stone dust and some blocks of limestone and even marble. There were masonry tools piled here and there but the place seemed unoccupied.

'The gallery must lead from the end of this hall, beyond those doors,' pointed Eadulf in satisfaction.

The doors were unlocked and, as Eadulf opened them, both Fidelma and he drew a quick breath as they surveyed the long passage that spread before them. It was broad but seemed narrow because of the vaulted roof rising some fifteen metres from the floor level, supported by ten tall pillars on either side, fluted like great Roman columns, pushing upwards. An arch connected each pillar. Behind the arches, some ten metres from the floor, a gallery seemed to run, its floor level with the base of the arch. In the centre of each arch stood a statue of some sort, five of them along each side. They seemed to be of men in the military attire of Ancient Rome. The floor of this passageway was of small coloured pieces of stone, an intricate mosaic as they had seen in Rome. At the far end was a large arch that looked as though doors had once stood beneath it but now it was blocked by stones that had obviously been placed there recently.

'It looks as if Brother Sigeric was right,' Eadulf observed, as they walked along the forty metres of the passage. 'This way has been blocked off.'

They paused before the stone-filled doorway.

'Leodegar is certainly a fanatic about segregating the sexes,' mused Fidelma. 'I wonder why he fears women so much?'

'Does his attitude mean that he fears women?' asked Eadulf, puzzled.

'Trying to deny equality, trying to denigrate women or, indeed, denigrating anyone is a sign that you really fear them,' she said. 'This blocking off of parts of this old building to segregate women from men is ridiculous. Anyway, I have seen enough.'

'What did you hope to find?'

'It was really a question of making sure, that's all. But I confess I did have an initial thought that this might still be a means of access between the two communities. But I was also interested because it was the only area that no one showed us or even mentioned until Sigeric.'

They turned and began to walk back along the corridor.

Eadulf suddenly became aware of a slight noise, a scraping sound. He did not know what it was nor why he reacted as he did. He leaped suddenly to one side of the narrow passageway, shouting a warning to Fidelma who was walking in front of him. Her reactions were also quick. Jumping into a space between the pillars to one side, she pressed herself against one of them.

A moment later, something smashed onto the spot where Eadulf had been standing and splintered into a thousand fragments. One of the fragments bounced from the mosaic floor and struck him in the back of the leg. It was painful and caused him to cry out in anguish, stagger a pace and fall. There was dust and debris everywhere, choking his throat and causing him to cough and gasp for clean air. He could not breathe properly and thought he was going to pass out.

It seemed a long while but in reality it was only a matter of seconds before a silence descended and the dust began to settle.

With a sob Fidelma turned and rushed from the pillar, which had sheltered her from the falling stone, and ran into the dust and debris.

'Eadulf!' she cried as she searched wildly for him.

A figure stirred among the grey stone dust and retched. She was bending beside him, trying to wipe the dust from his eyes and mouth.

'Are you all right?' she gasped.

His lips formed a crooked smile. 'Not exactly,' he replied.

She heaved a sigh of relief as he struggled to sit up.

'Are you hurt?' she demanded in concern, noticing how he winced suddenly.

'I think I was hit by something,' he said. 'Back of the leg. A rock or something.'

Fidelma turned and saw a large piece of stone that lay near by.

'It was a miracle that you were not hit by that,' she said, indicating it.

Eadulf blinked to get the dust from his eyes as he stared at it.

'It is the head from one of the statues,' he declared in astonishment.

Fidelma glanced up to the arched alcove that seemed directly above them.

'It was the entire statue,' she corrected. 'And it nearly fell on you. Look, you can see the plinth on which it stood.'

Eadulf shuddered. 'Dangerous,' he muttered. 'Maybe we should get out before something else falls down. Those statues must be several hundred years old.'

Fidelma was examining the back of his leg.

'You have a nasty gash there. I must get you to Brother Gebicca. Can you stand?'

'I'll try. I don't think anything is broken.' Using Fidelma's arm and one hand against the wall, he rose slowly, flinching as the weight was placed on his leg.

At that moment, Brother Benevolentia appeared at the doors through which they had entered. He paused and stared at them in surprise.

'I heard the crash,' he began.

'I need help, Brother,' Fidelma declared. 'Come and help support Eadulf.'

But Brother Benevolentia was still staring at Eadulf and did not appear to hear.

'What happened . . . ?' His voice trailed off as he saw the remains of the broken statue. His eyes went up to the spot where it had once stood. Then he turned to Eadulf. 'Have you been injured, Brother?'

'We must get the wound bathed and dressed,' Fidelma instructed. 'I don't think it is serious.'

'I will support him, Sister. Leave him to me.' He took the arm of Eadulf and, supporting him, glanced back at the debris. 'It looks like one of those ancient statues of the Romans. It has stood there for six centuries at least. It was a lucky thing that its fall missed you, Brother.'

Eadulf's calf was throbbing.

'I think that is an understatement,' he replied. 'A fraction closer and I do not think I would still be in this world.'

He suddenly noticed that Fidelma was looking intently at the remains.

'You go on, Brother Benevolentia,' she said. 'Take him to Brother Gebicca. I'll be with you in a moment.'

Brother Benevolentia hesitated. 'But, Sister . . . it may be dangerous here. This is an ancient part of the building and these old statues are known to be unsafe.'

'Eadulf is bleeding and the longer you delay, the worse it gets. I said I would be but a moment!' she snapped irritably.

Brother Benevolentia was unhappy but Eadulf, realising she wanted time to look at something, began to move forward, forcing his companion to go with him.

Fidelma stood for a moment looking at the pieces that had once constituted the marble statue. Then she peered up at the empty alcove that rose ten metres above them in the great vaulted passageway. There had been five statues along each side, and now one of them was missing.

There was a movement from the mason's room behind her. She turned to find that another young, dark-headed religieux had arrived; he was looking about him with dismay.

'What happened, Sister?' he demanded.

'One of the statues fell from its plinth up there,' Fidelma replied.

'One of the old statues?' echoed the Brother, sounding shocked.

'Have they all stood in those positions a long time?'

'They have been there since the time of the Romans. They have certainly stood in perfect safety for as long as I have been here. It is strange that one of them has fallen now. Perhaps it is an evil omen.'

'The omen would have been distinctly evil had it fallen on anyone,' Fidelma replied dryly.

'Then no one was hurt?'

She did not respond but looked up at the alcoves high above her. 'Tell me, is there any way one can get up to those alcoves? They seem particularly deep and I see light from behind them as though there is a space there.'

The religieux nodded. 'Indeed there is, Sister. There is a walkway along each side behind the places where the statues stand which the stonemasons used to use. In fact, they are still used for the upkeep of the roof and other high stonework.'

'Is it easy to get access to that walkway? How would I get to it from here, say?'

'You wish to go up there?' The religieux seemed surprised.

'I do.'

He looked around as if wondering what to do, and then said: 'Very well. I can show you.'

Just behind the doors through which they had entered, Fidelma now saw a narrow open doorway that her companion pointed to. There was a small circular flight of stone steps that moved upwards as if ascending some round tower. Fidelma took a step forward and peered up. She could see light at the top of the stairwell so she ascended a step before the cautious voice of the religieux halted her.

'Do you really mean to go up, Sister?'

'That is precisely what I do mean,' she replied firmly.

'It is dangerous. After all, if that statue has fallen, it shows that the stonework can be insecure.'

'I'll chance it.'

'I should come as well, just in case of danger. Let me lead the way.'

Fidelma shrugged and allowed the young man to ascend the spiral stone stairs before her. He did so nimbly and without hesitation.

It was not long before the stairs emerged onto what appeared to be a wooden-floored gallery. There was an outer wall to one side with windows giving onto the daylight while the other side consisted of the alcoves she had seen from below, containing the large stone statues, each nearly two metres in height. One alcove was empty and it was to this that she went directly.

The gallery continued on to another stairwell and vanished beyond.

'Where does this gallery eventually lead?' she asked her companion.

'Beyond that far wooden door is the *Domus Femini*, Abbess Audofleda's section of the abbey. But it is locked.'

Fidelma examined it for a moment. 'It is not blocked up like the main doors below.'

'It is simply locked. Only the bishop has the key. And no one comes here usually.'

She turned her attention back to the alcove.

The first thing she realised was that there was no way that the statue could have fallen of its own accord. Her eyes went to the plinth, which was still fairly intact but bore signs of indentations and fresh scratchmarks where a metal lever had been employed with brute strength to create a fulcrum by which the heavy stone statue could be tipped as they were passing.

She bent down to examine the marks more carefully, and a sudden chill went through her. Her suspicion had been correct. Someone had deliberately tried to kill them.

Whether it was some intuition or a reaction born of the years in which she had carried on the profession of a *dálaigh*, something caused the hairs on the nape of her neck to rise and she lunged swiftly to one side. The instinct had been right.

She saw the young religieux suddenly beside her, tottering for a second; his hands had been held out before him, ready to push her from the alcove into the passage below. His eyes bulged as he waved his hands in a desperate effort to recover his balance, and then with a great scream of fear he toppled and fell crashing down into the debris of the statue below.

Chapter Sixteen

Brother Gebicca was shaking his head as he peered at Eadulf's leg.

'You and Sister Fidelma certainly seem to be testing my abilities in the matter of healing leg wounds,' he frowned. 'Yes – what is it?'

His last remark was addressed to Brother Benevolentia, who was standing by looking impatient.

'Am I needed further?' Benevolentia asked. 'I have things to attend to, for Bishop Ordgar.'

It was Eadulf who dismissed him for there was no further assistance that he required.

Eadulf waited while the physician bathed his leg. With the blood washed away, Brother Gebicca regarded the wound.

'A small cut and some abrasions,' he commented. 'Nothing that won't heal quickly, but there will be some bruising. How did it happen?'

'I was in the old passage of statues and one of the statues fell.'

Brother Gebicca looked surprised. 'You were in the forbidden gallery?'

'I believe that is what it is called.'

'Bishop Leodegar has forbidden the brethren to use it. Why were you there?' the physician asked. Then, as Eadulf hesitated, he said: 'No, don't tell me. Hold still while I cleanse and bind this wound.'

Heart beating fast, Fidelma went on all fours and peered over the edge of the galley to the mosaic floor below. From the position of the head of the fallen religieux, there was no need to consider whether the young man was dead or not. Voices were calling from below and two of the brethren including, she noticed with surprise, Brother Benevolentia, were below, bending over the fallen body. Fidelma pulled back quickly in case they saw her, and breathed deeply to recover from the shock of what had happened.

Then she was on her feet and moving swiftly back along the gallery. She tried not to think of the young man. She had confirmed what she had suspected and, if further confirmation had been needed, she now knew that at least one of the brethren was involved in an attempt to kill them. Then she realised that there must be others. The thought made her pause as she came to the head of the stairwell. If she went down now, she would immediately be seen. Perhaps another potential killer was among them. It suddenly occurred to her that there was also only her word that he had tried to push her to her death.

She looked around, wondering if there was a way of avoiding the noisy group of religieux who had been joined by others around the dead body below. The wooden-floored gallery continued on beyond the stairwell. She followed it and after a while came to a second stairwell. This, surely, would place her beyond the view of the corridor. She made her way carefully down and, at the bottom, emerged into part of the abbey kitchens. Fortunately, there was no one about. She moved swiftly across to a door that provided an exit into the main courtyard before the chapel, then turned and hurried towards the apothecary's house.

Eadulf was having his wound dressed when she entered. He looked relieved to see her. There was a question in his eyes but she ignored him.

'Is it serious?' she asked Brother Gebicca.

'A fraction more and the muscle might have been sliced; a little further and Brother Eadulf would have been unable to complain,' he remarked cheerfully, as he applied a poultice of mosses to ensure that the blood coagulated in healthy fashion. Then he proceeded to bind it with strips of white linen. He stood back and glanced at Eadulf. 'I don't suppose it is any use to tell you that you should rest now to allow the healing process to start?'

'I shall walk with a stick if I have to,' Eadulf declared.

'I would advise against it,' Brother Gebicca replied seriously. 'You do not want to invite further injury or the bloodflow to turn bad. Wait a few days and allow the wound to heal. As for you,' he chided Fidelma, 'you should have rested for a longer period.'

Having finished binding the wound, Brother Gebicca excused himself to go in search of a salve that he said would help if applied to the other scratches that the falling stone had caused to Eadulf's leg.

Alone, Brother Eadulf was studying Fidelma's expression. Her look told him that she knew something but would not say anything until they had complete privacy. He was about to speak but, at that moment, Brother Chilperic came bursting into the physician's room. He stared anxiously at Eadulf.

'I heard that you had been injured by a falling statue.'

'It is nothing. Just scratches.'

'I was told there was a terrible accident in the . . . where the mason works. I was on my way there when one of the brethren saw you being helped here by Brother Benevolentia.'

'That is true. A statue fell and I was hit by fragments, that is all.' Just then, another of the brethren entered, obviously in search of Brother Chilperic.

'The stonemason has been killed,' he said without preamble. 'You must come quickly!'

With a muttered word, Brother Chilperic hurried out of the room.

Eadulf turned to Fidelma in astonishment. 'Did you hear that? The stonemason has been killed!'

'I think they have found the body of the young Brother who just tried to kill me,' Fidelma responded quietly. 'This religieux saw that I was suspicious when I went to examine the place from where the statue fell. He tried to push me from the same spot. Instead he fell and broke his neck.'

'What?' Eadulf could not help the exclamation.

Just then, Brother Gebicca re-entered bearing the jar of salve he had gone to fetch.

'Did I hear you cry out in pain?' he asked.

Eadulf nodded. 'I moved too quickly,' he lied. 'A moment's thoughtlessness.'

Brother Gebicca shook his head. 'I told you to be careful, Brother.'

He held up the clay pot of ointment. 'Now, from tomorrow you will apply this to your abrasions and they should heal quickly.'

As he handed the pot to Eadulf, there was a knock on the door and Abbot Ségdae entered. He looked anxious.

'There is a report that a statue fell and that a Brother was killed. I was told Brother Eadulf was brought here. Are you both all right?'

Fidelma nodded. 'As you see, Abbot Ségdae. Eadulf was nearly caught by the falling statue and is mildly injured by fragments but certainly not killed.'

'But one of the brethren has just assured me that he has seen a body . . .'

At that moment, Brother Chilperic re-entered slightly out of breath. Brother Gebicca frowned with annoyance.

'Everyone seems to be making free of my apothecary. Is this to be the new meeting hall?' he complained.

Brother Chilperic was trying to recover his breath. 'I came to get you, Brother Gebicca,' he gasped. 'Brother Andica has been killed. Please come at once.'

'Brother Andica – the stonemason?' Brother Gebicca looked amazed. 'How did that happen?' he asked, as he turned to find his physician's bag.

'It seems that he fell from the very alcove where the statue fell,' said Brother Chilperic. He was regarding Fidelma and Eadulf somewhat suspiciously. 'Did either of you see a member of the brethren in the alcove before you left?'

Fidelma decided that in the circumstances mendacity was a better path to follow. 'Apart from Brother Benevolentia who helped Eadulf here, there was no one. Perhaps this Brother . . . ?'

'Brother Andica. He was one of our stonemasons,' replied the steward. 'Brother Eadulf was asking about him only yesterday.'

'That is true,' admitted Eadulf. 'I had just met him coming from the women's community and wondered who he was.'

'He must have gone up to the gallery to investigate why the statue fell, lost his footing and gone over the edge to his death,' suggested Fidelma.

'This is a great tragedy.' Brother Chilperic was clearly upset.

'Some of the brethren heard a cry and when they rushed into the corridor, he was lying in the debris with his neck broken by the fall.'

Brother Gebicca sniffed. It seemed a habit with him.

'*I* will say what is broken and what is not. I am the physician and no one has consulted me yet. I am finished with the Saxon Brother so I will go to have a look at Brother Andica. Rest as much as you can, Brother Eadulf. And you, Sister Fidelma, should also be resting with that leg of yours. Come, Brother Chilperic.'

Brother Chilperic gave a deep sigh. 'I thought Brother Andica was too experienced to make a mistake like that,' he said as he was leaving. 'He has been working on the roof and towers of this abbey for many years.'

'It is just sad when a young man falls to his death before he has had time to live,' Fidelma reflected.

Brother Gebicca called impatiently and the steward turned again with an apology and left.

'Another death in the abbey,' Abbot Ségdae said, 'but at least this one is clearly an accident.'

Eadulf, who had been sitting patiently, now stirred.

'Forgive me, I feel quite fatigued,' he said. 'I must go to our room and rest a while.'

At once, Abbot Ségdae was apologetic and helped Eadulf negotiate the stairs of the *hospitia* to their chamber.

After they had been left alone, Fidelma turned with some eagerness to him and told him exactly what had happened. Eadulf was horrified.

'He actually attempted to kill you?' he gasped. 'But why? What reason could there be? And why push the statue down on us in the first place?'

She looked at him sorrowfully. 'Aren't we investigating a murder?' she asked. 'If this Andica was involved, then that is reason enough. It means, also, that we are close to our quarry.'

'But why would the local stonemason be mixed up in Dabhóc's death?'

'To be honest, I cannot see the connection between Dabhóc's death and the disappearance of the women from the *Domus Femini*. All right, Sister Valretrade was on her way to meet Brother Sigeric, or Sigeric was on his way to meet her, when the body of Dabhóc was discovered. She disappeared after that. But it seems she was not the only one to do so.'

'Often, in an investigation, one gets a feeling that something is not right. One has to follow that feeling until it is explained or dismissed,'

Eadulf said, and then contradicted himself. 'Of course, intuition can also be wrong,' he added.

'Often the feeling is not intuition but the accumulation of facts in the dim recesses of the mind,' Fidelma said. 'They remain there in shadows until another fact or event causes them to fit into place. For instance, the disappearances, the behaviour of the abbess and her steward, the connection with Lady Beretrude and our friend Verbas of Peqini, Brother Andica's attempt to kill us and the missing reliquary box . . . I see the strands, but they need something to connect them all together.'

'Maybe there is no connection,' pointed out Eadulf.

'Then we must establish that and move on,' Fidelma replied. 'But how?' She suddenly groaned. '*Ron baithaigeis hí!*'

'And why do you consider yourself a great fool?' Eadulf asked, surprised.

'Lord Guntram.'

Eadulf was none the wiser and said so.

'I had forgotten about him,' Fidelma said. 'Remember, he was in the next chamber to where the murder was committed? He is also the son of Lady Beretrude. We haven't even bothered to question him.'

'From what Brother Chilperic said, he was drunk. So drunk he could not even return to his fortress that night. We were told that he had not seen or heard anything because he was in no condition to do so.'

'That's assumption, Eadulf,' Fidelma rebuked. 'You know that it is my philosophy that one must never assume facts. And I nearly fell into that error. That is why I am a fool.'

'We will have to find out where Guntram can be found.'

'Easily done.' She stood up quickly. 'Rest here and recover a while. I will be back shortly.'

Before he had time to protest, she was gone.

Eadulf limped to the adjacent wash room, removed his dusty and torn clothing and washed the dirt of the statue from his body before putting on a clean robe and stretching out on the bed.

Fidelma, meanwhile, had made her way to the *anticum*. Brother Chilperic was there. His expression was moody.

'It seems that Brother Gebicca agrees that the death was an accident,' he greeted her. 'Brother Andica must have gone to examine how the statue fell, lost his footing and plunged to his death. It is very sad. He was a patriotic Burgund and he was a very good stonemason. The Lady Beretrude will be upset when I send her word.'

Fidelma tried not to show her sudden interest; an interest that made her almost forget the point of her coming to find the steward.

'Why would Lady Beretrude be upset?' she enquired.

'Because she has employed Brother Andica to do some work on her villa. I do not think the work is finished. He has spent much time there during the last two weeks.'

Fidelma absorbed the information and then murmured some appropriate condolence about the stonemason's death before asking: 'Do you know where I might find the Gaul, Brother Budnouen?'

Brother Chilperic peered round distractedly, as if searching for the man in question.

'You have just missed him, I think. He was in the square with his wagon a moment ago. What do you . . . ?'

But Fidelma was already gone through the great doors and into the main square.

In fact, Brother Budnouen was still outside the abbey doors, tightening the straps on the harness of his mules. He face wore his usual affable grin as he saw her racing towards him.

'You look in a hurry, Sister Fidelma.'

Fidelma halted breathlessly. 'Have you made your trip to Lord Guntram's fortress yet?' she gasped. 'You said the other day that you were due to go there to do some trade.'

'Lord Guntam, is it? I thought you would want me to take you back to Nebirnum. I wouldn't blame you if you did, not after what I hear about the happenings in this dark place.'

'Please, have you been yet?' pressed Fidelma, trying to keep her impatience in check.

He shook his head. 'I go tomorrow, just after first light. Why?'

'Is his place far from here?'

'Not at all. It is ten kilometres to the south west.'

'Will you take us? Will you take Eadulf and me there and bring us back?'

Brother Budnouen's expression clearly showed that he thought her mad but he agreed anyway.

'I never refuse the offer of company on these trips,' he said. 'I depart immediately after sunrise but I do not wish to stay long at his fortress. Long enough simply to deliver my goods and collect my money. I want to be back before nightfall.'

'That would suit us well enough. Where shall we meet you?'

'Right here, in the square.'

'Then until tomorrow at sunrise,' confirmed Fidelma. She was feeling much better now. It was not just because she wanted to see if Lord Guntram could remember anything of the events of the night of the murder, but also because he was Lady Beretrude's son – and she wondered whether he could provide a key to unlocking the mystery which connected the events at the abbey.

Chapter Seventeen

After the events of the last few days it was actually pleasant to ride again on the wagon of Brother Budnouen and listen to his gossip as he guided his mule team south from Autun. The weather was pleasant; the sky blue with only a few fluffy white clouds seeming to hang unmoving high in the sky indicating there was no wind. The track moved through grassy fields dotted with grazing cattle and sheep. Before them was the dark edge of a forest. It seemed to stretch away in both directions towards the east and also to the west.

They had not left the city walls that far behind when they saw, beside the track, a stone cabin and a forge with smoke rising from the chimney-stacks. They could hear the smack of iron on hot iron before they saw a man beating at a glowing bar on his anvil while a small boy was working the bellows at the fire. As the wagon trundled past, Brother Budnouen raised his hand in greeting.

'Give you a good day, Clodomar,' he called.

The smith thrust the iron bar back into the fire and rested his hammer.

'You have not been by in many months, Brother Budnouen. Can you not stop for a cup of wine and an exchange of news?' he called.

'I am going to Lord Guntram's fortress but will try to stop on the way back later,' replied the Gaul.

The smith raised a hand in acknowledgement.

'That was Clodomar the smith. He comes from a family of smiths. His brother has a forge in the city.' Brother Budnouen jerked his thumb back to Autun. 'Clodomar has chosen a good place to do business there, for many local farmers do not want to go into the confines of the city to get their work done.'

They continued on towards the forest. As they entered its canopy, it was like moving from bright sunshine into a dank gloom.

'This seems a large forest. How far does it stretch?' asked Eadulf, interested in his surroundings.

'From this point one can ride south and east and west for many days. There are some large clearings, of course. Lord Guntram has his fortress at the head of a valley whose surrounding hills are partly denuded of trees which, in fact, were used to construct his fortress.'

'How far is this place?' asked Fidelma.

'About five kilometres now, a straight run along the track. I have made the journey many times.'

'So you know Lord Guntram well?'

Brother Budnouen laughed. '"Well" is not a word I would choose. How can a lowly transporter of goods come to know a mighty lord like Guntram, a descendant of the Burgund kings?'

'It seems several folk claim to be descendants of these Burgund kings,' commented Fidelma dryly. 'Do you know what manner of person Guntram is? We have heard one or two stories of his youth and drinking.'

'His excesses are whispered everywhere in Burgundia. He is certainly a young man overly fond of strong drink, of women, and of hunting. Beyond that, I think he cares little for anything else.'

'Then he must be a disappointment to Lady Beretrude,' commented Fidelma.

'That he is.'

'Does he interfere in religious life in Autun?'

Brother Budnouen grinned. 'He wears religion like another person wears a coat. He can put it on and as easily remove it.'

'He was staying in the abbey a week ago,' Fidelma pointed out.

'I have heard Bishop Leodegar is somehow related to him,' Brother Budnouen nodded.

'Somehow? I thought Leodegar was a Frank.'

'He is indeed. Leodegar's father was called Bobilo, of high rank at the court of King Clotaire . . .'

'King Clotaire? I thought the Frankish king was a young man,' Eadulf intervened. 'I am confused.'

'I speak of the second king of that name who ruled the Franks some forty years ago. The current King Clotaire is the third of the name to be king here. It is said that Bobilo, Leodegar's father, had a young Burgund cousin who is Lady Beretrude. I do not know what his exact relationship was, to be honest. I repeat the stories that are told. Both Leodegar's parents were of high rank – that was Bobilo and his wife Sigrada. So Leodegar is connected with the ruling families both Frank and Burgund. That is why, before he was rewarded with being bishop here, he served Queen Bathild, the mother of the current King Clotaire, at the royal court.'

'So this royal connection is what gives Bishop Leodegar his autocratic air,' Eadulf reflected. 'And gives us a reason for caution,' he added softly for Fidelma's ears only.

'We are always cautious, Eadulf,' she replied, before turning back to Brother Budnouen. 'So you think that Guntram and his mother have a good relationship with Leodegar?'

'I have heard so,' the Gaul replied, 'but, as I have also heard, Beretrude and Guntram's relationship is wanting.'

'In what way? Because of her son's style?'

'Lady Beretrude is ambitious but Guntram is indolent. As I say, he spends more time in hunting, or . . .' Brother Budnouen cast an embarrassed look towards Fidelma. 'Or certain divertissements. Good wine and ladies of easy virtue. I only tell you what is common knowledge,' he added, almost defensively.

'Sometimes common knowledge is mere speculation,' pointed out Eadulf.

'There is some truth in that, Brother Eadulf,' agreed the Gaul. 'However, in this matter it is the truth.'

They had come to the edge of a large area of grasslands that had been denuded of trees and stretched away up into a series of small hills.

'Guntram's fortress is at the head of a horseshoe valley that opens just beyond the shoulder of that hill,' Brother Budnouen said, indicating before him with one hand.

They fell silent as the wagon moved slowly forward along the track.

Hardly a moment passed before they were hailed and a young warrior on horseback came riding out from the cover of a hill to a point that intersected their route. Brother Budnouen evidently knew the man, and a few brief words of greeting were exchanged before the warrior waved them forward and then returned whence he had come.

'Just one of the sentinels that Lord Guntram maintains on the route to his fortress,' explained Brother Budnouen.

The wagon continued along the track, through the grasslands and towards the valley between the low-lying hills.

The fortress of the Lord Guntram was a curious construction made of stone and timber. High walls surrounded the buildings. Along the walls were tall turrets, presumably for sentinels. It seemed an alien construction to Fidelma. It was obvious that this type of building would never be found in her native land. It was of sharp rectangles rather than flowing curves and circles. Once inside, beyond the walls, they found a complex that surprised them. There was a large villa that compared easily to that of Lady Beretrude's Roman construction. Obviously, it must have been built by the Romans and maintained over the centuries since it had first been constructed as well as being enclosed by the fortifications.

Lord Guntram believed in security for there were young warriors at the great wooden gates and one or two pacing the walkways along the walls. Brother Budnouen seemed well known, however, for cheery smiles and cries of greeting welcomed him. As they entered into the inner court of the villa, Brother Budnouen halted his wagon and a man came forward who apparently was the *major domus* of Guntram's household.

'Greetings, Brother Budnouen,' the man said as the Gaul clambered down. 'What goods do you bring us from Nebirnum this time?'

There followed a short and rapid conversation in the language of the Burgunds, but so quick were the words spoken that Eadulf admitted he lost track of what was being said, except that he and Fidelma were mentioned a few times. The *major domus* examined them keenly for they had both climbed down from the wagon and now stood hesitantly behind Brother Budnouen.

'So you wish to speak with Lord Guntram?' he asked after a pause, his voice low in heavily accented Latin.

Fidelma answered: 'We do. Would you tell him that it concerns the events in the abbey at Autun?'

'So I understand,' the man replied with a slight nod towards Brother Budnouen. 'Come with me.'

'Once I have unloaded my wagon, I shall be waiting here for you to join me for the return journey to Autun,' Brother Budnouen called as they followed the steward into the main building.

The stone-faced *major domus* told them to wait in an antechamber while he went in search of Lord Guntram. It was a room that filled them with some amazement after the hard stone confines of the abbey. The room was lined in pink stucco plaster displaying old frescos of scenes of satyrs, a man playing pipes and of young men sporting with girls. Although their colours were fading, the pictures were quite astonishing. There were chairs before a log fire but they had barely seated themselves when the *major domus* returned.

'My lord Guntram bids you welcome and apologises for a little delay in being able to receive you. You are welcome to partake of some refreshment while you wait.'

'Your pardon.' Eadulf rose looking slightly embarrassed and anxious. 'It has been a long trip on Brother Budnouen's wagon. Would you mind if I used your *necessarium*?'

The *major domus* looked puzzled, apparently not knowing the word. Eadulf made gestures and resorted to his own language, using the word *abort*.

'Ah,' grunted the man. 'Behind the stables to the left.'

The *major domus* left Fidelma with a beaker of apple wine and some dried fruit before leaving. Eadulf was gone some time and when he re-entered, he had no time to sit down before the man returned and beckoned them into the adjacent room.

A thin-featured young man was standing before a blazing log fire, even though the late summer day was moderately warm. In spite of the sharpness of his features, his blue eyes and curly black hair were handsome, or so Fidelma thought as she studied him. It was only Guntram's jaw line and his red lips, as if he had squeezed red berry juice over them as was the custom with some of the well-born women of her own land, that displayed a certain weakness. One could see a resemblance to Lady Beretrude immediately, just as she had seen it in the features of Sister Radegund. Then she paused: surely she had seen similar features elsewhere? Beretrude, Radegund and now Guntram – but who else?

Guntram stood with his hands behind his back, feet slightly apart, his pale eyes scrutinising them. Then he glanced to the steward, who announced their names.

'I have heard that you are investigating the death of Abbot Dabhóc at the request of the bishop,' began the young man, speaking in a fluent Latin. Then he frowned. 'Autun is within my feudal domain and Bishop Leodegar did not ask my permission about this matter.'

Fidelma's eyes widened slightly in reaction but her expression did not change.

'We have no wish to impose ourselves where we are not wanted, Lord Guntram. When we arrived at Autun, our assistance was requested and presumably the Bishop Leodegar was under the impression that, as the matter was concerned with the abbey, he had a right to commission us to investigate. Are you questioning that right?'

The young man was silent for a moment.

'I am Guntram, prince of the Burgunds and lord of this land,' he said, articulating it like a prayer. 'I am the direct descendant of Gundahar, who was the first great leader of the Burgunds and who defeated the Roman general Aetius. Our lineage was ancient before the ancestors of Clovis the Frank learned to write their own name. I am the ultimate law here.'

Fidelma bowed her head gravely. 'A great prince is known by his actions and not by a recitation of his ancestors,' she replied pointedly.

Eadulf suppressed a shiver. Fidelma's forthrightness might not be wise among these Franks and Burgunds who seemed so sensitive of their ancestry and rank. He saw Guntram's eyes narrow as if in anger. Then the young man began to shake. To his astonishment, Eadulf realised that he was laughing.

'Well said, Fidelma of Cashel. I have heard of the ready wit of your people. Let me offer you refreshments from your journey and please be seated.' He clapped his hands for attention.

As if from nowhere, servants appeared and drew chairs before the fire. Trays of sweetmeats and drinks were brought for them to choose from.

'My spies have told me all about you. I have heard that you are sister to the king of your country in which women are judges and lawyers. Amazing. You are a lucky man, Eadulf of Seaxmund's Ham.'

Eadulf could think of nothing to say in rejoinder. The young man was continuing to speak.

'It is true that I am the ultimate law and true, too, that Bishop Leodegar should have consulted with me on this matter. But, then, Franks often forget to consult with Burgunds. Of course I have no objections to your investigating this tiresome matter.'

'Tiresome matter? We talk about the death of an abbot of Hibernia,' interposed Eadulf, slightly outraged by the other's nonchalant tone.

'The effects are tiresome, not the act itself,' qualified the young lord.

'In what way tiresome?' Fidelma asked.

'Tiresome in that it disturbs the tranquillity of my land and my people. That there is a council, in which representatives from many lands have come to participate, is tiresome enough. That the council brings an envoy, Nuntius Peregrinus, from Rome here is also tiresome. Then comes a murder of a foreign delegate. That will mean that Clotaire will doubtless blame me for the disturbance in tranquillity and that is even more tiresome. Our Frankish king is youthful and sensitive as to how his image appears in Rome.'

'Why would he blame you?'

'The Franks are always blaming the Burgunds and seeking ways to destroy what little power we have.'

'I am not concerned with your internal affairs but with how the abbot of my country came by his death.'

The young man looked serious. 'Then, at least, we can join in that ambition. How may I help?'

'I am told that you were in the abbey on the night that it happened.'

Guntram nodded agreement. 'Not only in the abbey but in the very next chamber to where the body was discovered.'

Fidelma felt it was a good start that the young man was honest.

'And did you see or hear anything that aroused your suspicions that night?'

The young man suddenly burst out laughing and then seemed to catch himself.

'I am sorry, Fidelma of Cashel, but in all honesty, I was in no condition to see or hear anything. You must have been told of that. Yes, the truth is that I had over-indulged myself with the fruits of Bacchus.'

'You were drunk?' pressed Eadulf.

'*Mea maxima culpa!*' declared Guntram.

'Do you remember anything at all about that evening?' Fidelma insisted.

The young man seemed to reflect for a moment.

'Well, I had gone to the city to collect my feudal dues. I maintain only a dozen bodyguards and a dozen servants to upkeep this fortress. Not a great deal but money is essential. Every new moon, I receive the *taxa*, a sum due to me for overseeing the security of my people. So I collect this sum from the *maire principalté*, the chief officer of my lands, who gathers it on my behalf. He would prefer it if he worked for my mother,' he added with a disapproving tone. 'I am sure that he does not pay me the full due but rather allows her the first access to the money and between them they pay me enough to keep me content.'

He paused, frowning as he thought about it and so Fidelma interrupted his meditation.

'I understand you had imbibed more than was good to commence the journey back here. Your mother, Lady Beretrude, has a villa in Autun. Why did you not stay there?'

Guntram sighed languidly. 'Because we had had one of our interminable quarrels.'

'About anything in particular?' queried Fidelma.

'Her favourite subject. My lack of ambition.'

'You are lord of this area, what other ambition should you have?' demanded Eadulf.

'According to my mother, I should be raising armies to avenge the death of Sigismond and Gundomar . . .' He saw their puzzled expressions and explained: 'They were kings of the Burgunds who were defeated by Clovis of the Franks.'

'Are you saying that your mother wants you to raise an insurrection against the kings of this land?' asked Fidelma.

Guntram was amused. 'And I with only twelve men-at-arms! They are more my hunting companions than an army. I am afraid my mother has notions of grandeur; notions that the Burgunds will rise again. We are no longer a powerful nation, and the first duty of a ruler of such a people is to recognise that fact; recognise the strengths and weaknesses of his people and carve their role in the world according to what they may usefully achieve. That is essential for any leader. It is no good setting out to bring destruction down upon us for the sake of the wild dreams of ancient times.'

They sat in silence for a while.

'So this was the subject of the argument that you had with your mother?' Fidelma said. 'Is it why you chose to stay at the abbey and not at her villa?'

'The abbey is always preferable to staying with my mother. Every time I stay with her I have to listen to her criticism that I am not like my father or that I am an unworthy descendant of Gundahar and the line of the Burgund kings. I would rather a monk's uncomfortable cell than a bed in her luxurious villa.'

'Did Bishop Leodegar approve of your staying in the abbey under such conditions? My understanding is that he is a man of strict views.'

'I have known Leodegar for many years. There is some ancient family connection. I know not what because he is a Frank. But he is also my confessor. I went to him to talk about my frustrations.'

'Very well. What then?'

'We dined well that night. I recall Leodegar saying that the day had been most trying in that he had had to deal with arguments between the delegates attending the council. He was exhausted. In fact, he invited me to dine away from the refectory in his private rooms where we talked, played chess and ate our fill. The wine circled well and, I confess, I over-indulged. I was too busy trying to drown my mother's accusations about my lack of ambition and how the elder son did not always merit the inheritance of office. I remember feeling extraordinarily tired and sitting back in my chair. Then I was waking in a small chamber and it was late morning. There was movement outside. That was when I discovered that the abbot from Hibernia had been killed by some of his fellow religious.'

Eadulf leaned forward. 'In what way did you discover that?'

The young man shrugged. 'From Brother Chilperic. I had slept through it all. In fact, he had carried me out of Leodegar's apartments on the previous night just as that Saxon bishop, who is now suspected of the crime, arrived. I still had a sore head and was in no condition to take it all in. I had to get a balm from Brother Gebicca, the apothecary, before I could set out on my journey here that morning.'

Eadulf was disappointed. 'So you heard and saw nothing during that night?'

Guntram shook his head. 'You have had a wasted journey here, I am afraid, if you thought I could provide some testimony about the death of this abbot. The plain truth is that I was drunk and slept throughout all these events.'

'No journey is ever wasted, Guntram,' replied Fidelma gravely.

'All you have learned is my weakness,' the young man said ruefully.

'That you have acknowledged it as a weakness is a strength,' she replied philosophically.

He raised his eyebrows momentarily in surprise. 'You should be my confessor, but I am afraid it would be an unrewarding task. I do not think I can now change my habits. My mother has told me that I will come to nothing.'

'And you believe her?'

'She is a powerful woman. In her eyes I could never succeed. My father died when I was ten years old. I was the eldest son but, try as I might, I could never be his successor. By the time I was of the age of maturity I had ceased to even try to measure up to my father in her eyes.'

'We should only try to measure ourselves against our own standards, not other people's,' Fidelma said, not unkindly. 'We are all individuals.'

'That is what my Cousin Radegund says. She was left an orphan by the plague. Rather than live with my mother, she married. Then she went into the abbey. There she remains, safe from family cares. I envy her.'

'So she married Brother Chilperic?'

Guntram pursed his lips as if he disapproved. 'Much against my mother's wishes. But then that was before Leodegar came along and changed things.'

'Is your dispute with your mother the reason why you bury yourself in this forest fastness with your companions?'

'I certainly have no wish to dwell in Autun in proximity with my mother and her acolytes. Here I am free to hunt, drink and . . .' He had the goodness to hesitate.

'I understand,' Fidelma said. 'But this is not merely an escape from your mother but an escape from your responsibilities. Being the *toisech*, a chieftain, as we would call it in my land, is a matter of responsibilities as well as the privilege of rank.'

'Responsibilities?' countered Guntram. 'What if I do not want those responsibilities?'

'You can hand over your office to someone else.' Fidelma was thinking of the customs of her own land when she said it.

Guntram was shaking his head. 'I am the eldest son. To whom should I hand over that right? I have a young brother who is a sanctimonious religious somewhere and not interested in temporal affairs. My mother even used to call him "Benignus" as a pet name. Not only does it signify well born but good and gentle. That, indeed, was his pious nature. I have not seen him in twenty years.'

'I am sorry. I forgot this custom of your people that is what you call the law of primogeniture. Personally, I think it is a bad custom.'

In her own land the eldest son did not inherit as an automatic right. The *derbhfine*, the electoral college of the family, would meet to elect whoever was to be chief or provincial king or even the High King himself. Sons did not necessarily succeed fathers. Brothers, cousins and even daughters or sisters could fulfil office.

She hesitated for a moment and then asked: 'Does your mother ever indulge in trade with merchants?'

Guntram showed his amusement at the idea.

'I doubt it. She would consider it beneath her dignity as a noble.'

'And apart from her niece, Radegund, she does not have much to do with the *Domus Femini*?'

'To be truthful, I think she hates the abbess and would rather Radegund held the office.'

Outside in the courtyard, waiting for the reappearance of Brother Budnouen, Eadulf seemed resigned.

'It appears that we are still left with the same choice again. It keeps coming back to it. Who do we believe is guilty of Dabhóc's murder – Cadfan or Ordgar? The murder of the abbot must be coincidental to these other matters about the missing women. We are asked to discover his murderer and no more.' Eadulf suddenly realised that Fidelma was not listening to him but looking around with a close scrutiny. 'What are you seeking?'

'I was just checking to see what sort of household Guntram runs here. It is true that I see only a few warriors about the place.'

'You doubted him when he said he employed no more than a dozen?' asked Eadulf, puzzled.

'In such cases I tend to doubt most people until I see proof,' she replied easily.

'Well, I also checked this out before we saw Guntram,' he confided.

'You did what?' she asked in surprise.

'That was why I made the excuse that I needed to go to the *latrina*. I took the opportunity to look around the stables. It is true that there are only a dozen horses in his stables and I have seen fewer than that number of warriors. So far as I could see, Guntram appears to be what he says he is. No great military chieftain but a young man indulging himself.'

The rumble of a wagon came to their ears and around the corner of the building appeared Brother Budnouen, guiding the team of mules.

'Have you finished here?' he greeted them as he halted the wagon.

'We may leave as soon as you wish,' Fidelma assured him, leaping nimbly into the back of the wagon while Eadulf climbed beside the loquacious Gaul.

'That is good,' replied Brother Budnouen. 'We'll be back in Autun while it is daylight. Even if we halt briefly to hear the news at Clodomar's forge.'

Fidelma saw that the back of the wagon was fairly empty. Brother Budnouen caught her examination.

'The fortress of Guntram produces little in trade goods.' He tapped a bag at his side that clinked with metal. 'I trade here in coinage for my goods.'

'A profitable trade?'

'At least my family eat. In these times, that is all one can ask for. Thanks be to God.' He flicked the reins and the wagon moved off towards the gates. A warrior came forward to swing them open and acknowledge their departure with a wave.

They moved out of the fortress and along the track through the grasslands towards the woods.

'Was your business with Lord Guntram also successful?' asked Brother Budnouen, breaking in on their silence after a while.

Fidelma glanced up from where she had been deep in thought.

'Let's just say it was fruitful,' she admitted.

Brother Budnouen seemed sensitive to the fact that she did not want to talk and so he fell silent as they entered the darkness of the forest. He kept the team at a steady pace and the earth of the track was fairly hard so that the journey was easy for the team of four mules.

It was the sound of the birds that first drew Fidelma out of her thoughts. Eadulf also had raised his head as he heard the cacophony of alarm cries and the rustle of undergrowth. A wild boar and its litter stampeded through the long grasses and across the track ahead of them. Even Brother Budnouen glanced uneasily around him at the previously quiet forest's sudden eruption into sound.

They were startled by a shout from near by and out of the undergrowth emerged the dishevelled figure of a youth. He could not even have been twenty years old. He held a sword in his hand but did not appear to have an aggressive intent towards them. With the other hand he was frantically waving as if to attract their attention. In spite of his torn and mud-splattered clothing, and a cut above the eye that was bleeding, the man was, or had been, well dressed. He wore a gold chain of office around his neck.

Brother Budnouen exclaimed and began to check the forward momentum of the wagon.

'Don't stop! Don't stop!' cried the young man in Frankish, clambering on the back of the still-moving wagon with the agility of a young athlete. 'For God's sake, whip up your team!'

Chapter Eighteen

The dishevelled figure of the young man had leaped onto the back of the wagon, rolled over and lay gasping at the sky for a moment or two to recover his breath. He was quite handsome in a saturnine way, with his dark eyes, black hair and the dark-blue hint on his clean-shaved jowl. For a moment he regarded Fidelma, for she was seated in the back of the wagon, before rising and moving towards the driver's seat where Brother Budnouen, with Eadulf seated beside him, held the reins. Already the Gaul was urging the four mules into a fast trot.

The newcomer spoke rapidly to Brother Budnouen in the language of the Franks and then turned and said something to Fidelma. When he saw her frowning, he switched to Latin.

'Forgive me startling you, Sister, but I am pursued. Robbers. They shot down my servant – an arrow in the heart, poor devil. I turned to flee and they brought down my horse – confound their impudence! But they are close on my heels.'

He glanced back into the forest before addressing Brother Budnouen. 'Can you get more speed from your team, Brother?'

'I'll try my best, Sire,' replied Brother Budnouen, obviously recognising this young man.

'Sire?' Fidelma queried the style of address.

'I am Clotaire, ruler of this realm,' explained the young man.

Fidelma and Eadulf had no time to react to this news as Brother Budnouen had whipped up the mules and they had to hang on to the swaying wagon for balance as it surged forward. Fidelma could not believe the usually plodding animals could move so fast.

'There is a fork coming up on the track ahead,' yelled the young man. 'Take the right-hand path. God willing, we should soon meet some of my guards.'

Brother Budnouen, bending over the reins, merely grunted.

The wagon careered round onto the right-hand fork almost on two wheels. For a moment Eadulf thought it must overturn. They all clung on fiercely but, with a thump, it pitched back on its four wheels again and they were speeding down a dark avenue of trees. Eadulf later admitted that he had never seen a mule team moving so fast. But mules are not as fast as horses. The warning came from Clotaire.

'They're gaining!' he roared, glancing over his shoulder.

Some way behind them, half a dozen horsemen had emerged from the cover of the trees and were racing after them, heads down close to the arching necks of their steeds. To Fidelma's expert eye, she could see that the pursuers were trained horsemen.

'Let's hope your guards are not too far ahead,' cried Eadulf apprehensively.

'Your prayers in that direction would be appreciated, Brother,' Clotaire responded grimly.

Then he unslung a hunting horn from his side and blew several long blasts on it. A moment later, he turned to Fidelma. 'Sister, I would advise you to get down in the wagon and find better cover. They have bowmen with them and at the moment you present a good target.'

Fidelma did not need any further explanation. She lowered herself just below the driver's box where Clotaire also sheltered. She was about to suggest that Eadulf follow her example when it happened.

There was a whistling sound and Brother Budnouen gave a startled cry. It all seemed to happen in slow motion. Brother Budnouen was still sitting on the driver's box in absolute stillness, like a statue. Then blood began trickling from his mouth and down his chin and, as Fidelma's gaze followed the stream of blood, she saw that an arrow head and part of a shaft were sticking out from where Budnouen's Adam's apple would have been, while the remainder of the arrow protruded from the back of his neck.

Then, with the reins dropping from his nerveless hands, Brother Budnouen slipped slowly sideways and pitched from the bouncing wagon.

The way Eadulf seized the reins and recovered the momentum, moving into the seat that the unfortunate Brother Budnouen had occupied only a split second before, startled even Fidelma. He had moved so quickly that he had grasped the reins even before the Gaul had fallen from the wagon.

'Keep down!' cried Clotaire. 'Damn them to hell! Someone will pay for this outrage!'

Fidelma pushed down into the wagon to try to make herself as small a target for the bowman as possible.

'Let us hope we survive to see it,' she muttered.

Clotaire gave a sardonic laugh. 'Well said, Sister.'

He glanced up at Eadulf, who had slid down in the driver's seat so that he had the backboard as a protection, nodded his approval and said grimly, 'Damned thieves. They *will* pay.'

Two more arrows whistled in the air and thudded in the board of the driver's seat just above them.

Once more, Clotaire blew several urgent blasts on his hunting horn.

Fidelma could not help but say: 'Thieves they might be, but that bowman is exceptional. To deliver those shots from a galloping horse is not a skill you will find in most robber bands.'

Clotaire stared at her, a thoughtful look coming over his features.

'You know something of these things, Sister?'

'I know a little,' confessed Fidelma.

The horsemen were getting close now, and within a few more seconds would overtake the straining mule team.

Then Eadulf gave a sudden shout. 'Riders in front of us!' he cried.

Fidelma saw the leading pursuers suddenly hauling their horses to a standstill and trying to turn back. There were a few moments of confusion before they were galloping away.

Clotaire stood up in the wagon as nearly fifty riders streamed around.

'Brother,' he shouted to Eadulf. 'You can halt now.' Then he turned to the leader of the newcomers, shouting instructions in his own language.

The leader raised a hand and waved to his followers, after which they set off in pursuit of the robbers, leaving a group of twenty warriors behind as guards.

The young man next addressed three warriors that he had picked out. As they moved off in turn, Clotaire turned to Fidelma and Eadulf, a sombre look on his face.

'I have sent them along the path to find your companion. I've told them to see what can be done for him. If nothing, to bring his body back here and with all reverence. He gave his life in saving mine. Now, I thank you for your timely assistance. I am sorry that it has caused the loss of your companion, Sister . . . ? You are a Sister of the Faith, are you not?' He continued to speak in a fluent Latin.

Fidelma bowed her head with gravity.

'I am Sister Fidelma of Hibernia. This is Brother Eadulf. The man who was slain, for I have little hope that he lives from such a wound, was a Gaul named Brother Budnouen.'

The names had a surprising effect on the young king. A look of incredulity formed on his face.

'Fidelma of Hibernia? Fidelma of Cashel? Eadulf her companion? Are you Fidelma the famous lawyer and sister to the King of Mew-in?' It was a good attempt to try to pronounce the name of Muman.

Fidelma exchanged a surprised glance with Eadulf.

'I am of Cashel, which is the capital of my brother, Colgú, the king. And I am a *dálaigh*, that is an advocate of the law of my country,' she replied.

The young man seemed pleased. 'Then your reputation precedes you at my court, where many of your countrymen have come as teachers and advisers to my people. They speak highly of your deeds.'

Fidelma was almost lost for words. 'They flatter me. But it is providential that we happened to be passing through this forest.'

'Were you on your way to Autun?'

'We were returning there from Guntram's fortress.'

The young King sighed. 'We have been hunting in the south and were on our way to pay an unexpected call on Lord Guntram. Then I must make an appearance at this council in Autun. Are you also attending the council?

I didn't think that old Bishop Leodegar approved of women expressing their views.' He grinned broadly at her.

'You have not been told that the council has not yet begun its deliberations?' Fidelma asked. 'Or of the murders there?'

Clotaire frowned. 'I have learned that a foreign abbot was killed – but that was a week ago. Is there still danger there?'

'I would certainly advise caution,' confirmed Fidelma.

The three warriors now returned with the body of Brother Budnouen. As Fidelma had surmised, with such a wound he had probably been dead before his body hit the ground.

Clotaire stared down compassionately at the man.

'If there is anything I can do,' he said, 'anyone to notify . . . ?'

'We barely knew him,' Fidelma confessed. 'He transported us from Nebirnum on our journey to Autun. And then from Autun to see Lord Guntram. I think we will have to leave this matter in the hands of Bishop Leodegar who will probably have information on Budnouen and his family.'

The young King gave a half-nod and ordered the body to be placed in the back of the wagon. Then he said: 'My men and I were planning to take advantage of Guntram's hospitality for this night at least before coming to the city. Do you think that is a wise course?'

She was about to reply when they were interrupted by the sound of more horses. It was the main body of warriors returning. Their leader, an elderly man, rode at their head. He called out something.

Clotaire translated. 'They have all been killed.'

'All dead?' she demanded. 'No one spared? A pity.'

The elderly leader stared at her for a moment, startled.

'A pity that robbers are dead?' he retorted in Latin. 'You cry pity for those who would kill our King? Do you know in whose company you are, woman?'

'I say it is a pity, because dead men cannot give us information,' replied Fidelma coldly.

Clotaire grinned at the irritated man on horseback.

'She has a good point, Ebroin. By the way, this is Fidelma, sister of King Colgú of Cashel,' he explained. 'She is the famous lawyer of Hibernia. Fidelma. this is Ebroin, my adviser and chancellor. Oh, and this is Brother

Eadulf, of whom you may also have heard in connection with the deeds of Fidelma of Cashel.'

Ebroin looked slightly less irritated.

'Your pardon, Lady Fidelma. However, I am at a loss to understand your meaning. Why would highway robbers have anything useful to tell us?'

'She does not think that they were robbers at all but professional warriors,' Clotaire said slyly. 'Am I right?'

Ebroin regarded Fidelma with a frown.

'I confess that they were well armed and defended themselves with the bearing of trained men, but there is nothing of significance to say they are not robbers. Many former warriors turn to robbery on the highways. My men are searching the bodies now to see if there is anything that might identify them.'

'Is this something to do with the affair at the abbey?' Clotaire asked.

'Perhaps we could rest somewhere more comfortable and then discuss what we must do next, Imperator,' Fidelma suggested, using the respectful form of address for the King.

'There is a woodsman's cabin a short way back along the track,' pointed out Clotaire. 'Let us go there.'

'It will be as you say, Majesty,' Ebroin replied. Turning in his saddle, he instructed some of the warriors to ride forward to secure the woodsman's cabin and signalled the others to form a circle around them.

'Come, ride with me, Fidelma,' cried the young King. He signalled two of his men to dismount, hand their horses to Fidelma and himself, and take charge of the wagon, into which the body of Brother Budnouen was carefully laid. 'Tell me, Fidelma of Cashel, are the stories that your countrymen tell about you true?'

The barrage of questions from the young man embarrassed Fidelma.

Riding behind them in the wagon, Eadulf felt a growing irritation. Almost from the first he had been ignored, but he remained silent. He accepted that his rank was of little consequence compared to Fidelma, as sister of a king, in the eyes of Clotaire. He noticed that Ebroin, the elderly adviser to the young King of Austrasia, rode behind them in silence but also with a suspicious countenance.

They soon reached the cabin, to be welcomed by a warm fire and subservient hospitality by the woodsman and his wife.

Before the fire, and with mulled ale to help the story along, Fidelma repeated the main details of what had happened in Autun. She left out her suspicions and merely put forward the basic facts.

'Do you think there is a danger to our King?' Ebroin leaned forward in his chair, fixing Fidelma with a sharp interrogative gaze. 'I have never liked Bishop Leodegar. He was very close to Clotaire's mother when he was at court, which is not to my liking.'

'I cannot say for certain who is behind these matters,' confessed Fidelma. 'However, Leodegar seems to govern the abbey quite firmly and has fixed ideas. I must investigate further before I can point the finger of accusation or fully explain the deaths at Autun.'

Ebroin made a curious spitting gesture.

'Pah! A few minutes with one of my men and a sharp knife and we would get the truth from any man. I have always been suspicious of Leodegar.'

Fidelma looked shocked at his suggestion.

'I am uncertain of the ways of your country, Ebroin, but in my country we calmly investigate and when we find evidence, *then* we accuse the person concerned. They are then given a chance to defend themselves. Confession born of pain and fear is no confession at all but merely a cry for the pain to end.'

Clotaire was looking worried. 'There is a truth in what you say, Fidelma, but if there is danger in Autun . . .'

Ebroin too looked concerned. 'Do you know if the Nuntius from Rome is still there?' When Fidelma nodded, he shook his head. 'Rome expects you to attend, Majesty. You are to endorse the decisions made at Autun and, in return, the Holy Father will recognise your title as Emperor of all the Franks.'

'How will we know if there might be danger from Leodegar?' asked the young King.

'Might be?' muttered Ebroin. 'I remember when your father, Clovis, died and your mother, Balthild, found the regency thrust on her. Didn't your mother seek advice from Leodegar because he had been raised at the royal court due to the high rank of his parents? He had a taste for power then. Perhaps he enjoyed it too much to part with it.'

'But he was instrumental in educating me and my brothers,' Clotaire pointed out.

'He persuaded us to enter into a thankless war with the Lombards – and we saw the defeat of our armies by Grimuald of Benevento,' argued Ebroin. 'Shame on our arms! We are now hard pressed to defend our very borders from the vengeful Lombards.'

'That was why my mother sent him away from the court.'

'Aye, to be bishop at Autun,' Ebroin grumbled. 'And now what grief is he stirring up in Autun?'

Fidelma cleared her throat noisily to interrupt them, but before she could speak, one of the warriors came in, holding something in his hand.

'This was the only thing of interest we found on one of the bodies of the robbers, Imperator.' He held it out. It was an emblem of sorts – a bronze circle in whose centre was a jagged saltire cross.

'I have seen that design before,' ventured Fidelma, trying to remember where. 'What is it?'

Ebroin glanced at it and shrugged.

'Nothing of significance in this part of the world. It is the cross of Benignus, much favoured by the Burgunds. You would see it in many places.'

'It is a Burgund symbol?' pressed Fidelma.

'Of course. It was used on the shields of their kings before they accepted the rule of the Franks.'

Fidelma gave a soft sigh and Clotaire met her gaze expectantly.

'Does this mean something to you, Fidelma?'

'It might mean a conspiracy against you, Imperator,' she said. 'But I cannot be definite.'

'So what are you suggesting we do?'

'I suggest that Eadulf and I return to the abbey. It will allow me to bring to a conclusion some lines of investigation that I need to follow.'

'I am against it!' snapped Ebroin. 'It may give warning to whoever is behind—'

'Behind what, exactly?' Clotaire interrupted. 'We do not know. And what is your suggestion, Ebroin?'

'Ride down on Autun, seek out the conspirators harboured by Leodegar and burn them as rebels to teach the city a lesson.'

Fidelma forced herself to laugh. It was an unnatural laugh and sounded hollow, but it was the only way she could express her disapproval of Ebroin's attitudes with sufficient force. She had the young King's attention again.

'What use would that be?' she demanded. 'To seize hapless people who may or may not be guilty of a crime. Do you want to leave a legacy among your people as a tyrant? That would be one of the easiest ways. But if you want to be hailed as a king who is concerned with justice, then allow us to find the guilty first before you punish a city indiscriminately.'

Ebroin snorted in disgust but Clotaire held up his hand to silence any further comment.

'As I have said, I have spoken with teachers from your land and they have told me of your system of law and justice. It would be my wish to emulate it one day.' He turned to Ebroin. 'You have been a good mentor, my friend. I fear you do not yet deem me adult enough for the decisions that I must make as King. However, old friend, in this matter, I know what I should do. That is to listen to the wise advice of this princess from Hibernia.'

Ebroin started to say something and then shrugged as if resigned to his master's wishes. The young man turned to Fidelma.

'What is it that you propose we should do?'

'Is there any reason why you should not delay here for a few days? You say you had a plan to stay with Lord Guntram. Do so. When I am ready, I can send you word to come to the abbey. Indeed, perhaps I might need the support of your warriors.'

'I have only fifty fighting men with me but they are my best guards.'

'But if there is rebellion brewing, we will need more men,' Ebroin said.

'Someone can ride back to my palace and bring more men-at-arms if needed.' Clotaire dismissed the objection.

'What about Guntram?' demanded Ebroin of Fidelma. 'Is he part of whatever this conspiracy is?'

'I do not think the problem will come from Guntram,' Fidelma assured him. 'And he has only a dozen men at his hunting lodge. In fact, my suggestion is that you and your men continue on to Guntram's lodge, as you had planned. Stay there until I send for you. The presence of your warriors will also keep Guntram in order, if I am mistaken about him. But I believe that he does not care for much else besides his comforts. No, the danger will be in Autun itself.'

'But how long do you expect us to remain at Guntram's fortress?' queried Clotaire.

'No more than a few days. I think I am very close to uncovering the main culprits, for there have been attempts on our lives already. That is a sure sign that we are near to the answers to this riddle.'

'Then surely it is dangerous for you and Eadulf to return to Autun?'

'It would be more dangerous for you if we did not. One or other of us will bring you word when you should enter the city.'

CHAPTER NINETEEN

It was Eadulf who drove the wagon back to Autun. It was a slow and sombre journey, undertaken in silence for the greater part. The body of Brother Budnouen was wrapped in a blanket in the back of the wagon. Fidelma sat thoughtfully at Eadulf's side, seemingly lost in her own world until they came to the great paved square in front of the abbey. Leaving the wagon tethered outside, they went in search of Brother Chilperic. The young steward was shocked when Fidelma told him of Brother Budnouen's death.

She left out all references to Clotaire and Ebroin and their men, simply saying that they had been chased by robbers who had killed Brother Budnouen but had finally abandoned the chase. She did not see it as a lie but a matter of being frugal with the facts.

'You were lucky to escape in that slow old wagon with a mule team,' Brother Chilperic commented, and then added unctuously, 'but poor Brother Budnouen . . . *requiescat in pace*.'

'Can you contact his family to give them the sad news?'

'I believe so. Bishop Arigius at Nebirnum would know about such things. Brother Budnouen was due to leave here shortly for the return journey there. We will have to find a volunteer to return the wagon and his trade goods there. We will bury our poor Brother here in the abbey grounds.'

They were about to turn away when Brother Chilperic said: 'The bishop has been asking where you were. He wishes to see you urgently.'

Bishop Leodegar scowled as the couple entered his chamber.

'Sister Fidelma, I have been asking for you. Where have you been?'

'To see Lord Guntram. Brother Budnouen is dead. He was driving us back when we were attacked by robbers. He was killed but we escaped,' she replied tersely. 'We brought his body back. Brother Chilperic is attending to matters.'

'Brother Budnouen was a good friend to this abbey,' the bishop declared, showing sorrow and astonishment at the news.

'He was certainly a friend to us,' she replied.

'Death seems to follow your footsteps, Fidelma of Cashel,' muttered the bishop.

'When investigating unnatural death, one often finds more violent death.'

'Days have passed and you have still not come back to me with a decision on whether Cadfan or Ordgar killed Abbot Dabhóc. Even the Nuntius Peregrinus grows impatient. What is your decision?'

'You will be the first person to hear it when I make it,' Fidelma replied.

'You refuse to give a decision on the matter?' Bishop Leodegar asked ominously.

'I did not say that,' snapped Fidelma. 'I have said that I require more time. There is more to this matter than asking me to make a simple toss of the dice.'

'I have been very patient with you, Fidelma of Cashel.' The bishop's voice was heavy. 'I acceded to the request of Abbot Ségdae who said you were a great lawyer in your land. I overlooked the fact that you are a woman and that your culture has refused to accept the celibacy that we, in this abbey, have decided upon. I allowed you to stay here in the abbey with your . . . your companion, Eadulf. All these things I accepted, even giving you authority to do as you would under your own laws and system. All I asked in return was a quick decision on the murder so that the council could meet and progress those matters that have to be discussed so that the decisions can be sent to Rome. What has happened?'

When Fidelma drew herself up, Eadulf hoped that she would not lose her temper against the bishop's tirade, but she spoke coolly and carefully.

'What has happened, Bishop Leodegar of Autun – *what has happened* is that more deaths have occurred in this abbey and that attempts have been made on our lives.'

'More deaths?' sneered the bishop. 'Do you speak of the Hibernian monk Gillucán, Brother Andica, and now of the Gaul Brother Budnouen? How can they be related to the abbot's murder? The Hibernian monk was killed and robbed after leaving this abbey. Brother Andica, a stonemason, fell in an accident. Now you say Brother Budnouen was killed by robbers. As for the attempt on your life . . . are you saying that the statue fell by design? It was an accident and you were in a place that I have forbidden even the brethren to go to because of the dangers of the ancient masonry. That has nothing to do with the murder of Abbot Dabhóc! Come, this is prevarication.'

Fidelma met his eyes with grim determination.

'You seem to know more than I do. If you do, then the decision is your own to make and I wash my hands of it. I will inform Nuntius Peregrinus that you want to make the decision yourself.'

Bishop Leodegar hesitated, his lips compressed for a moment.

'I need a decision from *you*,' he repeated.

'I shall not be rushed into a judgement before I have assured myself that I have all the facts,' replied Fidelma stubbornly, whilst realising that she might push the bishop into removing her and Eadulf from the investigation.

Bishop Leodegar seemed to be struggling to control his anger.

'I will tell you what I shall do. I shall compromise.' He gave a tight smile. 'In two days from now, we celebrate the feast day of the Blessed Martial of Augustoritum who brought the Faith to the Lemovices. If you are not willing to resolve this matter by then, I shall pronounce on the case myself so that we may go forward upon Rome's business.'

Fidelma gazed into the dark eyes of the bishop. She knew that she was facing an immovable object.

'Then two days hence it shall be.' She muttered to Eadulf: 'Let us waste no further time here.' Without another word, she turned on her heel and left the room.

Outside, he gave her a look of gentle remonstrance.

'Isn't a little diplomacy a better way of securing what is needed?' he asked.

Her angry frown disappeared and her features softened.

'You tell me what diplomacy can be used against such a man as Bishop

Leodegar and I will pursue it,' she tried to joke. 'Besides, let us not think that Leodegar plays absolutely no part in these events. He seems a close friend of Beretrude, not to mention of Abbess Audofleda – both of whom have some culpability in these affairs.'

'Do you really think there is a conspiracy here to assassinate Clotaire when he arrives?' asked Eadulf. 'I cannot see the connection. And what of the disappearance of not only Valretrade but all the married religieuse and their children from the *Domus Femini*?'

'They are being kidnapped to be sold as slaves.'

Eadulf had suspected as much but had not wished to believe it.

'But with the approval of the abbess and the others?' He made it into a protest.

When Fidelma made no reply, he asked: 'And how can it be linked with Abbot Dabhóc's murder?'

'I need some proof to support my suspicion.'

'You think you know who is guilty?'

'I *suspect*. That is not the same thing. I need proof.'

Eadulf shook his head in bewilderment. 'We have run out of time.'

They fell in step and Fidelma guided him back towards the main entrance of the abbey.

'As we cannot progress logically,' she told him, 'our next step is to create a catharsis – an action by which the enemy will react in such a way that they give themselves away.'

Eadulf halted in mid-stride.

'What are you suggesting?' he demanded with a frown. 'I fear it is something dangerous.'

'I am not sure yet what I am suggesting. First I am going to change into some simple garments so that I will not be noticed. Then I want to have a close look at Beretrude's villa. The answer is there, perhaps in that cellar room where you saw Verbas of Peqini take the prisoners.'

Eadulf was horrified. 'I . . . I forbid it. Absolutely! You know Verbas is there. You believe the affair of the poisonous snake was deliberate. If anyone goes to examine the villa, it must be me.'

'I have a plan,' she replied. 'It needs you to remain here.'

'And am I to know what your plan is?'

'Do you remember that Brother Budnouen pointed out that seamstress shop not far from Beretrude's villa? I shall get some local clothes there. I'll disguise myself and then do what we call *cúartugad* – a reconnoitre.'

'But we saw Sister Radegund go into that very seamstress,' Eadulf reminded her. 'It is too dangerous. What do you hope to find, anyway?'

'I am not sure. I have to keep an open mind – that is why I, not you, must go. I want to explore the place where you saw Verbas of Peqini bring in the manacled women and the child. Perhaps these women are being held there. If not, I must find out where Verbas is. He is not merely a merchant. I believe he trades in slaves and Beretrude is involved with this.'

'I still don't see how it connects with Abbot Dabhóc's murder.'

'Poor Brother Gillucán supplied us with the connection. Think about it. But first things first. We have little time.'

'Time? We have only two days. Two days and Leodegar will make his announcement,' muttered Eadulf moodily.

'Then we must push events towards a rapid conclusion.'

'You cannot go on your own,' Eadulf insisted.

'One person can go where two can't. A local woman wandering around the streets near the villa might pass unnoticed but a man and a woman would not. Besides, you must remain here in case I fail to return. In that case, find Ségdae and let him know everything you can. It will then be up to him. There is also a question you must ask Ségdae that has been troubling me. Unfortunately, there is no time to find him now.'

'What question?'

'Benén mac Sesenén of Midhe, Patrick's comarb, whose name is on that missing reliquary – I am sure that he also adopted a Latin name but it eludes me. I need you to find out. I think it will tell us much.'

'I will do so,' Eadulf replied. 'I am still worried about you going. Anything could happen to you, alone in the dark and—'

'I don't intend to go in the dark,' replied Fidelma confidently. 'I intend to go now, while it is still daylight. I hope to be back before dark. Don't worry. I *will* be back. That's a promise.'

Eadulf was about to protest again but she had turned and was gone.

* * *

Fidelma left the abbey and walked quickly across the great square, down the series of streets with which she was now familiar. In this part of the city, away from the main commercial centre, there were few people about and only one or two riders on horseback. An occasional wagon trundled by, passing through the narrow thoroughfares. Those people who passed gave her a courteous nod or muttered a greeting.

It was not long before she turned into the broad street that she knew led to the Square of Benignus and Lady Beretrude's villa. On the top right-hand side of the street was the shop which sold dresses and other garments. The place was easy to find. She was confident that she could obtain some local clothes here with which to disguise herself. Clothes were hanging up, presumably ready for sale, dresses, scarves, skirts, cloaks, all manner of items. Fidelma hesitated on the doorstep and peered into the darkness behind. An elderly woman rose from her chair, laying aside a garment, and said something to her in the guttural language of the Burgunds. Fidelma presumed it was a greeting or merely a question of what she wanted.

'Do you speak Latin?' she asked.

It was the old woman's turn to look puzzled.

Fidelma tried her basic Saxon with similar results. Then she pointed to some hanging garments.

'I want to buy some clothes,' she said slowly.

The old woman stared at her, looking her up and down with curiosity, for although her clothing was not that of the religieuse of the abbey, she wore her crucifix, and the manner of her robes indicated she was a religieuse.

Fidelma realised that communication was going to be difficult. Again she pointed to a dress which she considered might be useful and raised her eyebrows in interrogation.

'How much?' She used Saxon again, thinking the simple words were probably the same.

The old woman held up her hand, one finger raised as if in admonishment before turning to a door at the back of the room and calling to someone inside.

There was a movement and a young religieuse came in.

Although they had only met in darkness by the light of the candle, Fidelma recognised the girl at the same time that she recognised Fidelma.

'Sister Inginde. I did not know you were allowed to leave the *Domus Femini*?'

The young girl regarded her in surprise for a moment or two and then her features re-formed in a smile of greeting.

'Sister Fidelma! This is my aunt. I was given special permission to visit her, as she has not been well lately.'

'Indeed?'

'What brings you here, Sister Fidelma? Have you news of Valretrade?'

Fidelma decided to answer the second question first.

'I have no news but I have not given up. And, as a matter of fact, I came here to buy some clothes.'

Sister Inginde looked puzzled. 'My aunt does not generally make clothes for the religious, although she does some mending for us.'

'It is not religious clothes I want,' replied Fidelma. 'I want something in which I can move freely about the city so that none may know my true identity.'

The girl regarded her curiously.

'I need some simple clothing that may help me pass without comment in a place where I can find out some necessary information,' Fidelma explained further.

'Then by all means, we must help you.' Inginde spoke rapidly to her aunt. The old woman regarded Fidelma critically. Then she said a few words. Sister Inginde nodded as if in agreement. 'My aunt says that you should not wear colours that are too bright. Your hair is red and that is bright enough. She advises some sombre colours, a dress, and a cloak with a hood to cover your hair.'

The old woman took a drab brown dress from a peg and held it against Fidelma's body.

'My aunt thinks that it is your size,' explained the young woman.

Some more items of clothing were chosen and Fidelma was able to change into them, using a scarf and hood to disguise her red hair and fair skin.

Sister Inginde looked on with approval.

'There, you may wander the streets of the city freely without exciting interest.'

Fidelma regarded her reflection in the mirror that the elder woman held before her.

'It will do,' she conceded. She had kept her cross under her clothing and she pointed to her *ciorbolg*, her comb bag that contained some toilet articles that all the women of her country used. 'I will take that with me but leave my clothes and pick them up when I have done.'

'Where are you going?' Sister Inginde asked curiously.

'Better if you did not know,' replied Fidelma.

The young woman seemed concerned. 'Perhaps I can help,' she pressed.

Fidelma shook her head. 'You will surely be expected back at the *Domus Femini*. How much do I owe your aunt for the clothing?'

The girl spoke rapidly to the old woman.

'My aunt says that there is no payment since you are helping to find a friend of mine. She will keep your own clothes here until your return.'

Fidelma thanked them both and left the shop, proceeding with a leisurely gait, head bent forward a little, as she had seen the women in the city do, and headed down the street in the direction of Lady Beretrude's villa.

Two or three people passed with a nod or called out a greeting in the local tongue that Fidelma could now recognise and could respond to. She began to feel easy in her disguise.

At the Square of Benignus, she looked beyond the splashing fountain to the gates of the villa. The symbol on the stone pillars on each side of the gates reinforced her suspicion. The single sentinel stood there as usual. Fidelma walked slowly across the square, trying to maintain her leisurely pace as if she were heading for the side street that skirted the high wall of the villa.

The street seemed deserted – but then she heard the sound of running footsteps across the square. A man's voice called out in challenge. Then the gate was opened and some voices were raised. She stood still for a few moments but no one appeared, no one followed her. After a while she began to walk along the entire length of the villa's outer wall. At one point she noticed an iron-barred gate, set in an arched entrance in the wall. It must have been through here that Verbas brought his charges when they disturbed Eadulf. Glancing round quickly, she tested that it was locked, before continuing on. With the gate locked, there seemed no way through or over the outer wall into the grounds of the villa without being seen.

She was beginning to think that her plan to reconnoitre the villa was not going to be a success – certainly not unless she could get inside. There was no way to sneak into the villa, and even if she could persuade one of the servants to let her in, what language could she use to communicate with them? Having decided to walk round the villa and return along the other side, she soon reached the narrow alley at the back. Here she hoped to find another means of entrance, so that she could double back to the place where Eadulf had seen Verbas taking his prisoners. However, there was nothing – no gate, not even a place where one might scale the wall.

As she came to the end of the path, she was aware of menacing shadows on either side of the exit. Several men suddenly launched themselves at her. As she turned to attempt to flee, there was a moment of pain at the back of her skull and then everything went black.

Eadulf was pacing the *calefactorium*, pausing every now and then to glance up at the darkening sky.

Abbot Ségdae had been talking to one of his delegation and now finally turned to address Eadulf.

'Brother Eadulf, is something troubling you? I swear that if you continue to pace with such vigour, you will wear a groove in the stones beneath your feet.'

Eadulf paused in mid-stride.

'It is Fidelma,' he said in a low voice. 'The hour is growing late and she has not returned to the abbey.'

'She has a will of her own, as you well know, my son,' Abbot Ségdae pointed out. 'Is there a reason why she should have returned at this time?'

'I fear that something might have happened to her,' Eadulf murmured, leaning forward. 'She left the abbey this afternoon to go to see the Lady Beretrude. Well, not exactly to see her but to look over her villa without being observed.'

The abbot looked astonished. 'Why should she do that?'

Eadulf wondered how much he should confide in the abbot. However, he realised that he needed an ally if Fidelma had been incapacitated.

'The fact is, she believes that Beretrude is somehow connected with these deaths here and with some other matters affecting this abbey.'

Abbot Ségdae continued to look astounded.

'I do not understand. How could Lady Beretrude have been responsible for the death of Abbot Dabhóc when . . .'

Eadulf himself was uncertain of Fidelma's logic so he decided to use the facts that the abbot would appreciate.

'Do you recall how we had an encounter at Tara with a foreign merchant named Verbas of Peqini, a slave owner? Well, that man is here and at Lady Beretrude's villa. He swore that he would have revenge on Fidelma one day. If he has encountered her . . .'

Abbot Ségdae knew Eadulf well enough to know that he was not given to unnecessary alarms.

'When was Fidelma supposed to return here?'

'She said her visit would not take long and that she would be back before nightfall.'

'The sky is only just darkening,' Abbot Ségdae said.

'I am still fearful. The sun is below the rooftops and she has not returned.'

'We must not act precipitately,' advised the abbot. 'I think it very unwise of Fidelma to have gone out alone.' His voice held a tone of accusation in it.

'Do you not think that I am accusing myself of folly in letting her go?' Eadulf cried. 'I should have insisted on going with her.'

Abbot Ségdae laid a hand on Eadulf's shoulder.

'*Aequam memento rebus in arduis servare mentem*,' he said kindly, advising Eadulf to keep calm in the difficulty.

'We must act,' Eadulf fretted. 'I promised her that I would remain in the abbey so that I could summon help from a friend, if need be. But I don't want to leave here without someone knowing what is happening.'

'Let us wait until the sky has fully darkened, my son. Then you must do what you have to, but I will go to Bishop Leodegar and demand that he accompany me to Lady Beretrude's villa.'

'Every moment that passes I feel she is in danger,' protested Eadulf in anguish.

'Calmly, Brother. We will succeed with calmness,' replied the abbot gently.

Chapter Twenty

When Fidelma swam through the black mist that had engulfed her into consciousness, she found a young woman bending over her. There was a concerned look in her pale blue eyes. She had apparently been dabbing at Fidelma's forehead with a damp cloth. Fidelma blinked and felt an ache on the back of her head. Her mouth was almost painfully dry. She tried to sit up and groaned immediately, feeling nauseous.

The young woman held out a cup and spoke in the local language. Fidelma could guess what she was saying and took a sip or two, resisting the urge to swallow mouthfuls. The water was cold and almost sweet. She closed her eyes in appreciation for a moment.

Glancing round, she found she was lying on straw in a corner of a gloomy, vault-like room. There was only one exit, a door approached by four broad stone steps. There was a small window at one side, high up in the wall, but outside it was dark. A few candles provided a flickering, shadowy light. Becoming conscious of murmurs and the higher-pitched tones of children, she tried to struggle up and the young woman bent forward to place an arm behind her shoulders to help her sit. She spoke again but Fidelma could not understand what she said.

'Latin,' Fidelma muttered. 'Do you speak Latin?'

'Of course,' was the immediate reply. 'I asked you how you felt?'

'My mouth is dry and my head hurts.'

The cup was again placed against her lips. Fidelma took another swallow and then the cup was withdrawn. Fidelma whimpered and sank back on the straw.

'What happened?' she asked. 'Where am I?'

'You were carried in here a few hours ago. I became worried when you did not recover quickly.'

Fidelma raised a hand to her head. It had been bandaged. The girl followed the motion.

'I dressed your wound. It was bleeding, but the cut was superficial. There is a little swelling. I would rest awhile. How did it happen?'

'I think someone hit me from behind. Where am I?'

The girl's expression was serious as she said, 'A cellar. I have been here a week, some of us as long as three weeks.'

'You don't know exactly where we are?'

'The villa of Lady Beretrude in the city of Autun.'

Fidelma now turned her head slightly and saw there were about thirty or more women sitting around the room, and several children. They sat on piles of straw, or spoke together in whispers. Now and then one of the children demanded the attention of one or another of the women. There was no furniture, only a few jugs and cups in one corner, and a pile of blankets and straw. She realised that most of the women were dressed soberly in the manner of religieuse. Clarity of thought slowly returned to Fidelma.

'You are dressed in local costume but you are a stranger to this place, aren't you?' said the young woman.

'I am from the land you call Hibernia. I am Sister Fidelma.'

'A religieuse from beyond the edge of the world.' The woman who had nursed her held out the cup of water again. 'What did you say your name was?'

'I am Sister Fidelma. It is a name of my country.'

'And why are you clad in those clothes of the local country folk?' She stared curiously at Fidelma's clothing.

'A long story,' she replied. 'Who are you?'

'I am Valretrade,' answered the young girl.

Fidelma's eyes widened in surprise. 'Sister Valretrade . . . of the *Domus Femini*? The friend of Sigeric?'

It was now the girl's turn to stare in surprise. 'What do you know about me?'

'I know Brother Sigeric,' Fidelma said. 'I was helping him try to find out what had happened to you.'

The girl breathed out sharply. 'Sigeric? Is he well?' Her voice was anxious.

'He was well last time I saw him. He was frantic with anxiety though. What happened to you? The story that Abbess Audofleda put out was that you had decided to leave the abbey a week ago. You were supposed to have departed because you disagreed with the Rule and left a note to that effect.'

'Audofleda? God's perpetual curse on that one!' Valretrade replaced the cup and examined Fidelma critically. 'But you were not in the *Domus Femini* when I was there. Have you but recently come to Autun? Oh, you must have come for the Council.'

Fidelma moved herself into a more comfortable position. As briefly as possible, she told the girl the circumstances that had brought her to Autun and what she had found, how she had become involved with Brother Sigeric and his search for her. Valretrade said nothing until Fidelma came to the end of her narrative.

'I fear the worst,' the girl said at last.

'Then perhaps you will explain what the worst is,' replied Fidelma. The throb in her head was ebbing and her concentration on telling her story had gone some way to curing her headache.

'We are all related to religieux and priests, and those are our children. In my case, I think I stumbled on something that I was not meant to see. We have all been forcibly removed from the *Domus Femini*, brought as captives and blindfold to this place.'

'What did you see and how were you brought here?'

'In recent weeks, I began to notice that some of the women of the community were disappearing.'

'Did you enquire why?'

'It was natural to ask why. I was told that they had decided to leave the abbey because they did not agree with the Rule.'

'Who told you this? Abbess Audofleda?'

The girl shook her head. 'Abbess Audofleda was too unapproachable. She would not directly address members of the community. It was Sister Radegund – she was the one who told us.'

'And did you accept her explanation?'

'Had it been one or two women leaving, then it would have been a feasible explanation. But then all the married women were leaving us and all in the same sudden manner, without warning. They were women whose husbands were still in the abbey. Then we heard from a visiting Sister that other married women, in other local communities, were also disappearing.'

'So what did you do? You didn't mention this to Sigeric at your secret meetings?'

'What could I say to him?' Valretrade shrugged. 'I had no facts. No, I thought it better to see if I could obtain advice. I did not trust any of the local prelates, and wasn't sure who to speak to – but then I met a woman from your country who was the wife of one of the delegates. I asked what person should I seek advice from. She was sympathetic even though I did not tell her all that I knew. She suggested I speak to an abbot from the north of your country.'

'Abbot Dabhóc?' Fidelma asked immediately.

'The name sounds right. I am uncertain with these foreign names – your pardon, Fidelma.'

'That's all right,' conceded Fidelma. 'So when and how did you meet him?'

'I was one of the few asked to look after the foreign women.'

Fidelma nodded. It confirmed what the abbess had said.

'Go on.'

'He was pointed out to me from a distance at the old amphitheatre. I had been told to show some of the foreign women around it – those women who had come with the delegates to the council. He had been speaking to another foreign man who was dressed in the robes of high office of the Church.'

'Nuntius Peregrinus?'

'I did not know his name. He had turned away from this abbot . . .'

'So you spoke with him?'

'I wondered afterwards if he really believed it when I said that women were disappearing from the abbey. To be honest, he was patronising and told me to go away and speak to my abbess about what he called "my fears". It was then that I decided to talk it through with Sigeric.'

'Go on.'

'It was that evening that I arranged to see Sigeric. I signalled my intention by . . .'

'Sigeric told me your method of contact. Had you told anyone else about this meeting?'

Valretrade shook her head.

'Not even Sister Inginde, who shares your chamber with you?'

'I made my signal to Sigeric by candlelight and, as she shared my chamber, she would have known that I was going to see him. But I told her nothing about the reason *why* I was going to see Sigeric that night. I told no one. Sigeric was late in acknowledging my signal. Thankfully, Sister Inginde was not in the chamber as I sat waiting for his answering signal. But then I saw his candle, we exchanged our signals, and I went to our meeting place at the prearranged time. Sigeric was not there, but a man and a woman were in his place. I came on them unexpectedly as they appeared to be hiding something in the sepulchre where we were to meet. They threatened me and I was gagged and bound. They brought me back through the *Domus Femini* to a side entrance where I was blindfolded and carried by the man, who was very strong, and conveyed here. As I say, I have been here about a week.'

Fidelma was grave.

'At the very time that you went to keep your appointment, the Abbot Dabhóc was murdered. Sigeric was on his way to meet you when he saw the body and raised the alarm. By the time he was able to come to your meeting place, you had been taken away and perhaps that delay in his arrival might have saved his life. Who were the man and woman that you saw in the vault?'

'They wore cowls over their heads but I could tell their sexes easily enough. At least I recognised one of them.'

'Who was it?' demanded Fidelma eagerly.

'The stonemason, Brother Andica. He was the one who carried me here.'

Fidelma was slightly disappointed. 'I am afraid he is dead.'

Sister Valretrade was shocked for a moment, and then she went on.

'I did not recognise the woman. Perhaps it was Radegund. After all, she is Beretrude's niece. And she is the only married one in the community who has complete freedom.'

It was a moment or two later when there came the sound of the scraping of bolts at the door. Everyone turned expectantly as it swung open. A thickset warrior entered and paused on the steps. He surveyed them all for a moment with a smirk on his bearded features. Then he spoke first in the local language and then in bad Latin.

'It is your last night here. Tomorrow, before first light, you will be transported south.'

There arose an immediate chorus of protests from the women. The warrior called a sharp warning to quiet them.

'Where are we being transported to?' demanded one woman. 'And why?'

'To the slave markets to which your unChristian marriages and liaisons have condemned you.'

Several women cried out in anguish.

'Under what law does it say our marriages are unChristian? By what right do you hold us prisoners?' entreated another one of the women.

'This is the law now.' The warrior tapped his sword in a significant manner. 'Resign yourselves to it. Be ready to commence your journey. You are being placed in good hands.'

Another figure appeared at his shoulder – a tall man, richly clad, swarthy but clean shaven. He was examining the women captives in speculation. Fidelma had no sooner looked at him than she turned her face and drew the hood over her hair. In the darkness of the cellar she hoped to avoid identification by this man. She herself had no difficulty in recognising Verbas of Peqini, the slave owner, with whom she had had the confrontation at Tara. She prayed that he had not seen her.

'This merchant is your new master until you are disposed of,' the warrior said. 'Be obedient and you will be well treated. Create trouble and you will be punished.'

A woman, one of the older ones, had taken a pace towards him.

'Shame on you! And shame on your mistress, Beretrude! We recognise you, warrior, and who you serve. We are freeborn women of this city. We have no masters. We freely entered the calling of the Faith and joined with our husbands to work in its service. By what right do you do this heinous act . . . ?'

Her words ended with a scream as the warrior moved down the few stone steps, raised his hand and struck her across the face, sending her spinning to the floor. A low, ominous sound came from the women and the man drew his sword.

'Back, you whores!' he snarled. 'It is your choice whether you wish to leave here alive or dead. I will not speak to you again. You made the choice to have liaisons with male clerics and religious. Councils in many lands have now ordained that this is an affront to the Faith. All wives of the religious are to be rounded up and sold as slaves for the greater good of the Faith. That is your Fate. Accept it.'

Verbas of Peqini turned and left, although the warrior, still with his sword at the ready, backed slowly up the steps after the merchant – and then the door swung shut and was bolted behind him.

Many of the women, joined by the children, had burst into tears, uttering piteous cries of lamentation.

Valretrade turned to Fidelma. 'Why did you not want that merchant to see you?' she asked.

'Verbas of Peqini? I encountered him some months ago in my own land, bested him in argument, managed to free one of his slaves and sent him without compensation from our kingdom. He would be delighted to see me again, for his last words to me were a promise of revenge. I believe, if he saw me, he would enjoy fulfilling his promise.'

'Then he will doubtless have his revenge tomorrow. Once it is daylight and we leave this gloomy cellar, you will not be able to hide for ever, not with that red hair.'

Fidelma compressed her lips. 'Then I must ensure that I am not here tomorrow.'

'Escape?' Sister Valretrade laughed without humour. 'Do you think that I have not been looking for a means of escape during this last week?'

'What happens when they take you for the ablutions?' Fidelma asked. 'What are the possibilities there?'

Valretrade looked wearied. 'None, because there is a bucket in that corner which is what we have to use. They also bring us buckets of water for our washing. I have not been allowed out in a week. The others have been in here since their incarceration.'

Fidelma was aghast. 'This is inhuman.'

'Not for slaves, it is not.'

Fidelma rose carefully to her feet, steadying herself on the arm of Valretrade.

'Help me walk around the chamber to get my balance,' she said.

A slow walk around convinced Fidelma that it was hopeless to even waste time contemplating the idea of trying to seek ways to escape from the cellar. However, the walk had helped to make her feel normal again. The ache in her head had eased and her confusion was gone.

'Perhaps there will be a chance on the journey,' suggested her new companion.

'Every moment it is daylight there is a chance Verbas will recognise me,' replied Fidelma. Her mind was working rapidly. 'From Berctrude's villa, he will probably want to transport us through the streets of the city before daylight,' she said, thinking aloud. 'That is why they have ordered us to be ready to leave before dawn. It may mean that they do not want anyone in the city knowing what they are doing. That might be a weakness that we can exploit.'

Valretrade was looking at her in puzzlement. 'What weakness?'

Fidelma glanced around at the others. One or two of the women were looking at them with curiosity.

'Keep your voice low, Valretrade, for we need to discuss this between ourselves before we can involve anyone else.'

'Very well,' whispered the girl. 'What weakness?'

'Consider. What would be their intention? To take us to the river and transport us from there? If so, there are two possibilities. They may pile us into a wagon or they may force us to walk through the city streets. Escape from the wagon would be difficult, but if we are on foot there might well be a chance.'

Valretrade was not convinced.

'They will probably bind us together – perhaps use manacles,' she said. 'I have seen it done in the slave markets.'

'If they want us to walk, they will not bind our legs,' Fidelma asserted.

'The narrow streets of the city in the darkness before dawn . . . it would be our only chance . . . How well do you know this area of the city?'

'I know it well,' replied Valretrade. 'I was born and grew up here. But even if there was a possibility of escape – what then? Where would we go? Certainly not back to the abbey, for how would one know friend from foe?'

'I have friends at the abbey who will help. There is also Brother Sigeric. But first things first. Let us think about escape, before we think of where to escape *to*.'

'If it is of any help, I have a sister who still lives close by and I am sure, if we can reach her house, she will shelter us until we can contact your friends. Her husband is a local blacksmith.'

Fidelma nodded absently. 'Much will depend on the route we take. Verbas of Peqini comes from the east. I suspect he will want to go south to the Mediterranean Sea.'

'Then the journey will be a long one. Most merchants travel by boat. I am sure we will be taken to the river.'

'Do the rivers go right through this land?' asked Fidelma. 'I thought they rose on mountains in the centre?'

'We would go along the Liger, which means a journey against the flow of the river. Mules usually pull boats as far south as a town called Rod-Onna – a Gaulish name. The Liger is navigable south to this trading centre. After that, there are narrow gorges and the river winds up at its source on the Massif Central. No large boat can navigate it.'

'And is that near to the southern sea?'

Valretrade shook her head. 'No, but from there some tributaries and waterways can be crossed from the Liger to a city called Lugdunum.'

'And from Lugdunum?'

'There is a great river called Rhodanus that runs from it and, going with the tide, a boat can reach the open sea within days.'

'Rhodanus?' Fidelma smiled. 'That is a good omen for it means Great Danu. Danus was the mother of all the pagan gods of our land.'

Valretrade said nothing, waiting as she saw Fidelma had relapsed into thought.

'Once out to the southern sea, we shall be lost,' Fidelma finally said.

'It seems that the weakest part of the journey is leaving this city to get to the Liger.'

'The river that runs by this city joins the Liger at a point further upstream to Nebirnum. I think this man Verbas will want to avoid Nebirnum, since Bishop Arigius there has long campaigned to stop traffic in slaves along the river. Of course, Verbas may use wagons to transport us to the Liger.'

'Then we must seize any opportunity to escape before we leave this city,' Fidelma announced firmly. 'So let us get some rest for we will need our strength later tonight.'

Bishop Leodegar gazed from Brother Eadulf to Abbot Ségdae, a look of disapproval on his face. He had not been pleased when Ségdae and Eadulf had come disturbing him with the news that Fidelma was missing. Nor was he pleased that the abbot was supporting Eadulf in the demand that he confront no less a person than the Lady Beretrude.

'I would weigh your words carefully, Brother Eadulf, when you affront the reputation of a noble lady. And as for you, Abbot Ségdae of Imleach, you should consider what support you give to the insinuations and demands of this Saxon.'

Abbot Ségdae reached out a hand to grasp Eadulf's arm and hold him back as he moved impulsively towards the bishop. The bishop's steward, Brother Chilperic, also took a step forward as if to intercept Eadulf, should he threaten the bishop.

'Bishop Leodegar!' Abbot Ségdae's voice sounded like the crack of a horsewhip. 'It is quite clear what Eadulf of Seaxmund's Ham is asking of you. I see no need for me to reconsider my support of him. Fidelma, who is the sister to King Colgú, ruler of my own land, went out with the declared intention of visiting the Lady Beretrude, whom she suspects of some involvement in the matters which she is investigating on your behalf. It is now after midnight and she has not returned. Let me say, Bishop Leodegar, that Fidelma is not only dear to her husband, Eadulf, but to her friends as well as to her brother, the King. It might be construed as an unfriendly act to all Hibernia, should this matter be ignored.'

Bishop Leodegar stared at the abbot in surprise. He was not used to such challenges to his authority.

'That sounds very much like a threat, Ségdae of Imleach.' His voice was tight and angry.

'It was not intended as such, only as a warning of what feeling might be aroused if the matter is ignored. All we are asking is that we proceed forthwith to the villa of the Lady Beretrude and discover what has happened to Fidelma.'

The bishop's jaw was thrust out aggressively.

'You are aware of who Lady Beretrude is? She is of the line of Gundahar of the Burgunds. It may be that her indolent son, Guntram, besports himself with drink, hunting and women, but it is Beretrude who is the ruler of this land.' Bishop Leodegar let out an angry breath. 'You expect me to march to her villa and accuse her . . . accuse her of what? Do you think that I am mad, that I would make such an enemy here?'

Eadulf was tight lipped. 'So, you would rather be a coward than champion truth and justice?'

Bishop Leodegar's steward again moved threateningly towards him.

'Brother Chilperic!' The bishop waved his hand to motion the steward back to his side. 'Come, let us have no more of threats. We are too old and should be too sensible to come to such a misunderstanding. You must appreciate that what you are suggesting is offensive to the dignity of the rulers of this land.'

'So you will do nothing? Am I to tell the King of Cashel that you did nothing to protect his sister?' demanded the abbot.

Bishop Leodegar sighed. 'I will send my steward to Lady Beretrude's villa and ask if Sister Fidelma is there or has called there. That is all I can do.'

Abbot Ségdae glanced at Eadulf and his look admitted defeat.

'And if, as I suspect, the reply is in the negative?'

The bishop shrugged. 'Autun is a big city. It is unwise for a foreign woman to have wandered its streets alone at night, for there any many thieves and robbers.'

Chapter Twenty-One

Fidelma was awoken by the noise of several armed men entering the cellar. They were shouting orders and the women were jolted from their sleep in confusion. The young children started to cry and the warriors cursed and threatened them when they wouldn't fall silent, which only made matters worse. Valretrade was already awake and shivering slightly in the dawn chill. Fidelma rubbed the sleep from her eyes and glanced up at the window. She was satisfied to see that it was still dark, but the men had brought several lanterns. There was no sign of Verbas of Peqini among them.

'Stand in line here,' shouted one of the warriors. Fidelma thought it was the burly man who had addressed them on the previous night. He held several lengths of chain in his hand with manacles on either end. The length of the chain between the manacles was about a metre.

'What are you going to do?' demanded one of the women, a Latin speaker.

The guard grimaced evilly. 'You will be manacled together. So if you have any ideas of running away, you can forget them.'

Fidelma grabbed Valretrade and moved quickly to the line. Instructions were being given in Burgund and in Latin. At Fidelma's prompting, Valretrade asked the warrior: 'Are you not going to provide wagons for us to ride in?'

'Wagons for slaves?' The man chuckled in amusement. No, my lady, you will walk to the river and like it. From there you will have a nice trip by boat.'

Fidelma uttered a silent cheer. It meant there would be an opportunity to escape as they walked through the small streets and alleys of the city, but the manacles would create a problem. She tried to assess the attitude of the guard as he locked a manacle shut on one woman's right wrist and then fastened the other end to a second woman's left wrist.

The guard fitting the manacles was not doing it haphazardly, she could tell. He was choosing to place the strong with the weak-looking. He was obviously a clever man. There was a thickset and tough-looking woman standing just before her and Fidelma saw the guard considering her. She decided to gamble.

'I'd like to be shackled to her,' she said, moving forward and pointing to the woman.

The guard stared at her for a second and then burst out laughing as he viewed her would-be companion. Grabbing Valretrade's wrist, as she stood close behind Fidelma, he fastened one manacle on it and placed the other on Fidelma.

'I suppose you think that you stand a better chance of escape with someone who is so strong?' He spoke with a sneer in his voice. 'I say to whom you are to be shackled.'

As they were pushed back into line, Valretrade was clearly puzzled.

'Why did you want to be shackled to her?' she demanded in a whisper.

'I didn't, but I had to be sure that I was shackled to you. That guard was clearly choosing who was being joined to whom, and he might not have put us together.'

Valretrade still didn't understand.

'He obviously wanted to ensure that two fit-looking women were not placed together,' explained Fidelma patiently. 'I had to distract him by pretending I wanted to be placed with that woman, who stood out as being strong. He was so taken off-guard that he reacted and only saw that you were slimmer than the person I asked to be bound to. He thought he was thwarting my chances.'

Valretrade stared at the iron chain that united them by the wrists.

'I don't see how this will improve our prospect of escape.'

'We are going to be walked through the city to the river. The streets are narrow.'

'Some of them,' agreed the girl.

'Then we must ensure we are placed about the centre of the column. There will be guards at the front and at the back. We need to be the furthest away from them.'

'Then what?'

'Do you know any narrow lanes or streets where we have a chance to break away? We need to start running and get enough of a lead over our pursuers to have time to find a hiding place.'

Valretrade was suddenly thoughtful. 'It will depend which side of the villa they march us out from,' she said. 'Both afford some good opportunities, but we need to start soon. In daylight we will not have much of a chance.'

As if on cue, the door opened again and Verbas of Peqini stood on the threshold, legs apart and hands on hips. Fidelma had quickly thrown her hood over her head.

'Well?' he called to one of the guards in Latin. 'Are they all ready?'

'All ready, lord,' was the reply.

'Then take them outside and get them into a line. I want to be out of the city before daybreak.'

The guards herded the women through the door and up the stone steps into the side garden of the villa. Thirty women and seven children, one only a babe in arms, were shackled in twos. But there were other guards waiting for them outside.

'Children in the front, the rest behind. Hurry now!'

The women began to arrange themselves, and Fidelma and Valretrade hurriedly inserted themselves into the middle of the column that was forming.

A horse had been brought, and Verbas mounted it, staring disdainfully down at his charges.

'Anyone escaping will face the lash,' he called harshly. 'Guard, if anyone does not understand Latin, ensure that their companions tell them the penalty. You will move quickly and in silence. Is this clear?'

'Clear, my lord,' called the chief guard.

Without more ado, Verbas waved his hand in a forward gesture and moved slowly through the side gates of the villa.

The women were forced in a shuffling movement over the cobbled street.

'I am relying on you,' Fidelma whispered to her companion. 'Tell me when we approach the next small alley. We must run as we have never run before.'

Valretrade nodded surreptitiously.

They had traversed two streets, working their way from the villa and into a complex of intersections, when she said: 'Down this street, on the right-hand side is a small alleyway. It is like a maze, criss-crossing and with sometimes barely room for one person.'

Fidelma moved closer to her and gripped her hand. 'We will move together when I give the word.' Her voice was firm.

'Together,' agreed Valretrade quietly.

The alley loomed up in the semi-gloom too quickly for second thoughts. As they reached it, Fidelma snapped, 'Now!' and the two women suddenly leaped for its dark mouth. Holding hands to make the manacle more easily handled, they started running down the cobbled way. Behind them they could hear shouts and screams.

It had been well after midnight when Brother Chilperic had returned from his mission to report that the *major domus* at Lady Beretrude's villa had informed him that Sister Fidelma had not been seen. By the sound of it, the man had not even consulted his mistress but had cavalierly dismissed Brother Chilperic at the gates of the villa. This was exactly what Eadulf had feared.

It was Abbot Ségdae who had prevented Eadulf from going directly to the villa himself.

'It is no good. And if you think that the *major domus* is lying and, indeed, that Lady Beretrude is involved, then it could be dangerous for you as well as Fidelma.'

'But what can we do?' asked Eadulf in anguish.

'Let us wait until daylight. Things are always so much clearer in the morning hours. You need the rest.'

'Little rest I'll be getting,' muttered Eadulf.

'Relax and meditate. After the morning prayers we shall tell Bishop Leodegar that we mean to go to the villa and demand to see Beretrude.'

It was after some intense discussion and still with much reluctance that Eadulf agreed to return to the *hospitia* to rest. It is true that sleep did not come easily to him but, nonetheless, it came eventually and when he awoke it was just past dawn and a distant bell was ringing for the morning prayers.

As Fidelma and Valretrade ran into the darkened alley, the other women, seeing what had happened, began to block off the entrance with their milling bodies while the guards tried to get into the alley to pursue the escapees. Frustrated by the women in their way, the warriors started to lash out. Verbas of Peqini shouted useless instructions but then, two of the guards broke through and started to run after the pair.

Fidelma and Valretrade moved as quickly as they dared in the darkness of the confined space.

'Do you know where this alley leads?' gasped Fidelma, as they came to a maze of small passageways.

'Yes. Not far now. I know where we can hide,' replied her companion.

Then Valretrade twisted and turned through the dark passageways until Fidelma was hopelessly confused and had to put her faith entirely in the hands of the young woman.

Suddenly she halted, breathing hard, in front of a wooden gate set in the black stone wall.

'Here we are!' She reached for the latch and it gave with a groaning sound of wood against wood.

She went through it, dragging Fidelma with her. Then she thrust the gate shut behind them.

Fidelma saw that they were in a small yard; a few chickens clucked irritably but were not particularly disturbed while a tethered goat gazed at them with an expression that seemed to imply it resented their intrusion.

'There's a hay pile there,' gestured Valretrade. 'Let's catch our breath.'

They flung themselves down in a dark corner away from the gate.

It was not a moment too soon, as heavy footsteps pounded by. They could hear the stertorous grunt of the guards who had been chasing them, then the sound faded away. The women crouched in the corner listening, but the tethered goat had grown restless and its movements had disturbed the chickens that now decided to protest. Suddenly, a door opened and the figure of a muscular man appeared with a lantern in one hand and a large blacksmith's hammer in the other.

'Come out, you thieves!' he called. 'Careful, for I am armed.'

The light fell on them in the corner.

'Come out!' he called again.

It was Valretrade who moved first. 'Ageric – it is I!' she called softly.

The man stepped forward, the lantern raised. 'By the holy powers! Valretrade?'

The girl moved swiftly and caught him by the arm.

'Quickly, let us go inside and douse the light. Be as quiet as possible. There are pursuers near by. I have a friend with me.' Her words came out in a breathless whisper.

The man did not say anything more but turned and went inside the house, with Valretrade and Fidelma following. Once they were inside, he bolted the door.

'Who is it, Ageric? What is happening?' A woman entered from the adjoining room and paused when her eyes fell on them.

'Valretrade!' She grasped the girl in an embrace. As Valretrade went to respond, the woman saw the manacles that linked her with Fidelma, and she stepped back, eyes wide. The man had now set the lantern on a table. He heard the gasp and turned to see the reason for it.

'By the holy icons!' he muttered. 'Have you run away from the abbey?'

'It is a long story. This is Fidelma from Hibernia,' Valretrade said, indicating her companion. 'We must speak in Latin for she does not understand our Burgund tongue. Fidelma, this is my sister, Magnatrude and her husband Ageric.'

'I am afraid I know little of your language,' Fidelma apologised.

Algeric strained to understand her and then said: 'My wife and I have Latin. It is a *lingua franca* still among us, for this was once a province of the empire. Most people who have had some learning speak it a little.'

Fidelma was relieved.

Magnatrude was examining them with a worried expression Her features bore a strong resemblance to Valretrade's except that she was a few years older than her sister. Her husband was of the same age, a big man with strong shoulders and dark hair. There was something humorous about his expression, as though he were permanently amused with the world.

'What has happened? Why have you run away from the abbey? Why did they manacle you?'

Valretrade shook her head. 'It's a story long in the telling, sister. The truth is that I didn't run away. I was . . . we were . . . being taken to be sold as slaves. We escaped.'

Ageric stared at her in amazement. 'Sold as slaves? Have slavers raided the abbey, then?'

Valretrade smiled bitterly. 'I said it would be long in the telling. But two important things first. Can you remove these manacles, Ageric? And is there something to drink and eat? We can then tell you the story as we proceed.'

Magnatrude at once set about the refreshment while her husband examined the manacles critically.

'Not a hard job,' he said, inspecting the lock. Then he turned and left them, going into another room.

'Ageric is a blacksmith,' Valretrade reminded Fidelma.

'One of the best in the city,' confirmed her elder sister, returning with beakers filled with cider and some bread and goat's cheese.

As they drained their beakers, Ageric came back with several keys in his hands.

'No need to even break the locks, nor saw through the chains. I believe one of these will do the task.'

As he sat down and started to pick at the locks, Valretrade quickly told their story while they nibbled on the welcome bread and cheese. By the time Valretrade had ended, the manacle and chain lay on the ground. It was well past dawn and the bird chorus had died away.

'But if Bishop Leodegar and the Lady Beretrude are part of the conspiracy to sell the women off as slaves,' commented Magnatrude, 'who is there to appeal to for justice?'

'The only thing for you to do is to hide up for today and then leave the city tonight and get to some other place where the writ of Beretrude and her family and of Leodegar does not run,' advised Ageric.

Valretrade did not look happy.

'Leave the city I grew up in? Leave you, my relatives? And what of poor Sigeric? It is not a good choice.'

Magnatrude looked at Fidelma who had been following the conversation without comment.

'You are from Hibernia. You will want to go back there. Why not take our sister with you? I hear that life is good there. Perhaps Sigeric can follow later.'

Fidelma sighed. 'I am afraid that my duty is to remain in Autun for a while yet.'

'Your duty?' asked Ageric.

It was difficult to explain to them that she was a *dálaigh*, an advocate of the laws of her people, and what that entailed.

'There is someone I need to get in touch with in the abbey,' she began.

'Sigeric?' asked Valretrade eagerly.

'Not Sigeric; not yet. I need to contact Brother Eadulf, but it would be hopeless to return to the abbey and seek him out. There are too many enemies about and I would doubtless be captured before I came near him.' She looked speculatively at Ageric. 'Are you known at the abbey, Ageric?'

The blacksmith looked startled. 'Not exactly. I used to work for the old abbot before Leodegar took over, but I have not been there for some years now. All my business is in the town.'

'Then you might not be recognised as the brother-in-law of Valretrade?'

'I doubt if anyone knows that,' he agreed.

'It would help, Ageric, if you went to the abbey and sought out Brother Eadulf in order to give him a message. But don't make it obvious if you can avoid it.'

'If I am questioned, I could say that I went to see if the abbey had work for a blacksmith,' he volunteered.

'Good. If you can speak to Eadulf alone, tell him that I want him to return here with you. Of course, ensure that you are not followed. If you have to speak to him with others in the vicinity, tell him that you had heard Alchú misses him and arrange to speak alone with him. Remember the name . . . Alchú. He will know that you have come from me.'

Ageric repeated the name.

Fidelma glanced at Valretrade and caught her in mid-yawn. She was sympathetic for she, too, was exhausted by the recent events.

'We had little sleep last night,' she explained, 'so while you go to the abbey, we shall rest awhile.'

Magnatrude took her sister's arm in sympathy.

'You may use our bed for the time being until you have thought out what it is you want to do.'

It was Fidelma who asked: 'Does anyone at the abbey know that Valretrade is your sister?' She was worried in case Beretrude was able to trace them to her sister's home.

'It is some time since I have seen my little sister, so I have had no cause to speak of her to anyone recently.'

Valretrade yawned again. She was almost asleep on her feet.

In fact, both Fidelma and Valretrade were fast asleep by the time Ageric the Blacksmith left on his errand to the abbey.

It seemed that Fidelma had not been asleep but a moment when she felt her shoulder being roughly shaken. She came awake abruptly, heart pounding. Valretrade was already moving from the bed while Magnatrude was still shaking Fidelma.

'Lady Beretrude's warriors are coming along the alley,' she hissed. 'There's no time to lose. Follow me.'

She turned and led the way into what was apparently a storeroom off Ageric's workshop and forge. She went straight to a corner and bent down. Already they could hear the tramp of the warriors at the gate outside the building. Magnatrude pulled up a trapdoor and pointed down.

'A souterrain. I can think of no other hiding place. There is no more time.'

A harsh voice was calling, demanding entrance.

Fidelma dropped down into the dark food storage area and crawled further back so that Valretrade could follow her. A moment later the trapdoor swung shut and they were in total darkness. It was cold. Black and cold. Fidelma shivered at the sudden change from the warm bed to this icy darkness.

She heard something move over the trapdoor and guessed Magnatrude was trying to obscure the entrance by placing some object on top.

A moment passed before they heard the harsh voices again and Magnatrude's tones replying.

'My sister? I haven't seen her for over a year or so. She is a religieuse up at the abbey. Why don't you try there?'

The harsh voice replied.

Fidelma could not follow much of the conversation even though it was conducted in Latin. It was too muffled.

There was a lot of movement above them. It was obvious the warriors were looking around. Then voices were close by. They were very clear. Fidelma's jaw tightened as she waited for the trapdoor to be discovered. Suddenly she recognised the voice of one of the speakers, and shuddered. It was Verbas of Peqini. She was thankful that his common language with Beretrude's guards was Latin so that she could understand what was said. Verbas was not happy.

'This means another delay,' he was complaining. 'Why didn't the Lady Beretrude tell me that one of the prisoners was this Fidelma of Cashel! I knew the cunning vixen. I would have taken a special care of her.'

There was an apologetic cough and a gruff voice said: 'My lady did not know you knew the foreigner, lord.'

'Well, I am forced to leave now. It is up to Beretrude to kill or recapture that troublemaker. I would have liked to have done so myself, but I have a boat waiting on the river. It takes many days to navigate down to the southern sea and my ship. I cannot wait for ever.'

'A cargo of slaves fetches a good price, lord, so surely it is worth the wait until these women are recaptured?'

'And your mistress has collected a good price,' muttered Verbas of Peqini. 'No, I cannot wait any longer.'

His voice died away and it was obvious that the men had moved towards the door. It seemed an eternity before Magnatrude's voice came from above them.

'They have gone. Are you both all right?'

'We are cold and it is dark down here,' Valretrade called back.

'I am sorry, but it is best to leave you there for a short time in case they return to catch us out. I will let you up as soon as I think it is safe.'

Fidelma thought the woman was wise.

'Let us up as soon as you can,' Valretrade shivered. She was clearly not enjoying the confinement.

A good hour or so later, Magnatrude returned. She removed whatever it was covering the trap door and pulled it open, then helped Valretrade first from the narrow confines and then Fidelma.

'Your warning was very timely,' Fidelma told her as she stretched to get her blood circulating again.

'It was a lucky thing that this house has an upper floor and I was there in time to see the warriors approaching from the top of the lane,' Magnatrude told them grimly.

Valretrade was trembling, more from the effects of being in the claustrophobic souterrain than from near recapture by Lady Beretrude's warriors.

'Have they gone?' she whispered.

'Of course,' replied her sister. 'But not before a thorough search of this place.' She suddenly went pale.

'What is it?' asked Fidelma in alarm.

'The manacles!' Magnatrude stared with wide eyes. 'What if . . . ?' She scanned the workroom. 'Ageric brought them in here.'

Fidelma pointed with a smile.

'They say that the best way to hide something is to leave it in plain view.'

The workroom of the smith had several nails and hooks along one wall from which an assortment of chains and other devices were hanging. Among them Ageric had hung up the manacles and chain from which he had released Fidelma and Valretrade. They were so obvious that the warriors would not have taken any notice of them, thinking they were just part of the smith's equipment.

'Don't worry, Magnatrude. As soon as Eadulf gets here, we will not trespass on you much longer and put you in fear of this Beretrude.'

Magnatrude shook her head. 'You mistake my fear. My sister Valretrade is the only relative I have. I will do anything to protect her.'

'They say Beretrude has the second sight.' Valretrade was still nervous. 'How did she know to send her warriors here?'

'Second sight?' Fidelma was disapproving. 'For shame – and you a Sister of the Faith. Beretrude must have known or been told that Magnatrude was your blood sister. There is no mystery to it. But she has been remarkably well informed.'

'I told only my close friends like Sigeric and Inginde.'

'Not Sister Radegund?'

'Radegund knew as steward.' The girl looked deflated. 'She is Beretrude's niece. I should have realised.'

Magnatrude led them back to the other room and offered them a bowl of hot broth.

'The Lady Beretrude is said to have spies everywhere. She is a powerful woman. More powerful than her sons.'

'Her sons? Oh, you include the younger son who was sent away when he was young. I have spoken to Guntram,' Fidelma added, explaining her knowledge.

'Guntram is the elder son and technically, the ruler. In reality, it is Beretrude who controls this province,' replied Magnatrude.

'What of the other son?'

'No one knows what happened to him. He was sent away from home when he was young to enter the religious.'

'Do you know the story?' asked Fidelma curiously.

'Gundobad was his name, I believe. The story is that he went into the abbey there when he was seven years old because his mother rejected him. She wanted to lavish her attention on Guntram, being the heir to the lordship of Burgundia, but only succeeded in spoiling him and making him indolent.'

Magnatrude offered them more broth but sleep was catching up with them again.

'Let's hope Ageric returns with Eadulf soon.' Fidelma noticed that Valretrade had already fallen asleep again. But she herself was too nervous to sleep, and just wished Eadulf would come. However, she must have fallen asleep in spite of herself, for the next thing she knew, she awoke to hear Eadulf's anxious voice. Ageric had returned with him.

'You were not followed from the abbey?' she demanded after they had exchanged enthusiastic greetings.

'We were very careful, and no one saw Ageric contact me, except Abbot Ségdae, whom I have taken into my confidence. We were very lucky.

We were just setting out to search for you again when Ageric approached and asked where he might find Brother Eadulf.'

'So Ségdae knows where we are?'

'When you did not return by dark last night, I approached Ségdae and told him where you had gone. We went to Bishop Leodegar and demanded that he send to Beretrude to enquire if you were in the villa. We wanted to go ourselves in case there was trouble. Instead, he sent Brother Chilperic, who was told that no one at the villa had seen you.'

Fidelma's face was grim. 'Beretrude is guilty of selling members of the *Domus Femini* as slaves,' she told him. 'But I think I can now explain what has been happening here.'

'She has many warriors to back her.' Eadulf was no longer surprised at the news. 'What is your plan?'

'Are Ségdae and his companions still at the abbey?'

'I told him not to say anything further until I had spoken with you. I said I would get word to him as to what must be done.'

'Did you discover the answer to my question?'

'About Benén mac Sesenén?' Eadulf was surprised at what he saw as a sudden change of conversation. 'Oh yes. You were right. He did have a Latin nickname.'

'And Benignus was his Latin sobriquet?'

Eadulf looked surprised for a moment and then said: 'It was.'

Fidelma nodded slowly as if everything now fitted together.

'What of Bishop Leodegar – what was his reaction to my disappearance? Was he concerned, or do you think he knew what was happening?'

Eadulf paused for a moment's thought. Then: 'He is either very good at disguising his feelings, or he was more concerned at the reaction from Nuntius Peregrinus when he heard you were missing. Tell me what has happened to you.'

As briefly as possible, she told him the details.

Eadulf looked grim when she mentioned the role of Verbas of Peqini.

'My movement is restricted now, Eadulf, so I must rely on you. Tonight I need to re-enter the abbey unseen. Apart from Abbot Ségdae and his comrades from Imleach, there is no knowing who are our friends and who are our foes in the abbey. We must be prepared for all contingencies.'

She glanced towards Valretrade. Their conversation had been carried on in Fidelma's own language that they always spoke together.

'I think we can rely on Brother Sigeric to support us,' she added.

At the name Valretrade looked up quickly.

'Sigeric? Has anything happened to him?' she asked fearfully, resorting to Latin.

Eadulf was reassuring. 'He is well but frantic with worry about your fate.'

'Then tomorrow morning I shall attempt to resolve all these matters,' Fidelma said.

'Tomorrow morning?' Eadulf was astonished. 'Can it all be resolved by then?'

'That is if certain conditions can be met. Firstly, you must return to the abbey and see Abbot Ségdae. He must arrange to smuggle me back into the abbey as soon as darkness has fallen. Valretrade will come with me. No one apart from Ségdae must know of our return. You, however, will find a horse and ride to Clotaire. Bring him and his warriors to the abbey unseen. Make sure he has Guntram with him.'

Eadulf was astounded. 'Fifty warriors? How can they arrive in this city unseen, let alone enter the abbey?'

'That is where Brother Sigeric will play a part. In this you must instruct Clotaire carefully. Stand firm against Ebroin, as I am sure he is the sort of person who will raise objections. He may wish good for Clotaire but he does not believe in being subtle.'

'Tell me what I should do.'

'As you know, the abbey buildings stand in the south-west corner of the city, against the city walls there. Do you recall Sigeric telling us about the tunnel from the vaults under the chapel that leads beyond the outside walls? The door can be opened only from the inside. I will send Sigeric to open that door before dawn tomorrow morning. You will bring Clotaire and his men to the outside wall. Can you find where the entrance is?'

'We can if Sigeric will signal with a lantern to show exactly where it is.'

'A good suggestion. It shall be done.'

'But where will I find a horse to ride for Guntram's fortress?' asked Eadulf.

'Ageric,' she turned to the blacksmith, 'do you have a good horse or do you have access to one?'

'My brother is also a blacksmith. His forge is outside of the city on the road to Guntram's fortress. He has horses,' he replied at once.

'How far away?'

'Just to the south west, at the beginning of the forest. It is no more than a brisk walk away. His name is Clodomar.'

Fidelma turned back to Eadulf in satisfaction.

'That's one piece of good fortune. We passed Clodomar's forge. Do you recall the place?' And when he nodded, she turned back to the bewildered Ageric. 'I presume that your brother can be trusted to keep secrets?'

'He is my brother,' responded Ageric stoutly. 'But I will accompany your friend to make sure all is well.'

'Remember to bring Clotaire back to the entrance before dawn.'

Eadulf tried to hide his dismay at the thought of a nighttime ride on horseback through the forest. Horses were not his favourite mode of transport.

'Once inside, Sigeric will guide you through the necropolis and into the chapel. This will coincide when all are meeting for the morning prayers. The warriors must stand ready to take control by force.'

'I am not sure I follow the reasoning,' Eadulf said, 'but I will certainly convey all this to Clotaire.'

Fidelma looked apologetically at him.

'What I am planning is that tomorrow, at morning prayers, which are attended by both communities in the abbey, I shall commence unravelling this mystery. I shall use the chapel as I would a court before the Brehons back home. Before that, I have to get Valretrade here to show me where she was taken captive. By that sarcophagus, I am hoping to find a piece of evidence. Do you follow?'

'What if Bishop Leodegar will not allow you to speak?'

'He must, for I will ensure that the Nuntius Peregrinus will be informed what my intention is. Leodegar cannot openly deny the hearing, for that is what he has requested. And Clotaire will also be there to hear. More importantly, Clotaire's warriors will be there to ensure there is no interference in the matter.'

Eadulf looked gloomy. 'It could all go wrong.'

'Not if we all play our parts.' She glanced at Ageric who stood looking on with his wife and sister-in-law.

'It is time to set our plans into motion,' she said. '*Audentes fortuna iuvat*. Fortunes favours the daring and we must be daring. Tomorrow morning, if all goes well, we can put an end to the mysteries that have brought such fear and darkness on the abbey and on this city.'

CHAPTER TWENTY-TWO

It was just after dawn that Fidelma, with Valretrade at her side and flanked by Abbot Ségdae and the remaining Hibernian delegates, entered the abbey's chapel. There were glances ranging from astonishment to outrage among the brethren as they marched to the front of the chapel and sat down. The murmuring of protest grew loud but they ignored it. A similar disturbance was heard beyond the wooden screens that separated Abbess Audofleda and the members of her community. It was obvious that no one in the chapel was unaware of their presence. Fidelma had a momentary thought as to what would be going through Abbess Audofleda's mind and that of Sister Radegund at seeing Valretrade at her side. She knew that she would not have long to wait to find out.

Bishop Leodegar and Brother Chilperic now entered to perform the first service of the day. As the bishop turned to the altar to invoke the ritual of the first prayer, he seemed oblivious to the atmosphere. However, he eventually became aware of the commotion and turned with an angry frown towards the congregation. As he did so, a harsh voice cried from the women's section: 'I protest!'

Abbess Audofleda had risen so that she could be seen beyond the separating screen. One arm was flung out towards Fidelma and Valretrade.

Bishop Leodegar followed her pointing finger to where Fidelma was sitting. His jaw slackened. His eyes turned to Valretrade sitting next to her.

'What is this?' he demanded. 'Where have you appeared from, Fidelma of Cashel? I was told that you had disappeared, and Brother Eadulf and

Abbot Ségdae were protesting that you had been abducted. And what is that other woman doing here among the brethren when—'

'Those women mock the Rule of this abbey, profane this very holy chapel by their presence in the area designated for the brethren!' Abbess Audofleda interrupted.

Bishop Leodegar was plainly in a state of bewilderment.

'Explain yourself, Sister Fidelma. You have disappeared and now you reappear – and with a woman seated by you when you know that, while I gave dispensation for you, this abbey is segregated and that no other female has any right to be here.'

'I will explain.' Fidelma put a reassuring hand on Valetrade's shoulder. 'I was prepared to allow the morning prayers to finish before announcing our presence, but since you prefer the explanations now, so be it. I have come, and with witnesses, to resolve the mystery of what has been taking place here. And I claim your authority, Bishop Leodegar, to do so.'

'I cannot allow—' the bishop spluttered.

Abbot Ségdae rose at once.

'As senior delegate from Hibernia, I bear witness to your commission to Fidelma of Cashel and to Brother Eadulf to investigate and present her conclusions as to who is guilty of the murder of Abbot Dabhóc.'

He had been joined by the languid figure of the Nuntius Peregrinus who was standing next to his grim-faced *custodes*, his constant shadow.

'As envoy from the Holy Father in Rome, I remind you, Bishop Leodegar, that this was your commission,' he said. 'I bring with me Bishop Ordgar of Kent and Abbot Cadfan of Gwynedd who are each as anxious as you are to hear Sister Fidelma's words. I submit that you are in error in saying that you cannot allow this.'

Bishop Leodegar hesitated, clearly in a quandary as to what he should do.

'We, too, are anxious to hear what resolution Fidelma of Cashel has to offer,' cried one of the delegates, Abbot Herenal of Bro Erech. Several others now cried out in agreement.

Brother Chilperic moved forward and whispered into Leodegar's ear. The bishop's face grew long. Before he could speak, Abbess Audofleda was interrupting again.

'I claim Fidelma is a conspirator sent to disrupt our morning worship!'

'That is a silly claim designed to stop the truth being heard. By what right does she claim that?' Fidelma asked.

Another woman had taken her place beside Abbess Audofleda so that her head could also be seen above the screen partition.

'Her right is my authority!' the woman cried, then flung off the hood of her robe. There was a gasp as most of the assembly recognised Lady Beretrude.

Bishop Leodegar was even more startled at her appearance.

'Lady Beretrude,' he swallowed, 'these are matters for ecclesiastical authority. While your intervention is appreciated, you cannot . . .'

'*Cannot*?' The voice was threatening. 'You know my authority in this city and in this land of Burgundia, Leodegar. If it is not acknowledged, then I will have to demonstrate it.' She clapped her hands twice.

A dozen men clad in the robes of the brethren, who had been standing around the edge of the chapel, moved forward now and cast them off. Each one was a warrior; each one held a sword in his hand. There was momentary chaos.

Fidelma looked to the anxious Abbot Ségdae and smiled briefly in reassurance. The interruption was no more than she had expected.

'Some friends will be with us soon. Do not fear,' she whispered.

'Now, Bishop Leodegar, will you obey my authority?' demanded Lady Beretrude loudly.

'No, but you will answer to mine, Beretrude!' came a cold male voice.

The young King Clotaire, with Ebroin, Eadulf and Sigeric behind him, was walking slowly down the aisle towards the high altar. Behind them, appearing rather sheepishly, walked the young Lord Guntram with two of Clotaire's warriors. Bishop Leodegar and Brother Chilperic had become like statues, shocked into immobility with the rapidity of events beyond their control.

Fidelma glanced quickly around. Clotaire's men who, as if by magic, seemed to pour out of the dim recesses of the chapel with weapons at the ready, had already disarmed the dozen warriors of Beretrude. Only a couple of the warriors had resisted and their lifeless bodies lay sprawled on the floor of the chapel. The uproar was deafening among the community but

Ebroin had moved forward. He held up a staff of office that he thumped forcefully on the stone floor.

'Silence!' he called in a stentorian voice. 'Silence and recognise your imperator, Clotaire, the third of his name to govern the house of the Merovingian. Hail Clotaire! Hail our rightful King!'

The effect was to gradually still the assembly.

Ebroin signalled to his men to secure all the exits from the chapel. He then turned to Bishop Leodegar with an expression of satisfaction.

'With your permission, we will remove those screens that separate the women of this congregation so that they are not hidden from us. I am sure Lady Beretrude is anxious to join in this community?'

Without waiting for Leodegar's assent, he gestured to a couple of his warriors who quickly removed the folding wooden screens that separated the women's section from the rest of the community in the chapel. There was some nervous murmuring while this was being done. Fidelma saw that Beretrude was still standing, her face white and her features a mask of outrage. Abbess Audofleda was standing with head bowed beside her.

Clotaire took his place before the high altar and stood with folded arms gazing thoughtfully at the congregation. Gradually everyone fell into an expectant silence. Then he turned and glanced at Bishop Leodegar.

'A chair would be welcome, Bishop. There is much to be heard here and I have been on my feet these several hours.'

Brother Chilperic immediately fetched a chair and hurriedly placed it before the altar facing the congregation, for the King to be seated.

'We will keep to Latin as our *lingua franca* in this matter as it is, indeed, the common tongue between all who are gathered in this place,' he announced. 'Fidelma of Cashel, are you prepared to elucidate?'

Fidelma moved forward and turned to face the congregation, having bowed her head to Clotaire. 'Imperator, I am ready,' she replied. She murmured to Eadulf who stood near by, 'Well done. You see, fortune has favoured the daring.'

'Do you not have another saying – that time is a good historian?' Eadulf responded pessimistically.

Fidelma then murmured to Brother Sigeric, who stood by Eadulf's side, 'Sigeric, you may join Valretrade.'

The young man hurried to take his place beside Valretrade; the joining of their hands and joyous expressions told of their emotions.

'You may proceed, Fidelma,' Clotaire invited. 'We are ready.'

Fidelma was used to estimating a correct dramatic pause before commencing. She had learned the trick during the years that she had presented cases before the great Brehons of the five kingdoms. Now she stood, head slightly bowed and silent until the last ripples of noise died away in the abbey. She began softly, and slowly allowed her voice to gain power.

'I came to this place to attend a council at the behest of the abbot and chief bishop of my brother's kingdom which is that of Muman, one of the five kingdoms of the land you know as Hibernia. My role was to advise Abbot Ségdae in the law of Hibernia that might affect matters discussed in this council. I came in the company of my husband, Brother Eadulf, who is well known among my people as he is also a *gerefa* . . .'

She paused a moment.

'When we came here, it was through the intercession of Abbot Ségdae, as the senior surviving delegate from Hibernia, that Bishop Leodegar requested us to undertake an investigation over a death that occurred here. Abbot Dabhóc had been bludgeoned to death in the chamber of the Saxon Bishop Ordgar of Canterbury while both Ordgar and Abbot Cadfan of Gwynedd were in the same chamber. It seemed a simple enough task. We were supposed to decide which of the two – Ordgar or Cadfan – was guilty of this crime. Yet simplicity is often deceptive. So it was in this case.'

'It is still a simple decision,' muttered Bishop Leodegar loudly. 'One of the two is guilty. *Vel caeco appareat*!'

The remark brought forth an irritated gesture from Clotaire and the bishop fell silent.

Fidelma allowed herself a grim smile.

'Bishop Leodegar says it would be apparent even to a blind man. Praise God that I do not have any affliction and can use all of my senses. Some people here have all their senses but cannot use them.' There was a chuckle from some of the brethren. 'However, let the twine of truth begin to unwind. It became obvious that there were other matters of concern in this place that might or might not have been part of this apparently simple murder. There were, in fact, three matters that in some way were linked together.'

Lady Beretrude had recovered some of her poise.

'Majesty, I must be heard,' she called out. 'I came here because I had heard that this woman might try to accuse the good Sisters of the abbey and others – even *me* – with claims of wrongdoing. I speak for the Burgunds of this province. My role here is to represent the law of our people. This woman is *not* of our people. She has no status in law among us. She cannot be allowed to make judgements that condemn any one of us. She is a foreigner in our midst without rank or position.'

Clotaire stared bleakly back.

'The last I heard, Beretrude of the Burgunds, was that your son Guntram, who now stands beside me, was the lord of this province, ruling under my authority with the law of the Franks. Whose law do *you* claim to represent?'

Guntram shuffled uneasily at the side of the King.

'Be silent, Mother,' he muttered uneasily, as if embarrassed. 'Sister Fidelma speaks with the authority of the King and . . . and under my authority as lord of the Burgunds.'

'So now your protest is answered, lady,' Clotaire added sharply, 'Obey your lord and your King.'

Lady Beretrude's mouth closed in a thin line, her face suddenly red with mortification.

Fidelma waited until there was a silence again.

'I am aware that I can only point things out. I cannot say whether these matters transgress your laws. I know that they would transgress the laws of my own land but then each people have their own laws and their own customs. I must leave it to those who are in charge of the law of this land to consider what I say and, if they feel it incumbent upon themselves, to enact that justice which is their own.'

There was a murmur of some approval from the brethren of the abbey.

Clotaire waved a hand towards her.

'This is well understood, Fidelma of Cashel. Proceed. You said that there were three matters that needed to be dealt with.'

'Let me start with the one matter of which there is ample proof. A matter with several witnesses to testify that I speak the truth. It is the matter of slavery.'

Bishop Leodegar leaned forward immediately. 'There is no law forbidding slavery in our land, nor the buying and selling of slaves.'

Fidelma turned to him. 'Of that I have become painfully aware. I find it a detestable thing, as do my people. Yet I acknowledge it exists in other cultures. I do not argue that it is legal under your law and customs. However, I think that even under the laws you have in this land, the idea of abducting the freeborn and selling them into slavery is a questionable practice. I was kidnapped but two days ago and was about to be sold into slavery . . .'

This time it was Abbess Audofleda who interrupted.

'Freeborn you might have been, but you are a foreigner and that negates such law. If you were abducted by slave traders, then bring them before us.'

'You are right to make that distinction between freeborn and foreigners,' replied Fidelma calmly. 'However, many freeborn Burgunds and Franks, members of your own community, have been abducted from your care and were being sold into slavery. You demand that the slave traders should be brought here. They are here already.'

'A lie! A lie!' cried Sister Radegund, coming forward to the abbess's side, her voice rising above the hubbub that had broken out.

'It is no lie, and there stands Sister Valretrade who was one of the freeborn women of this city, who served in your community, who was betrayed and abducted. She shared my peril in our escape from Beretrude's villa.'

Clotaire was regarding the *abbatissa* grimly.

'Before you call it a lie, Abbess Audofleda, let me also tell you that some of my warriors encountered a barge on the Aturavos yesterday evening. There were thirty religieuse mainly from your abbey and their children being transported under the care of a merchant called Verbas of Peqini. They were all manacled and, had their journey continued, they would have been taken to the southern seaports to be sold in the slave markets. Sadly, for Vebras of Peqini, he and his men tried to dispute with the authority of my warriors. They are all dead but I am pleased to say that the women and their children have been escorted back to

Autun where they stand ready to give an account of their capture and imprisonment.'

Abbess Audofleda was shaking her head in apparent bewilderment.

'I don't understand. These women all left of their own free will,' she protested feebly.

'It is true,' declared Sister Radegund defensively. 'You cannot blame the abbess for what happened to these women after they left the protection of the abbey.'

'Oh, but they were taken captive *within* the abbey,' stated Fidelma. 'And they will doubtless tell you so if it is necessary for them to give testimony.'

'But it is impossible!' gasped Sister Radegund, looking at Abbess Audofleda who was white faced and shocked, as though she could not believe what she was hearing.

'Explain to your niece and her abbess how it is possible, Beretrude.' Fidelma's voice cut like ice across the gathering.

'Slavery is not illegal!' snapped Lady Beretrude, raising her head defiantly.

'You claim that you have a right to take women and children captive and sell them?'

'I am—'

'We know who you are, Beretrude, and now we know *what* you are,' snapped back Fidelma. 'You have arranged this trade in slaves with Verbas of Peqini.'

'I do not deny it. It is not against the law.'

'I shall be the judge of that,' interrupted Clotaire in a heavy voice.

'How long have you known Verbas of Peqini?' went on Fidelma.

'He came as a trader to Nebirnum several weeks ago. He was going south to rejoin his ship to sail for eastern ports. I was in Nebirnum and persuaded him to return here to Autun to trade.'

'To trade in slaves that you could supply him with. You had in mind the married women and children who were in the *Domus Femini*. Since Bishop Leodegar had segregated the abbey and forced those married religious to separate, to divorce their wives and reject their children, you felt that they would have no protection from the Church if they were abducted and sold. You knew that Abbess Audofleda, with her attitudes, would not protect them.'

Lady Beretrude was silent but she made no denial. It was Abbess Audofleda who protested once more.

'I am innocent of this,' she said again. 'I did not know the women and their children had been abducted.'

'Nor I, nor I,' wailed Sister Radegund. 'They left notes, they quitted the community in the night.'

'But you were pleased to be rid of them and did not question where they had gone nor why,' Fidelma said harshly. 'You, Abbess Audofleda, had the responsibility for their well-being. They were all freeborn.'

'I serve in the abbey under Bishop Leodegar,' replied the abbess, desperately trying to shift the blame. 'His is the ultimate authority.'

'I declare that I had no knowledge of what was happening in the *Domus Femini*,' Bishop Leodegar stated. 'Anyway, I do not see that any crime has been committed here. Even if these women and their offspring were seized to be sold as slaves, their union with the religious is against our Rule and the communities of this abbey have accepted this. Their removal from the female community could be seen as a worthwhile work. It was a . . . a cleansing of the abbey.'

Fidelma glared at him, her face tight with anger.

Clotaire saw the muscles around her mouth working and intervened before she could speak, saying in a quiet tone: 'Remember that it is not your place to utter judgement on the matter nor speak of morals to the bishop, Fidelma of Cashel. We will accept that the women were abducted from the *Domus Femini* and that it was Beretrude who entered into an agreement with Verbas of Peqini in this trade. The crime seems to lie in the fact that they were freeborn. I will also bear in mind, when it comes to the judgements that I shall give, that you, a distinguished guest, were also abducted.'

'I am innocent of having knowledge or conspiring in this matter!' wailed Abbess Audofleda.

Fidelma glanced at her without pity.

'As a matter of fact, I believe you,' she replied, to the surprise of everyone. 'I even believe that Sister Radegund was not privy to the plot of her aunt. But I shall come to that matter in a moment.'

'Indeed!' snapped Bishop Leodegar. 'This is time wasted on a matter unrelated to the killing of Abbot Dabhóc. It was that matter, and that matter only, which Sister Fidelma was supposed to investigate. Surely, Sire,' he turned to Clotaire, 'there is a limit to our patience?'

'I will say when my patience is ended, Leodegar,' replied the young King.

Fidelma ignored the intervention.

'I thought I had made it clear that these matters *were* related?' she said coldly. 'And if the selling of the religieuse and their children, freeborn or not, as slaves is not a crime according to the laws of this land, then we will come to the reason why Beretrude was raising money by the selling of slaves. That reason was not merely for personal gain.'

Beretrude raised her head suddenly; the whiteness and strain in her features seemed to increase. There was utter silence now in the chapel. Clotaire bent eagerly forward in his chair, watching Fidelma expectantly while Ebroin had taken a step forward as if in anticipation.

'Beretrude was raising money for an insurrection; a rising of the Burgunds against Clotaire and his Franks.'

There was an audible gasp. It echoed through the chapel.

Two of Clotaire's warriors moved closer to Lord Guntram, hands on the hilts of their swords. The young Guntram was staring at his mother, his blue eyes wide, his mouth working but no sound would come.

'Do you, Guntram, aspire to lead this revolt?' breathed Ebroin. 'The Burgunds would never follow a woman.'

'It's a lie!' The cry was wrenched from the young man's throat as Clotaire turned an accusing gaze upon him. 'I have *never* conspired in such a plot! I swear it.'

'Clotaire,' Fidelma called, 'Guntram is as you see him. A young man who spends his life drinking, hunting and pursuing women. He is not interested in leading revolts.'

'Then who else could claim the allegiance of the Burgunds against us?' demanded Ebroin. 'The Burgunds would only follow a male heir of their former kings.'

'There was another son of Beretrude,' Fidelma replied simply. 'Another descendant of Gundahar and the line of kings of the Burgunds.'

'I have only one brother – Gundobad,' Guntram objected. 'He was given as a child to the religious. My mother abandoned him to some abbey. I have no other brother.'

'That is so,' agreed Fidelma. 'Gundobad grew up in the abbey of Divio, an ambitious young man and more of a warrior than Guntram. But it was Guntram who inherited the title of Lord of the Burgunds from his father. Beretrude realised some time ago that she had abandoned her younger and stronger son to indulge and ruin the elder but weaker son. She decided to correct her mistake.'

'Are you saying that Beretrude was raising money by selling slaves so that her son in Divio could use it to plan an insurrection?' Clotaire demanded.

'Precisely so. It was only when I was told about this second son that everything began to fit into place.'

'So now we must send to Divio to discover this man,' sighed Ebroin.

'He is no longer at Divio. Beretrude's younger son is here in this abbey.'

For a while there was uproar.

'Who are you accusing, Fidelma?' demanded Bishop Leodegar. 'There are several who come from Divio in this abbey. Are you claiming this was the person who killed Abbot Dabhóc? I do not understand.'

'Bishop Ordgar and Cadfan are both innocent of that crime,' confirmed Fidelma. 'In fact, they were victims of the same crime that was set up to distract suspicion away from the real killer and his intention. But I need to give some words of explanation before I identify the killer. With his mother helping him to devise the plot, Gundobad came to this abbey. Autun was going to be the base of the insurrection of the Burgunds against the Franks. Why? This very council provided the ideal opportunity It was known that Clotaire would come here to give his official approval to the decisions of the council before they were sent to Rome. What better place to assassinate the Frankish King and raise the symbol of insurrection?'

'The symbol?' queried Clotaire. 'What symbol?'

'I am told that the Burgunds hold a great teacher of the Faith in high regard both as bishop and martyr. His association with Autun is often spoken of with reverence – even Beretrude's villa stands in a square named after him – the Square of Benignus. The villa bears the symbol of what

I am told is the cross of Benignus. What if the leader of the Burgunds came forward bearing the relics of this Benignus before him, calling on the Burgunds to rise up and follow because God blessed this endeavour?'

'It would be a powerful symbol,' admitted Bishop Leodegar. 'But such relics do not exist.'

'Some people believe that they do. I heard from poor Brother Budnouen that there were rumours and stories about the relics of the Blessed Benignus. He told me that the peasants of this country already spoke of a leader who would carry them aloft and lead them to their former glory and independence.'

Fidelma paused, then went on: 'Brother Gillucán had told me that his abbot, Dabhóc, came to this abbey bearing a reliquary box containing the bones of the Benén mac Sesenén of Midhe, who was a disciple and successor of our great teacher, the Blessed Patrick. The relics were to be a gift for Bishop Vitalian of Rome.'

The Nuntius Peregrinus interposed in a languid tone, 'Oh, come, Fidelma. What has your Hibernian bishop to do with Benignus of Autun?'

'Just this. Benén Mac Sesenén also used the sobriquet of Benignus. On the reliquary box that was to be the gift to the Holy Father, his name was carved on one side, and on the other – clearly in Latin – was his name in religion . . . Benignus.'

There was a moment's silence.

'I think you have missed the point,' countered the Nuntius Peregrinus. 'This Benignus of Hibernia was certainly not the Benignus who brought Christianity to the Burgunds.'

'I agree with you, Nuntius,' replied Fidelma at once. 'But that did not deter the conspirators. Imagine how delighted they were on hearing that the abbot from Hibernia actually had an ancient reliquary box on which was inscribed the name of Benignus for all to see? How many followers would debate whether the bones inside were those of their apostle Benignus or that of some obscure Hibernian with the same name?'

'And you believe that this is why Abbot Dabhóc was slain?' queried the Nuntius. 'Because of that reliquary box?'

'I think you already know it,' she replied.

The Nuntius looked uncertain. 'What do you mean?' he demanded.

'Abbot Dabhóc had told you, when he met you at the amphitheatre, that he had the reliquary box which he would present to you at the end of the council. Then he was murdered. When you heard this, you went to his chamber in search of the reliquary box but could not find it. There was, in your mind, only one person who knew about it and that was Dabhóc's steward, Brother Gillucán. You and your bodyguard, the *custodes* who stands beside you now, *initially* searched his room but did not find it. Still certain that Gillucán must have hidden it in his possession, you both visited the poor young man in the dead of night and threatened him with physical violence unless he told you where the reliquary box was. He could not, and such was his fear that you finally believed him.'

The Nuntius Peregrinus was staring at her in amazement.

'Truly, you have remarkable powers of deduction, if deduction it is.'

'Do not fear, Nuntius. It is no more than deduction. Poor Brother Gillucán. He was sick with fear and decided to leave the abbey after he had spoken secretly with me. However, the Burgundian conspirators thought he was leaving for other reasons. They believed that he knew something and would betray them. Curiously enough, what made him even more fearful was the cries of the children being abducted from the *Domus Femini* which he overheard late one night when he was in the *necessarium*. And it was in that same *necessarium* that he was killed, his naked body shoved into the effluence from where it was finally washed into the river and discovered. That was why, when he was found, there was excrement on the body.'

The entire gathering was now hanging onto her every word.

'So what has happened to this missing reliquary box?' asked Bishop Leodegar. 'Who has it?'

'It had been stolen by the conspirators when Dabhóc was killed, of course.'

'But why did Abbot Dabhóc take this box to Bishop Ordgar's chamber?' the bishop wanted to know.

'He did not. Abbot Dabhóc was killed in his own chamber from where the box was stolen.'

'I am confused,' Clotaire confessed.

'It is a complicated story,' admitted Fidelma. 'When Beretrude's ambitious son came here he had two confederates apart from his mother. One was Brother Andica, the stonemason, who tried to kill both Eadulf and myself. Fortunately, the statue he pushed down on us did not kill us as intended. While Eadulf was taken to Brother Gebicca, the physician, to have his injury seen to, I went up to look at the plinth from where the statue had fallen. I wanted to make sure whether it had, indeed, fallen of its own accord or whether someone had pried it loose as we passed underneath. My assumption that it had been deliberately pushed down on us was proved correct. Now, a young man, afterwards identified as the stonemason Andica, had offered to show me to the gallery from where the statue fell. As I was examining it, he tried to push me from the galley, misjudged and fell to his death.'

There was a gasp from her listeners. The physician, Brother Gebicca, coughed dryly, dispelling the moment of drama.

'Are you also saying that the bite of the viper which you received was another attempt to kill you?'

Fidelma shrugged, glancing at Beretrude.

'No one can say. I will not pursue it. I am sure Beretrude has other matters of importance to deal with. The murder of Abbot Dabhóc might have commenced as a simple robbery. Our killer could have been in Dabhóc's chamber, attempting to steal the reliquary box, when Dabhóc returned unexpectedly. His bad timing cost him his life. I do not believe it was so, because the killer would have reasoned that, with the reliquary box stolen, Dabhóc would have raised the matter with the bishop and the relics of Benignus of Hibernia would become known. No, Dabhóc was killed to keep him silent, as was Gillucán when the killer thought he knew about the relics.

'So Dabhóc was killed and the box stolen. Then what? Leaving Dabhóc in his own chamber and the reliquary box missing might lead to too many questions. Why not camouflage the intent as well as the action? We see a devious mind at work. Bishop Ordgar had not returned to his chamber so his wine was easily drugged. When he was unconscious from its effects, the body of Dabhóc was taken into his chamber. But why would Bishop Ordgar want to kill the abbot? This is where the tortured mind of the chief conspirator devised a complication that really confused everyone. The murderer had heard of the row at the council earlier that evening. He went to Abbot Cadfan's chamber, put a note under the door and knocked to rouse him before disappearing. As Cadfan truthfully told us, the note invited him to Ordgar's chamber at once. He went there and was clubbed unconscious by the waiting killer. The note was removed. Then Dabhóc's body was brought to the chamber and the scene was set. The murderer had tidied Dabhóc's own chamber. The reliquary box was given to Brother Andica, who went to hide it in the vaults below the abbey. Everyone would now think that either Ordgar or Cadfan had murdered Dabhóc as part of the continuation of their quarrel.'

'Are you saying Brother Andica was Gundobad?' sneered Bishop Leodegar. 'That is not true. I knew Brother Andica well and he was certainly not the son of Beretrude.'

'And Andica was not from Divio,' confirmed Fidelma. 'Andica was just one of the main conspirators. He used his skill as stonemason here to maintain regular contact with Beretrude who was raising warriors to support the insurgency. There were, as I have said, two other conspirators in the abbey. The third was female; she it was who arranged the abduction and selling of the married women and their children.' Sister Fidelma waited while those present absorbed her words before continuing.

'Even in the best-laid plans, something may go amiss. In this case, it was the assignation of Sigeric and Valretrade. Passing by Ordgar's chamber, Sigeric saw the door open and discovered the situation. His delay in rousing the bishop saved his life. Valretrade, on her way to meet him at the sepulchre where they always met, found herself confronted by Andica and his female co-conspirator. Luckily, they decided not to kill Valretrade but to place her with the other women to be sold as slaves. It was a more practical and profitable way to silence her than killing her.'

'And who *is* this female conspirator?' asked Clotaire.

'Sister Valretrade will tell us. She was the witness who saw two of the conspirators hiding the reliquary box.'

Valretrade looked towards her with a puzzled expression.

'I told you that I only recognised the stonemason, Brother Andica, who was carrying the reliquary box. The second figure was holding the lantern. I knew only that she was a woman, a religieuse. I was tied up, gagged and blindfolded, and only freed from those bonds in Beretrude's cellar.'

'So when I went to meet her in the vaults,' Sigeric interrupted, 'Valretrade had already been made a prisoner?'

'Exactly so, Brother Sigeric,' affirmed Fidelma.

Clotaire sighed impatiently. 'Are we going to learn who this female is, Sister Valretrade? Fidelma claims that you know.'

'Well, I suspected it was Radegund. But I could not see her.'

Sister Radegund heaved a sob and muttered: 'It is not true. Not true.'

'Valretrade, think back,' pressed Fidelma. 'You told me that you left your chamber to keep the assignation with Sigeric that night. Your custom was to light the candle as your signal. But that night you unwittingly changed the custom. What did you do that you had not done before?'

Valretrade frowned as she mentally went through her actions.

'I left the candle alight,' she said suddenly. 'I had taken it from the window to my bedside to look for something and did not extinguish it as was my custom before I left the chamber.'

Fidelma was now looking in one direction.

'But one person did not realise that you had made that mistake, did they?'

Sister Inginde was shrinking back as if she was making ready to flee, but with a nod from Fidelma, two of Clotaire's warriors had seized her by the arms. She went limp and gave no resistance.

'Sister Inginde told me that she knew that Valretrade had gone to see Sigeric. How did she know that? Valretrade told me she was *not* in the chamber when the signal was made. However, the candle was alight. Sigeric's candle had been rekindled, which indicated that she had not turned up at the meeting place. Inginde implied that she was in the chamber when Valretrade left. She was not, and could only have known that Valretrade had gone to keep an appointment in the catacombs that night if she, herself, was there. She was not only the third conspirator but also the principal contact with Beretrude. She was involved in the sale of the married women. She identified them and arranged their abduction. She also wrote the notes that Valretrade and the others were supposed to have written. So, as I said before, neither Abbess Audofleda nor Sister Radegund were involved in that matter. They accepted the appearance of the notes and were pleased to do so, as it solved their problem of what to do with the presence of married religious in the *Domus Femini*.'

Fidelma looked towards the tearful Sister Radegund.

'Initially I suspected you, especially when I followed you to the villa of your Aunt Beretrude. Then I learned of your relationship and that you often went to your aunt on matters of business.

'My suspicion about Inginde was finally reinforced in that I went to get a dress from a seamstress. I wanted to disguise myself while I looked at Beretrude's villa. Brother Budnouen had told me that this woman was related to a member of the women's community. Sister Inginde was in this place and told me that the seamstress was her aunt. She was helpful in selecting clothes for me. Thinking I was disguised, I was seized by the warriors of Beretrude and thrown into the cellar to await my fate with the others. I realised that Inginde had somehow informed Beretrude of what I was wearing and where I might be found. In fact, I believe I even heard Inginde running to the villa to inform Beretrude and her guards. It was remiss of me not to check.'

Nuntius Peregrinus interrupted again.

'One thing I must ask – the reliquary box of Benignus. Where is it now?'

'It is safe.' Fidelma nodded to Abbot Ségdae who took a sack from beneath his seat and drew out the box, holding it up.

'This is the reliquary body of the Hibernian teacher Benén Mac Sesenén whom we also call by the name of Benignus,' he said. 'He had no relationship with the Benignus of Burgundia that you know here.'

'This is all very well,' interrupted Bishop Leodegar impatiently. 'You say Abbot Dabhóc was killed, not in Ordgar's chamber but in his own, and this reliquary box was stolen. You have said why. You have also stated that two of the killers were Andica and Inginde. But you have yet to name the last of the killers, the head of the conspiracy, this second son of Beretrude whom you say is already in this abbey in disguise.'

'Guntram, tell us again what was the name of your younger brother before he was taken to be given to the religious life?'

The young man shrugged. 'It was Gundobad. But don't ask me if I would recognise him now. I have not seen him since he was a few years old.'

'But you told me that your mother had a pet name for him.'

'That will not help you either. She used to call him Benignus – the good one.'

'Of course, *Benignus*.' Fidelma smiled.

Bishop Leodegar sniffed in annoyance. 'We have no Brother Benignus here.'

'Think again. Think of someone with . . .'

With a sudden cry – '*Sic semper tyrannis!*' – Brother Benevolentia had drawn a knife and was running towards Clotaire.

There were two sounds, a swift whistling followed by a thud. Two arrows, loosed by warriors, had embedded themselves in the chest of Brother Benevolentia. He halted and, for a moment, it seemed he had turned into a statue. The knife dropped from his fingers and he slowly sank to his knees before toppling over sideways. Beretrude gave one long shriek and collapsed. One of the warriors raced to his side, pulled him over on his back and then spoke to Clotaire.

'Dead, Majesty.'

Clotaire, who had started from his chair, sat back and exhaled deeply in relief.

'A pity,' Ebroin commented dryly. 'We are cheated of a ritual execution. A quick death was too good for someone who likened himself to Brutus slaying Julius Caesar.'

'I do not follow.' Clotaire frowned.

'His last words, Majesty – words supposedly used by Brutus when he plunged his knife into the great Caesar. Thus ever to tyrants!'

Clotaire looked sad for a moment. 'I mean to govern justly, not as a tyrant.'

'Of course, Majesty,' Ebroin assured him. 'But remember that you are dealing with Burgunds. You must also be a strong and firm ruler.'

Bishop Leodegar strode forward to look down at the corpse of the young religieux. He glanced up at Fidelma.

'You knew it was Brother Benevolentia all the time?'

'I suspected him for a while. His features had remarkable similarities to those of Beretrude, Guntram and even Radegund – the same dark hair and blue eyes. He was also the only other person who had a real opportunity to drug Ordgar's wine – indeed, to carry out the entire deed. But I really began to suspect him when he turned up in the gallery, which was forbidden to the brethren, when Andica tried to kill us with the toppling statue. Why would he be there, and how did he know all about the statues and how long they had stood there? Then, of course, there was his name.'

'Benevolentia is another form of saying Benignus,' Bishop Leodegar muttered almost wonderingly.

'A synonym,' Eadulf confirmed, speaking for the first time since Fidelma's explanation had begun. 'Indeed, both names have the same meaning.'

Bishop Ordgar came to stare at the body of his former steward in bewilderment.

'I don't understand any of this. He was my steward. I chose him.'

'You told us,' Eadulf pointed out, 'that you had gone to Divio and that your own steward had died on the journey. You found your new steward, Brother Benevolentia, in the abbey in that city.'

'That is true.'

'But I wonder if you chose him or did he come to you to volunteer his services?'

'Why, he . . . yes, I suppose he sought me out,' admitted the Saxon bishop.

'So Gundobad or Benevolentia, a fervent Burgund and heir to the line of Burgundian kings, came here with his plan to assassinate Clotaire and lead an uprising,' Eadulf explained. 'Then, as Fidelma has told us, he heard about Abbot Dabhóc's gift of the Benignus reliquary. What a symbol he thought it would be! It didn't matter if the two holy men were confused. It was not the reality of the relics that mattered, but their symbolism.'

'An amazing story,' muttered Bishop Leodegar. 'A convoluted one, too.'

'Life is never simple,' Fidelma sighed.

'Those people who attacked me in the forest and killed that Gaulish Brother were Beretrude's warriors?' asked Clotaire, standing up and coming forward.

'They were warriors of Beretrude's house who were probably instructed to follow Eadulf and myself. Their leader carried the symbol of the cross of Benignus, the same symbol that is displayed on the pillars of Beretrude's villa. The warriors were probably going to ambush Eadulf and myself. It was clear that Benevolentia and his mother were worried that we had become a threat to their plan. Clotaire, you either disturbed them or they recognised you hunting in the forest and so took their chance to pre-empt the assassination plan.'

'So who are we left with so far, as the guilty ones?' demanded Ebroin. 'Beretrude and Inginde? Beretrude's warriors – and no one else? What of Guntram?'

The young lord was white faced with apprehension. Two warriors were still guarding him. Fidelma felt sorry for him.

'The only thing that Guntram is guilty of is being a bad lord; a young man more interested in self-indulgence than in the welfare of his people. But he had no design to overthrow you, Clotaire. His only concern was that his people continued to pay tribute to help him maintain his lifestyle.'

'And the Abbess Audofleda?'

'I accuse her of simply being unsuited to be head of a religious house, that is all. But that is a matter between her and her bishop.' She addressed Bishop Leodegar. 'You may now hold your council, Leodegar. Truly your ways are not the ways of my people, your laws not our laws, and the concepts you wish to promote as ideas by which our Faith can come under one universal Rule are not those that I would agree with. I can see those things that you support leading to great suffering rather than a universal brotherhood and sisterhood among the religious. Personally, I cannot wait to return to my own land.'

Bishop Leodegar had regained some of his former aplomb.

'I ask no more from you than what you have done.' He turned to Clotaire. 'Majesty, you may order your prisoners to be removed for punishment, and then I will declare the resumption of the council to start its deliberations tomorrow. I do not think that our debates will last long now.'

Clotaire nodded absently, glancing to where Lady Beretrude and Sister Inginde had been placed under guard with the dozen or so warriors loyal to them.

'See to the prisoners, Ebroin.'

'Do you want them removed for trial, Majesty?' asked his chancellor.

'Trial?' Clotaire stared at the man as if he had made an improper suggestion. 'They have already received a trial. No! Take them out and execute them, and don't bother me with the details.' He swung round to the white-faced Guntram. 'You may go back to your fortress and your pursuits, but never let me hear that you have taken an interest in the governance of this province.'

He turned to look for Fidelma but she and Eadulf were gone.

Nuntius Peregrinus was standing talking with Abbot Ségdae.

'The sister of your king is an amazing woman,' Clotaire said to the abbot.

'She is certainly held in high regard, Imperator,' Abbot Ségdae informed him.

'I suppose you agree with her views about our laws and what Bishop Leodegar hopes to achieve here for the Faith?'

'At the risk of impertinence, I do, Sire. And I think you will find that those delegates from the churches of the Britons, Armoricans and Gauls will join us in that outlook, for we all share similar values.'

Clotaire started to chuckle and clapped the abbot on the shoulder.

'I suppose that is why the good bishop has ensured that there are twice as many representatives of the churches of Neustria and Austrasia attending here as those from the other lands.'

'We will make our protest,' Abbot Ségdae solemnly assured him, 'and then we will return home to what we know and feel comfortable with. There is an ancient saying in my land. *Níl aon tintean mar do thintean féin.*'

'Which means?'

'There is no hearth like your own hearth.'

Epilogue

Autumn had cast its russet and yellow colourings across the countryside surrounding Cashel. Clouds of grey smoke from chimneystacks showed that already the fires were constantly alight. Heavy woollens and animal furs had replaced the lighter linen and silks affected by those who served at the court of Colgú, King of Muman. Fidelma was stretched lazily in a chair before a blazing log fire. There was a lantern on the table to give extra light, for the day was dark even though the sun, had it been able to shine through the dark scudding clouds, had not yet set. Fidelma was trying to read a letter that had just been delivered by a returning religious who had spent two years wandering among the Franks.

Fidelma was excited when she saw the name of the writer, so excited that she could not wait for Eadulf to return from the business that had taken him to the abbey of Imleach. Breaking the seals, she spread out the vellum on her knees, seeing – with gratitude – that it was written in Latin. The letter was dated four months earlier, and was sent from the city of Nebirnum. She frowned. Why not Autun? But it had been over five years since she and Eadulf had departed from Autun.

> 'From Sigeric and Valretrade, servants in the Faith of Christ Jesus, to Fidelma of Cashel and Eadulf of Seaxmund's Ham, her faithful companion, greetings.
>
> 'We pray this finds you both dwelling in peace and happiness and in the contentment of our Faith. We send you greeting in remembrance of the great services that you rendered to us and our people at Autun.

'Since you departed our land, a great unhappiness has overcome it and all within the space of two years. Firstly, it was in the spring two years ago that Clotaire our young King died, acknowledging the Faith in his last breath, and he lies buried in the basilica dedicated to the blessed bishop and martyr, Dionysius of Paris. Clotaire's brother, Theuderic, succeeded him as King, but treachery struck as many suspected it might. Bishop Leodegar conspired with others to place another brother, Childeric, on the throne. Theuderic was arrested and imprisoned in an abbey, while Ebroin, who had continued as adviser to Theuderic, was also imprisoned. Ebroin eventually escaped to exile.

'There followed such horrors that we can only thank God for our decision to remove ourselves from the cursed abbey of Autun and for our safe delivery from such Fate as befell friends and family. Leodegar and Audofleda enforced their Rule and those who disobeyed were physically degraded, and not just those among the religious communities suffered. All throughout the kingdoms, even those nobles who did not obey Childeric, a young, intolerant ruler guided by the ambitious Leodegar, were mutilated or hanged.

'It was inevitable that Childeric and his wife Bilichild, both the subject of such hatred for the hurt they were inflicting, would attract the desire for vengeance. Whilst out hunting one day they were assassinated and no one claimed to know by whom.

'With Childeric's death, Theuderic was released from his monastic prison and he sent for Ebroin to become his adviser again.

'Ebroin was not a man of forgiveness for he raised an army and marched on Autun, which was still under the control of Bishop Leodegar. The attack on Autun was fierce and the suffering great. Abbess Audofleda perished, as did her companion Sister Radegund. Many of the religious died in the onslaught on the abbey. Finally Bishop Leodegar surrendered to Ebroin.

'Leodegar was not treated with courtesy. We are told that his eyes were put out with red-hot pokers and that his tongue was torn out and other unspeakable things were done to him. Yet he survived and was dragged for trial before the court of Theuderic. There, he was further degraded and condemned, albeit, we must in fairness say, as he had so often condemned others without compunction. On Ebroin's orders he was taken to a forest and hanged.

'There is a rumour that many of the religious claim him as a martyr. There are now several places that would follow his Rule; indeed, that same Rule decided at that now infamous council in the city of Autun. Even in Autun there are some who are asking that his relics be placed with them as objects worthy of worship. Alas, how short memories are.

'Valretrade and myself, with our two little ones, were saved from the worst of these atrocities for we were away from the city at the time of Ebroin's attack. Yet of her sister's family, only poor Magnatrude survived.

'So what does the future hold for us? We, together with Magnatrude, have decided to commence our journey westward. We are already at Nebirnum. We are going to seek a new home, a new life, in the land of the Armoricans. We are told that there is a land called Domnonia, a land by the sea, in the north of that country, where we shall start our new life. Perhaps we shall find a plot of land to farm or an inn to run for pilgrims.

'All we know is that we can no longer serve these new religious communities that are now following the ideas propounded by Leodegar. We maintain our Faith in the Christ Jesus but not in men who would try to claim dominion over us and regulate our lives with petty rules that are unnatural to human life. We deny those disciplines for we are human, no more but certainly no less. We are as the Creator made us and, if there is truth in religion, we are as we were meant to be.

'If Fate and Our Lord Jesus are kind to us, we will meet again with you. If not, accept forever our sincere and dearest wishes for peace and goodwill to attend you all the days of your lives.'

There followed a list of the names of the family of Sigeric and Valretrade.

Fidelma sighed deeply and found herself wiping away a tear.